Bad Timing
AND OTHER STORIES

Bad Timing
AND OTHER STORIES

Molly Brown

BIG ENGINE

Big Engine
PO Box 185
Abingdon
Oxon OX14 1GR
United Kingdom
www.bigengine.co.uk

This collection copyright © Molly Brown 2001
Individual stories copyright © Molly Brown
as detailed opposite

Cover artwork by
Deirdre Counihan

Typeset by
Paul Brazier, www.brazier.mistral.co.uk

ISBN 1 903468 06 X

All rights reserved.

The right of Molly Brown to be identified as the author of this work has been asserted by her in accordance with the Copyright, Designs and Patents Act, 1988.

This book is sold subject to the condition that it shall not, by way of trade or otherwise be lent, resold, hired out, or otherwise circulated without the publisher's prior consent in any form of binding or cover other than that in which it is published and without a similar condition, including this condition, being imposed upon the subsequent purchaser.

'Bad Timing,' first published in *Interzone*, December 1991.
   Copyright © Molly Brown 1991

'Feeding Julie,' first published in *Interzone*, October 1995.
   Copyright © Molly Brown 1995

'Community Service,' first published in *Interzone*, May 1996.
   Copyright © Molly Brown 1996

'Agents of Darkness,' first published in *Interzone*, October 1992.
   Copyright © Molly Brown 1992

'Doing Things Differently,' first published in *Interzone*, September 1996.
   Copyright © Molly Brown 1996

'The Vengeance of Grandmother Wu,' first published in *Interzone*, July 1992.
   Copyright © Molly Brown 1992

'Return of the Princess,' first published in *Villains*, edited by Mary Gentle and Roz Kaveney, Penguin/Roc, 1992. Copyright © Molly Brown 1992

'No Better Than Anyone Else,' first published in *Interzone*, April 1993.
   Copyright © Molly Brown 1993

'The Psychomantium,' first published in *Interzone*, February 1997.
   Copyright © Molly Brown 1997

'Star,' first published in *New Crimes 3*, Robinson, 1991.
   Copyright © Molly Brown 1991

'A Sense of Focus,' first published in *Constable New Crimes*, Constable, 1992.
   Copyright © Molly Brown 1992

'Choosing The Incubus,' first published in *Bad Sex*, Serpent's Tail, 1993.
   Copyright © Molly Brown 1993

'Asleep At The Wheel,' first published in *Phantoms*, November 1996.
   Copyright © Molly Brown 1996

'Rules of Engagement,' first published in *Substance* Magazine, Autumn 1995. Copyright © Molly Brown 1995

'Women On the Brink of a Cataclysm,' first published in *Interzone*, January 1994.
   Copyright © Molly Brown 1994

'Learning To Fly,' first published in *Interzone*, February 1993.
   Copyright © Molly Brown 1993

'The Final Rushlight,' copyright © Molly Brown 2001

'Doris and Angie and Me,' first published in *The Hardcore #8*, 1992.
   Copyright © Molly Brown 1992

'Angel's Day,' first published in *London Noir*, Serpent's Tail, in 1994.
   Copyright © Molly Brown 1994

'Neon Nightsong,' first published in *After Hours*, Spring 1991.
   Copyright © Molly Brown 1991

'Ruella In Love,' first published in *Interzone*, October 1993.
   Copyright © Molly Brown 1993

To Margretta Brown and to Brandon

Thanks to (in alphabetical order) Chris Amies, Tina Anghelatos, Liz Holliday, Ben Jeapes, Andrew Lane and Gus Smith for reading and commenting on very early drafts of most of these stories.

Thanks to David Pringle and Maxim Jakubowski for being among the first editors to publish my work when I was starting out, and to Sonny Mahlli and Erica Fuentes for their recent help.

Author's note:
Some of the stories in this collection ("Return of the Princess", "The Vengeance of Grandmother Wu", "Doris and Angie and Me" and "Angel's Day") have been slightly revised or updated since their original publication.

Visit Molly Brown's web site at
www.mollybrown.co.uk

Contents

Bad Timing *1*
Feeding Julie *19*
Community Service *35*
Agents of Darkness *55*
Doing Things Differently *71*
The Vengeance of Grandmother Wu *93*
Return of the Princess *115*
No Better Than Anyone Else *119*
The Psychomantium *133*
Star *151*
A Sense of Focus *157*
Choosing The Incubus *165*
Asleep At The Wheel *177*
Rules of Engagement *185*
Women On the Brink of a Cataclysm *191*
Learning To Fly *222*
The Final Rushlight *235*
Doris and Angie and Me *237*
Angel's Day *243*
Neon Nightsong *253*
Ruella In Love *255*

bad timing

"Time travel is an inexact science. And its study is fraught with paradoxes."   *Samuel Colson, b. 2301 d. 2197.*

Alan rushed through the archway without even glancing at the inscription across the top. It was Monday morning and he was late again. He often thought about the idea that time was a point in space, and he didn't like it. That meant that at this particular point in space it was always Monday morning and he was always late for a job he hated. And it always had been. And it always would be. Unless somebody tampered with it, which was strictly forbidden.

"Oh my Holy Matrix," Joe Twofingers exclaimed as Alan raced past him to register his palmprint before losing an extra thirty minutes pay. "You wouldn't believe what I found in the fiction section!"

Alan slapped down his hand. The recorder's metallic voice responded with, "Employee number 057, Archives Department, Alan Strong. Thirty minutes and seven point two seconds late. One hour's credit deducted."

Alan shrugged and turned back towards Joe. "Since I'm not getting paid, I guess I'll put my feet up and have a cup of liquid caffeine. So tell me what you found."

"Well, I was tidying up the files – fiction section is a mess as you know – and I came across this magazine. And I thought, 'what's this doing here?' It's something from the twentieth century called *Woman's Secrets*, and it's all knitting patterns, recipes, and gooey little romance stories: 'He grabbed her roughly, bruising her soft pale skin, and pulled her to his rock hard chest' and so on. I figured it was in there by mistake and nearly threw it out. But then I saw this story called 'The Love That Conquered Time' and I realised that must be what they're keeping it for. So I had a look at it, and it was…" He made a face and stuck a finger down his throat. "But I really think you ought to read it."

"Why?"

"Because you're in it."

"You're a funny guy, Joe. You almost had me going for a minute."

"I'm serious! Have a look at the drebbing thing. It's by some woman called Cecily Walker, it's in that funny old vernacular they used to use, and it's positively dire. But the guy in the story is definitely you."

Alan didn't believe him for a minute. Joe was a joker, and always had been. Alan would never forget the time Joe laced his drink with a combination aphrodisiac-hallucinogen at a party and he'd made a total fool of himself with the section leader's overcoat. He closed his eyes and shuddered as Joe handed him the magazine.

Like all the early relics made of paper, the magazine had been dipped in preservative and the individual pages coated with a clear protective covering which gave them a horrible chemical smell and a tendency to stick together. After a little difficulty, Alan found the page he wanted. He rolled his eyes at the painted illustration of a couple locked in a passionate but chaste embrace, and dutifully began to read.

It was all about a beautiful but lonely and unfulfilled woman who still lives in the house where she was born. One day there is a knock at the door, and she opens it to a mysterious stranger: tall, handsome, and extremely charismatic.

Alan chuckled to himself.

A few paragraphs later, over a candle-lit dinner, the man tells the woman that he comes from the future, where time travel has become a reality, and he works at the Colson Time Studies Institute in the Department of Archives.

Alan stopped laughing.

The man tells her that only certain people are allowed to time travel, and they are not allowed to interfere in any way, only observe. He confesses that he is not a qualified traveller – he broke into the lab one night and stole a machine. The woman asks him why and he tells her, "You're the only reason, Claudia. I did it for you. I read a story that you wrote and I knew it was about me and that it was about you. I searched in the Archives and I found your picture and then I knew that I loved you and that I had always loved you and that I always would."

"But I never wrote a story, Alan."

"You will, Claudia. You will."

The Alan in the story goes on to describe the Project, and the Archives, in detail. The woman asks him how people live in the twenty-fourth century, and he tells her about the gadgets in his apartment.

The hairs at the back of Alan's neck rose at the mention of his Neuro-Pleasatron. He'd never told anybody that he'd bought one, not even Joe.

After that, there's a lot of grabbing and pulling to his rock hard chest, melting sighs and kisses, and finally a wedding and a "happily ever after" existing at one point in space where it always has and always will.

Alan turned the magazine over and looked at the date on the cover. March 14, 1973.

He wiped the sweat off his forehead and shook himself. He looked up and saw that Joe was standing over him.

"You wouldn't really do that, would you?" Joe said. "Because you know I'd have to stop you."

——•——O——•——

Cecily Walker stood in front of her bedroom mirror and turned from right to left. She rolled the waistband over one more time, making sure both sides were even. Great; the skirt looked like a real mini. Now all she had to do was get out of the house without her mother seeing her.

She was in the record shop wondering if she really should spend her whole allowance on the new Monkees album, but she really liked Peter Tork, he was so cute, when Tommy Johnson walked in with Roger Hanley. "Hey, Cess-pit! Whaddya do, lose the bottom half of your dress?"

The boys at her school were just so creepy. She left the shop and turned down the main road, heading toward her friend Candy's house. She never noticed the tall blonde man that stood across the street, or heard him call her name.

———•——O——•———

When Joe went on his lunch break, Alan turned to the wall above his desk and said, "File required: Authors, fiction, twentieth century, initial 'W'."

"Checking," the wall said. "File located."

"Biography required: Walker, Cecily."

"Checking. Biography located. Display? Yes or no."

"Yes."

A section of wall the size of a small television screen lit up at eye-level, directly in front of Alan. He leaned forward and read: Walker, Cecily. b. Danville, Illinois, U.S.A. 1948. d. 2037. Published works: "The Love That Conquered Time", March, 1973. Accuracy rating: fair.

"Any other published works?"

"Checking. None found."

Alan looked down at the magazine in his lap.

"I don't understand," Claudia said, looking pleadingly into his deep blue eyes. Eyes the colour of the sea on a cloudless morning, and eyes that contained an ocean's depth of feeling for her, and her alone. "How is it possible to travel through time?"

"I'll try to make this simple," he told her, pulling her close. She took a deep breath, inhaling his manly aroma, and rested her head on his shoulder with a sigh. "Imagine that the universe is like a string. And every point on that string is a moment in space and time. But instead of stretching out in a straight line, it's all coiled and tangled and it overlaps in layers. Then all you have to do is move from point to point."

Alan wrinkled his forehead in consternation. "File?"

"Yes. Waiting."

"Information required: further data on Walker, Cecily. Education, family background."

"Checking. Found. Display? Yes or –"

"Yes!"

Walker, Cecily. Education: Graduate Lincoln High, Danville, 1967.

Family background: Father Walker, Matthew. Mechanic, automobile. d. 1969. Mother no data.

Alan shook his head. Minimal education, no scientific background. How could she know so much?

"Information required: photographic likeness of subject. If available, display."

He blinked and there she was, smiling at him across his desk. She was oddly dressed, in a multi-coloured tee-shirt that ended above her waist and dark blue trousers that were cut so low they exposed her navel and seemed to balloon out below her knees into giant flaps of loose-hanging material. But she had long dark hair that fell across her shoulders and down to her waist, crimson lips and the most incredible eyes he had ever seen – huge and green. She was beautiful. He looked at the caption: Walker, Cecily. Author: Fiction related to time travel theory. Photographic likeness circa 1970.

"File," he said, "Further data required: personal details, i.e. marriage. Display."

Walker, Cecily m. Strong, Alan.

"Date?"

No data.

"Biographical details of husband, Strong, Alan?"

None found.

"Redisplay photographic likeness. Enlarge." He stared at the wall for several minutes. "Print," he said.

— —•— —O— —•— —

Only half a block to go, the woman thought, struggling with two bags of groceries. The sun was high in the sky and the smell of Mrs Henderson's roses, three doors down, filled the air with a lovely perfume. But she wasn't in the mood to appreciate it. All the sun made her feel was hot, and all the smell of flowers made her feel was ill. It had been a difficult pregnancy, but thank goodness it was nearly over now.

She wondered who the man was, standing on her front porch. He might be the new mechanic at her husband's garage, judging by his orange cover-alls. Nice-looking, she thought, wishing that she didn't look like there was a bowling ball underneath her dress.

"Excuse me," the man said, reaching out to help her with her bags. "I'm looking for Cecily Walker."

"My name's Walker," the woman told him. "But I don't know any Cecily."

"Cecily", she repeated when the man had gone. What a pretty name.

——•——O——•——

Alan decided to work late that night. Joe left at the usual time and told him he'd see him tomorrow.

"Yeah, tomorrow," Alan said.

He waited until Joe was gone, and then he took the printed photo of Cecily Walker out of his desk drawer and sat for a long time, staring at it. What did he know about this woman? Only that she'd written one published story, badly, and that she was the most gorgeous creature he had ever seen. Of course, what he was feeling was ridiculous. She'd been dead more than three hundred years.

But there were ways of getting around that.

Alan couldn't believe what he was actually considering. It was lunacy. He'd be caught, and he'd lose his job. But then he realised that he could never have read about it if he hadn't already done it and got away with it. He decided to have another look at the story.

It wasn't there. Under Fiction: Paper Relics: 20th Century, sub-section Magazines, American, there was shelf after shelf full of *Amazing Stories, Astounding, Analog, Weird Tales* and *Isaac Asimov's Science Fiction Magazine,* but not one single copy of *Woman's Secrets.*

Well, he thought, if the magazine isn't there, I guess I never made it after all. Maybe it's better that way. Then he thought, but if I never made it, how can I be looking for the story? I shouldn't even know about it. And then he had another thought.

"File," he said. "Information required: magazines on loan."

"Display?"

"No, just tell me."

"*Woman's Secrets*, date 1973. *Astounding*, date ..."

"Skip the rest. Who's got *Woman's Secrets*?"

"Checking. Signed out to Project Control through Joe Twofingers."

Project Control was on to him! If he didn't act quickly, it would be too late.

It was amazingly easy to get into the lab. He just walked in. The machines were all lined up against one wall, and there was no one around to stop him. He walked up to the nearest machine and sat down on it. The earliest model developed by Samuel Colson had looked like an English telephone box (he'd been a big *Doctor Who* fan), but it was hardly inconspicuous and extremely heavy, so refinements were made until the latest models were lightweight, collapsible, and made to look exactly like (and double up as) a folding bicycle. The control board was hidden from general view, inside a wicker basket.

None of the instruments were labelled. Alan tentatively pushed one button. Nothing happened. He pushed another. Still nothing.

He jumped off and looked for an instruction book. There had to be one somewhere. He was ransacking a desk when the door opened.

"I thought I'd find you here, Alan."

"Joe! I… uh… was just…"

"I know what you're doing, and I can't let you go through with it. It's against *every* rule of the Institute and you know it. If you interfere with the past, who knows what harm you might do?"

"But Joe, you know me. I wouldn't do any harm. I won't do anything to affect history, I swear it. I just want to see her, that's all. Besides, it's already happened, or you couldn't have read that magazine. And that's another thing! You're the one who showed it to me! I never would have known about her if it hadn't been for you. So if I'm going now, it's down to you."

"Alan, I'm sorry, but my job is on the line here, too, you know. So don't give me any trouble and come along quietly."

Joe moved towards him, holding a pair of handcuffs. Attempted theft of Institute property was a felony punishable by five year's imprisonment without pay. Alan picked up the nearest bike and brought it down over the top of Joe's head. The machine lay in pieces and Joe lay unconscious. Alan bent down and felt his pulse. He would be okay.

"Sorry, Joe. I had to do it. File!"

"Yes."

"Information required: instruction manual for usage of…" he checked the number on the handlebars, "Colson Model 44B Time Traveller."

"Checking. Found. Display?"

"No. Just print. And fast."

The printer was only on page five when Alan heard running footsteps. Five pages would have to do.

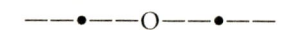

——•——O——•——

Dear Cher,

My name is Cecily Walker and all my friends tell me I look just like you. Well, a little bit. Anyway, the reason that I'm writing to you is this: I'm starting my senior year in high school, and I've never had a steady boyfriend. I've gone out with a couple of boys, but they only want one thing, and I guess you know what that is. I keep thinking there's gotta be somebody out there who's the right one for me, but I just haven't met him. Was it love at first sight for you and Sonny?

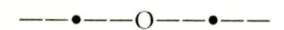

——•——O——•——

Alan sat on a London park bench with his printout and tried to figure out what he'd done wrong. Under Location: Setting, it just said "See page 29." Great, he thought. And he had no idea what year it was. Every time he tried to ask someone, they'd give him a funny look and walk away in a hurry. He folded up the bike and took a walk. It wasn't long before he found a news-stand and saw the date: July 19, 1998. At least he had the right century.

Back in the park, he sat astride the machine with the printout in one hand, frowning and wondering what might happen if he twisted a particular dial from right to left.

"Can't get your bike to start, mate?" someone shouted from nearby. "Just click your heels three times and think of home."

"Thanks, I'll try that," Alan shouted back. Then he vanished.

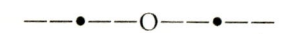

——•——O——•——

"I am a pirate from yonder ship," the man with the eye patch told her, "and well used to treasure. But I tell thee, lass, I've never seen the like of you."

Cecily groaned and ripped the page in half. She bit her lip and started again.

"I have travelled many galaxies, Madeleine," the alien bleeped. "But you are a life-form beyond compare."

"No, don't. Please don't," Madeleine pleaded as the alien reached out to pull her towards its rock hard chest.

Her mother appeared in the doorway. "Whatcha doin' hon?" She dropped the pen and flipped the writing pad face down.

"My homework."

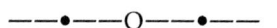

——•——O——•——

The next thing Alan knew he was in the middle of a cornfield. He hitched a lift with a truck driver who asked a lot of questions, ranging from "You work in a gas station, do you?" to "What are you, foreign or something?" and "What do you call that thing?" On being told "that thing" was a folding bicycle, the man muttered something about whatever would they think of next, and now his kid would be wanting one.

There were several Walker's listed in the Danville phone book. When he finally found the right house, Cecily was in the middle of her third birthday party.

He pedalled around a corner, checked his printout, and set the controls on "Fast Forward". He folded the machine and hid it behind a bush before walking back to the house. It was big and painted green, just as in the story. There was an apple tree in the garden, just as in the story. The porch swing moved ever so slightly, rocked by an early summer breeze. He could hear crickets chirping and birds singing. Everything was just the way it had been in the story, so he walked up the path, nervously clearing his throat and pushing back a stray lock of hair, just the way Cecily Walker had described him in *Woman's Secrets*, before finally taking a deep breath and knocking on the door. There was movement inside the house. The clack of high-heeled shoes across a wooden floor, the rustle of a cotton dress.

"Yes?"

Alan stared at her, open-mouthed. "You've cut your hair," he told her.

"What?"

"Your hair. It used to hang down to your waist, now it's up to your shoulders."

"Do I know you?"

"You will," he told her. He'd said that in the story. She was supposed to take one look at him and realise with a fluttering heart that this was the man she'd dreamed of all her life. Instead, she looked at his orange jumpsuit and slapped her hand to her forehead in enlightenment. "You're from the garage! Of course, Mack said he'd be sending the new guy." She looked past him into the street. "So where's your tow truck?"

"My what?" There was nothing in "The Love That Conquered Time" about a tow truck. The woman stared at him, looking confused. Alan stared back, equally confused. He started to wonder if he'd made a mistake. But then he saw those eyes, bigger and greener than he'd ever thought possible. "Matrix," he said out loud.

"What?"

"I'm sorry. It's just that meeting you is so bullasic."

"Mister, I don't understand one word you're saying." Cecily knew she should tell the man to go away. He was obviously deranged; she should call the police. But something held her back, a flicker of recognition, the dim stirrings of a memory. Where had she seen this man before?

"I'm sorry," Alan said again. "My American isn't very good. I come from English-speaking Europe, you see."

"English-speaking Europe?" Cecily repeated. "You mean England?"

"Not exactly. Can I come inside? I'll explain everything."

She let him come in after warning him that her neighbours would come running in with shotguns if they heard her scream, and that she had a black belt in Kung Fu. Alan nodded and followed her inside, wondering where Kung Fu was, and why she'd left her belt there.

He was ushered into the living room and told to have a seat. He sat down on the red velveteen-upholstered sofa and stared in awe at such historical artefacts as a black and white television with rabbit-ear antennae, floral-printed wallpaper, a phone you had to dial, and shelf after shelf of unpreserved books. She picked up a wooden chair and carried it to the far side of the room before sitting down. "Okay," she said. "Talk."

Alan felt it would have been better to talk over a candle-lit dinner in a restaurant, as they did in the story, but he went ahead and told her everything, quoting parts of the story verbatim, such as the passage where she described him as the perfect lover she'd been longing for all her life.

When he was finished, she managed a frozen smile. "So you've come all the way from the future just to visit little ole me. Isn't that nice."

Oh Matrix, Alan thought. She's humouring me. She's convinced I'm insane and probably dangerous as well. "I know this must sound crazy to you," he said.

"Not at all," she told him, gripping the arms of her chair. He could see the blood draining out of her fingers.

"Please don't be afraid. I'd never harm you." He sighed and put a hand to his forehead. "It was all so different in the story."

"But I never wrote any story. Well, I started one once, but I never got beyond the second page."

"But you will. You see, it doesn't get published until 1973."

"You do know this is 1979, don't you?"

"WHAT?"

"Looks like your timing's off," she said. She watched him sink his head into his hands with an exaggerated groan. She rested her chin on one hand and regarded him silently. He didn't seem so frightening now. Crazy, yes, but not frightening. She might even find him quite attractive, if only things were different. He looked up at her and smiled. It was a crooked, little boy's smile that made his eyes sparkle. For a moment, she almost let herself imagine waking up to that smile... She pulled herself up in her chair, her back rigid.

"Look," he said. "So I'm a few years behind schedule. The main thing is I found you. And so what if the story comes out a bit later, it's nothing we can't handle. It's only a minor problem. A little case of bad timing."

"Excuse me," Cecily said. "But I think that in this case, timing is everything. If any of this made the least bit of sense, which it doesn't, you would've turned up before now. You said yourself the story was published in 1973 – if it was based on fact, you'd need to arrive here much earlier."

"I did get here earlier, but I was too early."

Cecily's eyes widened involuntarily. "What do you mean?"

"I mean I was here before. I met you. I spoke to you."

"When?"

"You wouldn't remember. You were three years old, and your parents threw a party for you out in the garden. Of course I realised my mistake instantly, but I bluffed it out by telling your mother that I'd just dropped by to apologise because my kid was sick and couldn't come – it was a pretty safe bet that someone wouldn't have shown – and she said, 'Oh you must be little Sammy's father' and asked me in. I was going to leave immediately, but your father handed me a beer and started talking about something called baseball. Of course I didn't have a present for you…"

"But you gave me a rose and told my mother to press it into a book so that I'd have it forever."

"You remember!"

"Wait there. Don't move." She leapt from her chair and ran upstairs. There was a lot of noise from above – paper rattling, doors opening and closing, things being thrown about. She returned clutching several books to her chest, her face flushed and streaked with dust. She flopped down on the floor and spread them out in front of her. When Alan got up to join her, she told him to stay where he was or she'd scream. He sat back down.

She opened the first book, and then Alan saw that they weren't books at all; they were photo albums. He watched in silence as she flipped through the pages and then tossed it aside. She tossed three of them away before she found what she was looking for. She stared open-mouthed at the brittle yellow page and then she looked up at Alan.

"I don't understand this," she said, turning her eyes back to the album and a faded black and white photograph stuck to the paper with thick, flaking paste. Someone had written in ink across the top: Cecily's 3rd birthday, August 2nd, 1951. There was her father, who'd been dead for ten years, young and smiling, holding out a bottle to another young man, tall and blonde and dressed like a gas station attendant.

"I don't understand this at all." She pushed the album across the floor towards Alan. "You haven't changed one bit. You're even wearing the same clothes."

"Did you keep the rose?"

She walked over to a wooden cabinet and pulled out a slim hardback with the title, "My First Reader". She opened it and showed him the dried, flattened flower. "You're telling me the truth, aren't you?" she said. "This is all true. You risked everything to find me because we were meant to be together, and nothing, not even time itself, could keep us apart."

Alan nodded. There was a speech just like that in "The Love That Conquered Time".

"Bastard," she said.

Alan jumped. He didn't remember that part. "Pardon me?"

"Bastard," she said again. "You bastard!"

"I… I don't understand."

She got up and started to pace the room. "So you're the one, huh? You're 'Mister Right', Mister Happily Ever After, caring, compassionate and great in bed. And you decide to turn up now. Well, isn't that just great."

"Is something the matter?" Alan asked her.

"Is something the matter?" she repeated. "He asks me if something's the matter! I'll tell you what's the matter. I got married four weeks ago, you son of a bitch!"

"You're married?"

"That's what I said, isn't it?"

"But you can't be married. We were supposed to find perfect happiness together at a particular point in space that has always existed and always will. This ruins everything."

"All those years… all those years. I went through hell in high school, you know. I was the only girl in my class who didn't have a date for the prom. So where were you then, huh? While I was sitting alone at home, crying my goddamn eyes out? How about all those Saturday nights I spent washing my hair? And even worse, those nights I worked at Hastings' Bar serving drinks to salesmen pretending they don't have wives. Why couldn't you have been around then, when I needed you?"

"Well, I've only got the first five pages of the manual..." He walked over to her and put his hands on her shoulders. She didn't move away. He gently pulled her closer to him. She didn't resist. "Look," he said, "I'm sorry. I'm a real zarkhead. I've made a mess of everything. You're happily married, you never wrote the story... I'll just go back where I came from, and none of this will have ever happened."

"Who said I was happy?"

"But you just got married."

She pushed him away. "I got married because I'm thirty years old and figured I'd never have another chance. People do that, you know. They reach a certain age and they figure it's now or never... Damn you! If only you'd come when you were supposed to!"

"You're thirty? Matrix, in half an hour you've gone from a toddler to someone older than me." He saw the expression on her face, and mumbled an apology.

"Look," she said. "You're gonna have to go. My husband'll be back any minute."

"I know I have to leave. But the trouble is, that drebbing story was true! I took one look at your photo, and I knew that I loved you and I always had. Always. That's the way time works, you see. And even if this whole thing vanishes as the result of some paradox, I swear to you I won't forget. Somewhere there's a point in space that belongs to us. I know it." He turned to go. "Good-bye Cecily."

"Alan, wait! That point in space – I want to go there. Isn't there anything we can do? I mean, you've got a time machine, after all."

What an idiot! he thought. The solution's been staring me in the face and I've been too blind to see it. "The machine!" He ran down the front porch steps and turned around to see her standing in the doorway. "I'll see you later," he told her. He knew it was a ridiculous thing to say the minute he'd said it. What he meant was, "I'll see you earlier".

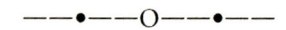

——•——O——•——

Five men sat together inside a tent made of animal hide. The land of their fathers was under threat, and they met in council to discuss the problem. The one called Swiftly Running Stream advocated war, but

Foot Of The Crow was more cautious. "The paleface is too great in number, and his weapons give him an unfair advantage." Flying Bird suggested that they smoke before speaking further.

Black Elk took the pipe into his mouth. He closed his eyes for a moment and declared that the Great Spirit would give them a sign if they were meant to go to war. As soon as he said the word, "war", a paleface materialised among them. They all saw him. The white man's body was covered in a strange bright garment such as they had never seen, and he rode a fleshless horse with silver bones. The vision vanished as suddenly as it had appeared, leaving them with this message to ponder: *Oops*.

——•——O——•——

There was no one home, so he waited on the porch. It was a beautiful day, with a gentle breeze that carried the scent of roses: certainly better than that smoke-filled teepee.

A woman appeared in the distance. He wondered if that was her. But then he saw that it couldn't be; the woman's walk was strange and her body was misshapen. She's pregnant, he realised. It was a common thing in the days of over-population, but he couldn't remember the last time he'd seen a pregnant woman back home – it must have been years. She looked at him questioningly as she waddled up the steps balancing two paper bags. Alan thought the woman looked familiar; he knew that face. He reached out to help her.

"Excuse me," he said. "I'm looking for Cecily Walker."

"My name's Walker," the woman told him. "But I don't know any Cecily."

Matrix, what a moron, Alan thought, wanting to kick himself. Of course he knew the woman; it was Cecily's mother, and if she was pregnant, it had to be 1948. "My mistake," he told her. "It's been a long day."

——•——O——•——

The smell of roses had vanished, along with the leaves on the trees. There was snow on the ground and a strong northeasterly wind. Alan set the thermostat on his jumpsuit accordingly and jumped off the bike.

"So it's you again," Cecily said ironically. "Another case of perfect timing." She was twenty pounds heavier and there were lines around her mouth and her eyes. She wore a heavy wool cardigan sweater over an oversized tee-shirt, jeans, and a pair of fuzzy slippers. She looked him up and down. "You don't age at all, do you?"

"Please can I come in? It's freezing."

"Yeah, yeah. Come in. You like a cup of coffee?"

"You mean liquid caffeine? That'd be great."

He followed her into the living room and his mouth dropped open. The red sofa was gone, replaced by something that looked like a giant banana. The television was four times bigger and had lost the rabbit-ears. The floral wallpaper had been replaced by plain white walls not very different from those of his apartment.

"Sit," she told him. She left the room for a moment and returned with two mugs, one of which she slammed down in front of him, causing a miniature brown tidal wave to splash across his legs.

"Cecily, are you upset about something?"

"That's a good one! He comes back after fifteen years and asks me if I'm upset."

"Fifteen years!" Alan sputtered.

"That's right. It's 1994, you bozo."

"Oh darling, and you've been waiting all this time –"

"Like hell I have," she interrupted. "When I met you, back in 1979, I realised that I couldn't stay in that sham of a marriage for another minute. So I must have set some kind of a record for quickie marriage and divorce, by Danville standards, anyway. So I was a thirty-year-old divorcee whose marriage had fallen apart in less than two months, and I was back to washing my hair alone on Saturday nights. And people talked. Lord, how they talked. But I didn't care, because I'd finally met my soul-mate and everything was going to be all right. He told me he'd fix it. He'd be back. So I waited. I waited for a year. Then I waited two years. Then I waited three. After ten, I got tired of waiting. And if you think I'm going through another divorce, you're crazy."

"You mean you're married again?"

"What else was I supposed to do? A man wants you when you're forty, you jump at it. As far as I knew, you were gone forever."

"I've never been away, Cecily. I've been here all along, but never at the right time. It's that drebbing machine; I can't figure out the controls."

"Maybe Arnie can have a look at it when he gets in, he's pretty good at that sort of thing – what am I saying?"

"Tell me, did you ever write the story?"

"What's to write about? Anyway, what difference does it make? *Woman's Secrets* went bankrupt years ago."

"Matrix! If you never wrote the story, then I shouldn't even know about you. So how can I be here? Dammit, it's a paradox. And I wasn't supposed to cause any of those. Plus, I think I may have started an Indian war. Have you noticed any change in local history?"

"Huh?"

"Never mind. Look, I have an idea. When exactly did you get divorced?"

"I don't know, late '79. October, November, something like that."

"All right, that's what I'll aim for. November, 1979. Be waiting for me."

"How?"

"Good point. Okay, just take my word for it, you and me are going to be sitting in this room right here, right now, with one big difference: we'll have been married for fifteen years, okay?"

"But what about Arnie?"

"Arnie won't know the difference. You'll never have married him in the first place." He kissed her on the cheek. "I'll be back in a minute. Well, in 1979. You know what I mean." He headed for the door.

"Hold on," she said. "You're like the guy who goes out for a pack of cigarettes and doesn't come back for thirty years."

"What guy?"

"Never mind. I wanna make sure you don't turn up anywhere else. Bring the machine in here."

"Is that it?" she said one minute later.

"That's it."

"But it looks like a goddamn bicycle."

"Where do you want me to put it?"

She led him upstairs. "Here," she said. Alan unfolded the bike next to the bed. "I don't want you getting away from me next time," she told him.

"I don't have to get away from you now."

"You do. I'm married and I'm at least fifteen years older than you."

"Your age doesn't matter to me," Alan told her. "When I first fell in love with you, you'd been dead three hundred years."

"You really know how to flatter a girl, don't you? Anyway, don't aim for '79. I don't understand paradoxes, but I know I don't like them. If we're ever gonna get this thing straightened out, you must arrive before 1973, when the story is meant to be published. Try for '71 or '72. Now that I think about it, those were a strange couple of years for me. Nothing seemed real to me then. Nothing seemed worth bothering about, nothing mattered; I always felt like I was waiting for something. Day after day I waited, though I never knew what for."

She stepped back and watched him slowly turn a dial until he vanished. Then she remembered something.

How could she have ever have forgotten such a thing? She was eleven and she was combing her hair in front of her bedroom mirror. She screamed. When both her parents burst into the room and demanded to know what was wrong, she told them she'd seen a man on a bicycle. They nearly sent her to a child psychiatrist.

Damn that Alan, she thought. He's screwed up again.

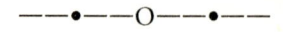

———•——O——•———

The same room, different decor, different time of day. Alan blinked several times; his eyes had difficulty adjusting to the darkness. He could barely make out the shape on the bed, but he could see all he needed to. The shape was alone, and it was adult size. He leaned close to her ear. "Cecily," he whispered. "It's me." He touched her shoulder and shook her slightly. He felt for a pulse.

He switched on the bedside lamp. He gazed down at a withered face framed by silver hair, and sighed. "Sorry, love," he said. He covered her head with a sheet, and sighed again.

He sat down on the bike and unfolded the printout. He'd get it right eventually.

feeding julie

Hannah was standing at the front of a long bus queue when she saw him coming towards her. He stumbled along the pavement, buffeted from side to side by an unyielding and unstoppable torrent of people – thousands and thousands of people, every one of them in a hurry. The man probably wasn't much older than her – and she was only twenty-four – but his face was pale and haggard, his clothes were in tatters. She averted her eyes and concentrated instead on searching the distance for any sign of a bus. There wasn't one, of course. Only cars and trucks, gridlocked in a seemingly endless jam that stretched as far as she could see.

Then the man was right in front of her, his face only inches away from hers. He stank of sweat and sickness. Hannah wrinkled her nose and raised a hand to her mouth, trying not to inhale.

Why me, Hannah thought; of all the thousands of people in the street this morning, why did he have to pick on me?

The traffic started moving again; her bus was finally coming. The man stood where he was, trembling. Hannah thought she saw him mouthing the words: "Help me", but she couldn't be sure. The bus pulled up to the stop and the crowd shoved her forward. She got on and paid her fare.

There were no seats on the bus; she would have to stand. She always had to stand. She pushed her way down the aisle, towards the back.

Craning her neck to look out the window, she saw the man get knocked aside by the surge of people scrambling for a place on the bus.

She saw him fall to the ground, saw him struggle to get up, saw him fail. He seemed to have lost all control of his body.

Hannah closed her eyes and imagined biting into something hot, something greasy and chewy and filling. She opened them again when a man shoved his elbow into her ribs, nearly knocking her off her feet. She was about to say something when she noticed a woman in a worker's uniform, about thirty, with light brown hair cut very short, shoving her way down the aisle. *Oh no*, she thought, *not her again.*

The other woman came to a stop directly in front of Hannah, positioning herself so that they stood face to face, their bodies pressed together in the crush. The woman said nothing, but her expression implied some kind of challenge; she stared at Hannah coldly, without blinking. Exactly the way she had stared at her yesterday, and the day before that. Hannah sighed and turned her head slightly, trying to focus her attention on the scene outside the window, still just visible over the woman's right shoulder. The man on the ground had stopped struggling; he lay perfectly still, head thrown back, mouth open wide. "One less to worry about," said a man sitting next to the window.

As the bus pulled away she heard the wail of a siren.

It was dark when Hannah rode back again. She fought her way to the front of another crowded bus and leapt off, inhaling acrid smoke that made her eyes water.

A group of teenagers huddled around a fire burning inside a metal rubbish bin, their painted faces eerie and garish in the orange glow of the flames. Hannah hurried past them, relieved that they ignored her.

Stepping over a bundle of rags with its hand outstretched – she couldn't be sure if the bundle was a man or a woman – she crossed the street to avoid a group of Hare Krishnas and came across some children who seemed to be robbing a corpse. She averted her eyes and kept walking; only four blocks to go.

Hannah climbed the five flights of concrete steps leading up to her one-room apartment, a ten by twelve box with a kitchenette against one wall. She stopped outside her door and felt around inside her bag, searching for her key. The hall was dim and full of shadows; the only source of light was a single bare bulb, blinking at the far end of the corridor. She couldn't see what she was doing. "Damn," she said out loud.

She heard movement behind her: footsteps. She turned and thought she saw a pinhole of light briefly appear in the middle of the door across the hall, as if someone had lifted the cover off the peephole. Could someone be in there, watching her? She told herself not to be silly, that apartment was empty, but beads of sweat still formed on her forehead and upper lip.

She found her key and turned it in the lock. The key felt slippery; her palms had started sweating as well. The door wouldn't open. She looked up and down the corridor, then back to the apartment across the hall. Everything seemed quiet. She knocked, calling softly, "Julie. Julie, open up. It's me."

There was a rustle of movement behind the door. The sound of something being dragged across the floor. An eye staring out from the little glass peephole. Then the sound of a metal bolt, sliding, followed by another, then another.

Hannah turned her key again, and the door swung open. Julie picked up the little plastic footstool she had to stand on to reach the peephole, cradling it in her arms like a baby. She was still in her pyjamas, the little folding cot she slept on wasn't made, and there were no lights on in the apartment.

Hannah took a deep breath and struggled to compose herself; Julie must not see that she was nervous. She dumped her bag on the floor and switched on the electric lamp next to the sofa that served as her bed. "How come you're in the dark? I told you you can put the light on, so long as you keep the curtains closed."

"Someone knocked at the door," Julie whispered. Hannah stiffened. "When?"

"This morning," Julie said. "After you left for work. Just after. They woke me up."

Hannah bent down on both knees, grabbing the girl by both shoulders. "You didn't answer it, did you?"

Julie shook her head, her eyes wide and serious. Hannah took another deep breath and told herself to stay calm. "Well, that's all right, then. You know what I've told you about answering the door: just be very quiet and wait for them to go away."

Julie's eyes filled with tears. "I did! I waited and waited, but they wouldn't go!"

"How do you know they didn't go away? Did they try to break in? Were they making noise?"

Julie shook her head "no". She pointed at the space beneath the door. "I could see feet."

There was a knock at the door; Hannah raised a finger to her lips. Julie leapt onto her cot, hiding beneath the covers. The knocking continued for at least a full minute, then the doorknob began to twist.

Hannah grabbed a knife from a drawer beneath the sink. "Who's there?" she demanded sharply, trying – and failing – to keep the edge of fear out of her voice.

"Hello!" said a man's voice, "I'm your new neighbour."

Hannah moved to the door and pushed the peephole cover to one side. She looked out and saw a short, round-bellied man with dyed black hair plastered close against his skull, and several wobbling chins. He wore an embroidered jacket over a baggy white shirt and frayed black trousers as shiny as his hair. His deep-set eyes were ringed with black kohl. His fingernails were a brilliant red. Hannah guessed he was at least fifty. He smiled, baring a full set of yellow teeth, and winked, blowing a kiss at the peephole.

Hannah slid a metal chain into place before opening the door by a couple of inches. "Why were you trying to open my door?"

The man looked surprised, and a little hurt. "I'm sorry. It's just that I saw you go in, and when you didn't answer I was worried. I thought you might be ill. You might be lying on the floor, unconscious, with no one to help you. You might have been murdered for all I knew."

"What do you want?"

"I just wanted to meet you, that's all. I mean, since I'm going to be living just across the hall from you ..." He stepped aside, gesturing to the open door behind him. "I thought I'd offer you my services. If you need anything, that is."

"We don't need anything."

The man raised one eyebrow. "We?"

Hannah cursed herself, thinking quickly. "My husband is asleep right now."

"Oh." The man leaned forward, lowering his voice. "Then we mustn't wake him, must we?"

"No, we mustn't," said Hannah, pushing the door closed.

The man's hand shot out, holding it open. "But we've hardly had a chance to get acquainted." He tilted his head towards the open door across the hall. "Don't you want to know how I came to be your new neighbour? Don't you want to know what happened to the old one? The woman who lived in my room?"

Hannah's mouth went dry; she forced herself to shrug. "I didn't know her," she said. "I only saw her once or twice."

The man leaned forward, raising a hand to his mouth. "They say she was murdered." He raised one eyebrow, giving Hannah a significant look. "Now you see why I was concerned about you."

"I didn't know her," Hannah said again, a chill running down her spine. "In this building, we keep to ourselves."

"I hear it was terribly gruesome," the man said with a theatrical roll of his eyes.

"Please keep your voice down."

"Oh yes, the sleeping husband," the man said, winking conspiratorially. "They say she was all chopped up, into tiny little pieces, and that the flesh had been sliced clean away from her bones. That's all they found, apparently: pieces of bone and gristle. And her head; the skull was more or less intact, with a lovely cascade of long brown hair, though it seems the maggots got her eyes. I didn't know maggots liked eyes, did you?" He winked and pursed his lips. "Though I imagine they must love internal organs. I mean, doesn't everyone love organs? Anyway, they went in and found the body when she fell behind on the rent. Of course they killed all the flies; the first thing they did was call the exterminators. But they never bothered to sweep out the bodies, the flies' bodies I mean. They left that little job to me. You should have seen them! They covered the floor from wall to wall, like a crunchy black carpet. Can you imagine it? Every step another little crunch."

He looked up and down the hall before continuing. "And would you believe I am still finding blood stains? They're everywhere, my darling, simply everywhere. Just when I think I've got them all, I find another little splash. You don't have any bleach I could borrow, do you?"

Hannah swallowed hard, trying to keep her voice steady. "You're trying to make me sick, aren't you?"

The man's mouth dropped open in surprise. "Oh no, not at all. I just thought you'd be interested."

"Well, I'm not. Except..." She hesitated a moment before continuing. "Do they know who did it? Has anyone been arrested?"

"Search me," the man said, flicking his tongue suggestively around his lips. "I wouldn't object." He tossed his head to one side, regarding her curiously. "You really didn't know about this? The police never asked if you saw or heard anything?"

"No, they didn't," she lied. Of course the police had questioned her; they questioned everybody in the building. But Julie had been asleep – very deeply asleep – and Hannah had been convincing; the police never asked to search her room.

"Strange they didn't bother," said the man.

Hannah snorted. "Not in this neighbourhood."

A door swung open down the hall. A grey-haired woman stuck her head outside, scowling at the man through thick wire-rimmed spectacles. The blare of a television set briefly filled the corridor with inane chatter from a local talk show, then the woman closed her door and all was quiet again.

"Must dash," the man said, looking down the hall where the woman had stood. He turned back to Hannah. "And to think, you never told me your name. I'll bet it's as pretty as you are."

Hannah said nothing.

"Well, my name is John, and I'm just across the hall if you need me." He winked and bared his yellow teeth once more. "I'd be very surprised if you didn't. This seems like a dangerous building; I think I'm going to like it here."

Hannah slammed the door and slid all three metal bolts across. She pushed the peephole cover aside and watched the man re-enter his own apartment. She didn't move until she saw his door close behind him. Julie stayed hidden beneath her blanket. "It's all right, he's gone," Hannah said.

The blanket shifted and the child's head reappeared: a tiny skull, all eyes and hollow cheeks. Blonde hair that would eventually go brown – if she lived long enough – and translucent skin lined with tiny blue veins. She was small for her age, Hannah thought, much too small.

Hannah pointed at her bag, which was still on the floor where she'd dropped it. "I couldn't get any meat," she said, "but there's other stuff if you want it."

Julie lunged from her cot and turned the bag upside down, spilling its contents across the floor: a chunk of stale bread and a tiny piece of hardened cheese. She swallowed the cheese in one gulp, then grasped the bread with both hands and sat cross-legged on the floor, grunting and tearing the bread with her teeth.

Walking to the bus stop in the morning was like climbing over an obstacle course of beggars' hands. Every step brought another outstretched palm to block Hannah's way. She knew it was her uniform that made her a target, a uniform made it obvious she had a job. But having a job didn't mean she had money; by the time she paid for her rent and her fares, there was almost nothing left. Certainly nothing for strangers. Not even for herself. Not while she had Julie to feed.

She gritted her teeth and forced her way forward, imagining she was clearing a path through a jungle, swinging a razor-sharp machete at a tangle of overgrown fronds shaped like human fingers.

She had to hurry. She'd left home later than usual that morning; Julie had screamed and sobbed and begged her not to go, until the only solution was to give her a larger than normal dose of sedative. Hannah was always very careful about the dosage, using a razor blade to slice the pill into four equal quarters. Most days – now the child had come to trust her – she only ground one segment into a powder which she sprinkled in a glass of synthetic milk. Today she ground three. Julie was dozing on the couch when she left.

The short-haired woman was already waiting at the bus stop; she gave up her place in the queue and moved to the back, to stand behind Hannah.

Hannah was scrubbing the floor on her hands and knees, when her boss's son, Lovell, came into the kitchen.

She looked up and saw him leaning back with both elbows resting on the counter. Lovell was a blonde-haired Adonis who liked to dress up as an old-fashioned country squire, and today he looked as if he was going on a fox hunt. He had the hat, the jacket, everything. Even the boots, which Hannah noticed were covered in mud. A line of black footprints led from the door to the point where he was standing now. "So how are we today, Hannah?"

Hannah wrung out her sponge in the bucket of soapy water that sat beside her on the floor. "Wonderful," she answered dryly.

"Good," he said. "That's what we like to hear." He pushed himself away from the counter and walked across to the refrigerator, leaving another set of tracks. He opened the door and the light went on inside, revealing shelf after shelf of brightly coloured food: crispy green and yellow vegetables, shiny fruits in shades of orange and red and purple, meat oozing blood like sweet dark wine.

Everything in the fridge was carefully inventoried. No one took anything out without signing for it: a necessary measure to stop servants, such as Hannah, from helping themselves.

Lovell selected a steak – a large one, at least an inch thick – and laid it across a marble cutting board before signing his name to the inventory sheet mounted on the wall. He carefully sliced the steak into bite-sized chunks and then tossed them into a bowl, which he placed on the floor. "Here, boy," he said, opening the back door to a small black and white dog that scurried, yapping, towards the bowl of steak and thrust its head in, gulping and slobbering. "Good boy," said Lovell, leaving the kitchen.

Hannah reached for the bowl the second Lovell was out of the room. The little dog growled and bared its teeth at her. She lifted the bowl off the floor. The dog sunk its fangs into her arm, tearing the skin beneath her sleeve. "You little bastard!" she screamed, standing up and knocking the dog across the room.

The dog came at her again, barking and growling and snapping at her ankles. She kicked it out into the yard, closing the door behind it. It threw itself against the door. She could see it through the glass, its dripping mouth curled back into a snarl. She would have liked to wring its neck.

She took what was left of the meat over to the sink and rinsed it under the tap before wrapping it in a bit of newspaper. Once it was cooked it would be all right.

She heard running footsteps. She fell to her knees and grabbed the sponge. She was busily scrubbing when Lovell stormed back into the room.

"What the hell's the matter with that dog?" he demanded, crossing to the outside door.

"I don't know," Hannah said, "I put him outside so I could finish the floor. I guess he didn't want to go."

Lovell opened the door and the dog leapt for Hannah's throat.

Her new neighbour's door swung open the instant she reached the top of the steps; his greasy head poked out into the hall, and he smiled at her, licking his lips. "Come into my parlour, said the spider to the fly."

If Hannah was quick enough, she could get inside her room before he even managed to cross the hall. She reached into her bag for her keys and placed her hand on a chunk of raw steak. The newspaper she'd wrapped it in had disintegrated, and now the meat was rolling around loose inside her bag. She took a deep breath, told herself to be calm, and kept feeling for her keys – they had to be in there somewhere.

She still hadn't found them by the time she reached her door. "Tough day?" said her neighbour. "I know a way to relax you."

She snorted and turned her back on him, still desperately searching for her keys.

"How's your husband by the way? Still sleeping?"

"He's at work; he'll be home any minute."

"If you say so."

She turned around to face him. He was leaning against one side of the doorframe, holding a bottle of unlabelled brown liquid; it was more than half empty. He raised the bottle and shook it. "Sure I can't tempt you?"

"No thanks."

"Your loss, dear. I could have helped you, you know. Whatever happens, just remember that I could have saved you." He tapped his chest. "Me. And I might have – if you'd only been a little bit nicer to me." He stepped back inside and closed his door.

Hannah breathed a sigh of relief.

"You won't believe what I've brought you," she announced a moment later. "I've got some steak!"

Julie stayed where she was on the couch. "I'm not hungry."

"What?" Hannah reached down and felt Julie's forehead. "Not hungry? You?" She bent over, tickling her around the ribs. "The bottomless pit?"

Julie giggled and squirmed. "I'm not hungry!"

Hannah was worried now. She'd left some bread on a plate for Julie's lunch; it was still there. "Look," Hannah said, "you're going to eat this steak, and you're going to love it. You have no idea what I went through to get it for you!"

"I don't want it," Julie said, pouting.

Over the next few weeks, Hannah began to notice that the girl was getting less and less dependent on her. It wasn't as easy to get her to take her sedative; she actually complained the milk made her sleepy. And strangest of all, she seemed to be putting on weight.

"Julie, what do you do all day when I'm not here?"

Julie was sitting on the floor in her pyjamas, drawing circles on a piece of paper. Those pyjamas were getting tight on her, Hannah told herself; she wasn't imagining it.

"Nothing."

"But you don't mind when I go out to work now, do you?"

"No."

"You used to mind. You used to mind a lot." Hannah knelt down beside her. "Julie, is everything all right? Julie, are you listening to me?"

Julie continued drawing circles, large and small. "I'm listening."

A woman lay dead in the street outside Hannah's building, surrounded by a haze of buzzing flies. "None of them shall remain, nor of their multitude. Neither shall there be any that weep for them," said a voice close to Hannah's ear. Hannah turned and saw the woman from the bus, walking quickly alongside her. It was the first time she had ever heard her speak.

"Huh?" Hannah said, stepping up her pace.

The other woman speeded up as well, keeping in step beside her. "Ezekiel, chapter seven, verse eleven. More or less."

"I don't know what you're talking about. Why don't you just leave me alone?"

"Everyone has to die," the woman said. "I know that. And I can accept it. But it's the how I sometimes find hard to take. And the who. I mean, it's far easier to accept the death of a stranger – a nameless, faceless stranger, no matter what the circumstances, no matter how they might have suffered – than say, the death of your only sister. Or your niece. Don't you think?"

Hannah lengthened her stride, walking even faster. To her dismay, the woman kept up with her. As she joined the massive line of people waiting for a bus, the woman was right behind her.

"I mean, there's too many people in the world. We all know that," the woman continued. "If any other animal multiplies beyond what the environment can support, nature provides a predator to cull the herd. The weak and the old must die, so the strong can live, that's nature's way, isn't it? But what if it's your sister that gets ripped apart by a predator? What if it's your sister's child?"

Hannah swung around to face her. "What is it with you? You've been following me around for weeks, not saying a word, and now you won't shut up. Just what is your problem? What the hell do you want?"

"I wanted to be sure," the woman said. "I wanted to be sure you were the one. And now I know, I promise you, you're going to pay for what you've done."

Hannah found it difficult to breathe; her clothes were damp with sweat. *Pull yourself together*, a voice screamed inside her head, this woman knows nothing. She's just some street crazy; she doesn't know what she's talking about.

But there was something about the woman's face, something about her eyes and mouth. Then she realised: the woman looked a lot like Julie. "Pay for what?" Hannah said. "I don't know what you're talking about."

The woman turned and walked away.

She'd been at work less than an hour when the police came. They took her to the station for questioning, and then they put her in a cell.

They showed her a picture of Julie, only they called her by a different name. She told them she'd never seen her. They showed her a picture of the woman who used to live across the hall. Hannah shook her head and said she didn't know her. They showed her a picture of the woman's body as they'd found it: some bones and a pool of sludge, crawling with insects. They asked her what she'd done with the woman's child. She told them she'd done nothing.

When they were taking her from one interrogation room to another, she saw a woman seated behind a window at the end of the hall. The woman from the bus. The woman who looked like Julie. It seemed she was the dead woman's sister.

She was with a man, short and fat, with painted nails and dyed black hair.

They shone lights in Hannah's eyes; she didn't speak. They slammed her against a wall; she stayed quiet. They punched her and they kicked her and they threw her to the ground. And then they had to let her go – with black eyes and broken teeth and ribs that hurt so bad she was sure they were broken – for lack of evidence.

Julie wasn't there when she got home. Julie's things were gone, too. Her pyjamas, her cot, her drawing pad.

She did a frantic search that only lasted a minute or two – she couldn't search for long in a ten by twelve room. She crossed the hall and pounded on the door. "Julie!" No answer. She kicked it, over and over. It wouldn't budge.

She went back to her own room and took out the axe she'd always kept hidden on a shelf where Julie couldn't reach it. She went back across the hall and started to chop through the wooden door. Each swing of the axe seemed to wrench her broken ribs apart, sending shock waves through her body, so intense she had to scream.

Doors opened on chains up and down the hall. Dozens of eyes peered out, some in fear, others in interest. "What do you think you're doing?" a woman called out.

Hannah ignored her and kept chopping at the door until she'd made an opening big enough to step through. The room was empty. Hannah threw her head back and howled.

She had often heard strange noises coming from the apartment across the hall. Then one night, almost a year ago, she'd heard a woman's voice chanting, interspersed with sobs. She'd gone out into the hall to investigate; it was definitely coming from the room across the hall. She knocked on the door, and everything went silent. There was a tiny flash of light as the peephole cover was drawn aside, and then a bloodshot, crazy eye. "What do you want?"

"Are you all right? I thought I heard someone crying."

"What business is it of yours?"

Hannah shrugged and started to turn away. "Look, I was just trying to help."

"Wait! Perhaps you'd better come in."

The door opened slowly, gradually revealing the tableau of a small, unconscious body strapped to a table surrounded by candles. "What?" Hannah said out loud, stepping forward instinctively, to free the child. And then the woman leapt from behind the door, swinging an axe at Hannah's head.

Hannah ducked and grabbed the woman's wrist, bending it back until it snapped. The woman dropped the axe, screaming in agony. Hannah swooped down to pick it up; the woman tried to kick her, but she lost her balance and fell over backwards, hitting her head against the wall.

Hannah went over to the table and saw an angelic little girl, as thin and fragile as a twig. She felt for a pulse; the girl was alive, but heavily drugged.

Hannah looked at the woman struggling weakly to her feet. "Just what the hell is going on here?"

The woman started shaking. She was almost as thin as the child. "I lost my job. I can't pay the rent and we are starving, both of us. In another week, we'll be out in the street. Look at me! I'm sick and I'm weak; how long do you think I'm going to last out there? Huh? How long?"

Hannah shrugged.

"Now look at her! She's my daughter! How long do you think she'll last out there without me? Do you know what they do to children like her? Children with no one to protect them? Do you?"

"I've heard stories," Hannah said.

"Then you know," the woman said. "You know what'll happen to her, once certain people get a hold of her. And they will!"

"I still don't know what you were trying to do here."

"Look," the woman said, walking towards her, trying to smile but keeping her eyes on the axe. "If it's going to happen to her anyway, then isn't it better it's done by her own mother – whose flesh she was in the beginning – than by a total stranger?"

Hannah shook her head in disbelief. "You don't mean ...?" The woman leapt forward, growling like a dog, and that's when Hannah used the axe.

Hannah had a daughter who'd died as an infant; her name was Julie. So the little girl from across the hall became her Julie; she was even the right age.

Of course the girl was frightened and prone to hysterics at first – screaming she wanted her mummy, screaming so loud that Hannah had to gag her, screaming so often that Hannah was almost tempted to let the child know exactly what her beloved mummy had had in store for her – but she soon discovered pills kept the screaming under control.

And the poor girl was so thin – it seemed only right that the mother should be used to feed the child. Of course the meat didn't last very long, but the little girl seemed happy enough, especially those last few weeks.

Then Hannah's little girl – she was Hannah's little girl; Hannah had claimed her for her own – was gone, and everyone said she had murdered her. They told her she'd killed the girl a long time ago, at the same time she'd killed her mother.

No, she told them, she hadn't killed her, she had saved her. She'd taken her in, she'd fed her and lived with her for months. "I was saving her," she told them, over and over.

They told her it was all self-delusion to cover guilt; they gave her pills and injections and electric shocks to make her remember what she had done. And finally she began to believe them. Finally she told them yes, I remember, and they released her onto the street, with no place to sleep and one month's supply of medication.

One night, as she lay shivering in a doorway, wrapped in a tattered blanket, she heard a familiar voice. "Oh, my dear! It's been much too long, hasn't it?"

She looked up and saw him looking down, kohl-rimmed eyes sparkling with something that might have been triumph. He was older than she remembered, and thinner. He knelt down beside her and gently took hold of one hand. "My poor darling, what has become of you? You were such a pretty thing, weren't you? But then so was I, once."

Hannah blinked several times, trying to bring him into focus, to be sure he was really there. "I didn't do it, did I? It wasn't me, after all. I knew it wasn't me; I knew it all along."

He chuckled. "I used to slip her all sorts of goodies through the letter slot. She was fat as a pig by the time I was through with her."

"But I saw you with that woman – her aunt."

"It seems Auntie just assumed the child had been dead for quite some time, and who am I to disillusion a woman in mourning? Women in mourning are so vulnerable, you know. I find them quite irresistible." He sighed and pulled his hand away. "Pardon me, dear. But I really must dash." He stood up, walked a few steps, then turned around and came back. "Why do you think they let you go the first time? It was because of me. They had nothing to connect you to her – not a shred of evidence – because I went into your room and cleared it all away. Some people might have thanked me for that, and some people might have ended up a bit differently. But not you, dear, not you. You should have been nicer to me, you know. Though I'll tell you one thing for nothing," he winked and smacked his lips, "she was delicious."

"I'll kill you!" Hannah screeched, writhing beneath her threadbare blanket. "I swear, I'll tear you apart with my bare hands!"

"Of course you will, my dear."

She tried to pull herself up to a standing position, but didn't have the strength. She collapsed back onto the ground, and lay there, helpless, choking back tears of rage.

The man reached down to pinch her on the cheek. "You're just mad because I got to her first." Then he turned, and disappeared into the crowd.

community service

Prologue

Kathy Lopez was asleep in her cardboard hut on the bridge between the twenty-fourth floors of two buildings protected by the Spiders when she was wakened by the sound of spinning blades. No, she thought, it can't be. She stuck her head through the little flap that served as her door onto the walkway and looked up, but it was hard to see what was happening in the perpetual twilight of the ramps, far below the thick web-like netting that had been draped from roof to roof. Then to her horror, the sunlight broke through. She raised a hand to shield her eyes and saw the net had been sliced in half. Beyond it, dozens of blue and gold helicopters hovered, guns trained on the people below. "Terrorism will not be tolerated. Surrender now," a voice bellowed from a speaker as the choppers began their descent, "and you will be treated fairly."

The bridges swayed wildly from side to side as people ran towards the buildings.

Windows were flung open up and down the towers as Spider soldiers ushered the bridge people in to safety. Then the helicopters opened fire. Several walkways collapsed, plunging homes and businesses and screaming people to the ground. Kathy stumbled along the bridge, wheezing and gasping for breath. She'd just reached a window when the footpath fell away behind her. A Spider soldier caught her by the shoulders and pulled her inside. "You okay, Kath?"

The soldier was a corporal named Raymond and she'd known him all her life. They'd grown up together; he'd been her younger brother's best friend, before her brother, Louie, had been captured and executed. The room she was in was a food store the Spiders maintained for the bridge dwellers. It was filled with row upon row of metal shelves holding bags of flour and stacks of cans. She sank down onto the floor and reached inside her jacket pocket for her inhaler.

"Come on, Kath," Raymond said, kneeling beside her. "You gotta keep moving. Everybody's supposed to head for the basement. We've been in contact with the Cobras; they're gonna open up the tunnel."

She shook her head; she couldn't do it. She'd never make it down all those flights of winding stairs.

"You can't stay here, Kath."

The roar of engines became louder than ever; a helicopter appeared outside the window. Raymond pushed Kathy's head down and leapt to his feet, reaching for his gun. The room had been strafed with gunfire before Raymond could manage a single shot.

Kathy lifted her head to see Raymond lying only inches away from her. His blood was in her hair and on her clothes and she was covered in debris from the shelves; there was spilled food everywhere. Outside the window, the helicopter rose slightly, disappearing from sight. Keeping close to the floor, Kathy slowly began to edge backwards, towards the door. Then she heard someone coming through the window.

"Freeze, terrorist."

Kathy froze where she was.

"Now stand up."

She lifted her head to see a man in blue and gold armour pointing a very large gun at her with one hand while he unhooked a rope from the harness around his waist with the other. She couldn't see much of the man's face behind his helmet, but she'd know that voice anywhere. No, she told herself, it wasn't possible. She carefully got to her feet, raising her hands in surrender. She was still clutching her inhaler.

"Drop it," the man ordered her.

"It's just –"

"Drop it!"

The inhaler hit the ground.

"Against that wall," the man said. "Now!"

Molly Brown

She stood gaping at him, open-mouthed. It wasn't just his voice, it was his mouth, his chin, the way he stood, the way he didn't hold his head quite straight. If only she could see his eyes, then she would know beyond doubt…

"I said move!" the man barked.

"Louie? It *is* you, isn't it?"

The man raised his gun to her forehead. "Move!"

"Louie, what are you doing? It's me, Kathy, your sister…" He pulled the trigger.

—•— 1 —•—

I was working the day shift at Traffic Control when I noticed that someone was making obscene finger shadows on one of my computer screens. I turned around and saw a couple of the guys standing at the back of the room with a flashlight. "Very funny," I said, turning back to the screen. Then a rubber band bounced off my head. I knew who'd done that, and I was determined to ignore it.

Jimmy Rodriguez slid his chair over next to mine. When I still ignored him, he nudged me with his elbow. "Hey, Nora!"

I looked up from my terminal, giving him my iciest stare. I was furious at Jimmy that morning, though it seemed he hadn't figured that out yet.

He pointed to a crack in the left front wall, between two banks of screens displaying a line of nearly stationary cars stretching across most of the fifteenth sector. That was Angela Greenman's sector, and she was just about tearing her hair out trying to get things moving again. Rather her than me, I thought.

"Is it my imagination," Jimmy said, "or is that crack getting bigger?"

Jimmy had been calling maintenance about that crack for the last two months. And he was right, it was definitely getting bigger. But I wasn't going to tell him that because I wasn't speaking to him. I just shrugged.

I turned back to my own set of screens. I had a bottleneck forming in Valley View Road; I reduced vehicle speed to 20 kph and diverted every second car to an alternate – longer – route. I zoomed in on one particular driver, watching his face contort as he tugged at his steering wheel, trying to pull it the opposite way. It didn't do him any good; I was the one in control and he was taking the scenic route, whether he liked it or not. The man finally let go of the wheel to shake a fist at the camera.

Jimmy laughed and patted me on the back. He loved it when drivers tried to resist, and the more upset they got, the more he loved it. I couldn't blame him for that. The poor guy was stuck monitoring sector nine, the most boring sector you could imagine. Semi-rural. Nothing ever happened in sector nine.

The look on that man's face as he shook his fist at me was so comical I almost started laughing myself. Then I remembered I was supposed to be angry. I bit my lip and stared straight ahead at my screen.

Jimmy got out of his chair and sat down on top of my desk. He bent forward, blocking my view of the terminal. "Nora, is something the matter?"

I shook my head "no".

"So how come the silent treatment?"

"Silent treatment?" I asked innocently.

"You've hardly spoken a word to me all morning."

Hurrah, I thought. He'd finally noticed. "Haven't I? Well maybe I just thought you might be all talked out after your long conversation with Officer Stone last night."

Jimmy's mouth dropped open. "You mean Francie? Is that what this is all about?"

"All *what* about? And will you please get off my desk before I punch out all your teeth?"

He switched back to his chair. "Don't be like that, Nora! We were only talking about work."

"So that's why the two of you went off to sit alone in a booth, is it? So you could talk about work?"

"Exactly." He lowered his voice to a whisper. "There's things going on that we're not supposed to know about. Since Francie's moved upstairs, she's overheard some pretty amazing stuff."

"Like what?"

"Apparently there's some big-" Jimmy stopped mid-sentence. "I'll tell you another time," he said, nodding towards something behind me.

I turned and saw a man in the blue and gold torso armour of the Airborne Patrol walk into the room.

Everyone looked up. As far as we were concerned, this guy was one of the elite; his uniform had shoulders out to *there*, and it looked as if he had enough firepower hanging from his hip to blow up an entire block.

The airborne cop took off his helmet, revealing an angular face framed by a tangled mop of curly black hair, and began to move slowly up and down the rows of terminals, as if he was looking for someone or something.

I directed my attention back to the bottleneck in my sector. A truck had started backing into Valley View Road. Great, I thought, just what I do not need.

I looked up a minute later and saw the airborne cop looming over the back of my terminal. He looked about twenty-five – a couple of years younger than me – with large dark eyes and full lips. Dishy. "Can I help you, Officer?" I asked him.

He raised a hand to his forehead, then hurried from the room.

The guy was waiting in Larry's Bar when we got off shift. I didn't recognise him at first, without the blue and gold. He was sitting at the bar, staring straight ahead, a half-empty glass in front of him. Dressed like a typical cop off duty: jeans and a leather jacket, loose-fitting enough to conceal a shoulder holster. He was alone.

I was with about eight or nine others from the office. Other than the airborne cop at the bar, we were the only customers, but it was early yet. Things would pick up later, when the Armoured Vehicle Patrol changed shifts. Then the place would be a madhouse; those guys knew how to party.

"Hey," Jimmy said as we all sat down at our usual table, "isn't that the guy who came nosing around this morning?"

"He wasn't nosing around," I said. "He just took a wrong turn or something."

"He could take a wrong turn with me anytime," one of the women said. "Whoever he is, he's absolutely gorgeous."

I agreed with her, just to annoy Jimmy.

"Never seen the guy before," Jimmy muttered, "now we see him twice in one day." He tapped his nose. "He's not from our area, and even if he was, since when do airborne cops come slumming it down in traffic? You ask me, there's something funny going on."

"Funny like what?" I asked him.

"I don't know. It's just a feeling I have." Then he turned away and started talking to Angela Greenman.

Okay, I thought, two can play at that game. I got up and walked over to the bar, planting myself on the stool next to the airborne cop. I reached into my bag for a handful of credit chips and stacked them in front of me on the bar. "Buy you a drink?"

There was a mirror behind the bar; I could see Jimmy and the others reflected in the glass. Angela was talking to someone else now, but Jimmy still seemed to me making a point of ignoring me. He got up, walked over to the holovid box and pressed some buttons. I sighed in dismay as a woman in a low-cut dress at least two sizes too small for her appeared on a tiny stage at the far end of the room, in full colour 3D. She began squirming and gyrating, her digitalised voice screeching inane lyrics at a decibel level that shook the walls. He had to be kidding; did he really think he was gonna make me jealous with a holovid?

The airborne cop downed the last of his drink in one gulp, grimacing as if he was in pain.

"Are you all right?" I asked him.

"Headache," he said.

I turned to call across the room, "Turn it down a little, will ya?"

Jimmy didn't hear me. He was up on stage with the holovid, doing something that looked like a rain dance.

There was a bowl of nuts on the bar. I popped a handful in my mouth. They were coated in salt, of course. As if the guy who owned Larry's really thought cops needed encouragement to drink.

The airborne cop slid his empty glass across the bar. "My name's Rico Salvo. I work helicopters out of South Central. Does that offer of a drink still hold?"

"Sure."

"Then I'll have a triple Scotch," he said. "Neat."

"Cheap date, aren't you?" I reached into my bag for more credit chips. "Hey, Freddie," I called down to the bartender. "One triple Scotch and one beer."

Freddie poured the drinks, then counted the stack of chips I'd placed on the bar. He took every single one of them.

"Cheers," Rico Salvo said. He gulped down the contents of his glass, then swivelled around to face me, his head tilted slightly to one side. "Do I seem drunk to you?"

"No."

He sighed. "I didn't think I was. Though it's not for want of trying." He pointed to the glass he'd just emptied. "I've had four of those within the last hour, all triples, but nothing seems to work."

"Really?" I said. I could still taste those salty nuts. I took a long drink, swirling the beer around my tongue before I swallowed. "And I came over here thinking I would drink you under the table."

"How long you been working traffic?"

"Forever."

"And how long's forever?"

"Six years."

"Six years?" he repeated, his eyes widening slightly.

"Well, almost. My anniversary is next week. Depressing, isn't it? All that time I spent in the academy, all that riot training and target shooting and unarmed combat, and where do they send me on graduation? To an office where I do nothing but sit on my butt all day, staring at a bank of screens. What kind of work is that for a cop, I ask you?"

"But you weren't always working Northwest, were you? You used to work in another area and got transferred here within the last couple of months, right?"

"No. I've always worked Northwest."

He looked back at the table where the others were sitting. "And what about them? How long have they been working traffic here?"

"Most of them were already around when I started." I shrugged. "We've all been here for years."

The guy practically turned green.

"You sure you're okay?" I asked him.

"Yeah, I'm fine." He stood to leave. "Thanks for the drink."

"Hey, wait," I said. "I buy you a triple Scotch and you don't even ask me my name?"

"All right, what's your name?"
"Nora. Nora Kelly."
"Thanks for the drink, Nora Kelly."
He walked out the door without looking back.

Freddie came over to clear away the glasses. He gave me a sympathetic look, then poured me a beer on the house. "Forget him, sweetie. He wasn't your type anyway."

"So who is?" I asked him.

He nodded towards the stage. "You know that better than me, honey."

The holovid came to an abrupt end, leaving Jimmy alone on the little platform, his lips puckered into a kiss. "Ah, hell," he said, stepping down to put more chips in the machine. Then he saw I was alone. He crossed over to lean against the bar. "Well?"

"Well what?"

He rolled his eyes. "What did you and that guy find to talk about? Was it love at first sight?"

I shrugged. "What's it matter to you?"

"Oh please don't be like that, baby." He gave me one of his little boy lost looks. "You know how I feel about you, so how come you always wanna fight about everything, huh?"

I could never resist him when he looked at me like that. "Let's get outta here," I said.

Next morning at work, all anyone could talk about was the news that a cop bar in Northeast had been bombed the previous night. The local branch of the Spiders had claimed responsibility, saying it was in retaliation for a police raid in South Central, which they referred to as "an unjustified massacre of the poor and homeless". The death toll so far was in the thirties, but expected to rise to at least fifty, which would bring the number of police killed so far that year to nearly four hundred.

There was a jam building up in my sector. I started to divert a couple of trucks, and then I stood up.

"Something the matter, babe?" Jimmy asked me.

There was something the matter, all right. My father and my brother had both been killed by the terror gangs, and this latest atrocity by the

Spiders had brought it all back. I hadn't become a cop so I could sit in a basement monitoring traffic while terrorist scum were getting away with murder. "Cover for me, will you?"

I went upstairs to the personnel office and demanded a transfer to patrol. "I don't belong behind a desk," I told them. "I should be out there on the streets, where I'm needed."

"Sit down, Officer Kelly," the woman behind the desk said, "and let's have a little talk."

—·—2—·—

I was ordered to report to a room at East Central Headquarters, where a woman in a Captain's uniform asked a couple of routine questions before telling me that I was being assigned to Armoured Vehicle Patrol in the seventeenth sector.

Vehicle patrol! I couldn't wait to tell Jimmy. The captain pressed a button on her desk. "Send Kopalski in."

There was a knock at the door, then a tall man entered, wearing the blue and white torso armour of a vehicle cop, his helmet tucked beneath one arm. He was in his late twenties or early thirties, with pale blonde hair, cut very short. His face was round and boyish, and his eyes were the brightest shade of blue I'd ever seen.

"Officer Kopalski," the Captain said, "this is Officer Kelly. I'm assigning her to be your partner."

Kopalski grabbed hold of my hand and shook it up and down. "Nice to meet you, partner."

"Officer Kopalski," I said, wincing. The guy had quite a grip. I pulled my hand away and turned to face the Captain. "When do I start?"

"Tonight. Report to sub-station four at twenty-one hundred hours."

"But I left all my stuff –"

"That's all been taken care of," the Captain interrupted. "Your possessions should be en route to your new quarters within the hour." She reached into a desk drawer and handed me a key. "Accommodation Block B. It's just around the corner."

The elation I'd felt a few moments earlier had vanished. Everything was happening so fast. I'd thought I'd have at least a couple of days to arrange everything. I'd thought I'd be able to spend some time with Jimmy and say good-bye to all my friends and maybe have a big farewell bash at Larry's, and now it looked like I wasn't going do any of those things.

And I didn't like the thought of strangers in my room, going through all my things.

I dumped four heavy bags on the lobby floor of Accommodation Block B and held my ID out to the clerk behind the desk. "Ah yes, Kelly," he said, checking the name against a list on his computer. "Been shopping, have you?"

I turned the key in the door of my new quarters on the thirty-first floor and switched on the lights. Not only had my possessions been delivered in my absence; they'd been unpacked. I blinked several times, shaking my head in disbelief. Everything was exactly the same, the same standard furnishings, the same light blue paper on the walls. I could have been back in my room at Northwest Area, if it wasn't for the fact that this place was so much cleaner.

But that won't last long, I thought, flopping onto the bed. I rolled onto my side was asleep within seconds.

Officer James Rodriguez
Room 1728
Accommodation Block A
Northwest Area

Dear Jimmy,

I must have written you at least a dozen times over the last two months, so how come I haven't heard anything back from you?

Everything's okay this end, though I miss you and the rest of the old traffic gang something terrible. None of them have written to me either. What the hell's going on, huh?

Bruce (I told you about him, he's my partner) and I get along just fine, but – this is going to sound corny – he just isn't you. Goofy, huh? I can almost hear you laughing over the net.

Please Jimmy, please please write back.

        Nora

I re-read the letter I'd typed on my bedside screen before I pressed the key to mail it. I'd tried to keep it short and light this time; my last couple of letters had sounded kind of desperate. But what was I supposed to do? This not hearing anything was driving me crazy.

I got up and made a cup of coffee.

A couple of hours later, I opened a bottle of Scotch. Jimmy still hadn't written back.

Kopalski knocked on my door a little after eight. He lived a couple of floors above me, and we'd got into the habit of leaving for parade together. But this was our night off.

I opened the door, holding the Scotch bottle in one hand. It was only half empty; I still had some way to go. "What do you want, Kopalski?"

"Looks like I've come at a bad time," he said, eyeing the bottle.

"You think there's any such thing as a good time?" I stepped aside to let him pass. "Come on in."

He sat down at my kitchenette counter. "You okay, Nora?"

"I'm fine."

"It's just... you seem upset."

I took a long swig from the bottle. "Do I?"

"Maybe it's none of my business..."

"It isn't."

"But as your partner... and I hope... your friend..." He sighed and shook his head. "Drinking alone out of a bottle is not what I'd call a good sign."

"Kopalski, what I do on my night off in my own room is my own damn business, okay? And for the record, it doesn't affect me." I held out my hand to show him. "See? Steady as a rock. I could drink five gallons of this stuff, it wouldn't be any different."

"Sounds like an even worse sign," he said.

"What do you want, Kopalski? Just tell me what you want, okay? And then you can piss off outta here and leave me alone!"

He stood up. "I'm going."

Damn, I thought, why am I doing this? We got along fine when we were on duty. I liked the guy. I put down the bottle and spread my arms to block his way. "Look, I didn't mean that, okay? Sit back down, I'll make us some coffee."

He nodded and sat down.

I went around behind the counter and started heating up some water. "So what brings you knocking on my door tonight, Bruce?" I asked him, keeping my voice light and casual so he'd know we were still friends. "Don't usually see you on a night off."

"I knocked on your door because I wondered if you might like to go out for a pizza or something," he said, looking away.

"Go out with you?" This wasn't the same as going for a drink at the end of a shift; I wondered what he was getting at. "Why?"

"No reason," he said. "It's just that it's my birthday, and I felt like maybe going out or something and I wondered if you'd like to come." He threw up his hands. "Just forget it, okay? I'm sorry I bothered you." He stood and started walking towards the door.

I glanced at the blank screen of my bedside computer. Jimmy would have been off shift for hours now. I knew he wasn't going to write back. Not ever. "Wait," I said.

Kopalski kept walking.

"Bruce!"

He stopped and turned around.

"Why didn't you tell me it was your birthday? I woulda got you a present or something."

"Oh yeah?" His cheeks turned pink. "What would you have got me?"

"Something cheap." I reached for my coat. "So where you wanna go?"

A week later we were called to a disturbance near the Heights, a housing estate the locals referred to as "the Fortress" because its hilltop location had made it a stronghold for the East Central branch of the Spiders. Cops never went into the Fortress, but this was just a domestic tiff in the no man's land on the outskirts near the bottom of the hill, too easily accessible from outside to be much use to the terror gangs.

It was my turn to do the driving. The sun was setting as the car approached the hill. I couldn't resist the urge to gaze up at the high dark towers of the Fortress set against a glowing red sky. While other terror gangs like the Cobras and the Blades had moved their operations to underground tunnels, the Spiders had taken to the air. They were famous for the huge nets they draped across their roofs and their networks of suspended walkways. They said there were people in the Fortress whose feet had never touched the ground. The Fortress represented everything I hated, everything I was sworn to fight against – but at that moment I couldn't stop thinking that those tall black silhouettes also had a kind of strange, almost thrilling, beauty. I noticed that Bruce was looking up at them too, and I couldn't help smiling.

A group of children appeared out of nowhere and started pelting the car with rocks. I gritted my teeth and kept driving; children with rocks were just one of those things you got used to on vehicle patrol.

The address we'd been given turned out to be a converted garage at the end of an alley. I stepped on the brakes, rolled down the window and listened. "No sound of breaking glass, no yelling. Maybe they've already kissed and made up."

"Let's hope so," Bruce said.

We got out of the car and walked towards the door. I reached up to ring the bell and a window above my head flew open. There was a sound like an explosion. Bruce toppled forward, clutching at his chest. "Officer down!" I shouted into my radio. "We need help! Now!"

There were more shots from overhead. Spirallers: those spinning rocket-type bullets with a tail of flaming propellant that can burn a hole through nearly two inches of solid steel. This was no domestic call; this was an ambush. I crouched down with my drawn weapon in one hand, trying to shield Bruce's body while I dragged him back to the car. "Don't die on me, damn you," I warned him. "Don't even think about it."

A spiraller spun past my head, melting a hole in the side of my helmet. I fired several times into the window the shots were coming from. There was a moment's silence, then a spiraller grazed my arm, scorching the sleeve of my jacket. Another grazed my leg.

I kept tugging at Bruce with my one free arm until I managed to get him around the back of the car. I fired over and over at that upstairs window, tears streaming down my face. Bruce wasn't moving.

Suddenly the air was filled with the hum of spinning blades. There was a loud burst of gunfire, then a figure in blue and gold slid down a rope, landing directly behind me. I turned to see a woman holding a hypodermic needle. "Just relax," she told me, "you'll feel better if you just relax."

—•— 3 —•—

I woke up in some kind of clinic, with an acrid smell of disinfectant in my nostrils and a terrible chemical taste in my mouth. A man in a white coat stood at the foot of my bed. "What's your name?" he asked me.

I had to think about that. I noticed a jug by the side of the bed and sat up to pour myself a glass of water. "Kelly," I said finally. "Nora Kelly."

"And what do you do for a living?"

That was easy. "I'm a police officer."

"Do you remember anything else?"

I suddenly became aware of a throbbing pain behind my forehead. "My father worked Armoured Vehicle Patrol in West Central," I said, reaching up to rub my temples. "He was killed on duty when I was just a kid. I entered the academy the year my brother was shot."

The man shone a narrow beam of light into one of my eyes, which made the pain in my head even worse. "Then what?"

I raised a hand to block the light. "Six years of boredom in Traffic Control. What am I doing here?"

"You had a little accident, but you're all right now. Good to have you back with us, Officer Kelly," the man said.

I was assigned to a small station in the seventeenth sector at Southeast, which immediately erupted into full-scale war between us and an alliance of the Cobras and the Blades. I remember the next few months as a blur of shootings and bombings. The fourth time I was wounded, they gave me a medal. And then they told me to get myself a set of blue and gold because I was being transferred to airborne.

I had to go back to Northwest Area, one last time. I had to show them.

I went down to the basement and found myself in a room full of strangers. A man looked up from his terminal. "May I help you, Officer?"

"I'm looking for someone," I said. "Do you know an Officer James

Rodriguez?"

He shook his head.

I started to wonder if I was in the wrong room. Then I saw the jagged stripe of mismatched plaster where someone had finally filled in that crack Jimmy always used to complain about. I mentioned some other names of people I had worked with.

"Try Personnel, on the second floor."

"I'll do that," I said. "By the way, how long have you been working Northwest Traffic?"

"About eight years."

"Eight years? Here? In this room?"

He laughed. "Sad, isn't it?"

I went across the street to Larry's Bar, but it wasn't there. A squat prefab stood in its place. A sign above the door read: "Colette's Lounge".

I went inside. No one in Colette's had ever heard of Jimmy Rodriguez. They hadn't heard of him at his old accommodation block, either.

I spent the long drive home trying to make sense of it all, but I couldn't.

I got off the elevator at the twenty-ninth floor and opened the door to my quarters. Though the room was dark, I couldn't miss the outline of that familiar figure standing in the shadows beside my window. "Jimmy!"

I raced across the room and threw my arms around him, words pouring out of my mouth in a rush. "Jimmy, for God's sake where have you been? Why didn't you write? And what are you doing here? Oh God, it's so good to see you!"

He pushed me away and switched on the lights. When I saw his face, I was horrified. There were deep lines around his eyes and mouth and his hair was streaked with silver. He looked like an old man. "Jimmy, what happened to you?"

"Hand over your weapon, Officer."

It was then I noticed he was wearing a Captain's badge. "When did you make Captain?"

"I said hand over your weapon, Officer! Now!"

"Okay, Jimmy." I handed him my gun. "What's going on?"

"You've been breaking regulations, Officer. Leaving your own area without permission is strictly prohibited, even the greenest rookie knows that. But you went to Northwest today, didn't you?"

"I only went to see you, you jerk," I said, playfully punching him on the shoulder.

He batted my hand away as if he couldn't stand the thought of me touching him. "Don't do that again."

"Jimmy, why are you acting this way? This is me you're talking to! Me, Nora. Remember?"

"Don't you dare," he hissed. "Don't you dare!"

My eyes filled with tears. "Jimmy, please. This isn't like you…"

He slapped me across the face, hard. "Shut up, you murdering terrorist scum!"

"What?" I croaked. The tears were rolling down my cheeks now; I couldn't stop them.

"Scum, that's all you are. You used to make bombs for the Spiders in a tower in North Central. But you don't remember that, do you, Officer?"

I cursed myself for giving up my weapon. Jimmy had gone crazy. I took a step backwards and found I was up against the wall. "Jimmy, you need help…"

"Don't move," he said, pointing my own gun at me. "You really think you're Nora, don't you? But then so did all the others; you must be the fifth or sixth by now. I remember the second one used to bombard me with letters, the stupid bitch. But you're the first to actually come looking for me."

"Jimmy," I said, keeping an eye on the gun, "you're not making sense."

"Aren't I? Then let me explain. Officer Nora Kelly agreed to take part in an experiment –"

"I remember that," I interrupted. "I went up to Personnel to demand a transfer and they asked me if I would be willing to take part in some new programme, then they sent me to some doctor for a physical, but all he did was some kind of brain scan or something…"

He scowled, then carried on. "Nora Kelly's memory was downloaded into a computer. Everything she'd ever learned, done, seen or felt."

I didn't remember that part.

"She died in a terrorist blast at Larry's Bar seven months later. That was twenty years ago, and they've been making new Noras ever since. She's just one of hundreds we re-use every three or four years."

"What?"

"What other choice did we have? Fatality rates for police were at an all time high; and thanks to the anti-police propaganda being spread by Spiders and the other terror gangs, recruitment had never been so low. So we started taking convicted criminals and terrorists who'd been sentenced to death, wiped out their previous identity and programmed them with the memories and personalities of dead cops, then sent them into the most dangerous sectors. They were disposable, like cannon fodder. It didn't matter if they got killed on duty – matter of fact, that's what was supposed to happen. Rather than putting them on the chair or giving them a lethal injection, the courts gave us approval to make some use of them before they died. Of course it's always been very hush hush; it's hardly the sort of thing you make public. But I'd say at least half the force at any time – on patrol, that is, not on desk jobs – are convicted criminals doing community service."

I thought back to that long ago evening in Larry's Bar; it seemed like yesterday. "I remember an airborne cop came into the room while we were working at Northwest Traffic. He seemed confused, like he was looking for someone... Like I felt today, looking for you. I remember I bought him a drink that night, while you were dancing with some holovid. He was so sad... He said his name was Rico Salvo. Was he...?"

Jimmy finished the question for me. "Another ex-Spider with implanted memories of working at Northwest Traffic?"

I nodded.

"His real name was Louie Lopez, and he couldn't follow regulations, either," Jimmy said. "Though in his case, what happened wasn't really his fault. It seems some idiot in dispatch screwed up and assigned the guy to South Central, which happened to be his home area and I guess somebody there recognised him, which completely blew his programming. Assignments are supposed to be carefully orchestrated; no one is ever stationed any place where they might encounter past associates. And that includes other cops who might have known an earlier version of the implanted personality. But whether Lopez was the victim of an administrative fuck-up or not was not the issue. Insubordination was the issue: it's the one thing we cannot and will not tolerate." He sighed. "His original sentence was carried out the next day."

I felt my eyes widen. "You can't mean what I think you mean…"

"Don't look so upset. You never even met the guy. You only remember that particular incident because it happened to the real Nora before her memories were downloaded, and we still haven't figured out how to edit the damn things." He sat down on my bed, keeping the gun pointed at me the whole time. "How about a guy named Bruce Kopalski? Remember him?"

I shook my head.

"Of course you don't. No more than the current Kopalski remembers a woman named Nora Kelly. Though word is that once upon a time, those two became quite friendly, if you catch my drift." He picked up the empty bottle I'd left on the bedside table. "This was despite the fact the third Kopalski was more than a little concerned about the second Nora's drinking." He laughed. "The original Nora liked a drink now and then, but she could never handle her liquor. The times I had to carry her home from Larry's…

"Doesn't affect you though, does it? And drugs don't do anything for you guys, either… There's always stuff it's better not to leave to chance." He dropped the bottle, letting it crash into pieces at his feet. "Your name used to be Martina Wiley, by the way. Just in case you were wondering…"

He clicked back the hammer on my gun.

"Jimmy, please don't do this. No matter what you say, I know what I remember and the one thing I can't forget is that I've always loved you."

His face softened briefly. "I doubt it's any consolation, but after you there won't be any more Nora Kellys. She wasn't a bad cop, but she was too emotional. This isn't the first time a Nora's caused problems."

I brought one leg up in a sweeping kick, knocking the gun from Jimmy's hand. As he bent forward to pick it up, I brought a hand down on the back of his neck; I heard it crack.

He crumpled onto the floor. I knelt down beside him, cradling his head in my arms. "Oh Jimmy, Jimmy, why?"

My world was falling apart. Jimmy, my best and only friend, the man

I loved more than I'd ever loved anyone, had tried to murder me.

He wasn't breathing.

"No," I sobbed, rocking his head like a baby. "Don't be dead. Don't leave me!"

Something fell out of his jacket. I picked it up and saw a faded photo of a redheaded woman, with large green eyes and a round face dotted with freckles. Written across it were the words: *To Jimmy, love forever, Nora.*

She wasn't me.

I heard the sound of running feet out in the hall. I reached for my gun and stood, letting Jimmy's head drop to the floor. Someone pounded on my door, and then they tried to kick it in.

I climbed out onto the window ledge and started making my way around the outside of the building. I seemed to have a head for heights.

agents of darkness

On Martha Carson's first day at the John Winters Literary Agency, the second post brought a large parcel with no return address, which landed on Samantha Charlton's desk. Samantha sighed, tossed the unopened package to one side and told Martha she was going out to lunch.

"Oh yeah, so where does everybody usually go?" Martha asked Samantha's back. She got no answer.

Martha reminded herself that her analyst back in New York had warned her about her tendency to paranoia, so she decided that Samantha just hadn't heard her. She'd speak a bit louder in future.

And all that shouting she'd heard through the wall a little while ago – when Samantha was in John's office yelling that she couldn't stand that awful American woman, and what was she doing in London anyway? – Samantha could have been talking about almost anybody. Maybe she was talking about Ruby Wax. Martha would just have to stop being so paranoid.

Though she wished she hadn't made such a fuss that morning when Samantha had tried to shake her hand. But she couldn't help screaming like she did, and she did try to explain, "I can't shake hands, not without gloves, anyway, and I forgot my gloves – just ran out without them. You see, I'm incredibly ticklish! Sometimes I can't stand to be touched – I get hysterical. My hands and arms are bad, but my neck is worse. Someone touches my neck, I go crazy. My analyst says this is an outward sign of hidden insecurities." Samantha had looked at her like she was some kind of madwoman.

She put on her coat and hugged herself tightly. She could actually see her breath. Why didn't the English believe in central heating? Or any heating at all for that matter?

John had told her that Samantha would help her get into the swing of things, but all she'd done so far was suggest Martha take the bottom two drawers of the file cabinet. Martha felt very cold and very hungry. She wondered for a moment if it was genuine hunger or just a neurotic craving for affection disguised as a pain in her stomach. She'd read an article about that on the plane.

She didn't want to overfeed a neurotic craving for affection; she'd just get a carton of yoghurt. She was supposed to be on a diet anyway.

She found a deli right across the street. She bought a carton of yoghurt. She also bought a salt beef sandwich, a bag of crisps and three slices of chocolate cake. Then she found another shop where she could buy real filter coffee, next door to a place that sold electrical goods.

The smell of freshly brewed coffee filled the air as Martha warmed her feet in the orange glow of a two-bar electric fire. Now she was ready to do some work. Her first task was to mount her collection of inspirational posters on the walls. The largest, a picture of a man tearing out his hair with the caption, "You don't have to be crazy to work here, but it helps," was given the place of honour: just above eye level, directly facing the door. She stood back and gazed around the room in satisfaction.

Samantha had been gone for almost two hours. Martha couldn't help noticing that the package on Samantha's desk was not addressed specifically to her; it was just addressed to the agency. She stared at it for at least two full minutes, and then she touched it, lightly running one finger around its edges. "Why not," she said out loud.

She ripped off the brown paper wrapping and looked at the title page: *Confessions Of A Vampire* by Count Henry Vladimir. She sat down at Samantha's desk and started reading.

The first thing Samantha said upon her return was, "It's like an oven in here." The second was, "Kindly take your feet off my desk." And the third was something to do with the fact that Martha had opened her mail.

Martha's reply to the first two was simply, "Sorry." But her reply to the third was that she could see Samantha was terribly busy, and she was just trying to be helpful.

Samantha raised one eyebrow. "I'm sure you have much more important things to do, like taking down those posters." She dabbed a delicate lace handkerchief over her face. "And opening a window."

A few weeks later, Samantha sat down in her living room with a stack of manuscripts and a pot of very strong coffee. She read the first five or six pages of each one before tossing it aside. Finally, she picked up the one that began:

> *I'd be the first to admit that being a vampire in the modern world is far from easy. It's not like you see in the movies, we're not all idle rich, we're not all devilishly handsome, though of course I wish we were. We don't live in big creepy mansions with hunchbacked servants to cater to our every whim. Some of us have jobs, though of course we work the night shift. A lot of us are on the dole. Some of us are homeless. A lot of what they say about us isn't true. A lot of it is. My name is Henry Vladimir, and this is my humble attempt to set the record straight.*

There was a pale glow on the eastern horizon as Samantha composed a letter to the author, suggesting that they meet.

"Dear Count Vladmir," the agency receptionist typed one month later, "I am sorry to inform you that my colleague Samantha Charlton has been taken ill, so if you have no objections, I will be handling your novel, *Confessions of a Vampire*, which I have read and very much enjoyed. However, there are a few suggestions I would like to make and I think it would be useful if we were to arrange a meeting. Please contact my office to set up a convenient time. Yours, Martha Carson."

Martha re-read the letter before she signed it and told the receptionist to put it in the post. It was the middle of winter, but the office was lovely and warm since Samantha had gone away; Martha left the heat on all the time. And it was great not having to listen to all those sarcastic cracks about her being a "hothouse flower". And there was a marvellous satisfaction in tearing up the supposed "gift" Samantha had given her on her third day: a poster of a chimpanzee sitting on a toilet seat. "I do hope you like it. I saw it in Athena and I instantly thought of you." Martha had thanked her profusely and instantly mounted it on the wall directly facing Samantha's desk. Samantha's only response was a frozen and slightly sick-looking smile. She could never come out and say what she meant; stiff upper-lip and all that.

Everyone had been shocked when she had her breakdown. Everyone except for Martha. She'd seen it coming. Those stiff, repressed types always crack sooner or later. But even Martha was surprised at how thoroughly Samantha had cracked. Found wandering in a graveyard at three a.m., wearing nothing but a bloodstained nightdress and mumbling incoherently. The doctors said she was terribly anaemic; Martha wondered if that could have anything to do with Samantha's memory loss. She'd check her medical encyclopaedia when she got home.

It was pouring rain by the time she left the office, and she'd forgotten her umbrella. She got thoroughly soaked and woke up with a sore throat the next morning.

Two days later, she was certain she was coming down with pneumonia. Henry Vladimir phoned just after sunset and said he could meet her any day she chose. "Oday," she said through her heavily stuffed-up nose. "Dow about eleben o'dlock Friday morning?"

"Sorry?"

"Dow about eleben o'dlock Friday morning?"

"I'm afraid I couldn't possibly make it that early. How about five-thirty? The sun will have been down for an hour by then."

Martha felt too ill to argue.

On her way home that night, she bought two large bulbs of garlic. Her herbal specialist in New York used to swear by garlic, eaten raw, as a treatment for colds and flu.

Dinner that night was a garlic sandwich: three chopped raw cloves spread between two slices of bread. By morning she felt a little better. Breakfast was a garlic omelette.

The next two days, she had lunch at a little Italian place around the corner from the office and just asked the waiter to bring her a large glass of orange juice and whatever dish had the most garlic in it. By Friday afternoon, she was completely cured and didn't care if anyone ever came within three feet of her again or not.

At five fifteen she prepared for her meeting by sucking on a large extra-strong mint pastille. At five forty-five there was a knock on her office door.

She quickly slipped on a pair of gloves and stood up to greet her visitor. He was a small man, barely bigger than her. Like her, he wore large spectacles that almost covered his face. Unlike her, he was losing his hair. What was left of it formed a fine dark ring around his skull. He wore a black raincoat over a dark turtle-neck sweater, jeans, and jogging shoes. It was impossible to tell his age; he could have been anything from twenty to forty-five. Martha wondered if he'd been ill; he was awfully pale.

The man's lips brushed across her gloved hand; she wanted to giggle, but suppressed it. "Please have a seat, Mr Vladimir. Would you like a cup of coffee?"

He shook his head "no".

"I'm not sure what, if any, agreement you reached with my former colleague. I'm afraid no one's been able to get much out of her. I mean, she's been in hospital and I don't like to disturb her."

"She invited me to come here, as you have invited me. She expressed an interest in representing my book, but then I heard nothing more from her," he replied with a shrug.

"That's quite an accent you've got there. Where are you from?"

"That's quite an accent you've got. Let's just say I'm from Europe."

Martha began to feel uncomfortable; he wasn't just looking at her, he was staring. Intently. She had to suppress another giggle before getting down to business. "I personally think it's a nice touch, writing a work of fiction as if it were straight autobiography, but first person is usually harder to sell. I was thinking that you might want to re-write it in the third person."

"Never."

"Huh?"

"Why should I write in the third person when I live in the first?"

"Well, we can come back to that later. There's another thing I want to discuss with you. There's a lot of violence in here." She tapped the manuscript with one finger. "Throats ripped open by razor-sharp fangs, the undead rising from their graves to rip innocent passers-by to pieces, lots of gore, lots of blood. That's all great, but what's missing is the heavy breathing."

"The heavy breathing?"

"Yeah, you know." Martha could see by the puzzled look on Henry Vladimir's face that he didn't know. "The sex," she explained. "Where's the sex? You haven't got a bit of sex in here, and let's face it, sex is the vampire's main selling point."

"Sex?" Henry said, raising both eyebrows.

"What else? Think of any vampire movie you've ever seen. Vampires are very seductive. Female vampires wear tight-fitting dresses, have long flowing hair and lure men to their doom. A male vampire is a snazzy dresser who comes in through the bedroom window and heads straight for the bed where he rips his large-breasted victim's bodice. Then, as he sinks his teeth into her neck, we see a close-up of her eyes widening in an expression of pure ecstasy. The whole idea is a lot more's getting sunk into her than just his teeth, if you get my drift."

"I see," Henry Vladimir said. He was blushing. "But I say at the beginning, a vampires' life isn't like the movies. I wanted to reach people, to tell them the truth."

"Of course you want to reach people, Henry. We all do. But how many people do you want to reach? Two or three thousand? Or two or three hundred thousand? It wouldn't take much, just a scene or two... tastefully handled, of course."

"I'll see what I can do."

"I knew you'd have a professional attitude. Now, if you'll excuse me, it's getting a bit late..." She stood up and walked around to the front of her desk.

"I do apologise, Miss Carson." Henry stood and kissed her gloved hand once more. "I tend not to notice things like the lateness of the hour. It is only the sunrise I fear."

"No problem. I'll show you out." She pulled her hand away and headed towards the door. She could see both their shadows on the opposite wall. The way he was moving didn't look right; it was almost like he was gliding instead of walking. His shadow grew impossibly large. And why was he raising his arms like that? She could have sworn that he was leaning his head towards her neck. She blinked and shook her head, silently scolding herself for having such an overactive imagination. Just because he'd written a book about vampires! She put her hand on the doorknob and turned to say goodnight.

Three days worth of garlic chose that moment to make a return appearance. Martha belched a cloud of it right into Henry Vladimir's face and he fell over backwards.

She knelt beside him on the floor. "Oh my God, I'm so sorry! Mr Vladimir, speak to me! Are you okay?"

"I'll be all right." His voice was barely a squeak. He struggled to get up, shielding his face with one hand. Martha helped pull him to his feet, then dusted off his clothes. He kept his face turned away from her the whole time.

"I can't tell you how sorry I am! You sure you're all right?" she asked him again.

"Fine," he said, still holding up one hand. "I'd better be going now."

"Okay, you write those sex scenes, and then I'm going to put the book up for auction. You're going to be a rich man, Henry Vladmir."

"Wonderful," he wheezed, hurrying out the door.

Two weeks later, Martha opened her post and read a vivid description of an orgy in a desecrated church.

The book was duly sold to the highest bidder. Martha got a nice letter from someone at the *Guinness Book of Records*, asking for details of the author's advance.

A few days later, she asked John if there was any news about "poor dear Samantha". He frowned and told her that she'd been moved to a violent ward after biting one of the nurses. Martha shook her head and frowned along with him. Then he told her about a strange recurring dream he'd been having: "I wake up and find Samantha hovering outside my window – and you know I live in a third floor flat – then everything goes blank and the next thing I know, the alarm goes off and it's morning and I feel more exhausted than before I went to bed."

"You're under an awful lot of stress, John," Martha said. "Have you tried aromatherapy?" Then she left for an appointment at the hairdresser's.

It was a total disaster. Every time the stylist tried to trim the hair around her neck, she burst out laughing and hunched her shoulders all the way up to her ears.

"Will you please hold still? I can't possibly cut your hair if you won't stay still," the stylist told her repeatedly. "You're worse than a two-year-old child."

"I can't help it; my neck is extremely sensitive. My analyst says it's an outward manifestation of suppressed anxiety after a particularly traumatic divorce," Martha said between giggles. "Ouch!" she said a minute later.

The stylist dropped his scissors, wailing, "I told you to stay still, didn't I?"

The next day, she got a letter from Henry Vladimir asking if he could come see her; he had some questions about his contract. She phoned him immediately, and as usual, she got his answering machine. He never answered the phone during the day. She left a message that she would be happy to meet him whenever he liked. He wrote back that it would have to be evening; the days were getting longer all the time now.

Martha sighed at her client's peculiarities and it was arranged that he would come to the office at eight o'clock Thursday evening. She ran out for a bite at six, and discovered a new deli she hadn't noticed before. The largest sausage she had ever seen was hanging in the window.

She went inside and was surrounded by the overwhelming aromas of meat and spice. The place was just like one around the corner from her apartment in New York. She suddenly felt an overwhelming surge of homesickness. Her eyes became misty as she bought herself a loaf of French bread and a three-foot long salami. It was the next best thing to booking a flight.

The man behind the counter carefully wrapped the salami in cling film before placing it in an extra-large plastic bag. She took her prize back to the office and waited for Henry Vladimir to show up, which he did at ten past eight.

He had several worries. He couldn't possibly go to lunch with her and the publisher; it would have to be dinner, and a late one at that. Martha sighed and said she would fix everything. Then there was the problem of publicity photos.

"Why is that a problem?" Martha asked him with what she was certain was the patience of a saint.

"I can't be photographed," he told her.

"But why not? Believe me, they'll bring in an expert and you'll look wonderful."

"No, you don't understand. I can't be photographed." He looked at her imploringly, and saw that she still didn't get it. "I don't show up on film," he told her.

"Well, maybe with a bit of make-up."

"I'm telling you I don't show up on film. I don't reflect in a mirror, either."

"Ah," Martha said, enlightened. So he was one of those. That explained a lot. She knew there were people who actually believed they were vampires; like any true hypochondriac she owned enough medical books to fill a library, and she'd read about this particular condition in one of her many volumes on psychiatry. It was a recognised psychosis; it had a scientific name and everything. She frowned and tried to remember the name of the condition. Unfortunately, most of her psychiatry books were still in her apartment in New York. She could have kicked herself for leaving them behind, but she was certain she'd read somewhere that these people really do drink blood. It would be great publicity.

"So photographs are going to be a problem," she said sympathetically.

"I'm afraid so. And they can forget about that signing tour of America."

"How come?"

"Haven't you read the book? I can't cross water!"

"Not even first class?" Martha asked jokingly.

"Well, there is one way. I'd have to travel in a coffin filled with unhallowed earth."

The publicity! Martha tried to keep her voice calm as she told him that everything would be arranged; he shouldn't worry. That record-breaking advance was beginning to seem like peanuts. She had a great idea for the launch party: waiters in black capes and white make-up would serve Bloody Marys and little heart-shaped hors-d'oeuvres with stakes through them, then Henry would make his grand entrance in a coffin. She'd phone the publisher's PR people first thing in the morning.

"Anything else you worried about, Henry?" she asked him, casually pushing a bit of hair behind her ear.

"What's that? On your neck?"

"Huh?" Then she realised that he must be talking about the plaster just below her ear. It was only a little cut, and it had been her own fault. "You mean this?" she asked, pointing at it.

Henry nodded, licking his lips.

"It's nothing. Just a little accident while I was getting my hair trimmed."

"Was there any blood? Let me have a look at it." Henry rose from his seat and moved towards her.

Martha looked into Henry's eyes and felt as if a huge weight was pressing down upon her. All her strength and her energy seemed to drain away. She sat perfectly still, unable to move or speak. Henry removed the plaster and leaned forward with his mouth open wide. Martha's eyes glazed over. Somewhere, faraway, voices called her name, inviting her to join in an eternal dance.

But the spell was broken the instant a wisp of Henry's thinning hair brushed against the bare skin at the base of her neck. She shrieked and brought her shoulder straight up to her ear, laughing hysterically. "Don't do that! I'm ticklish!"

Henry jumped back a little, holding his nose. Martha's shoulder had snapped up and hit it hard. The way it was swelling, it was probably broken.

Martha's giggling stopped immediately. She had seen Henry's face. His skin had turned a horrible shade of greenish-grey, and chunks of it were hanging loose, revealing the bones underneath. His eyes had taken on a yellow glow. His lips were a deep shade of purple, and somehow, in less than thirty seconds, the man had managed to grow a set of fangs.

Henry's breath was deep and noisy. There was a horrible smell in the office. Martha knew what it was, and it was the knowledge, even more than the smell itself, that made her gag. It was the smell of a rotting corpse.

"Henry, let's be reasonable," she said, rising carefully from her chair and edging around behind it.

Henry shrieked and lunged towards her. She raised the chair and swung it across his face. Once again, he stopped to hold his nose. A piece of it fell to the floor.

Martha's mind raced desperately. What did she know about vampires? There were three things that would repel them: a cross (fat chance of finding one in the office), holy water (ditto), and garlic. Garlic!

Count Vladimir glided menacingly towards her, shielding what was left of his nose. He looked angry. Extremely angry.

Martha dived for the bag she'd stored beneath her desk. The Count dived after her. Then he shrieked in horror.

Martha was brandishing a three-foot long salami that must have contained at least a dozen cloves of garlic. "Back off," she said. "I'm not afraid to use this." She tore at the cling-film wrapping.

Henry backed off.

"Siddown!" she barked, waving him towards a chair with the salami.

Henry sat down.

"I think it's time we laid down some ground rules," she said, stroking the salami. "First: don't you EVER, and I mean EVER, try that with me again or you'll have a stake through your heart before you can say 'American paperback rights'! And then I'll cremate you! Got it?"

Henry Vladimir, whose appearance was beginning to return to normal, nodded contritely.

"Second: from now on you do exactly what I tell you. With worldwide distribution, magazine serialisations and a TV mini-series in the offing, I'm not gonna let you blow this deal. You are going to be on perfect behaviour at all times. That means no attacking your editor, either."

Though Henry sighed and nodded, Martha resolved to send Henry's editor a garlic necklace by motor-cycle courier.

"Third: from now on you are on time for appointments. That's twice you've been late!" She paused for a moment, and then she added in her most menacing tone, "Don't you even think of crossing me. Whatever you do, you don't wanna make me mad. 'Cause when I get mad, I get ugly. You may think you're a tough guy, stalking little villages in Transylvania. But let me tell you something Buddy, you don't even know the meaning of tough 'til you've lived in New York City."

The fact that there were no photographs of the author only added to the aura of excitement that surrounded the book.

As the release date drew near, bookshops across Britain agreed to open at midnight for special late-night autographing sessions.

Martha accompanied Henry to every interview and distributed homemade garlic bread to everyone present, insisting that they try some. Those who refused were given a cross to hold. Everyone said it was a marvellous publicity stunt.

The publisher arranged for Henry to appear on a live television programme three days before the book's release.

"I can't do it!" Henry moaned, pacing circles around Martha's office.

She yawned and glanced at her watch. Eleven-thirty p.m. Henry was difficult in the summer; too little darkness made him cranky.

"I can't go on television!" he said again.

"It ought to be all right, Henry," Martha told him.

"I don't show up on film. I can't be photographed."

"But it's not going to be on film. It's a live broadcast."

"You think that makes a difference?"

"Yeah. It should do, anyway."

"What about the make-up?"

"What about it?" Martha asked tiredly. She was exhausted. She had other clients as well, especially since John had gone away on holiday and left her to run the agency single-handed. Henry didn't seem to realise this, and lately he'd been keeping her up until an hour before dawn almost every night.

"They'll sit me in front of a mirror, won't they?"

She'd forgotten about him and mirrors. "Er, I'll think of something." She yawned loudly. "I know, I'll tell them you have extremely sensitive skin and can't have any make-up or you break out in a rash. Okay?"

"Okay," he said, sounding doubtful. "Are you sure this is going to be okay? Martha?"

She was snoring.

The Chatter Box was a late-night live interview and variety show that specialised in the strange and tacky. The guests appearing the same evening as Henry included a sculptor who liked to work with dead rodents and a rock band called Sick Pay. The host, Tony Hitchens, was young, sarcastic and known for his amusing taste in clothing.

The studio audience, which had been suitably warmed up in advance and had practised applauding when the floor manager clapped his hands above his head and cheering when he spread his arms wide, did exactly what they were supposed to, and cheered loudly when Tony Hitchens appeared in a huge black cape. He waved and smiled, revealing a false set of fangs, which he then removed.

"Sorry ladies and gentlemen, I can't talk with those things in."

"Then put 'em back in!" someone yelled from the audience.

"I can see we're off to a great start tonight. That's my producer, ladies and gentlemen," Tony said, vaguely waving in the heckler's direction. "It's going to be one of those nights," he said with an exaggerated sigh. The audience loved it.

After exactly one minute and forty-five seconds of monologue, the floor manager cued Tony to introduce his first guest of the evening. "I don't suppose there's anybody in Britain, or even the world today who hasn't heard about what's got to be the most publicised book ever written: *Confessions Of A Vampire*. Everybody but everybody is talking about this book, and it isn't even in the shops yet! Up 'til now, the author has been a little bit of a mystery man. Nobody even knows what he looks like. But I know what he looks like, ladies and gentlemen, and in a moment, so will you. Let's have a really warm welcome for my first guest this evening: Count Henry Vladimir!"

The studio audience went wild as Henry Vladimir poked his head through the curtain, blinking uncertainly. Tony Hitchens rolled his eyes and made a big deal of walking over to the curtain and saying, "You can come out now, Count."

"Good evening." Henry stepped out from behind the curtain.

"Just over here, Count," Tony said, indicating the desk and sofa at one end of the stage. "Walk this way." He pushed his knees together and waddled over to his desk. The audience howled in appreciation.

Henry bowed to the studio audience and walked over to the sofa in a dignified manner.

"Sit down, Count. Make yourself comfortable."

Up in the control room, the director was tearing out his hair. According to the image on the monitors, Tony Hitchens was talking to himself.

"So Count, let's get right down to brass tacks, shall we? I understand from your publicity people that you claim that you are a genuine vampire and that your book is one hundred per cent true."

"Well, not one hundred per cent," Henry admitted.

"AHA! So the truth comes out! Now look, just between us, since we're such good friends and everything, what part isn't true?"

"Well, I've never actually been to an orgy. Though I've been to some pretty good parties."

The studio audience shrieked with delight. The station switchboard lit up with calls from viewers demanding to know what was going on. The technicians in the control room pushed every button they could find. Still no Henry Vladimir.

"But you're not really a vampire, are you?" Tony winked and nudged the Count with his elbow.

"Yes I am."

"Come on, Count."

"But I am."

"Okay, if you're really a vampire, then why don't you bite me?"

"What?" Henry asked breathlessly.

"If you're really a vampire, I want you to bite me. I'm sure we'd all love to see how it's done. Wouldn't we, ladies and gentlemen?"

The studio audience cheered.

"What a bunch of ghouls!" Tony rolled his eyes at the camera before turning back to Henry. "Really, we'd all love to see a real vampire at work." He took off his cape. Then he undid his tie and the top button of his shirt. "Go on," he said, pointing at his neck. "I don't mind. Really." He ignored the insistent shouting in his earpiece, something about the Count is invisible, cut to commercial. It sounded like his director had gone stark raving mad. "Bite me," he said.

"No, thank you," Henry replied.

"I knew you were a fake. All that business with your manager handing out garlic bread and crosses back stage. I wouldn't have any of that stuff. Garlic is strictly for the French."

"You didn't have any garlic then?"

"Of course not."

"And you are carrying no cross?"

"Now what do you think? Well, Count baby, I'll tell you what I think. I don't think you're going to bite me, are you?" He turned to the audience. "Well, he's a fake, ladies and gentlemen. I knew it all along. This vampire business is nothing but a load of media hype. And if anybody should know about media hype, it's me!"

"Well, if you insist," Henry interrupted.

"So you're going to bite me after all?" Tony said mockingly.

"With pleasure," Henry answered, swooping down over his host.

The studio audience laughed hysterically as Henry, deprived of human blood for so long, greedily drank his fill. They laughed even louder when a woman ran onto the stage waving something that looked like a giant sausage and screamed, "Stop it, Henry! Stop it!"

Viewers around Britain wondered why they couldn't see Tony Hitchens any more, either. He was there a few seconds ago. The station announced they were having technical difficulties and cut to a commercial for cat food.

The sated vampire swung around, faced the studio audience, placed his hands across his stomach, and belched. Large sections of his skin were hanging off; his fangs were dripping blood. The audience and crew watched open-mouthed as Count Vladimir changed into a bat and flew away, leaving the woman angrily shaking her fist and Tony Hitchens sprawled across the floor with his throat torn open. Then they burst into a spontaneous round of applause.

Two weeks later, Martha's office door opened. She looked up from the pile of manuscripts on her desk.

"Henry! I've been trying to get hold of you for weeks! You were such a hit on the Tony Hitchens show, everybody, but everybody, wants you as a guest. Jonathan Ross, Clive Anderson – they're phoning five times a day. Wogan wants you to co-host the Eurovision Song Contest. And do you know the entire first print run of your book sold out within forty-eight hours and the second printing sold out before it even hit the shops! Coppola and Spielberg are fighting over the film rights, and Jack Nicholson has told everyone in Hollywood that he's desperate to play you."

"That's very nice, Martha. But I'm afraid I have some bad news for you."

"Bad news? What do you mean?"

"I'm afraid you won't be representing me any more. Of course, you've been very helpful, but I believe there are other agents better equipped to deal with my – how can I put this? – special needs."

Samantha and John walked into the office, wearing matching black capes. They both had yellow, glowing eyes and purple lips. Samantha smiled at Martha, revealing a perfect set of fangs.

"You can't do this, Henry. We have a contract."

"I think you'll find my contract is with the agency and not with you personally. And these two," he indicated John and Samantha with a sweep of his hand, "are the agency. Not you."

"But I'm the one who got you the biggest advance for a first novel in history! I'm the one who contacted Hollywood! I'm the one who's been negotiating the contract for your second book…"

"I know all this, Martha," Henry said. "And I'm very grateful. Really, I am. But it's just that these two… well, we have more in common. They understand me. If you know what I mean."

"Oh," Martha said. "You mean…" She pointed at her neck. Henry shrugged and nodded.

"Damn it, Henry! You're going to be one of the biggest authors of all times, and with your immortality there's just no end in sight. For one thing, you'll never go out of copyright. And if you think I'm giving up my ten per cent, you're crazy. I'll do whatever it takes to keep you."

"You mean…?"

"If that's what it takes." She dropped her head back, exposing her jugular vein. "But just be careful, okay? You know how ticklish I am."

doing things differently

"Mr Viner," said a woman's voice, "it's time to wake up now."

Josh Viner drove down a winding country lane, eventually pulling to a stop in front of the rose covered cottage he shared with Mary Lou and the children. The kids – Ben and Annie – rushed up to meet him, demanding to know what he had brought them. Then Mary Lou appeared in the doorway, her hands white with flour – she'd been baking again – her belly distended with their third child, due any day now...

That can't be right, a voice at the back of Josh's head said. This was a man's voice; it sounded like his own.

He was fifteen. It was the night of the sophomore dance and Mary Lou was sitting on a folding chair next to the wall, her long black hair tied back with a scarlet ribbon. He walked across the room, took her hand and led her out onto the floor. From that moment, they each knew there would never be anyone else...

It wasn't like that, said the voice in Josh's head, *it never happened. You were too scared to ask her to dance, too scared to even say hello.*

You were a misfit. You didn't dress like the others. You didn't like the right music or have the right haircut. The year you turned fifteen, your skin erupted like a volcano. The night of the dance, you stood alone in a corner, talking to no one. Mary Lou caught you staring at her and you looked away. A month later, your father was transferred to Moonbase and you were glad to go.

Shut up, Josh told the voice.

"Time to wake up, Mr Viner," the woman repeated. After the dance, Josh and Mary Lou walked hand in hand along the river, then sat down to watch the sun rise...

No.

Josh leaned back on his data couch and plugged into work, a baby gurgling happily on his lap.

"I'd better take him," Mary Lou said.

"It's all right; he's not in my way."

... No, no, no! Listen to me! This isn't real!

"Mr Viner, do you hear me?" asked the woman's voice. It was a warm summer evening. Josh and Mary Lou sat on the front step of their cottage, watching the children play in the red glow of the sinking sun. Tim, the youngest, toddled towards them on chubby legs, clutching a bouquet of dandelions. "Sometimes I wonder what life would have been like," Mary Lou said, "if we'd never met."

Josh took a deep breath, inhaling the smell of freshly cut grass. He closed his eyes, listening to the chirping of crickets under the porch, the call of a bird soaring high overhead, the bark of a neighbour's dog. "I can't even imagine it," he said.

"Mr Viner... Mr Viner!"

"Hmmm?"

"Mr Viner, you must wake up now."

"Mary Lou?" Josh tried to open his eyes. They felt as if they'd been glued shut. He raised a hand to wipe the crust from his lashes, then blinked several times, trying to get his vision into focus.

He was naked, cocooned inside a padded plastic capsule. There were tubes attached to his arms and legs. Beyond the open capsule lid was a low metallic ceiling; beyond an open panel in the ceiling was a camera lens. "Where am I?"

"You're disoriented," the woman's voice observed. "Completely understandable. You've been asleep more than a hundred years."

A hundred years? "Who are you?" he demanded. "Where are you?"

"I'm your ship's computer, Mr Viner, and we've just landed on New Eden."

"New Eden?" And then it all came back to him. "Oh God."

Josh sat in a small basement office at the Moonbase headquarters of the

New Eden Foundation, facing the white-haired man who had introduced himself as Doctor Herman. "I'll be perfectly frank with you, Mr Viner. The position was offered to two other candidates before yourself, both of whom turned it down once they realised the long term commitment it entailed." The elderly man shrugged. "We are a privately funded non-profit organisation with no connections to the government or the military, Mr Viner. We can't order someone to give up the equivalent of several lifetimes in order to prepare a distant planet for the benefit of future generations. What we need is someone dedicated to the ideals of the project."

Josh had read an article about the project – and the group behind it – a few months earlier. They said it was financed by a religious sect based on the teachings of a pacifist mystic with utopian socialist leanings. The new planet was to be developed as a home for the current generation's great great grandchildren. Josh supposed he had to give them credit for thinking ahead. "Does that mean you're offering the job to me?"

"You do understand that by the time you arrive at your destination, your loved ones will all be dead."

"I don't have any loved ones, doctor. Your ad specified someone with no ties or dependants, willing to relocate, remember?"

The doctor shrugged. "It's still a great sacrifice. One hundred years of deep sleep to get there, approximately another hundred years in stasis until the colonists arrive – interspersed with brief periods of wakefulness during which you will be expected to install and supervise various terraforming nanomachines. And one thing I must make clear to you is that the ship you will be travelling in is only capable of a one-way journey. Once you land on New Eden, it will be impossible for you to leave."

"In other words, I won't be coming back... ever?"

"That is correct, Mr Viner."

He felt like telling the doctor there was nothing for him to come back to anyway; at the age of thirty-five, he was still a low-grade nanotechnician with little or no prospects for advancement, living alone in a basement efficiency. But saying that might jeopardise his chances of being selected for the mission. Instead, he said he was enthusiastic about the long-range vision for the future of humankind that the New Eden Project represented.

It was a lie.

The only thing he was enthusiastic about was the chance to start life over again, in a new place with new people – people who hadn't even been born yet, people who would come later, in an armada of gleaming ships to populate a world that he had created especially for them. They would wake him from his long sleep on the planet's surface, knowing nothing about him except that he was the nanotech who had gone ahead to pave the way, the pioneer who had terraformed a new world from scratch. In the future, he could re-invent himself, become a different person. No one would remember the nobody he'd once been; to the gentle pacifists of New Eden, he would be a hero.

He leaned forward, looking earnest. "I believe in everything the project hopes to achieve and I think I have a contribution to make."

The doctor stood up and extended his hand. "Welcome aboard, Mr Viner."

"You should eat something solid," the computer told him as he unhooked the last of his tubes. "But not too much; your digestive system – "

"Please spare me the details."

"Solid food has been stored in the – "

"I know where it is."

"Don't sit up too fast," the computer warned him.

"I'm all right," he said, pulling himself into an upright position and climbing out of the capsule.

"It might be better if you didn't try to stand just yet. Your blood pressure reading is low – "

"Computer, you're getting on my nerves, you know that?"

"My only concern is for your well-being."

The panel in the ceiling closed as one in the wall facing him slid back, revealing another lens at eye level. Josh suddenly felt uneasy in his nakedness, despite the fact he knew there was nothing behind that lens but circuitry. He supposed it was the voice that made him feel self-conscious. They would give the computer a woman's voice, wouldn't they? "Do you have to watch me all the time?"

The wall panel slid closed.

Josh crossed over to the cupboard where his clothing had been stored. And then he looked out the window. "I don't believe it," he said.

Panels all over the ship flew open. "Is something wrong, Mr Viner?"

"Give me a surface analysis of the planet," he said, gazing out at a landscape of rolling hills covered in lush vegetation bathed in the glow of two brilliant red suns.

The computer began a litany of percentages of various gases in the atmosphere.

"Just tell me: is it breathable?" Josh interrupted.

"Yes." It then began a list of chemical and mineral components in the soil, which Josh ignored in his rush to get outside.

He leapt out of the airlock, spreading his arms. New Eden was a paradise. The blue cloudless sky gradually gave way to pink and purple around the twin setting suns. The evening air was warm with a slight breeze carrying a heady mix of exotic, musky scents from brightly coloured flowers and huge striped fruits unlike anything he had ever seen. The planet was perfect as it was; it didn't need terraforming at all. There was hardly anything for him to do. But the colonists didn't need to know that, he reminded himself.

"Computer," he said as he re-entered through the airlock, "transmit this message immediately: Have arrived safely, stop. New Eden requires much work. Oxygen levels low – "

"Mr Viner," the computer interrupted. "My readings indicate oxygen levels are more than sufficient."

"Just transmit the message! Oxygen levels low, toxicity levels high, breathing apparatus required at all times, poor soil in need of enrichment, but will do my utmost to ensure habitability in time for colonists' arrival. Signed, Joshua Viner, chief nanotech."

"*Chief* nanotech?"

"Who's Mary Lou?" the computer asked as Josh sat down to his first solid meal in more than a century. Despite the abundance of fresh fruit growing just outside the airlock (which the computer was still running a number of tests on, even though it looked safe enough to Josh), on the computer's suggestion, he was limiting himself to a small bowl of rehydrated imitation chicken broth and a handful of easily digestible, tasteless crackers.

"What?" he said, spraying cracker crumbs.

"Mary Lou," the computer repeated. "It was the first thing you said when you woke up."

"I don't know any Mary Lou," he said, reaching for the soup bowl.

"Don't you?"

He raised the soup to his lips and lowered it again; too hot. "Well actually, now I think about it, there was a girl in high school... Mary Lou Johnson, that was her name. It was the year my father got sent to South Carolina. He was in the army, you see, and we were always moving from place to place, never staying anywhere for long. I doubt I was in that school more than six or seven months..." He blew on the broth to cool it, gazing in fascination at the little ripples this action created. Had it really been a hundred years since he had touched anything? "Funny I should still remember her after all this time. I mean, I hardly knew her, really. In fact, I doubt we ever spoke... Not even once."

"But you dreamed about her," the computer prompted him. Josh suddenly realised what was going on.

"I get it! This is some kind of psychology program, isn't it? Make me think I've got someone to talk to, is that the idea? Keep me from going insane?"

"Is 'going insane' something that concerns you, Mr Viner?"

"No it isn't."

"I'm glad to hear it," the computer said. "Now tell me about Mary Lou."

Josh destroyed all his stocks of unnecessary nanoware. With the nanos gone, the colonists would assume the breathable atmosphere and lush vegetation were thanks to Josh's diligence in distributing huge amounts of microscopic self-replicating machinery across the planet's surface. The oxygen producers, soil enhancers, toxicity filters, all of them could go straight into the disposal unit.

There was one type of nano he didn't throw out. It gradually ate away at the ground, flattening even the steepest hills: a handy way of creating a landing pad for the armada of ships which should be arriving in about a century, by which time the nanos had been programmed to deactivate. He spent several days spreading the microscopic machines over an area of several square miles, marking the future spaceport's site with a radio beacon to guide the ships in to the prepared site.

Then he went back to bed, to await the day he would be hailed as a hero.

Josh stood at the back of the rented marquee at the bottom of the garden, sipping a glass of champagne as he surveyed the scene. No expense had been spared for Annie's wedding; Mary Lou had insisted on that. The band was no holographic simulation – he had hired a live ensemble. And there were flowers everywhere. Even the musicians had been bedecked with flowers. Hundreds of guests were eating and drinking and dancing, mostly relatives from his wife's side of the family. Mary Lou had a lot of cousins.

Ben was there, of course, with his wife and new baby. And Tim had come home from performance art school; he was on stage at the moment, singing with the band.

"Your son has a beautiful voice," a passing cousin remarked. Josh nodded and smiled, reaching for another glass of champagne.

"Mr Viner."

He turned to see who was speaking. The glass slipped from his hand, shattering into pieces on the ground. There was no one there.

"Mr Viner, I need you to wake up now. You have a visitor."

A visitor? That had to mean his centuries of sleeping had finally come to an end; the colonists had arrived at last. He leapt up from his capsule, zipped up his clothes, smoothed down his hair, sprayed his mouth with breath freshener, then pressed the button to open the airlock.

There was no one there.

He looked outside, expecting to see half a dozen huge ships disgorging thousands of people. There was nothing. "I thought you said the colonists were here."

"The colonists aren't due for another seventy-five years, Mr Viner. I said you have a visitor."

He closed the airlock door and turned back towards his sleep capsule, yawning. "I don't see any visitor. Maybe you should do a self-diagnostic or something."

"It's still there, Mr Viner."

"It?" He looked out the window. A small animal was peering up at the ship from a clump of bushes a few feet away from the airlock. "Seventy-five years to go, and you woke me up for some little beastie?"

"It has been examining the ship, Mr Viner."

The animal was about three feet long, with a chubby body. Its head and legs seemed to be covered in short brown fur, while the skin across its back was hairless and shiny black in colour. Josh leaned closer to the window and tapped on the glass. The beast rose up on its hind legs, revealing another large patch of hairless dark skin stretching across the front of its body. It had a large round belly and the most enormous eyes Josh had ever seen. "Examining the ship? Yeah, sure."

"It was trying to open the airlock door before I woke you."

Josh laughed and shook his head. "Was it really?" He could just imagine it sniffing curiously around the base of the ship, its little paws scrabbling away at the impenetrable hull.

The animal was really very cute, kind of like a living teddy bear. Josh could imagine the colonists going wild over these inquisitive little creatures, wanting them as pets. He tapped on the glass again. "Hello, little fella."

The animal took a hesitant step forward, its huge doleful eyes staring straight at Josh.

"Look at that!" Josh exclaimed. "He comes when you call him!"

Josh slipped a small stun gun into his pocket (just because the thing had a pair of big goo-goo eyes didn't necessarily mean it was harmless; it could have teeth like razors for all he knew), then stepped back into the airlock.

The beast leapt back into the bushes as the door slid open. "Here boy," Josh said, bending forward and snapping his fingers. "Nice boy, nice little fella."

The creature re-emerged from the bushes and Josh saw that what he had mistaken for a hairless patch of skin was actually a garment; the alien was wearing a kind of jerkin. And it was armed; a small wooden club hung from a belt around its waist.

"I bring you greetings from the people of Earth," Josh said, abruptly changing his tone.

The little native began shrieking a series of strange syllables. No one had prepared Josh for anything like this. They'd told him there was no evidence of intelligent life on New Eden. Or any other newly discovered planet, for that matter. They had told him humankind was alone in the universe.

And now he was being shouted at by a teddy bear. He shrugged and grimaced to show he didn't understand. The alien stamped a foot and pointed to something in the distance. Josh looked where the alien was pointing, and suddenly didn't need to understand the other's language to know what it was saying. The high, lush hills Josh had spread with nanos a quarter of a century earlier were now squat bumps on the landscape, topped with flat discs of reddish dirt that had been stripped of all vegetation. "I'm sure we can work something out, maybe some kind of compensation…"

The creature reached for its club, raising it high in a threatening gesture.

Josh pulled the stun gun from his pocket, then froze, horrified at the sight of the alien bringing the club down hard… on its own head.

"Stop that!"

The creature hit itself again.

"Stop it!" Josh screamed, trying to wrest the club away from the little native. It was impossible; the creature had a tenacious grip. As they were struggling, at least a dozen more club-wielding locals leapt out from the bushes. One of them shouted something that sounded like an order, and then they all started hitting themselves.

"Stop it!" Josh screeched, desperately trying to grab hold of a dozen swinging clubs at once. "Stop it right now!"

It was hopeless. He was surrounded by a group of living cuddly toys, apparently intent on mercilessly battering their own skulls. He watched them open-mouthed, his hands hanging uselessly at his sides. No matter how much blood they drew, they kept hitting themselves. Even as they lay on the ground, dazed and semi-conscious, they still raised a feeble arm to club themselves one last time.

A voice came from a speaker next to the airlock. "Mr Viner, please come inside at once!"

"Do something!" Josh shouted at the computer. "They're killing themselves!"

"If you wish to put an end this, please get inside the ship! Now!"

The carnage halted the moment Josh stepped through the airlock. He paused beside the window, watching the little creatures sprawl bleeding and exhausted on the ground.

"Oh my God," Josh muttered. "Oh my God. What are we going to do about them?"

"We do seem to have a problem," the computer admitted.

The situation rapidly escalated over the next few days. The original dozen wounded were joined almost immediately by another twenty demented little cuddlies, bearing supplies of food and sleeping bags.

And then the army arrived.

Suddenly, there were thousands of them. The land Josh's nanos had begun clearing for a spaceport was now a huge campsite, the flattened hilltops covered with row upon row of white tents stretching far into the distance. The ship was under constant guard, with troops of cute little spear-carrying beasts in red coats with shiny buttons, relentlessly marching up and down below Josh's window. He sat in a chair next to the control panel, staring helplessly at the scene being played out before him.

"Why don't you do something?" he demanded of the lens in the panel beside his elbow.

"And what do you suggest I do, Mr Viner?" the computer asked patiently.

Josh threw up his hands. "I don't know! Talk to them, I guess."

"In what language do you suggest I talk to them, Mr Viner? English? French? Japanese, perhaps?"

"In their own language, of course! Don't you have some kind of translation chip or something?"

"I have several," the computer replied. "For English, French, and Japanese."

"Oh, great. Digital sarcasm."

"Actually, lest you underestimate my abilities, Mr Viner, I am fluent in a total of fifty-nine languages all together, including several obscure regional and tribal dialects, none of which has the slightest resemblance to the language spoken by the native inhabitants of this planet. I am working on it, but I need more time."

"Time for what?"

"To analyse the apparent context of certain sounds, patterns of repetition, combined with posture and facial expression-"

"In other words, you need to hear them talk," Josh interrupted. "So let's get them talking." He leaned over the control panel, flicking the switch marked: Outside Broadcast. "Hello, everyone," he began, keeping his voice low and soothing. Even if they didn't comprehend the words, he hoped they would understand the tone. "I'm sorry we seem to have got off to a bad start, but it's never too late to put these things right. I mean, once you get to know me, you'll see I'm not such a bad guy, really. So why don't we sit down and have a little chat?"

He paused, waiting for some kind of reaction. There didn't seem to be one; the troops carried on as before, silently marching up and down with their little pointed spears.

"Is this thing working?" he asked the computer. It didn't answer.

He flicked the switch marked: Manual Override.

"I would advise you to be cautious, Mr Viner. Without sufficient knowledge of native mores and culture, you may find your actions do more harm than good."

"Hello, everyone," Josh said again. The guards marching below the window stopped in their tracks, looking up, while others poured out of nearby tents. "I'm really sorry we haven't had the chance to talk before now, but I'm hoping we can make an effort to get to know each other, become friends – "

"They are not computers with decoding chips, Mr Viner," the computer interrupted. "Just speaking English at them – no matter how loudly and clearly – will not make them understand you. You are wasting your time and theirs."

"Then I'll just have to try something else." He walked over to the airlock.

"What do you think you're doing, Mr Viner?" the computer demanded as the airlock slid open. "Mr Viner, come back here this instant! Josh!"

He stepped down onto the ground, watched by hundreds of chubby little beasties clutching spears and swords and daggers. Josh spread his hands, palms upwards, to show he had nothing to hide.

The computer's voice came from the outside broadcast speaker. "Mr Viner, trust me, my only concern now and always is for your well being. Please come inside before it is too late. Based on my observations of your previous behaviour and psychology, I must warn you: continuing with this course of action may make you extremely unhappy."

"Shut up," Josh hissed. One of the cuddly critters stepped forward to approach him. Its cape was bright red embroidered with gold and it wore a big floppy hat with holes for its pointed ears. It stopped in front of Josh, looking up at him with liquid eyes.

"Pleased to meet you," Josh said, holding out his hand. The alien drew the sword hanging from its belt, plunging it deep into its chest. It fell dead at Josh's feet.

Josh stared down at it in disbelief, still holding out his hand.

Then they were all at it, slashing their throats with daggers, throwing themselves onto their spears, thrusting pointed swords into their chests and abdomens.

Josh ran back into the airlock, screaming.

"I told you you'd only upset yourself," said the computer.

More reinforcements arrived the next day and this time they had guns. One by one, little furry beings with large sad eyes positioned themselves beneath Josh's window. And one by one they blew their brains out.

"What are they doing?" Josh demanded of the computer. "What do they want?"

"I think they want us to leave," the computer replied.

"This is how they get someone to leave? By killing themselves? But it's stupid; it's crazy!"

"It is also highly effective," the computer added. "Wouldn't you leave immediately, if you could?"

"All right, I would. But it's still crazy!"

"Perhaps," the computer admitted. "But suicide as a form of protest is not unknown on Earth – "

"All right," Josh said. "I get the point."

"In certain cultures, to kill oneself is to bring shame upon the one who provokes the act, rather than the one who commits it-"

"I said I get the point, computer!"

"So it would seem conflicts on this world are resolved by one party shaming the other into retreat," the computer went on blithely. "And as your ship is still here, they probably conclude you have no sense of shame."

Josh covered his face with his hands, groaning. "Why didn't we know they were here? Where were they hiding when we landed?"

"I do not believe they were hiding, Mr Viner. My guess is that – contrary to first impressions – this area is not typical of the planet's surface after all, but is rather, like some wilderness areas on Earth, a place you might refer to as: 'the back of beyond'. If you hadn't spread those nanos to change the landscape, they never would have known we were here."

"If just my presence provokes this kind of reaction, what's gonna happen when thousands of colonists arrive seventy-five years from now? They'll wipe themselves out, won't they? There won't be a single one of the little kamikazes left! We've got to contact the colonists, tell them not to come. Tell them to turn back."

"They are asleep, Mr Viner," the computer reminded him.

"So wake them up!"

"I doubt it would do any good, Mr Viner. Even if I did wake the colonists, and even if they did turn around, you would still be here. As long as this ship remains, the native population will continue to exterminate themselves in protest. And as you are well aware, there is no way this ship can leave the planet."

"Oh God," Josh moaned. "What am I going to do? I can't just sit here and watch this!"

"Then I suggest you return to sleep, Mr Viner. By the time you wake up, it will all be over."

The kids had been pressuring Josh and Mary Lou to sell the house and move into a retirement complex in the city. The place was too big for the two of them on their own, they said, the garden too much work for a man of Josh's age.

My age, Josh thought defiantly as he and his wife sat in their rocking chairs on the front porch. He felt as fit and energetic as he had in his twenties. He looked at Mary Lou, dozing beside him. Her long black hair had turned silver, her hands become gnarled with arthritis, but inside, she was still the teenage beauty he'd fallen in love with when they were both fifteen.

He nudged her gently. "Mary Lou, if you had it all to do over again, would you have done anything differently?"

"Like what?" she asked him, yawning.

"I don't know," he said. "Anything. Would you have made different choices along the way?"

"No, I wouldn't change a thing," she muttered, going back to sleep.

"And neither would I," Josh said, patting her on the hand.

"Mr Viner."

Josh grabbed hold of his wife's arm, shaking her. "Mary Lou! Mary Lou, wake up! I need you."

"Mr Viner."

"Don't let them take me, Mary Lou. I want to stay here with you, forever."

"Mr Viner!"

Josh moaned, afraid of what he'd find when he opened his eyes. "Don't tell me," he said. "The natives are dead and the planet belongs to us, hurrah. Well guess what? I don't want to wake up to the extinction of a race. I don't care if there's two thousand people waiting outside to meet me, I don't care if they wanna throw me a ticker tape parade, I wanna stay with Mary Lou."

"Excuse me, Mr Viner?"

"Just let me go back to sleep! I just wanna go back to sleep. I wanna stay asleep forever, okay? There's nothing for me to get up for, you hear me? Nothing!"

"Mr Viner, we've received an urgent message from Moonbase – "

He shook his head, thinking he couldn't have heard right. "Moonbase?"

"I have been monitoring all Earth and Moon transmissions since take-off, but this one is addressed specifically to you. Message begins: Political situation has undergone drastic change. Military coup has resulted in martial law in Europe and Asia. Fear factional fighting may spread to Moonbase. Military takeover appears imminent. Previous schedule has been abandoned, everything pushed forward. Colonists preparing for launch at earliest opportunity. Signed, Edgar Herman."

"Edgar Herman?" Josh repeated, suddenly wide awake. Doctor Herman had been an old man before Josh left Moonbase. "How long ago was this message sent?"

"Ninety-nine years, four months and thirteen days ago," the computer replied.

"What?"

"We are many light years from Earth's solar system, Mr Viner. Transmissions take time to reach us. That particular message was transmitted twenty-five years and twenty-seven days after your own departure. Their next launch window would have been four months after that, which means the colonists should be arriving seventy-four years earlier than expected, in approximately twelve months time."

Josh sighed and rubbed his eyes. "How long have I been asleep?"

"Two days."

"Only two days? No wonder I'm so tired." He pulled himself up, stumbling over to the window in time to see another cute little cuddly raise a gun to its head. He turned away as it pulled the trigger. "Computer, you know I didn't want to see this, so why bother waking me up? If they're going to commit mass hari-kari a year from now, I don't want to be a witness. I'd much rather sleep through it."

"Based on my analysis of the situation, I believe that if the natives are allowed to commit mass suicide, it will mean the destruction of the colonists as well."

"Huh? How's that?"

"I'm picking up the presence of explosives, Mr Viner. Enough to blow up the entire planet."

"Explosives? If all they ever do is kill themselves, then how come they've got explosives?"

"Under ordinary circumstances, I would assume they use explosives for such purposes as mining, Mr Viner. But these are not ordinary circumstances – to the natives of this planet, I am afraid this is war – and this morning I observed large amounts of explosive material being transported into the area."

Josh looked out the window in time to see a cuddly rush towards the ship carrying something that looked like a stick of dynamite. He averted his eyes as the stick exploded.

"Wake up the New Edenists and tell them to turn back," Josh said.

"Their fuel supply will be nearly exhausted. The New Edenists must land on this planet, they have nowhere else to go."

"And the minute they land, the cuddlies will blow the place up."

"Unless you do something to stop them, Mr Viner."

Josh sat beside a speaker, listening to the sound of sonorous chanting, accompanied by a slow drumbeat. The suns had gone down hours ago; through the window he could see fires burning in the darkness. Funeral pyres, he supposed. The ritual suicides below his window seemed limited to daylight hours, when he was more likely to observe them. Now, in the darkness, only two guards had been left beside the ship while the others went to chant around the fires at the campsite.

Josh crept over to the airlock and crouched down, ready to pounce. His plan was to capture the guards – or at least one of them – but they both swung around the instant the door slid open, managing to shoot themselves in the head before his feet even touched the ground.

So it was on to Plan B. Josh slunk away on tiptoe, cursing silently to himself. At least none of the others seemed to have been alerted to his escape; the chanting must have drowned out the sound of the gunshots.

A lantern glowed inside a tent at the edge of the campground; inside it, he saw a single reclining shadow. Josh positioned himself behind a tree, watching as the shadow inside the tent reached up to extinguish the lantern. He waited several minutes; no sign of any other cuddlies nearby and the one in the tent should be asleep by now. He hoped.

He stripped to the waist, then burst in through the flap, stuffing his shirt into the cuddly's mouth as he pinned it down with the weight of his body and wrapped it up in its own blanket.

He hurried back to the airlock with a thrashing bundle draped over his shoulder. Its arms and legs trapped, the cuddly's attempts to injure itself were reduced to repeatedly banging its head against Josh's back. He threw it into the sleep capsule while he went to look for some rope. When he came back, it was banging its head on the capsule lid. He lifted it out before it managed to knock itself unconscious, then tied it to a chair.

With its arms tied behind its back, it started kicking itself, so Josh had to tie down its legs as well. When it started banging its head against the backrest, Josh taped a pillow to the back of its head.

"Okay," he said, removing the gag from the cuddly's mouth. "Come on, yell at me. Tell me what a bastard I am, call me every name you can think of. Just talk, say something, anything, so that heap of junk that calls itself a computer can start figuring out your language."

"There's no need to be abusive, Mr Viner," said the computer.

The creature moaned, twitching as if it was in pain. Josh knelt down beside it, placing a hand on its furry arm.

"Please, don't look at me like that. I'm not trying to hurt you; I'm trying to stop you from hurting yourself. I'm trying to save your life. All your lives. I wish you'd understand."

It moaned again, tilting its head towards its bulging stomach, as if it was trying to indicate the source of its pain.

All the cuddlies had protruding bellies, but this one was enormous. He placed a hand on the creature's abdomen and felt something moving. So that was why the cuddly hadn't gone to the funeral with the others. "Oh my God," he said, turning towards the nearest lens. "I think it's in labour!"

The computer was silent.

"Help me!" Josh shouted. "What do I do?"

"Mr Viner, being programmed with a woman's voice does not automatically confer a knowledge of midwifery. In this situation, I fear you are on your own."

"But what do I do? Boil some water?"

"Why not untie her?" the computer suggested.

The cuddly hadn't tried to hurt herself since giving birth; Josh hoped it was a sense of responsibility for her babies that held her back, though he suspected it was merely exhaustion. "You get some rest now," he whispered, placing her three tiny offspring: Ben, Annie, and Tim, beside her in the sleep capsule, then gently draping a blanket across their furry bodies. "Good-night, Mary Lou."

"Mr Viner," the computer began one night about six months later, soon after Josh had finished telling the kids their bedtime story. "I think we need to talk."

"What's there to talk about?" Josh said. "I'm happy. For the first time in my life, I'm fully awake and I'm happy."

"Mr Viner, I must remind you, these creatures are not your family."

Ben's eyes were closed, but Josh could see his little ears twitching; he was listening. "Not in front of the children," Josh hissed.

He crossed over to Ben's makeshift cot, pulling the blanket up over his shoulders. "Go to sleep, son," he said, bending down to kiss him on the cheek.

"Mr Viner, you seem to have lost all touch with reality," the computer observed.

"You're jealous, aren't you? You think Mary Lou and the kids have taken your place. You think now I've got them, I don't need you any more! And guess what?" Josh pressed his face against the lens. "You're right!"

"Dad," Ben said as they sat around the table for dinner one evening about two months before the colonists were due to arrive.

"Wait 'til your brother's finished saying grace," Josh told him.

"Oh Lord make us truly grateful for the bounty we are about to receive," Tim said. "Amen."

"Amen," Ben and Annie chorused.

Josh passed a bowlful of dry crackers to his oldest son. "Now what did you want to ask me?"

"Mom says you're an enemy to our people."

Josh laughed and shook his head. The things kids came out with. "Now you know that isn't true," he said, giving Mary Lou an exasperated look.

Mary Lou, tied to a chair next to the control panel, said nothing.

"But Mom says you're responsible for the deaths of thousands."

"If they want to kill themselves, it's nothing to do with me."

Mary Lou said something to Annie. Of all the kids, Annie was closest to her mother.

"Mom says you have no shame," Annie announced, reaching for another bowl of dry crackers, which she hand fed to her mother.

"It's not a matter of shame," Josh explained. "It's a matter of doing things differently. For example, where I come from, you don't drive away your enemies by killing yourself."

"You don't?" the kids chorused, wide-eyed.

"No, we don't."

"Then what do you do?" Ben asked.

Josh took a deep breath. All the months of teaching the young ones his language, getting them to bond with him, to trust him, had led up to this moment. Now he would tell them that humans didn't have enemies, they were friends to every living thing, and there would be more of these friends arriving soon. He would indoctrinate them with the New Edenist creed of live and let live, then tell them to go out and convince the others to stop this madness of self-destruction. And for once, he thought, he really would be a hero.

"Well, son," Josh began, only to be interrupted by the computer.

"Mr Viner, I'm monitoring some transmissions from Earth."

"So? You're always doing that, aren't you?"

"Yes, Mr Viner, but I think this is one you should hear."

Josh made a face and winked at the kids. "All right, computer. Go ahead if it makes you happy."

"News report. Moonbase in chaos after latest round of fighting. Reports of widespread looting and thousands of unidentified dead. Headquarters of religious group due to embark for colony world said to have been destroyed by fire; survivors believed to have escaped on interstellar craft – "

"That's enough," Josh said, silencing the computer. He looked at his adopted family, the children staring up at him with their innocent eyes, their mother still making an occasional half-hearted attempt to bash her head against the control console. Who would be coming to join them in eight weeks time? Had the gentle pacifists who'd employed him really managed to escape the destruction on Moonbase? Or someone else?

For the first time he considered the possibility that there might be more than one kind of hero. He took several sheets of paper and a pencil from a cupboard, then sat down to make several drawings. When he was finished he stood up, lifting Ben onto his shoulder, and crossed over to the window, looking out over the thousands of campfires burning in the night. These little creatures were smart; the young ones had picked up his language in no time. He hoped they would understand his drawings. "I'm going to tell you something very important now, son. I want you to remember it, and then I want you to go out there and tell everyone else exactly what I said, you understand?"

"Yes, Daddy."

"The most important thing where I come from is self-preservation. You don't harm an enemy by killing yourself, you harm them by staying alive. And you do that by killing them before they kill you. Now I want you to repeat that."

"Kill your enemy before they kill you."

Josh put the little cuddly down and handed him the drawings. "Show these to someone who will know how to use them," he said. Then he bent over to untie Mary Lou. "I want you to go now, kids, and tell everyone what I told you." The minute Mary Lou's hands were free, she started slapping herself across the face. "And take your mother with you."

"But I want to stay with you, Daddy," little Tim protested, wrapping his arms around one of Josh's legs.

"No, Tim, I want you to go with the others. And don't forget to practice your singing, okay?"

Ben took hold of Tim's hand, solemnly leading him towards the airlock.

"I don't understand," Annie wailed. "Why do you want us to go?"

"Because I love you," Josh said, kneeling down to look into her huge dark eyes.

"I still don't understand!"

"You will some day, I promise." He pressed the button to open the airlock and ushered them outside.

He watched from the window as Ben spoke to a couple of heavily-armed sentries.

That night he went to sleep for the last time, to dream about the other Mary Lou.

"What do you think?" he asked her as they rocked side by side on the porch. "Did I do the right thing?"

"You did what you had to," she said, taking his hand. And suddenly she was a young girl again, a scarlet ribbon in her long black hair.

They sat by the banks of a river, watching the sun rise, each knowing there would never be anyone else.

"It's time to go now," Mary Lou said as the sky began to brighten. "Are you ready?"

"As long as you're with me."

"I'll always be with you," she said, fading into transparency. "Always."

He opened his eyes.

"Mr Viner? What are you doing up? I didn't wake you."

"I know. I woke myself. How long have I been asleep this time?"

"Three weeks."

He started to pull himself up from the capsule.

"I wouldn't look outside, Mr Viner. The situation would only upset you."

Josh ignored the computer and walked over to the window. Something that looked a lot like a missile launcher was pointed directly at him. "It's okay," he told the computer.

the vengeance of grandmother wu

Strips of coloured paper covered in Chinese writing hung suspended over a Soho doorway and flapped in the early autumn breeze. Wayne McKenzie sighed when he saw them. They meant that she was at it again. He'd find her upstairs, muttering something he couldn't understand and filling the apartment with smoke.

He wished his mother was still alive. She hadn't been able to control the old woman, but at least she could communicate with her. He spoke enough Cantonese to get by, but not enough to make his grandmother understand him when she didn't want to.

Like the time she'd started a bonfire in the middle of Shaftesbury Avenue. It took him ages to sort that one out with the police, and even longer to sort it out with her. She protested that the spirits would be angry if they didn't get their offerings, and Wayne explained, more in sign language than in Cantonese, that she must not burn her offerings in the street. He felt a sense of triumph when she nodded and went back upstairs, but his triumph was to be short-lived. From that day on, she burned her offerings in the living room.

Wayne nearly choked as he opened the door. She was standing in the middle of the sitting room, holding at least a dozen sticks of burning incense in one hand. With the other, she was dropping little rectangles of paper, hand-painted to resemble English money, into a small fire which raged inside a metal rubbish bin. "Grandmother, please! Someone will call the Fire Brigade."

She ignored him and dropped the remaining paper rectangles into the fire. She did this all the time. First she would cut the paper into pieces of the right size and shape. Then she would paint them green and draw the symbols for £5 or £10 or even £100 in the corners. Finally, she would burn them in the rubbish bin, adding to her grandson's conviction that she must be crazy.

Wayne often wondered how this woman could have given birth to his mother. They were so totally different. His mother had been soft and gentle. He used to think of her as fragile and almost translucent, like the dust on a butterfly's wings. Her death from cancer had seemed inevitable; she was never really meant for this world. But this woman standing before him, his mother's mother, was four and a half feet of solid rock, strung together with wire. Ninety-six years old, with hair the colour of steel and eyes like two black raisins, she seemed as much a part of the earth as a mountain. She looked up as she dropped the last paper rectangle into the bin and told him that dinner would be ready in a minute.

"You know you don't have to cook for me, Grandmother," he said, following her into the kitchen. "I keep telling you we can have anything you want sent up from the restaurant."

She chose not to understand a word he was saying, and busied herself hacking vegetables into tiny pieces with a cleaver. Wayne walked back into the living room and opened all the windows. He stuck his head outside and took several deep breaths. How could the old woman stand all that smoke? His eyes and throat were burning, but it never seemed to bother her. If anything, she seemed to thrive on it.

The chopping in the kitchen stopped and he heard her half-singing some of her usual mumbo-jumbo. He knew what she was up to. She was putting some food aside for the spirits. His father would never have put up with all this nonsense. Fifteen years in the Orient hadn't even made a dent in his practical and totally materialistic view of life.

Wayne was 17 when his father died, nearly 20 years earlier. He was there when it happened: he watched in amazement as his mother calmly addressed the corpse in the hospital bed and apologised for the fact that it would be impossible to cut a hole in the roof, but she would open a window for him. "Mother, what are you doing?" he asked her, thinking she'd gone mad with grief.

"Your father's spirit needs to be let out or he will stay trapped in this room," she explained, adding, "He has much farther to go yet. Soon we will help him on his way."

One night, several weeks after the funeral, Wayne's mother woke him hours before dawn and told him to get dressed, they were going out. She was wearing her most expensive suit, her best pearls and her highest heels. The leather bag she carried was her largest.

It was a clear, warm summer night. They walked for what seemed like ages, each wrapped up in their own thoughts. Wayne's thoughts were to do with his mother's mental state. First she'd insisted he go for a walk with her in the wee small hours, then she'd insisted he wear a suit. He really started to worry when they reached Hyde Park. Despite his insistence that she shouldn't go walking through the park at night, she kept on going. He had no choice but to follow her. She came to a halt at the edge of the Serpentine.

"Mother, why are we here?"

She signalled silence with a finger to her lips. She reached into her bag, pulled out a piece of cloth, and placed it on the ground. Then she adjusted her skirt and got down on her knees. She reached into the bag again and produced a little wooden boat with a sail made of paper. She placed this on the ground beside her and pulled out a candle and a box of matches. This was followed by several tiny gift-wrapped parcels and a folded one-pound note. Wayne watched intently as she carefully balanced the candle in the centre of the boat, surrounded by its gift-wrapped cargo. She whispered something that Wayne couldn't hear, lowered the boat into the water, and lit the candle. Then she gave the boat a gentle shove. The little boat floated away, and they eventually lost sight of it as the glow of the candle became indistinguishable from the light of the moon reflected on the water.

Finally, Mei-Lee McKenzie stood up and brushed a dead leaf away from her stocking. "Are you finished?" Wayne asked her. She nodded. "So what was all that about?"

Mei-Lee shook her head and then smiled a sad little half-smile at her son. "The flame of the candle," she began, "is your father's soul. I have launched him upon his journey to the world of the spirits."

"Mother," Wayne interrupted her, moaning in disbelief, "you've just launched a burning wax stick onto the Serpentine! Since when," he pointed across the water, "is Bayswater the world of the spirits?"

The telephone woke Wayne from his reverie. He answered it on the second ring.

"There's somebody here from Callahan's office. He's got the lease for number 24." It was Sammy Chong, calling from the restaurant.

"I'll be right down." Wayne popped his head into the kitchen just in time to see his grandmother set the spirits' portion of food alight. "I have some business to take care of. You go ahead and have dinner; I'll grab something downstairs."

She looked up from her chopping board. "Stop him, Siao-Te," a voice said. "For his own good, you must stop him."

Wayne was halfway down the stairs when he turned around and saw his grandmother coming after him, still holding her cleaver. "What's the matter?"

"Don't go," she told him.

"I don't understand. What do you want?"

"Don't go."

"Grandmother, please go back upstairs. Someone's waiting for me."

"No. Bad things will happen."

Wayne ignored her and kept walking. Within seconds, she was at his side.

"Go back upstairs."

"I'm coming with you."

They reached the doorway that led into his office. He pointed to the cleaver, saying, "Give me that. You can't go walking into the restaurant carrying that thing!" There was a brief tug-of-war before she gave in and handed it over. He hid the cleaver in a desk drawer and then they headed into the dining room.

Sammy Chong was sitting with a middle-aged and overweight Western man at a table by the window. "Here comes my boss now,"

Sammy said. The man stood up and shook Wayne's hand.

"Wayne, this is Joe Simpson. He's Mr Callahan's partner."

"Nice to meet you," Joe Simpson said, pumping Wayne's hand up and down enthusiastically.

"This is my grandmother, Mrs Siao-Te Wu," Wayne said. "I'm afraid she doesn't speak any English."

"I see," Joe Simpson said, nodding. The man's huge stomach nearly burst through his shirt as he bent over to take one of Wu Siao-Te's hands and shake it solemnly. "It's very nice to meet you, Mrs Wu," he said slowly and loudly.

"Why is this fat man shouting at me?" Siao-Te asked Sammy Chong, who spoke much better Cantonese than her grandson.

"He thinks because you don't speak English, you must be deaf."

"And my grandson wants to do business with this idiot?"

"What's she saying?" Joe Simpson asked.

"She says it's nice to meet you, too."

They all sat down at the table and a uniformed waiter brought them the "Special Dinner For Four." Siao-Te didn't touch the food. She sat, watching and listening. "What's all this about?" she whispered to Sammy.

"Wayne wants to open an amusement arcade. This is the man who owns the lease," Sammy whispered back.

"Amusement arcade?"

"You know, where people play with machines. Video games and fruit machines."

Siao-Te nodded gravely. She'd seen these machines. People put in lots of money, little pictures moved around and when they stopped, people put in more money. Wayne should become rich owning these machines. So why was she worried?

"This will lead him into danger," the voice told her. "Don't let him sign those papers."

"Wayne," she said, "Do not sign any papers."

"Excuse me, Mr Simpson," Wayne said before turning away to see what his grandmother wanted. "What did you say?" he asked her in Cantonese.

"Don't sign any papers," she told him again.

"Grandmother, please!" He turned back to Joe Simpson, who

handed him a pen. He signed his name in three places.

Siao-Te sighed and closed her eyes. Maybe it will be all right, she thought silently. "HMMPH!" said the voice.

The next morning, while Wayne was downstairs going over some invoices with Sammy, the old woman made her way into the street. Quite a few heads turned as the tiny woman in cotton pyjamas hobbled by on feet that had been tightly bound from infancy until the day that she had dared to pull off the bandages and cause a scandal. Just as she had ignored the villagers who condemned her as a wicked woman for unwrapping her feet, she ignored those who stared after her now. She had business to attend to.

That afternoon, an elderly man in a grey business suit walked into the restaurant, placed his briefcase on one of the tables, and introduced himself to Sammy as Mr Han. He took out a compass and a notebook and began to survey the room, walking in a slow circle. "I see the kitchen faces to the West," he said. "That's very good."

"Hey, what do you think you're doing?"

Mr Han stopped. "Aren't you Wayne McKenzie?"

Sammy shook his head. "No, he's not here right now. But I'm the manager. Perhaps I can help you, if you'll just tell me what you want."

"There's nothing I want," Mr Han said gravely. "I'm here because Mrs Wu asked me to come."

"She did?"

"Yes. I'm here to check your *feng shui*."

"Just a minute. I'll get my boss."

Wayne picked up the telephone and listened. "There's a *what* man downstairs?"

"A *feng shui* man."

"Oh God, more superstitious nonsense. Thank him and tell him we don't require his services."

"He says your grandmother asked him to come."

"I'll be down in a minute." He slammed down the phone and

shouted, "Grandmother!"

A short while later, Wayne, Sammy, Siao-Te and Mr Han were seated around a table. Wayne stared down at the table-cloth as Mr Han made notes on a pad and drew some diagrams. He explained that Wayne's desk was facing in the wrong direction; it should be turned around to encourage prosperity. He made some suggestions for symbols to hang on the wall and he was quite adamant about putting a fish tank at the front of the restaurant. That was very good *feng shui*.

Siao-Te interrupted to say that she wasn't worried about the restaurant; she knew it had good *feng shui*. It was the other place she was concerned about. Mr Han nodded. "Then I must look at this other place. Where is it?"

Siao-Te shrugged and said she didn't know. Then she turned and asked her grandson.

"Just down the street. At number 24."

Siao-Te and Mr Han joined in a simultaneous gasp of horror.

"What's the matter?" Wayne asked in English.

"Very bad *feng shui*," Mr Han said grimly. "Very bad. Number four means death. With two in front you get 'easy death'."

"You're joking!"

"No," Mr Han said. "I do not joke. You must not open a business at number 24."

"Look," Wayne said, trying to keep his voice level. "There's more to a place than just the address, isn't there?"

Mr Han nodded, and rose up from the table. Soon he and Wayne were heading down the street with Siao-Te hobbling along beside them.

Wayne opened the door to number 24 with a flourish. "See. It's a nice big room with plenty of natural light. Fruit machines will go all along that wall there, games over there. I've ordered all the latest ones, really popular with the kids these days. Fortune-telling machine in the corner there, and a simulated ride to Mars in the middle. It's gonna be great; a real money-spinner."

Mr Han looked around and sighed. Everything was wrong. The room was the wrong shape. The storefront faced the wrong way and was at the apex of a T-junction: dreadful *feng shui*. A neighbouring building cast a shadow across it. And of course there was the number painted across the doorway; the number for easy death.

"Okay," Wayne said, humouring the man, "What do you suggest? How can I improve the *feng shui* here?"

Mr Han shook his head sadly and said there was nothing he could do; he wished he had been called in earlier, before Wayne had signed the lease. His only suggestion was that Wayne should lock the door behind him and leave the place empty.

Wayne shook his head and sighed. "All right, how much do I owe you?"

"Nothing. I cannot help you." Mr Han muttered an apology to Siao-Te and then he left.

Wayne would have nothing to do with Mr Han's advice; he sneered and called it superstition. He had invested a lot of money; he'd already ordered the machines from a firm in Essex. He would go ahead exactly as planned. The only concession he would make was to put a fish tank in the restaurant, and that was only because he thought it would look nice.

That night, when she was alone in her room, the voice in Siao-Te's head couldn't resist telling her, "I told you so."

Yes, Siao-Te thought tiredly, you told me.

"You had your doubts, but I knew best, now didn't I?"

Yes, you were right. I should never have doubted, she thought in silent apology. She was getting a little annoyed with all this nagging. He never used to nag; maybe old age was affecting him, too. No, she reminded herself, age could not affect him.

"My love, my love. How could you ever doubt me, my love? Haven't I always been truthful with you?"

There was something about the way he said "my love" that still made her body tingle. Yes, Siao-Te nodded, you have never tried to deceive me. From their very first encounter, all those long years ago, he had been totally honest as to who and to *what* he was.

She was married at fourteen to a farmer named Wu Fung-Lao. He was a widower in his late forties who wanted someone young and strong to work in the fields and around the house, so a deal was struck with Siao-

Te's parents, and the young girl found herself in the house of a stranger.

She spent her days bent over double in a field, and then she would enter the house towards evening, exhausted, and make the supper. Her husband barely spoke to her except to chide her for being lazy; his first wife had been a much better worker. When darkness fell, she would lie down beside him and grit her teeth at the feel of his hot sour breath and the clumsy mounting of her body. Later, as he snored beside her, she would dream the romantic dreams of a fourteen-year-old girl: of a heroic stranger who would rescue her from this living hell, of a man she could love.

The next day would bring the same routine: the daylight hours spent toiling in the fields, the evening with a man whose touch she despised, and the time of dreams, when she could be alone with the hero of her fantasies.

One evening, she came home from the fields, her back aching as usual and her husband waiting for his supper as usual, when an extraordinary thing happened. Her husband leapt into the air and stayed there, floating high above her head.

"Wu Fung-Lao!" she cried. "What are you doing?"

"I AM NOT WU FUNG-LAO!" roared a voice she had never heard before. She watched open-mouthed as the body of her husband turned cartwheels through the air and then stopped, hanging upside down. She cowered in terror as her husband's face became engorged with blood, the skin turning redder and redder, the eyes so huge she feared that they would pop right out.

"Stop!" she cried. "Please put him down."

Her husband spun right-side-up and dropped until he hovered only an inch from the ground. His mouth opened wide and a series of animal sounds came from his throat, everything from the cluck of a chicken to the roar of a lion. "DO YOU SEE MY POWER?" boomed the voice, the voice that was not her husband's.

"Yes, I see your power," she whispered.

"HA!" boomed the voice as the body of her husband touched the floor and stood with arms spread in a gesture of triumph.

"Who are you?"

"I AM A DEMON, COME FROM THE NETHERWORLD TO TORMENT THE LIVING."
Her husband's body rose into the air once again.

She ran to the door, but it wouldn't open. She tried to scream, but the scream stuck somewhere in the back of her throat. She collapsed to the floor, trembling. She clutched at her knees, and rolled herself into a ball, rocking back and forth with her eyes closed. There was a long silence, and then a voice said, "Please don't do that." Siao-Te froze. "Don't be afraid," the voice continued. "I won't harm you."

Siao-Te didn't move, didn't open her eyes. "Why," she whispered shakily, "why are you doing this to me?"

"I will do nothing to you. I can see you are just a child."

Her eyes snapped open. "I am not a child!"

The demon chuckled sadly. "You are. Even though I am condemned to wander as a demon, I will not torment a child."

"I am not a child. I am a married woman."

"Married to this?" The demon indicated the body of Wu Fung-Lao with a sweep of her husband's arm. He shook her husband's head and clucked in pity. "And I thought I was the miserable one."

Siao-Te straightened her back and looked directly at him. It was still her husband's face, but with an expression she had never seen. He looked almost wistful.

"I didn't think demons were miserable. I thought they were bitter and vengeful."

"I am that as well," the demon replied.

"Have you always been a demon?" Siao-Te's eyes were wide with interest. She'd totally forgotten to be afraid.

"No, not always." He looked at her and smiled, a sad little half-smile. "Come nearer, and you shall hear what I have told no other living person."

Siao-Te moved closer, and the demon told her the source of his bitterness and his misery: his name was Zhang-Cho and he had been a soldier and personal bodyguard to an emperor of the Wei dynasty. There was an attempt on the emperor's life, and Zhang-Cho alone fought off seven swordsmen. But the eighth drove a blade through his heart, wrenching his spirit from his body less than one week before the day he was to marry. The violence of his sudden death and the anger he felt about missing his wedding had combined to make him a demon, stalking the earth for victims to possess and torment.

"I had only twenty-two years before my life was stolen from me, and I never had a wife. Now those whose lives have not yet been stolen must bear my wrath."

"And this is how you show your wrath? To take another's body?"

"Yes."

"And do you ever give the body back?"

"Of course! That's the whole point."

"I don't understand."

"It's always the same. The victim and his family agree to worship me. Then they build an altar in the centre of the room with incense burning at all times, and I receive regular offerings of food and money."

"That makes you leave?"

"And I never come back."

Zhang-Cho, the demon, watched her through her husband's eyes while she sat on the floor with her chin in her hand, thinking. She had a problem. She liked the demon a lot more than she liked her husband, and he seemed to like her, too. And he'd said he was only 22 years old when he was killed.

"Demon," she said.

"Yes?"

"What do you look like?"

"I am a spirit."

"I know... but what *did* you look like? It's hard to know how to talk to you when all I can see is the body of my husband."

The demon told her to close her eyes once more. She did, and in her mind's eye he stood before her in silken robes and gleaming armour, brandishing a sword which he placed at her feet with an exaggerated bow. She felt as though she could reach out and touch his topknot of thick black hair. Then the demon raised his head and she saw into his eyes.

Siao-Te had fallen into a whirlpool and there was nothing she could do about it. She might scream and flail her arms, but she knew it wouldn't save her. She knew she was drowning, and she didn't care if she ever came up for air again. "Demon," she whispered.

"Yes?"

"If worshipping you will make you leave, then I don't want to worship you."

"Then it is my turn to ask you a question."

"Yes?"

"Why not?"

"Because I don't want you to leave."

"Why should I stay?"

"Because..." Siao-Te hesitated, gathering all her courage. "Because I want to be your wife."

One day, a Mrs Tan walked into her house to find her husband floating near the ceiling. "Tan Lo-Hua!" she shouted. "What do you think you're doing?"

"I am not Tan Lo-Hua," replied a weedy little voice nothing like her husband's. "I am Wu Fung-Lao, the farmer, and I have been cast out of my own home by my wicked wife and her demon lover."

"Puh!" Mrs Tan spit in disgust. "You lying spirit! I saw Wu Fung-Lao the farmer just today, in the village with his pretty young wife. It does my heart good to see two people so obviously in love. How can you tell such evil lies with her expecting a baby any time now?"

She sent for a priest, who prodded the possessed body with needles until the spirit of Wu Fung-Lao promised to go away and never come back. Meanwhile, people in the village began to talk. Wasn't it strange, they wondered out loud, the way Wu Fung-Lao looked younger every day? At forty-five, he'd been a scrawny matchstick of a man. Now at fifty-one, he had the strength of ten with muscles to match. And he'd always had such a scratchy little voice, nothing like the deep rumble he spoke with these days. Many in the village thought these were signs of evil doings. Others, like Mrs Tan, said these were merely the effects of love.

The time finally came when the body of Wu Fung-Lao could stand no more. The years had taken their toll, despite the best efforts of the demon. Skin shrivelled, arteries clogged, and bones became brittle. The heart that once belonged to a farmer named Wu Fung-Lao was worn out after seventy-nine years of beating, and wanted to stop.

Zhang-Cho told his wife that it was time for him to go. He lay down on their bed and closed his eyes.

"No, you can't leave me."

"I must. This body refuses to hold me."

"Then find another."

But he told her that though he did not want to leave her, he was no longer bitter and now swore that he would not take another's body against his will. He had found what he'd searched for through centuries of torment and wandering: the normal lifespan and the happy marriage he had once been robbed of. The last statement to come from the throat of the former Wu Fung-Lao was that he would always love her.

Siao-Te did not cut a hole in the roof for Zhang-Cho's spirit, or even open a window. Instead, she went around the house and sealed up every opening she could find.

"Zhang-Cho!" she called from the middle of the room, "You cannot leave me. I have blocked every exit so there is no way out. You said you would never take another's body against their will – I tell you now that it is my will. Make my body your new home."

A soft breeze blew against her ear. "How can I, my darling? I would never cast you out of yours."

"You don't need to. My body may be small, but I have room in here for two."

And that is how Zhang-Cho the demon came to live inside her head.

Wayne ordered a giant fish tank and an assortment of brightly-coloured tropical fish. When they arrived, they were given a prominent display just inside the front door. He even turned the desk in his office around and covered the walls with the various symbols suggested by Mr Han. He showed all this to his grandmother in an attempt to appease her, but she just shook her head and said it wasn't enough. He must abandon his plans for number 24. This was the one thing he refused to do.

The machines arrived and were installed. Two men, Colin and Ahmed, were hired to work alternate shifts making change and guarding against vandalism. Siao-Te said nothing, and waited.

The first few months were uneventful; the trouble began on the night that Colin caught someone breaking into one of the machines. Colin was a big man, and sometimes he got rough. He got rough that night. It was less than two hours before a gang of eight came in with crowbars. Every machine was emptied, and Colin was taken away in an ambulance.

There were demands for protection. Wayne refused to pay. Three men came in and held Ahmed down while a fourth smashed the simulated ride to Mars into pieces.

Wayne kept all this a secret from his grandmother. He didn't want to frighten her, and he didn't want to hear her say "I told you so." He hardly saw her, anyway. He was always either in his office or at the police station, trying to get them to do *something*. Siao-Te spent most of her time in her bedroom, alone with the voice in her head.

She didn't need Zhang-Cho to tell her something was wrong. She could see the worry in her grandson's eyes.

On a Wednesday night, at three minutes to midnight, eleven men in balaclavas rushed into the restaurant. They had long knives as long as swords and they had guns. Sammy Chong was knocked on the head with the butt of a pistol. Wayne was slashed by eleven knives before he was shot twice in the chest.

A waiter ran up the stairs, calling Siao-Te's name. "Mrs Wu! Mrs Wu!"

She stumbled to the door. "What is it?"

"Your grandson killed! Masked men shoot him!"

Her eyes went blank and she collapsed. The waiter was terrified the shock had killed her.

"Mrs Wu! Mrs Wu! Are you all right?" He grabbed her wrist and felt for a pulse. He should never have told her. He should have left it to someone else. Tears streamed down his face. "Oh, I'm sorry, Mrs Wu!"

A cold wind swept up the stairway and into the living room. The waiter's hair flew into his eyes, temporarily blinding him. A man's voice thundered from somewhere above him, "I HAVE SEEN HIM AND HE IS NOT DEAD!" The old woman's pulse leapt into action beneath the waiter's trembling fingers. She opened her mouth and the thundering voice came from her throat: "TAKE THE WOMAN TO HIM!"

The waiter screamed and ran, leaving the old woman lying on the floor.

Siao-Te rubbed her eyes and sat up slowly. "Don't worry, my love," the voice whispered, "I will help you downstairs."

She walked into the restaurant and into chaos. Tables were overturned, glass was broken, and men with notebooks were everywhere. Wayne's beautiful fish tank had been demolished. No one seemed to notice the old woman until she paused in front of a large red stain.

"Hey, get her away from there! How'd she get in here, anyway?"

One of the kitchen staff explained that she was the owner's grandmother.

"Oh, I'm sorry," one of the policemen told her. "Hawkins here will drive you to the hospital."

She shook her head uncomprehendingly, and someone was dragged over to translate. She nodded to the policeman named Hawkins. He took her arm and led her towards the doorway, pausing while she leaned over to pick up one of the tropical fish that still flopped its tail on the carpet.

Wayne hovered at the edge of a cliff. He heard voices. Many voices. Some shouted; some wept. Some called to him in Chinese and some in English. "Come to us," they told him. "Be one of us." He stepped off the edge and floated gently downwards. "Down you come, Wayne," the voices whispered. "Down to us who were forced from our bodies before our time. Down to us who stalk the earth and seek revenge. Down to..."

The voices stopped. Wayne stopped as well. Something had caught him in mid-fall. It was a hand; he was sure of that. He felt the fingers digging into his shoulder. For a moment he hung suspended. Then the hand tightened its grip and pulled him back up, to the edge of the cliff. A bed was waiting for him there.

It was three days before they let her see him. Even then, they warned her through an interpreter not to expect much. "You can go in and sit with him," they told her, "but don't try to make him speak. He needs his rest."

Siao-Te hobbled into the room where her grandson was wrapped up like a mummy and held together by tubes connected to bottles of coloured liquid. She stood by the side of his bed and looked down. His breathing was shallow and his eyes were closed.

"Zhang-Cho," she thought angrily, "look what they have done to your grandson. You, an honoured warrior and personal bodyguard to the emperor! You, a fearsome demon of the netherworld! Do not tell me you will stand for this!"

"NO!" the voice of Zhang-Cho thundered in her head. "I WILL NOT!"

Unable to speak, unable to move, with massive doses of drugs coursing through his system, Wayne's senses had never been more acute. He heard everything. He saw everything there was to see without even opening his eyes. He saw his grandmother now, standing beside his bed. And he saw the young man standing behind her. He'd never seen anyone like him.

The man's hair was long and black and tied into a knot upon his head. His beard was long also, and it was trimmed to a point. And his clothes! Wayne shook his head in amazement, though of course his head never moved. He'd only seen robes like that in a museum. Wayne puckered his lips to whistle in appreciation (though his mouth never moved), but then he thought better of it. The young man might take it the wrong way. Whoever the guy was, he certainly didn't seem in any mood to kid around. His thick brows were furrowed with anger and his teeth were bared in a snarl. Wayne could have sworn he saw sparks flashing from the young man's eyes, even though the logical side of his brain was aware that such a thing was impossible; he must be asleep and dreaming. Still the guy was *huge*. Dream or not, Wayne told himself, you'd have to be crazy to upset a guy like that.

As the old woman stepped into the street outside the hospital, the voice inside her head repeated for the third time, "YES! I agree our grandson must be avenged, but I am worried about you. I will not let you put yourself into danger."

"What do I care about danger? I am an old woman, and it is time for me to die."

"No, you are still the little girl who rolled herself into a ball with fear at the sound of a demon's voice."

"That little girl is dead. She died the day you left the body of Wu Fung-Lao the farmer."

"I will not let you do this."

"Zhang-Cho, I will do what must be done, and if you will not help me I will do it alone."

The demon had no choice but to give in. "All right," he said, "you shall have your vengeance."

There were preparations to be made. Siao-Te walked into the restaurant and asked the cashier for money. When she told him how much she wanted, he had to send a waiter to the bank. She made a mark on the cashier's receipt and took the money upstairs. She went into her room and lit several sticks of incense at the altar opposite the foot of her bed. She drew a portrait of Zhang-Cho, which she mounted on the wall. Then she drew a picture of a horse. She held a match to it, and dropped it into a metal bowl with flame and smoke seeming to pour from the animal's nostrils. Then she burned the money one note at a time.

"Rest now, my darling," Zhang-Cho told her. "Later we will need all your strength."

She lay down on her bed and closed her eyes while Zhang-Cho went to equip himself.

"Mother?"

"Is that you, Mei-Lee?"

"Mother, you must not do this."

"Mei-Lee, he is your son. Don't you want vengeance?"

"No, Mother. He isn't dead. He is going to live; I made sure of that."

"So it was you that caught him."

"He had no preparation for death. He would have become a demon."

Siao-Te said nothing.

"Mother, if you do what you are planning, you will become a demon yourself."

"Daughter, I am one already."

Zhang-Cho returned that evening with everything they needed. He had already seen the gang's headquarters; he would lead Siao-Te to it.

The old woman rose from her bed, washed her face, tied back her hair, and stepped into her tiny shoes. As she reached the street, Zhang-Cho told her one last time that she did not need to do this. She ignored him and kept walking. Soon she turned into a dark alleyway, walked past a sign reading "Keep Out" in both English and Cantonese, and headed down a flight of stairs. She stopped in front of a steel-reinforced basement door. She knocked three times. A panel slid back and a pair of eyes appeared. They crinkled in amusement at the sight of the tiny woman. The door opened.

"How can I help you, grandmother?" a man asked her with mock politeness. He spoke Cantonese; the dragon tattooed on his chest was clearly visible beneath his thin cotton shirt.

"I am looking for someone."

"You won't find him here, grandmother."

"I will look, just the same."

Someone laughed and said, "Let her come in, then."

The man who'd opened the door bowed as he let her past, and then bolted the door. The place was obviously an illegal drinking club; a bar ran along one wall. There wasn't much light; just a single bulb.

Siao-Te walked to the centre of the room and looked around. She counted eleven men, all young. All big. Most wore jeans and tee-shirts. Some wore leather jackets. Several of them were sitting on stools at the bar. Three sat around a table. The rest stood, glaring at her. One, who couldn't have been older than seventeen, spat at a spot on the floor only inches from the old woman's feet. Then he smiled and went back to cleaning his fingernails with a long knife that was more like a sword.

The twelfth man entered the room through a beaded doorway. He was older than the others, maybe forty. He wore a suit and a tie and a large jewelled ring. "What's going on?" he demanded. "Who let her in here?"

Zhang-Cho whispered in Siao-Te's ear, "This is the man who ordered our grandson's execution."

The man beside the door shrugged. "She said she's looking for someone."

"And I have found him," Siao-Te said, staring at the man in the suit.

The boy who'd been cleaning his fingernails giggled.

"Shut up! All right, old woman. Just who the hell are you and what do you want?"

"I come from The House of Wu restaurant, and what I want is vengeance."

Eleven knife blades glistened under the light provided by a single bulb. Eleven pairs of hands and feet moved closer.

The man in the suit contemplated the tips of his fingers. "I'm sorry. But you leave me no choice."

"NOW!" boomed the voice of Zhang-Cho. Siao-Te opened her mouth and a gleaming sword rose from the back of her throat, wielded by the arm of a giant.

Outside, the evening was mild, with just a hint of a breeze, and though it was quite late, the sun still hovered above the western horizon, giving the sky a brilliant pink and orange glow. It was the height of the summer tourist season, and the streets of Soho were packed with people from around the world. Three Germans were entering a pub, a group of Japanese were stepping off a coach, an Arab was hailing a taxi, and a married couple from Kansas were trying to decide on a restaurant. Then one of the West End musicals finished its evening performance and even more people spewed out onto the streets.

In such a crowd, no one paid much attention to the three men running frantically down the street. But one second later, the theatre crowd stopped dead in their tracks, the Germans ran back into the street, the taxi hailed by the Arab smashed into a lamppost, the Japanese reached for their cameras, and no one said a word except for the man from Kansas, who actually said three: "Oh my Gawd!"

A man was charging down Shaftesbury Avenue on horseback, a sword held between his teeth. His robes were silk of imperial yellow, embroidered with threads of solid gold. The last rays of the sun reflected in his metal helmet and breastplate with such intensity that it was painful to look at him. Still, no one turned away. Every head turned to watch him. Every eye devoured him. He was *magnificent*.

One of the three men tripped and fell. His head fell away with one swooping stroke of the warrior's sword as the horse, breathing fire, leapt over him. A second stroke sent another head rolling beneath the wheels of a number 19 bus.

The next stroke removed the third man's shirt. The dragon on his chest clearly visible, he shoved a messenger off his motorcycle and roared away, closely pursued by the giant on horseback.

"Golly," said the woman from Kansas. She watched the two of them turn right into a side street and then right again into the congested traffic of Regent Street.

There was utter chaos as cars, buses and people did their best to get out of the way. The horse leapt effortlessly over those that didn't. There was a roar of triumph that could be heard for miles and a final sweep of the gleaming sword.

The last severed head smashed through the window of Hamley's toy store and landed on the shoulder of a giant teddy bear. The motorcycle and its headless rider didn't stop until Oxford Circus.

The horseman turned back and vanished into a maze of side streets. The woman from Kansas ran to the corner to watch him go. Later, she swore that he became transparent and gradually faded from view. Her husband took her back to their hotel to lie down.

The police were on the scene within seconds, but found no trace of the man or his horse.

When Siao-Te got back to the restaurant, they had to help her up the stairs. "Mrs Wu, what happened? You're covered in blood." But she wouldn't answer.

A doctor was called, and he said she was suffering from shock and exhaustion. One of the waitresses came to stay in the flat and take care of her.

The papers were full of varying eyewitness accounts of the mystery horseman, and the fact that the police were linking the murders on Shaftesbury Avenue with the apparent "gangland revenge" slaying of nine men in a Soho basement. Most had criminal records, either in Britain or in Hong Kong, and each one had been beheaded. The first policeman to enter the basement fainted at the sight of nine severed heads impaled on empty lager bottles, lined up in a row across the bar top. Strangely, none of the many photographs taken of the horseman had come out, but there was an artist's impression of him on every front page as well as on television.

The police were regular visitors to Wayne's bedside. They showed him the artist's impression of the man seen riding around Soho on a fire-breathing horse, and demanded to know who he was.

"I have no idea who he is. I've never seen him before." He'd forgotten about his dream.

"Wasn't this a revenge killing, arranged by you?"

"How could I arrange it? I was unconscious."

Finally, the doctors decided that Wayne was well enough to go home. He arrived at the restaurant in a taxi. Sammy helped him get upstairs.

The first thing he did was to look in on his grandmother. He'd heard she was ill; but he wasn't prepared for what he saw. She was a skeleton only loosely covered by translucent flesh.

"Grandmother," he whispered.

She didn't need to open her eyes to see him. He was thin and weak and scarred, and there were stitches in his chest, but he would be all right. "Wayne," she said, "I have only struggled to hold this body so that I would see you once more, and know that you will be well again and not become a demon."

"What?" She's rambling, he thought. She must have a fever.

"The next time you die," she whispered. "You must be ready for it."

He caught a glimpse of Siao-Te's altar out of the corner of one eye, and then he turned to stare at it open-mouthed. He knew that she had one in her room and that she burned incense and left little offerings there, but he'd never noticed the drawing pasted on the wall. "Grandmother, who is this?"

She still didn't open her eyes. "Your grandfather."

He frowned. "My grandfather? No! The police came to the hospital. They showed me pictures of this man. He killed a dozen people! Who is he?"

"Help me to sit up."

He gently pulled her forward and piled some pillows behind her head. Paper. She was thin and light as paper. Where had those muscles of solid rock disappeared to?

"Now, grandson. I will tell you everything."

When the body of Wu Siao-Te would no longer hold her spirit, Wayne apologised to the corpse for the fact that he could not cut a hole in the roof for her, but explained that he would open a window.

Three weeks later, on a cloudless and chilly autumn night, Wayne knelt by the edge of the Serpentine and shoved a tiny wooden boat across the water. It carried two lit candles: one for his grandmother and one for the demon.

return of the princess

There had been rumours and rumblings for some time; some said a darkness was spreading across the world, some said an army was rising in the East. Not an army of men, but an army of unnatural creatures able to kill with a glance. Some spoke in whispers of one they called the Lord of Darkness, all-seeing and never-sleeping. There was danger to the East, they all agreed. But not to them. They were too small and poor to be of interest to anyone. They were too far away; all these distant goings-on had nothing to do with them. Besides, the kingdom of Tanalor had better protection than even the finest army: it was bordered on every side by mountains.

Then the princess disappeared.

It happened late one night. She was alone in her chamber, high atop the highest tower in her father's castle. She was lying in her bed, in her lacey white night-dress, but she wasn't asleep. She couldn't sleep, there was too much to think about with her wedding day so near.

She saw the hooded figure appear at her window. She watched him approach her. She didn't scream right away; she thought she'd wait and see what he wanted.

She never got around to screaming, but the castle guards did. They screamed, they shouted, they lit torches. They ran around in circles. The beloved princess Ruella, the pride and joy of her father's court, had been abducted, and someone had stolen their horses.

The princess was last seen hanging upside down from the shoulder of a dark rider on a dark horse, heading East.

"This way, Princess," said a rasping voice. She stumbled down a long dark corridor, far below the ground.

"Where am I? What do you want from me?" Something cold and hard prodded her from behind, pushing her forward.

"Keep moving, Princess."

Ruella kept moving. The rope around her wrists dug into her flesh, her lacey white night-dress was dirty and torn, her bare feet were nearly blue with cold. Still the harsh voice urged her on, further and further down.

There was a red glow ahead; the air was getting warmer.

"Where are you taking me?" she demanded.

"To your fate, Princess."

The room was carved from solid rock. Hooded figures gathered around a black iron cauldron suspended over a crackling fire. They chanted something in a language Ruella had never heard before. She watched as they poured bottle after bottle of brightly-coloured liquid into the steaming brew, and then she turned and saw the shelves carved into the wall behind her.

"What is this?" she asked the hooded figure with the rasping voice who had brought her there.

"Look closer," the rasping voice told her.

She took a few steps toward the shelves, and then she gasped in horror. The shelves were lined with row upon row of corked glass bottles, and inside each bottle there was a tiny man, shouting and pounding against the glass.

"Ruella!" shouted a squeaky little voice. "Dear lady, help me!"

She leaned forward and peered into the bottle the cry had come from. "Why, I know him," she told her abductor. "That's the Bishop Alphonse."

"Even your spiritual leaders are powerless against us," the hooded figure told her.

"Spiritual leader? Him? The dirty old bastard came to my room one night with a bottle of sacrificial wine." She giggled. "I broke it over his head."

"Behold your betrothed," the figure proclaimed, gesturing to a bottle on a higher shelf.

Ruella had to stand on her toes to see the Prince of Luria, sitting on the floor of his bottle, rocking back and forth and sucking his thumb. She lowered herself and turned to her abductor. "Can you believe my father actually expected me to marry that guy? Everyone at court said it would be a gesture of friendship, cementing the alliance of Tanalor with the people of Luria. The entire court are either liars or morons! The truth is, Daddy's had his eye on the Lurian gold mines for years. Well, that's fine, I said, if Daddy wants the gold, let Daddy sleep with the creepy prince, 'cause I'm sure not going to! Those were my exact words, I said that at a big tournament in front of everybody. Daddy's been furious at me ever since, but I don't care." She swung around and rose up on her toes once more. "The wedding's off," she told the shrunken prince. She turned to her captor once more, lowering her voice. "I won't say if that's the first time I've seen him naked; I just hope it's the last. I mean, well… there's little and then there's *little*, if you know what I mean."

The hooded figure paused for a moment. "Well, behold all these others then." He made a sweeping gesture.

Ruella walked up and down, inspecting the contents of the shelves. Several called out to her to save them. She shrugged. "So what do you want me to do? Stretch you?"

"Your attitude surprises me, Princess. The same fate awaits you."

Ruella stopped dead in her tracks. She tilted her head to one side and regarded the hooded figure with half-closed eyes. She'd been told men found this devastating. She would have completed the effect with a casual sweep of her hand across her thick dark hair, but she couldn't do that because her wrists were still tied behind her back. "Really?" she said. Her voice was a purr.

"Really," the hooded figure replied. He reached into his robes. "Behold your new home."

Ruella took one look at the glass bottle he was holding, and realised that the devastating look wasn't working. She changed tactics. "So who's the top man around here? You?"

"I am not a man," the rasping voice replied. He pulled back his hood, revealing a skinless, mis-shapen skull. Hundreds of worms wriggled out through the eyeholes. Some paused to bask on the hard bone surface, raising one end and swaying like tiny cobras, while others busily crawled back inside, some through the nose and some through the mouth.

Ruella gulped loudly. With an almost super-human effort, she managed to make the ends of her mouth curve upward. It was a pretty sickly imitation of a smile, but it would have to do. "Well," she said. Her voice cracked a little. "That's no reason why we can't do business. There's something I want more than anything, and you're just the guy I need to help me get it. I mean, you scratch my back..."

On a dark and moonless night, while Tanalor (including the castle guards) slept, two hooded figures prowled the castle grounds. They stopped beside a well, directly behind the kitchen. "Come on," the smaller one said. "I don't have all night." The larger took out a vial of brightly-coloured liquid and poured it into the water. The smaller one giggled.

The next afternoon, the entire court gathered in the throne room to help the king climb up the leg of his chair. The king, like the others, was dressed in a toga made from a knotted handkerchief. There was no sign of the guards. Most of them were trapped somewhere inside their suits of armour.

Just before sunset, a procession of hooded riders on dark horses approached the castle gate. They paused and turned to face the gathering crowd. "People of Tanalor," a rasping voice proclaimed, "Behold your new leader."

The smallest of the riders threw back her hood. "My beloved people," she said, "I think we're gonna get along just fine, don't you?"

no better than anyone else

It was a Friday night and I was part of a team working the booth joints in the West sector of Area 4. Another team was working the East. There'd been seven booth-related murders in the last four months; all dark-skinned women in their twenties, with shoulder length black hair, all known prostitutes, all mutilated. Two were black, one was oriental. The rest were Latino: three Puerto Ricans, one Mexican. I'd never done plain clothes before; I'd only been out of the academy three weeks. But I was twenty-two years old, and despite my blue-eyed Irish mother, I looked more like my Puerto Rican father. So I was assigned to Bruce Woods' team as a decoy.

My partner was Castilla Mae Jones, a six-foot-tall black chick with a red and green dragon tattooed on her right thigh. She wore a leopard-print leotard and ballet shoes; I wore a red rubber strapless dress. It was a bad choice, so tight I could hardly move and hot as hell. We each wore a single silver earring, which was actually a microphone. And of course we wore rubber gloves – Area 4 was a disease zone. Nobody went to Area 4 unless they were already infected, crazy, suicidal... or a cop.

I'd heard some of the uniform guys back at the station, saying why risk good cop lives over a bunch of broads who'd probably've been dead in a year or two anyway. But murder's still murder, isn't it? And you can't just ignore it, no matter who the victim was or how long she might have lived anyway. Doesn't matter if she wouldn't have lasted another year or even a week, she still had the right to that week. And I told them it was our job to get the bastard who'd stolen that week, or that day, or even that hour she might have had left. And they just said you're a fucking idealist, Gonzales, and nobody stays an idealist long on this job.

Bruce decided we'd hit this joint called Ricky's Dating Game Lounge first. It was eleven o'clock. There were maybe half-a-dozen people in the whole place, counting us and the bartender. We were the only women. All the booth joints were dumps, but this was a worse dump than most. It was just a long narrow room with a couple of tables and a bar, dark and smelling of stale beer and smoke. The mirror behind the bar was cracked. There was a black imitation-velvet curtain drawn across one corner at the back, next to the ladies' room. That's where the booth was. In the other back corner, there was a jukebox and a tiny stage where the bartender told us they were supposed to have a dancer. It didn't look like the dancer was going to show. Frankie O'Hara, our back-up, had gone in a few minutes ahead of us. He was sitting at the bar ignoring us, just like he'd ignored me back at the station. I didn't like the guy; on the way over, he'd rolled his eyes every time I opened my mouth. He was wired, too. A little microphone next to his chest.

Bruce stayed outside in an unmarked car, watching the front entrance and monitoring all three of us; he was supposed to come in if he heard anything suspicious, like gunshots or screaming, like he really thought screaming would be something unusual in a place like Ricky's. O'Hara said the reason Bruce stayed in the car was he was scared of infection – if he got out of the car at all, he'd be wearing a surgical mask. Looking around Ricky's, I wished I'd worn a mask myself, even though they said you couldn't get infected through the air.

Castilla had been a bit stand-offish back at the station. Bruce told me she'd told him no way was she gonna get stuck looking after some goddammed rookie who didn't know her ass from a hole in the ground. She wanted to work with Chrissie Lopez, but Chrissie got assigned to the other team. Castilla was stuck with me, and anyone could see she wasn't happy about it. But once we were hanging around Ricky's with nothing happening and nothing to do but talk, she started to get a bit friendlier. Especially after I told her I'd been with Dilation and Curettage.

It wasn't like I was bragging, it just slipped out. We'd given our glasses to the bartender to be filled and sterilised. He'd placed them back on the bar, using a pair of metal tongs, and handed us each an individually wrapped straw. Ordinarily, that should have been precautions enough, but I didn't like the look of the bartender – even in the dim light of Ricky's, I could see the guy had a pasty face and huge dark circles beneath his eyes. Of course, he might have just been tired, but I wasn't taking any chances; there was no way I was drinking anything poured by that guy, even through a sterile straw. We took our drinks and went to stand at the back of the room. I noticed Castilla wasn't drinking hers either.

She was leaning against the jukebox, smoking a cigar, when I noticed the box had one of the old Dilation tunes: "Cut Me, Baby". You know it. It's the one with the chorus that goes: Cut me, squeeze my veins dry, let me die in your arms, let me die real slow cause I love love love you. And then there's this instrumental part that's done with synthesisers and there's a woman's voice and it sounds like she's moaning. Well, that's me. I'm the one moaning, plus I sing back-up on the chorus. I was nineteen when we recorded that. I just couldn't help pointing the song out to Castilla. She was really impressed. "Quick," she said, "hand me some money so I can play the sucker!" She played the song and I sang along with the chorus. "That really is you!" she said. Suddenly her whole attitude towards me went through this complete transformation; it was like the old days, when Dilation were tops in the virtual charts and people used to recognise me everywhere I went.

She got all excited and said she knew she'd seen me somewhere before, I looked so familiar. She started going on about all the virtuals, like the one for "Cut Me", where Derek slashes me with a razor and then I rise headless out of a grave, wearing a blood-spattered gown. And of course, Satan's Child, which is most people's favourite. Everyone knows that one, it's where Dilation ride their Harleys into a derelict church and I'm strapped to the altar and suddenly the guitars turn into chainsaws and you get to choose whether they slice me up or have sex with me.

"Girl," she kept telling me, "anybody'd who'd leave a band like Dilation for this shit is crazy! You're fucked up in the head, you know that?"

"They can't sing, Castilla. I was the only one of them who had any kinda voice, but they just kept me in the background most of the time, like some kinda decoration. And in every single virtual, they killed me off! Between the ages of eighteen and twenty-one, I did twenty virtuals with them, and I got murdered twenty different ways. They hung me, they shot me, they electrocuted me, they cut off my head. You name it, they did it to me. That shit can get annoying."

"You can't take that stuff personally. Every virtual's gotta have somebody die. That's what sells the song. You should know that!"

I tried to tell her how Dilation's guitars were just fashion accessories 'cause none of them could even play an instrument, the computer did it all, and how they couldn't even work the computer themselves, there was this guy who did it for them. And she just said, "Who cares about music? They're such pretty little boys."

And then I tried to tell her how they're not little boys, they're in their forties and you wouldn't look twice at them if you saw them in the street, the computer pretties them up for the virtuals. And she said but you don't look any different in person, and I said of course not, I didn't need twenty years taken off of me. Then I told her that Derek Dilation's real name is Stan Bukowski and Clive Curettage is Sidney Harstein, and that Stan's got boils and Sidney's got bad breath. But she just said she'd slip old Sidney a peppermint anytime. I gave up.

Castilla nearly took a sip of her grapefruit juice, then realised what she was doing and put it down on top of the jukebox. She looked around the room, winked and tilted her head towards the front door. I turned slightly, trying not to be too obvious, and saw a man standing near the door, staring at Castilla. I could have sworn the guy was drooling.

"I still think you're crazy," she said, watching the man watching her. "What's it matter what anyone's like in real life anyway? Who cares if they're Derek or Stanley or Sidney or whatever, those guys are stars! I've got them on virtual and that's good enough for me. That's good enough for most people. Why'd you ever wanna leave them and come on the job?" I told her my Irish grandfather'd been a Captain. "Oh, God," she said. "So it's the family business. That explains a lot."

The man she'd been watching started walking towards us. She took a small gold compact from her bag, and started dabbing powder on her nose and chin. "What do you think, Rosie?" She called me Rosie. Fifteen minutes earlier, I'd been Gonzales.

"I think he likes you," I said. "That doesn't mean he's a slasher, does it?"

"We'll find out, won't we?" Castilla leaned back against the wall, striking a perfect pose. I glanced over at the bar and I saw the look on Frankie's face. Now I knew why the guy seemed like such a sullen bastard, he was in love. "He's getting closer, Rosie. This is where I get to be an actress, just like you in the virtuals. Lights, camera, action!" Castilla placed one hand on her bare dark thigh, long red nails drumming her tattooed dragon. I got out of the way.

Castilla and the guy talked for a few minutes; Castilla was laughing. Then they headed towards the black curtain. She wasn't supposed to do that. I looked over at Frankie O'Hara. His face had gone green.

We both lit cigarettes and waited.

They came out less than five minutes later. The man looked angry; Castilla looked ill. I rushed over to her. "You okay? Is that our guy?"

She mumbled something about leaving her alone, and stumbled into the ladies' room. I followed her in and found her kneeling in one of the stalls, heaving into the bowl. "You all right?" I said. "What happened?"

She staggered to her feet. "Shit," she said. She took a wad of toilet paper, sprayed it with disinfectant, and stuffed it under her leotard, between her legs. "I'm still bleeding."

"Bleeding? What'd he do to you? Oh my God, he's getting away!"

She waddled over to the sink. "Shut the fuck up, Rosie! He's not the slasher."

"Then what's going on? Why are you sick? Why are you bleeding?"

"Will you shut up?" she hissed, pointing at my earring. I finally understood; she didn't want Bruce to hear. She took off her earring and indicated that I do the same. Then she unstrapped the bag from around my waist, opened it up, and dropped both our earring mikes inside it. She placed my bag in the sink, and turned on the tap. "What are you doing?" I said. "My badge and my gun are in there!"

"Shut the fuck up, will you? Your bag's waterproof, I've got one just like it at home."

"You gonna tell me what's going on?"

Castilla nodded wearily and slumped to the floor, leaning her head against the pipes beneath the sink. "Lock the door," she told me. "I don't want any assholes walking in." There was a metal bolt; I slid it across.

She closed her eyes. "It wasn't like I expected. It wasn't what I thought it would be; it was nothing like the virtuals."

"What the hell are you talking about?"

"Before I went in that booth, I… you don't tell anybody about this, you hear? You don't tell anybody or you die. Got that?"

I nodded.

"Before I went in the booth, I was a virgin." I almost choked; it was an involuntary reaction. "Don't you laugh at me, bitch! Whatever you do, don't you laugh at me or I swear I'll knock your head upside the wall!"

"I'm not laughing at you, Castilla. I swear I'm not. But why the hell did you go inside the booth?"

"Why do you think? Because every woman who was murdered was murdered inside a booth! I'm a decoy; it's my job to go into the booth!"

"But why'd you take this assignment? You could have turned it down."

"Turn it down? Oh yeah? I've been on the force three years. You know what I've been doing all that time? I spent my first year searching the body cavities of women prisoners. The last two I've been touring schools, lecturing children about road safety."

This time I did laugh. "You mean you were an 'Officer Friendly'?"

"That's what the kids called us, yes. Will you stop laughing, damn you! This assignment was my chance to be a cop, a real cop. I couldn't turn this shit down."

Frankie O'Hara was pounding on the door. "Castilla, are you all right?"

"Go away!" Castilla shouted.

"Look, Castilla," I said, "if it's any consolation, I think technically you're still a virgin. I mean, what happens in the booth technically isn't… well, you know… because there's something between you the whole time."

"Will you shut your stupid face?" Castilla growled at me. "I don't need you to tell me about it, okay?" I didn't need her to tell me about it, either. My own first time had been in a booth, but at least I'd been with someone I knew, someone I even thought I was in love with. And it was terrible, with that dim red light and piped in music and vibrating walls, each in your separate padded compartment with a lubricated, disinfected – supposedly "infinitely stretchable, guaranteed never to tear" – latex wall between you the whole time so there was no contact and no chance of infection. The booths had been brought in after the epidemic of 2019, and now there were booth joints in every major city, except for Charlestown, South Carolina, where even virtuals were banned. Frankie was still pounding on the door, threatening to break it down. "Tell that boy to get out of my life."

I pulled the bolt aside and opened the door. "Castilla wants you to go away." He shoved past me and got down on the floor beside her. "Oh baby, baby," he said. "Talk to me."

"What? What do you want me to say to you, O'Hara?"

"Anything, baby. Anything."

He moved in closer to her. I saw her reach inside his shirt and pull out his little microphone. "Get outta here, Gonzales," O'Hara said.

My drink was on top of the jukebox where I'd left it. I picked it up and sat down at a table. My dress was digging into my stomach so bad I could hardly breathe. I was shifting around in my chair, trying to get comfortable, when the worst thing that could possibly happen to a rookie cop working undercover happened. Someone recognised me.

"Rosemary Gonzales!" he shouted for the whole bar to hear. Every head turned. Great, I thought. Everybody's having a good look at me, everybody in the bar knows my name. A guy about my age, dressed in black leather jeans and a tee-shirt, was walking straight towards me. "Rosemary Gonzales," he was saying, "Rosemary Gonzales. I can't believe it."

"I think you've got me confused with someone else." I looked at the ladies' room door in desperation. When were those two coming out?

He was standing over me, breathing on me. "Come on, you can't fool me! I'm your biggest fan. I've got ever virtual Dilation ever made – I've zoomed in on your face, close up, a thousand times. I know every inch of you, intimately."

"I'm sorry," I said, "but you've got me mixed up with someone else. My name is Sandra, and I've never been in a virtual; I don't even like them."

"Don't tell me that. It's me. Victor. You remember me, don't you?"

"Victor?" I took a good look at the guy, and then I remembered.

Orange-haired, pimply nutcase who used to send me flowers every day. And he used to write me letters, telling me how the two of us met and made love in his dreams every night, which he considered proof that we were lovers on the astral plane. I recognised him from the photos he used to send me, at least a dozen of them, all of him sitting alone in a room papered with pictures of me: close-up stills from every virtual I ever made. Even his ceiling was covered with them. I remembered he had a job somewhere, making dentures or something. A nutty, obsessive fan, but harmless. Dilation had loads of fans just like him, always writing weird letters and sending gifts. I figured it was better to admit who I was than to keep arguing with the guy – he probably just wanted my autograph; then he'd go away.

"Victor," I said, "of course I remember you. You used to call yourself Dilation's number one fan, didn't you?"

"Not Dilation, only you. I saw their latest virtual and it was crap – you weren't even in it. What happened? Did you quit or what?"

I shrugged. "Something like that."

"So what are you doing now, Rosie?"

"Not a lot. Look, Victor, I'd appreciate it if you didn't tell anybody you saw me here, okay?"

"Don't want people to know how you've come down in the world, huh?"

I stared into my drink, willing him to go away, willing Castilla and O'Hara to come out of the john, willing Bruce to get out of his goddamn car and come into the bar and tell us we were leaving this dump and moving on to the next one. It didn't work. Victor leaned even closer.

"You knew how I felt."

I shrugged and glanced at my watch. Barely two minutes had gone by since I'd left Castilla and O'Hara in the john. It seemed like a lifetime. "I don't know what anybody feels about anything," I said.

"You knew, but you didn't care, did you, Rosie? Didn't you get the flowers? I sent you flowers every day, remember?"

"That was years ago, Victor." I looked at my watch again. Another ten seconds went by; I know because I counted them, one by one. That rubber dress was killing me. I was sweating like crazy, and my skin itched all over.

"So how about it, Rosie?"

"How about what?"

"There's only one reason for coming to a place like this. You must want it bad."

I couldn't believe it; he actually expected me to go in the booth with him. He actually expected it. "No way, asshole," I said, "Fuck off."

Victor's eyes went narrow and hard. I felt a knife in my ribs. "That's not nice, Rosie. That's not nice, at all. Now stand up, real slow."

"Bruce," I said.

"What?"

"Bruce, come in right now!"

"Stop playing games, Rosie, before I get mad. Now get up real slow, like I told you, or I'll cut you right here."

Oh shit, I thought, Bruce couldn't hear me – my goddamn earring was in my bag, which I'd left in the ladies' room with Castilla. And so was my gun. I stood up slowly, like he said. He pressed himself hard against my left side, pinning down my left arm, and put one arm around my waist, pinning down my other arm. Positioning himself so that the knife was hidden from view, he pulled me to my feet and away from the table. I could feel the tip of the knife through my dress. If he was planning to take me outside, Bruce would see. But he didn't take me outside, he led me towards the imitation velvet curtain at the back.

Once we were behind the curtain, he manoeuvred himself around behind me and raised the blade to my throat. "Don't make a sound," he said, "don't even whisper." He fed a one hundred dollar bill into a slot beside the booth door. It slid open, and he pushed me inside. He came in behind me, squeezing us both into the same compartment. "You can scream now," he said as the door slid closed behind us. "The walls are soundproof."

Victor pushed me back against the wall, his blade digging into my throat, my right shoulder bending the latex wall at my side. Behind him, I saw the exit button glowing faintly, just out of reach.

"Hey, Victor," I said, quietly, "what's this all about, huh?" The wall behind my back was vibrating. Then the piped-in music started, a slow thumping beat with lots of synthesised groans and heavy breathing.

"I was so wrong about you, Rosie. I used to think you were something really special. Everything I ever did I did thinking of you. I dreamed of the day we would be together. You were beautiful, but you were arrogant. You thought you were too good for me, didn't you Miss Rockstar? But look at you now, in a booth joint in the middle of a fuckin' disease zone! No better than anyone else. Not even half as good."

"Who said I was a star? I was a back-up singer."

"Shut up!"

With that blade pressing into my throat, I didn't try to struggle, I just tried to keep him talking, until somebody noticed I was missing. "Come on, Victor," I said. "We're old friends, aren't we?" He spat in my face; I didn't dare raise a hand to wipe it off. I grimaced and fought back a wave a nausea as I felt the spit oozing down my cheek.

"Friends?" he said. "After what you did to me?"

"What do you mean? I never did anything to you."

"What about Atlanta?"

"Atlanta? What are you talking about? We never even played Atlanta!"

"You recorded a virtual there. Monarch Studios, Atlanta. I remember the date: April 23rd, sixteen months exactly tomorrow. I was outside the studio, waiting for you with a bouquet of roses. I always used to send you roses, remember? Roses for Rosie? And these five guys came up to me… I remember there were five of them. Five of them! And they grabbed the roses from me and they threw me up against the wall, and they told me, 'This is from Rosie', and they took turns punching me in the stomach and they knocked me to the ground and they kicked me and they told me if I ever came near you again, they'd kill me. I had four broken ribs; I spent a week in the hospital. I gave you my devotion, you gave me two black eyes and four broken ribs."

"I had nothing to do with it, I swear. I never even knew about it until now. I wouldn't have done that to you or anyone. Honest."

"You didn't know about it, huh? I looked up and saw Derek watching from a window. You think I don't know about you and Derek?"

I remembered now. Victor wrote me this crazy letter, he said he'd been to a ceremony just like the one in "Satan's Child", the devil had promised me to him for eternity, and he'd be coming to get me. I showed the letter to Derek and he said not to worry, he'd make sure the guy never got near me. I didn't get any more letters, so I forgot about it. It was a case of out of sight, out of mind. How was I supposed to know what had happened to him? Derek and I split up, I left the band, and I'd never given Victor a second thought. It was like he'd never existed. "I'm sorry, Victor. But it was nothing to do with me. I didn't know about it."

He didn't hear what I said, he didn't seem to be listening. His eyes moved to the blade at my throat. "Things would have been different if I'd had this. I'd a shown 'em not to mess with me. Nobody messes with me."

"How about putting that knife away?" I said.

"In your first ever virtual, you looked straight into my eyes and told me you loved me. I played it over and over, and each time you promised to be mine forever. I laid there in the hospital for seven days and seven nights and you never came to see me once. You never even sent me a card. Why'd you say you loved me if you didn't mean it?"

"Victor, those were only the words to a pop song! Words someone else wrote for me to say. And I didn't know you were in the hospital. I honestly never knew. Now please put the knife away."

"That's when I started to hate you, Rosie. That's when I really started to hate you. I wanted to kill you."

Victor had to be the booth slasher. The reason all the victims looked like me was because in Victor's mind, I was the victim. I was the one he wanted to kill and so far he'd killed me seven times. I wasn't going to let him kill me again. I pulled my head away, into the latex, and brought my knee up, hard.

He doubled over. The music speeded up, as it was programmed to do after the booth had been in use for ninety seconds. The groans got louder and the red light in the ceiling started to strobe. Victor screamed and struck out wildly, knocking me off balance.

I fell against the opposite wall. I tried to pull myself up, but the more I tugged at the latex, the further down it stretched. I managed to stand up just as Victor recovered enough to lunge at me with the knife. I brought my knee up again, knocking it from his hand, and reached for the door. He grabbed my arm and pressed my face down into the latex, so I couldn't breathe. He tried to twist me around, wrapping me up like a fly in a web, but the latex sprung back into position, twirling me around so fast I was dizzy. Victor got hold of the knife again.

"Police!" I shouted. "You're under arrest!" He brought the blade down in a sweeping movement; I raised my left arm to block him and punched him in the stomach with my right.

"I'm not joking, asshole. I'm a cop." I grabbed his right wrist with both hands, ramming the knife against the wall. It wasn't very effective, the blade just sunk into the padding. Victor knocked me back with his left arm. I landed next to the exit button. As I reached over to press it, I heard the sound of something ripping, and then my head was encased in transparent rubber. Victor pulled it tighter and tighter; I couldn't breathe. I kicked and flailed my arms, slamming my hand desperately against the wall where I knew the button was still glowing. The piped-in music faded out, and I heard the whoosh of a sliding door. Then everything went black.

I didn't even hear the first shot, but I heard the second, or maybe it was the third. All I know is, there was something sticky and wet all over me. Then there was something heavy. The heavy thing was pulled away, and I didn't feel anything. But I heard voices. Maybe I couldn't open my eyes, but I could hear.

Castilla was screaming that she'd never shot anybody before. O'Hara was saying he couldn't believe how stupid that fucking rookie had been, going into the booth without her gun.

There was a siren, then there were more voices. "This one's dead," a voice said. "What about the girl?"

"Still breathing," said another voice. "But only just. Oh shit!" There was a sudden shower of water and disinfectant; the automatic cleaning system had come on, and whoever was talking must have got drenched. I know I did.

I was moving; I heard more sounds, more voices. "We're gonna have a lot of explaining to do," O'Hara was saying. "That goddamn rookie's really dropped us in the shit."

The air felt cooler, I was outside. "Hey guess what?" Bruce was saying. "I just heard it over the radio. They got the slasher!"

I wanted to scream of course they got the slasher, I'm the one who got him, but I couldn't even open my mouth.

130

"Yeah," Bruce said, "they got him about an hour ago, in the eastern sector. Chrissie Lopez got the collar. He pulled a blade, she cuffed him, he confessed to all seven killings. That Chrissie Lopez, she's quite a cop, isn't she?"

"She's one of the best," O'Hara agreed.

I heard the ambulance doors slam, and I was driven away.

the psychomantium

By the time Samantha Stockard arrived in Meadow Lane the market was deserted, the traders gone, the stalls packed away, the road strewn with rubbish. She parked her car in front of the café.

She walked up to the window and looked inside. A man in a white apron was mopping down the floor. Behind him, a young woman sat alone in a plastic booth. She seemed to match the description supplied by Marcia Anson: late teens or early twenties, long yellow hair twisted into dreadlocks, jeans ripped at both knees, oversized jumper looking more than a little frayed, a rhinestone stud glinting in the flesh between her mouth and chin. A cracked mug sat on the table in front of her; she stared down at it without expression, oblivious to Samantha's presence on the other side of the glass.

Samantha stared at the other woman, transfixed. She'd seen her before, she was certain of it. But where? Perhaps it would come to her later, once they'd had a chance to speak.

She walked around to the entrance. It was locked. She knocked on the glass. The man in the apron waved her away. She knocked again, gesturing for him to come to the door.

He finally put down his mop and opened the door a crack. "Sorry, love. We're closed."

"I don't want to order anything; I just want to talk to that woman," she said, nodding towards the booth. "It'll only take a minute."

The man narrowed his eyes, taking in Samantha's neatly groomed bob and office-style clothing. "In some kind of trouble, is she?"

"Not at all," she assured him. "I just want to talk to her."

"All right." He stepped aside to let her pass, then touched her on the arm, lowering his voice to a whisper. "You mind yourself, love. Anna's a bit..." He tapped the side of his head with one finger. "Know what I mean?"

On the one hand, she was relieved to hear the other woman referred to as Anna; that meant she'd definitely found the right person. On the other, she didn't like the way the man kept pointing at his head. "I'm sorry?"

"She's got something wrong upstairs, love. I let her sit in the cafe sometimes, so long as she don't bother me customers, 'cause she's only young and I feel sorry for her, but I wouldn't credit anything she says if I were you. And I wouldn't turn my back on her," he added darkly.

She looked over at Anna and watched her set the cracked mug upside down on the table, then lean forward to sniff the base. "I'll keep that in mind."

She walked over to the booth and introduced herself. "I understand you knew a woman named Eleanor Burdon."

Anna glanced up at Samantha then quickly looked away. "You're surrounded by flickering shadows of forgotten ghosts, shrouded by the clinging remains of the person you were and the place you came from. You don't belong here."

"Come again?"

"Eleanor Burdon," Anna muttered, gazing down at the table. "Poor old dearie. Only met her the once, you know. She was just like you. Lost and confused and frightened. Gives me a headache to look at you, you know that? You're so blurred around the edges, you keep shimmering in and out of focus like a reflection in a rippled pool."

A stream of brown liquid was dripping off the edge of the table; Anna's upside down mug hadn't been completely empty. Samantha turned to leave; this was a waste of time.

"You don't belong here," Anna called after her. "You know that, don't you? Deep down inside, you know it. Or at least you suspect. You've started to suspect, haven't you? That's why you're here, isn't it?"

Samantha stopped and turned around. Anna was right: that was exactly why she was there. Maybe it didn't matter that the girl was obviously off her rocker; Eleanor Burdon had worried that she might be going mad, and now it was just possible that Samantha was losing her mind, too. Maybe it took someone crazy to understand what was going on; maybe that's why Eleanor had said that Anna had believed her and understood. Samantha had to take a chance; she had to tell her.

"I think something terrible happened to me this morning, but I can't remember what it was."

Samantha had tried to hide her nervousness as she followed her new boss, Janet Hale, down the dimly-lit tenth-floor corridor of the north London tower block where Eleanor Burdon had lived. The old woman's flat was all the way down at the end, then around a corner. Samantha had followed Janet's example and stepped into her hooded white coveralls in the hallway outside the flat. They had each put on rubber gloves, and then Janet had opened the door.

"Oh my God!" Samantha reeled backwards, raising a hand to her mouth.

"You're not going to throw up, are you?" Janet asked her. Samantha shook her head.

"Just try and hold your breath a minute," Janet said, "while I get some air into the place." She disappeared into the flat.

Samantha pulled her hood up, covering her chin length hair, then reached into her bag for a surgical mask.

She found Janet in the living room, opening every window. Walking into the dead woman's lounge was like walking into an oven. Samantha moved around the room slowly, sweating in the street clothes beneath her coveralls and trying not to breathe too deeply; despite the open windows, the pungent odour of rotted meat was overpowering.

Yellow foam erupted through the worn upholstery of the dark green settee. A bowl on the floor held several clumps of furry green cereal. A mug sat on top of the television, sprouting something that looked like asparagus and smelled like vomit. A folding metal table was buried under a mountain of yellowing paper: old newspapers, letters, God knew what. More paper overflowed from the half-open drawers of a small wooden cabinet. The threadbare carpet was littered with balls of hair and dust and foam from the sofa.

Janet shook her head and tsk'd, pursing her lips and deepening the furrows between her eyebrows. "Look at this place." She glanced at her younger companion. "All right, Sammy?"

Samantha gritted her teeth; no one had called her "Sammy" since she was ten years old. And she'd felt ill from the moment they'd picked up the key from the caretaker. Janet had introduced him as Hughie, adding that they'd known each other more than thirty years. He looked about Janet's age – mid to late fifties – with a shiny bald pate and thick tufts of reddish hair growing from his ears.

Hughie had insisted they have a cup of tea before going upstairs. Samantha had sipped her tea in silence, trying not to stare at the caretaker's ears – until he'd started regaling them with the story of how he'd come to discover the body, which he did in graphic detail. After that, she couldn't even drink her tea. And she still couldn't stop thinking about some of the things he'd said, like how he could have sworn the old woman was moving until he realised it was only the maggots wriggling.

"I'm fine," she lied.

Janet looked dubious. "You sure? You're awfully pale."

"I'm fine." This was Samantha's first case; she didn't dare admit to feeling sick for fear she'd end up back in the housing department where she'd spent the last three years as a typist.

"If you say so." Janet opened the door to another room and vanished inside. Samantha stayed where she was, not certain if she was expected to wait for Janet's instructions or impress her with her initiative. She was twenty-three years old, with an expensive haircut, a car and a mortgage, but Janet seemed to think she was some kind of naïve child. She decided to impress her with her initiative. She crossed over to the table to look through some of the dead woman's papers.

"Sammy, come here," Janet called from the other room. Samantha sighed. So much for initiative.

She walked up to the open door and saw that Janet was in the kitchen. "I want you to see this," Janet said, opening each and every cupboard. Apart from a jar of tea bags and a couple of glasses and plates, the shelves were empty. She opened the refrigerator. It, too, was empty, except for one carton of something solid that used to be milk. "No food," she said, shaking her head. "Not a crumb. You often find that." She lifted the flap to the ice-making compartment and stuck her hand inside.

"What are you doing?"

"Sometimes they hide things in there."

"Hide what?"

Janet shrugged. "Money, jewellery, whatever." She reached behind the fridge and unplugged it, then walked past Samantha to open another door, this time to the bathroom. Nothing there but a tub and a sink and an old fashioned gas water heater. A towel had been draped across the medicine cabinet. Janet lifted a corner of the towel, revealing the cabinet's mirrored front, and chuckled to herself.

"What's funny?" Samantha asked her.

"Hughie's covered all the mirrors again. He does it every time."

Janet left the room before Samantha could ask why. She shrugged and followed her back into the lounge. There was only one door left. As they approached it, Samantha thought she heard something: the whine of a distant motor, perhaps. Janet took a deep breath and reached for the handle. "This'll be it, then," she said.

"Bloody hell," she said a moment later.

The noise Samantha had heard was the buzzing of insects; the windows were covered with bluebottle flies. The moment the door opened, they swirled into the air, becoming a whirring black cloud heading straight for the two women. Samantha screamed, batting her hands wildly in front of her face. Janet calmly crossed the room to open the windows, shooing as many of them as she could outside. "Why don't you start on those papers in the lounge?" she asked, sounding tired.

Samantha didn't bother telling her that was what she'd been trying to do when Janet had called her into the kitchen. She was just grateful to get away from the flies and the sickening stench of death; the smell was even worse in the bedroom where the old woman had lain undiscovered for two weeks in the middle of a summer heatwave. She was beginning to have second thoughts about this job; maybe secretarial work wasn't so bad after all.

Janet followed her into the living room. "You know what to look for?"

"Yes."

The older woman pulled a chair up to the table and gestured for Samantha to sit down. "Insurance policy documents, a will, anything with an address… even just a name."

They'd been through this back at the office. "I know."

"Okay," Janet said, heading back into the bedroom. "Shout if you need me."

Samantha pulled off her gloves and started organising the chaos in front of her into tidy stacks. There were dozens of unopened envelopes, some addressed to Mrs E Burdon, others addressed to Occupier. Some said things like: *You may already be a lucky winner*. Others had the words: *Final Demand* printed across the top. She put them to one side, to look at later, then picked up a spiral bound notebook. She flicked through several pages. Nothing useful, just a lot of twee little rhymes written in a precise – if slightly shaky – hand, each ending with the words: *by Eleanor Burdon*.

She could hear Janet through the wall. Rummaging through the old woman's wardrobe and chest of drawers, looking for anything of value that might be passed on to a relative – if they could find any – or sold at auction to pay for the funeral. Then she heard Janet call her name.

She put down the notebook and looked into the bedroom. The remaining flies had settled into a huddle around a light fixture in the ceiling.

Janet was on her hands and knees beside the bed. "Help me with this."

Samantha knelt down beside her and saw a large trunk pushed up against the wall. She got hold of one end while Janet grabbed the other. They pulled it out only to find it wouldn't open. "You any good at picking locks?" Janet asked.

"I've never tried," Samantha said carefully, not certain if that was meant to be a joke or not.

"Then I guess we'll have to find the key." Janet stood and walked over to an old fashioned dressing table to look through the dead woman's jewellery box. The dressing table mirror had been covered with a sheet.

Further along the wall behind the dresser, a floor-length black curtain hung across a narrow doorway. Samantha wondered what was behind it. Then she looked down. "Oh God," she said, leaping to her feet.

Janet turned around. "What's the matter?"

Samantha pointed to the discoloured patch of floor that marked the spot where the old woman had lain as clearly as if her body had been traced in chalk. And she'd just been kneeling on it.

Janet made a little tsk'ing noise. "Poor thing, to lie there like that for so long with no one knowing. Trouble is, it could happen to any one of us, Sammy. Any one of us. I always used to tell my children, you won't let that happen to me, will you? But my son married a woman in California and my daughter's in Australia. I'll be lucky if I see my grandchildren once a year. So who'll miss me if something happens? Who'll even know?"

Samantha shrugged, feeling uncomfortable with the way the conversation was going. "They'd miss you at work," she said.

"But I'm retiring year after next, Sammy, remember?" She shook her head and smiled. "Sorry, I don't mean to come over so morbid. It's just…"

She turned back to the jewel box on the dresser. "I was younger than you when I started, you know." She laughed. "My first year, I nearly got the sack for wearing my skirts too short; they told me as a representative of local government, my knees had to remain covered at all times."

Samantha walked over to the black curtain and pulled it to one side, revealing a walk-in cupboard, empty except for a wooden chair and a full-length mirror on a metal stand.

"Janet, why does Hughie always cover the mirrors?"

"It's an old superstition. When someone dies, you're supposed to cover every mirror in the house so the soul of the deceased doesn't get trapped behind the glass. And one thing you don't want is ghosts getting stuck inside a looking glass, because you know what they do when that happens? They reach out and grab any person who becomes reflected in that mirror, and they take them far away."

"Away? Away where?"

"Bournemouth," Janet said. "Where do you think?" She smiled and raised an eyebrow. "Know why it's seven years bad luck to break a mirror?"

Samantha shook her head.

"Because it takes seven years for the soul to renew itself."

"Pardon me?"

"The idea is the reflection represents your soul, so if you shatter the reflection, it stands to reason the soul will be shattered as well. Then, as if that wasn't enough, what do think your shattered soul fragments go and do? They only get themselves imprisoned inside the shards of glass! Stupid things. No wonder it takes seven years to sort them out." She laughed. "So now you know."

Samantha giggled. "Now I know." She started to draw the curtain back across the mirror.

"Tah-dah!" Janet exclaimed triumphantly.

Samantha let go of the curtain and swung around, startled. "Told you I'd find it," Janet said, holding up a small key. Samantha knelt beside her boss as she turned the key in the trunk lock and suddenly everything else – the smell, the insects, even the outline of a neglected corpse only inches away from their feet – was momentarily forgotten. The trunk was full of treasures. Beautiful, sparkling treasures.

"Oh, it's gorgeous!" Janet gasped, carefully unfolding a floor-length red silk dress wrapped in tissue paper. It must have been fifty or sixty years old but it was in perfect condition. Beneath it, she found a ball-gown – white, embroidered with gold – and a long jet black sheath covered in shiny glass beads.

There were shoes and handbags, some leather, some alligator, some velvet studded with rhinestones. There were long white gloves, hats with veils, capes with fur-trimmed hoods, silk stockings with seams. In a large padded envelope at the bottom, they found a scrapbook full of press clippings and faded black and white photos of a beautiful dark-haired woman dancing in a variety of glittering costumes, sometimes with a male partner, sometimes as part of a chorus line, sometimes alone beneath a spotlight.

"So that was Eleanor Burdon," Janet said, carefully turning the brittle pages. "Sometimes I'm glad we don't know the future, Sammy. I mean, look at her, smug as the cat that got the cream, wasn't she? Would she have wanted to know how it was all going to end? And if anybody'd told her, you think she would have believed them for one moment? I doubt it. Bet she had the world at her feet in those days. Bet she thought she always would." She sighed and shook her head. "Poor thing."

"Poor thing," Samantha agreed, nodding.

Janet put the book to one side and picked up the black beaded dress. She stood, holding it in front of her; the hem dragged on the floor. "She was tall, that Eleanor. More like you."

"I'm only five seven."

"Taller than me. Taller than most of the old lady's generation." She told Samantha to stand up, then pressed the dress into her hands. "Now hold it up properly. Here, that really suits you. Have a look at yourself. Go on."

Samantha pulled down her mask and turned to face the mirror in the cupboard. She nearly laughed out loud; she looked ridiculous holding a beaded dress in front of a pair of baggy coveralls with a surgical mask hanging loose around her neck.

Then something went wrong. Everything reflected in the glass seemed to develop a kind of after-image, like a photographic double-exposure. Including her. She seemed to have two bodies, one superimposed over the other. She moved her head a few inches to one side; her duplicate head followed a fraction of a second later. She blinked several times, trying to clear her vision, but couldn't get her two sets of overlapping eyes to open and close in synch; one always seemed a millisecond behind the other.

Then everything went black. "Janet?" she said. No reply.

"Janet, where are you?" she said, fighting back panic. "Janet, I can't see!" She heard a sound of creaking hinges, then a beam of light cut through the darkness, moving in a graceful arc as it illuminated her surroundings, section by section.

She was standing on a bare concrete floor surrounded by black walls splashed with large red letters spelling something she couldn't make out. Then she realised why she couldn't read the writing: it was backwards. She had managed to decipher the first word – *Gateway* – when she was blinded by a torch beam shining into her eyes.

She heard at least two sets of approaching footsteps, and then the beam moved on. She stood rooted to the spot, unable to believe they hadn't seen her.

"Bloody hell," a man's voice said as the light fell onto a young woman with long blonde hair, slowly swaying in mid-air, a rope around her neck.

Samantha tried to run, but she couldn't move. She tried to scream, but no sound came out.

Janet suddenly crossed in front of her, pulling the curtain across the cupboard doorway. She seemed angry. "Are you mutt and jeff or something, girl? I've been telling you the last five minutes: stop admiring yourself and put that bloody dress away, we've got work to do!"

"Five minutes?" Samantha repeated. It seemed like less than ten seconds since Janet had handed her the beaded gown. She became aware of a tingling sensation in her hands. She looked down and saw they were clenched into tight fists, the knuckles white. And they were shaking. How could she have lost five minutes? She let go of the dress, carefully uncurling her aching fingers, and saw a line of deep ridges where her nails had dug into her palm.

Nothing about the room she was in seemed right, though she had no idea exactly what was wrong. She looked up at the light fixture in the middle of the ceiling, half-expecting to see a squirming mass of flies. There weren't any, of course; the flat reeked of insecticide. The chemical smell was so strong she could taste it.

She reeled over to one of the windows and stuck her head outside, gasping for breath. "I must have blacked out from the fumes. I'm sorry, I'm really sorry."

"Come on, girl," Janet said, "let's get you out of here for a bit."

They knocked on several of the neighbours' doors before they left the building. No one they spoke to knew anything about the old woman, though one suggested they try the residents' association.

There they found a man who knew Eleanor Burdon. He said she used to be quite active in the association, serving on the pensioners' committee, though she'd resigned three or four years ago. "She was eighty-odd and getting a bit frail," he explained. He also said she had a daughter somewhere: possibly Canada, though he couldn't be sure.

"Do you know the daughter's name?" Janet asked him.

He shook his head. "I only know it wasn't Burdon. Eleanor was widowed twice, and I'm sure she said the daughter was from the first marriage."

"Thanks for your help," Janet said, turning to leave.

"You know who you ought to ask about Eleanor," the man called after them. "They do a writing workshop at the community centre, down the north end of the estate. Eleanor was always writing poems and things."

The sign on the padlocked front door of the community centre read: *Closed as of 15 June due to lack of funding. If you are unhappy about this, write to the Council.*

They put Eleanor's trunk into a storage locker, then crossed the hall to the Arts Department, which the latest round of cuts had reduced to a single desk at the back of Social Services. Of course as funeral officers their "office" wasn't any better, consisting of two desks in the Environmental Services Department, sandwiched between Refuse Collection and Vermin Control.

It only took a minute to find the name and phone number of the woman who'd run the creative writing workshop on the Verdant Meadows Estate in the Arts Department files. Janet decided Samantha should be the one to make the phone call; the only way to learn was to do.

Samantha returned to her desk in Environmental Services, dialled the woman's number and introduced herself. The workshop leader, a Mrs Marcia Anson, confirmed that Eleanor Burdon had once been an enthusiastic member of her writing class, but had stopped coming the previous autumn. "Do you know how she died?"

"I think she had a stroke," Samantha said. "Something to do with her brain, anyway."

"Oh, dear," Mrs Anson tutted. "When did it happen?"

"Some time during the second week of June; I don't – "

"Well, she was still alive on the twelfth," Mrs Anson interrupted. "I saw her in the café in Meadow Lane Market, sitting in a booth beside the window. I would have stopped to say hello, but she seemed to be in the middle of a rather intense conversation and I didn't like to interrupt. Of course now I wish I had."

"Who was she talking to?"

"Some young girl; I doubt she was more than twenty. Looked a bit like one of those anti-road protester types, all torn clothes and messy blonde hair, with some kind of ring through her lower lip. I have no idea what she and Eleanor could have found to talk about, really. I mean, Eleanor always took such care of her appearance; what could those two possibly have had in common?"

"Ask her about Eleanor's family," Janet whispered.

"Did Mrs Burdon ever talk about her family?"

"Not really. I think she had a daughter somewhere, but that's all I know."

"Ask about friends," Janet prompted.

"Did Mrs Burdon have any friends that you know of?"

"I think she used to be involved in the residents' association. You might want to ask someone there."

"Well, we can strike that one off our list," Janet said as Samantha put down the receiver. She reached into one of the bulging carrier bags full of paper they'd brought back from the dead woman's flat. She pointed to another, on the floor beside Samantha's feet. "Look for anything with an address."

"I know, I know," Samantha said, emptying the sack onto her desk.

Most of the bag's contents turned out to be rubbish: junk mail, bills, old calendars, expired money-off coupons, recipe cards and so on, all of which could go straight into the bin.

A short while later, Janet stood up and put on her jacket. "It's almost five. Go home, girl, and forget about the dead until tomorrow."

Samantha yawned and rubbed her eyes. "All right." She slid her chair back from the desk and crossed over to the coat rack where she'd hung her jacket that morning. She glanced towards the doorway and saw that Janet was already gone; she hadn't waited.

Samantha sighed and shook her head. What did she expect? A slap on the back? A round of applause? After the way she'd passed out in the dead woman's flat that morning, she needed to prove herself more than ever. But how?

The only way she could think of was to keep working. She crossed back to her desk and started sorting through another mound of paper. There were several letters from someone named Pamela – no surname –

with a return address in Paris. She printed off one of their standard letters and put it in the "out" tray. Sending the letter made her feel as if she'd finally accomplished something, even though there was little hope of getting a reply – the most recent of Pamela's notes was dated 1975.

She found several black and white photographs of a man in a military uniform. She turned one over and saw the words: *Terry, home on leave, 1943.* Husband? Brother? Lover? She had no way of telling.

She put the photos into an envelope for safe-keeping, then picked up the notebook she'd seen on the old woman's table that morning and started flicking through it again. Nothing but page after page of handwritten verses. Completely useless.

She was about to put it down when the neat script of the previous pages suddenly gave way to an almost illegible scrawl.

Must hurry! Memory fading. Like dream, one moment so clear, the next, gone forever. Saw a girl. Room with black walls. Something written in red paint, letters backwards. Spelling? No, too late, already forgotten. The girl: blonde hair, eyes pale blue, wide open and staring. Rope around neck. Hanging from a pipe? Not sure. So young, so sad. Wearing jeans, I think. Getting vague now.

Just looked at clock. Lost four hours! How? Seems like minutes. Something is wrong. Room seems strange, everything strange.

Feels different. Can't say how. Knew a minute ago, but it's gone now. Whatever I thought I knew, gone.

Samantha put down the notebook, shivering. Something was nagging at the back of her mind, something about footsteps and a beam of light. She shook her head and forced her attention back to the notebook.

The old woman's writing reverted to her original precise hand.

11 June.

I just re-read the above and freely admit it sounds like the ravings of a madwoman. Yet twenty-four hours have passed and I am still unable to shake the feeling that I am in the wrong place and I don't know how I got here.

12 June.

I now know what has happened and I think I know how to fix it. I told

Anna everything...

Anna had to be the woman Marcia Anson had seen with Eleanor.

She not only believed me, she understood. We talked for hours about choices and probabilities, the physical and the mental and infinite numbers of universes. Then I brought her back here to see the psychomantium...

"The what?" Samantha said out loud.

... and she confirmed that it was hers. My only hope now is to go back the way I came.

The rest of the book was blank.

Anna nodded to the seat across from hers. "Sit down," she said quietly, "and maybe I'll tell you what you want to know."

Samantha sat. "Eleanor Burdon wrote in her notebook that she'd talked to you about your psycho... something."

Anna picked up a salt shaker and tossed it from one hand to the other, giggling. "Psychomantium. Never heard the word myself 'til I met the old woman."

"Well, what is it? What does it do?"

Anna emptied some salt onto her palm and licked it, glancing sideways at Samantha. "It's a mirror used for contacting the other side."

"The other side? You mean the dead? Eleanor Burdon was trying to contact the dead?"

"Well, she was that age, wasn't she? Not so long to go herself, wanting to know who or what was waiting for her. And it worked, of course. She did contact the dead. Only trouble was, the dead person she contacted was me."

Samantha threw up her hands. "Well, thank you for your time."

Anna put the salt shaker back on the table. "No, you don't understand." She pulled back one of her sleeves, revealing several scars across her wrist. "I've been out of hospital almost six months now; they closed my ward. I've got these pills I'm supposed to take, but they make my tongue swell up..." She shrugged and rolled the sleeve back down.

"Anyway, about three, four weeks ago, I found some rope in a rubbish bin. I imagined myself with it wrapped tight around my neck, my face bloated and purple, my lifeless body swaying in the breeze. I even imagined my soul, plummeting into hell. I saw myself writing a sign in big letters so everyone would know where I'd been all these years and where I was going. It would be so easy, I thought, so easy...

"But I didn't do it; I only thought about it, right? And then I guess I started walking. I don't remember where I went or what I did, but it felt like I'd been going in circles for hours. And then I get back to the place where I've been staying and it's been done over! Everything I own is gone, including this full-length mirror on a metal stand. A few days after that, some old dearie comes up to me, claiming she's seen me in this mirror she bought off a market stall. She said she'd been sitting in the dark, waiting for spirits to appear in the glass, when suddenly she sees *me*, hanging dead from a rope. I was gobsmacked. She gave me a perfect description in every detail of something I had considered doing but hadn't actually done.

"It was then I started to notice the way the old woman kept shifting in and out of focus, and I soon found that if I stared at her hard enough, she became almost transparent." Anna raised her pale blue eyes to meet Samantha's. "Just like you."

Samantha looked down at her arms and saw they were covered in goosebumps. Somewhere in the distance, she imagined she could hear the sound of buzzing insects.

Samantha sat on a folded blanket in the middle of a bare concrete floor. The room was dark and almost bare of furniture. A large pipe ran from one corner of the floor, up a wall and across the ceiling.

Anna lit a kerosene lamp and placed it on the floor before her. "Welcome to my place."

"I've been here before, haven't I? In a dream. I remember it from a dream."

Anna didn't answer.

"But the room was different then. The walls were painted black – there was something written on them, but I couldn't make out the words. I heard a window being forced open and then I heard footsteps. It was a dream, wasn't it? Or am I dreaming now?"

"Does it matter?"

"It matters to me. I don't understand where I am. I don't understand what's happening. The last thing I remember is looking in a mirror..."

Anna sat on a wooden crate, her face hidden in shadow. "How much do you want to bet there's at least one universe where you're the one who's dead, not me? Must be at least one, don't you think?"

"Universe?" Samantha repeated. "What do you mean, a parallel universe?"

"It's all about possibility, isn't it? I saw something about it on TV while I was in hospital. Every possibility has to happen somewhere. So sometimes I'm dead, sometimes you are, sometimes neither of us, sometimes both of us. And sometimes one of us is a ghost, trapped inside a mirror."

Samantha thought back to what Janet had said: that trapped spirits reached out to grab the living. "Are you saying I'm stuck inside a mirror?"

"I'm saying you're stuck inside a universe. Where that universe is, I don't know."

Samantha thought back to the last line in Eleanor Burdon's notebook: *My only hope now is to go back the way I came.* She must have tried to go back through the mirror. And it had killed her.

The sign outside the local library said that they were open until eight o'clock on Mondays and Tuesdays. Samantha glanced at her watch – nearly a quarter past seven – and hurried up the stairs to the reference section.

She found what she was looking for in a book on folklore and superstition: *The reflection in the mirror mirrors the soul. If the glass holding your reflection should ever be broken, expect seven years' despair and misfortune, for seven years be required for the renewal of the soul.*

To break the cycle and release the soul, the broken pieces must be collected together and buried in the earth.

It was after midnight when Samantha opened the door to Eleanor Burdon's flat and walked through to the bedroom, carrying a hammer and a sheet.

She wrapped the sheet around the mirror, lay it down on the floor and attacked it with the hammer, shattering the glass. She put on a pair of gloves before she picked up the sheet full of jagged splinters and carried it downstairs, placing it in the boot of her car.

Then she drove to the nearest park and buried all the pieces.

Samantha went into the office early the next morning. She picked up the dead woman's notebook and started going through it page by page. Nothing but twee little rhymes.

"Hello, Sammy," Janet said brightly when she came in half an hour later. "Quite the early bird, aren't you?"

Samantha sighed. "I'm still trying to find an address for Mrs Burdon's daughter, but so far, nothing. Not even a clue."

"What are you talking about, you silly thing? We wrote to her yesterday; don't you – " She was interrupted by a ringing telephone. "Janet Hale," she said, lifting the receiver. She listened a moment, then reached across her desk for a notepad.

They went out on a new case later that morning: a former psychiatric patient who'd hung herself three weeks earlier.

Samantha followed Janet into a dark ground floor room with a bare concrete floor. The walls were painted black with the words: *Gateway To Hell* splashed across them in huge red letters. The room was empty of furniture.

Janet shook her head. "Can you credit it? They reckon somebody burgled the place with the poor girl's body still hanging from that pipe. I sometimes wonder what kind of world it is we're living in, Sammy, what kind of world."

"I wonder," Samantha agreed, nodding.

star

When Leslie woke up, John was just leaving. It was one of those tiny New York flats without internal doors, where you had to walk through the bedroom to get to the kitchen, and the bedroom was in full sight of the front door. "Where you goin'?" she asked sleepily.

He paused in the doorway and walked back to the bed. "To get some food," he said. "I've just looked in the kitchen, and the cupboard is bare!" He indicated the kitchen with a sweeping, dramatic gesture. Typical actor, never off-stage for a moment.

"That's all right. I'm not hungry, anyway."

"But I am," he said. "There's a deli on the corner. It'll just take me a minute to pick up some eggs and bread and stuff, and then I'll come flying back to you." He leant over to kiss her, and she giggled. "Make yourself at home. I'll be right back."

"Aren't you afraid to leave me here alone? How do you know I won't steal the family silver?"

His face hardened. "You couldn't if you wanted to," he said, sounding serious. Geez, she thought, didn't he know I was kidding? "There's a pot of coffee in the kitchen, help yourself. I want you awake." The front door closed and he was gone.

I want you awake. What was that supposed to mean? She shrugged and stretched, then she hopped out of bed and walked through the kitchen into the bathroom. She had a quick shower, and went back into the bedroom. She rummaged through his closet until she found a shirt to suit her, a pale blue to complement her eyes, nicely over-sized, very sixties' movie. She went back in the kitchen and poured herself a cup of coffee. One swig and she spat it into the sink. God, it was strong! No wonder the guy was so hyper.

She opened the refrigerator. There was one small carton of half-and-half, nothing else. She checked the freezer section, empty as well. He hadn't been kidding about bare cupboards. She sighed and held her cup under the hot water tap. Once she'd watered the coffee down enough so that she could drink it, she added a bit of the half-and-half and went back into the bedroom to wait.

John was sure taking his time. Maybe the deli was busy; it was a Saturday morning after all. She wandered into the living room, still sipping her coffee, and looked around. He didn't have much. A sofa, two metal folding chairs, a wooden table. Plain white walls. No pictures, no books, no stereo, nothing. The bedroom furnishings consisted of one double bed, one television set, and one video. About a dozen cassettes were piled on the floor beside it. No sign of anything else.

The lack of pictures surprised her – she'd never known an actor who didn't have loads of pictures of himself. Her apartment, down in the Village, was positively buried in pictures of herself. Publicity stills of her as Helena in *A Midsummer Night's Dream* in Central Park, Frenchie in a touring company of *Grease*, the wife in a dinner-theatre production of *Deathtrap*, and the time she'd been a background singer in one of the "I Love New York" TV ads.

But then he'd told her he didn't do much stage work, he worked mostly in film. Cheap videos, he'd told her, ones that never make the cinema. But it was regular work, and it paid the rent.

They met at an audition for an off-off-Broadway revival of *Streetcar*. She read Stella to his Stanley, and they had a cup of coffee afterwards. He phoned her a few days later to find out if she'd made the call-backs, but she hadn't. He hadn't either. He suggested they meet for a drink and some mutual consolation. That's when he told her about the videos.

"In a way, it's an actor's worst nightmare," he told her. "I've been completely typecast. I play the same role, over and over. But there's a huge demand for the damn things, so they keep churning them out, and I keep working."

"So what's the role you keep playing?"

He took a sip of his drink and looked around the bar. No one was within hearing distance. "Oh," he said casually, "I'm usually a mad slasher. Though sometimes I get to shoot someone."

Leslie giggled. "You're making video nasties!"

"Do you disapprove?"

"Nah! In this biz, you gotta take work where you can find it. You know what I did last year?" She leaned forward, lowering her voice to a confidential tone. "I did the voice for a porno flick. They got this big-chested bimbo to play the lead, right? But she couldn't talk! I mean, she had a voice like Minnie Mouse. So my agent phoned me up and asked me if I'd do it, just record her lines so they could dub them in. Well, all my politically correct friends would have killed me if they knew, but it was anonymous, and I was broke. Mostly, all I had to do was moan and say stuff like, 'Ooh, don't stop!' Besides, if I didn't do it, someone else would."

"That's exactly how I feel," he said, nodding. "If I didn't do it, somebody else would."

He phoned her the next day. "I'm doing another video," he said, "and they need someone like you. Are you interested?"

"Sure. What do I have to do, send them a photo, go to a casting, what?"

"Why don't I tell you all about it over dinner?"

Across a candlelit table in an Italian restaurant, he told her he'd fixed everything. Not only was she going to be in the next film, she was going to be the star. *I wonder if Katharine Hepburn started like this?* she thought ironically. But what did she care? Work was work.

They went back to his apartment after dinner. "You're going to be a star, Leslie," he told her. "You're going to be a star."

He'd been gone a long time now. She was getting hungry. She went through all the drawers and cupboards in the kitchen. Empty. Except for one box of cereal, way at the back of a shelf. That would do. She poured some into a bowl and screamed. It was crawling with worms. "Damn," she said, tossing it in the bin.

She watered down some more coffee and took it into the bedroom. She turned on the television and flicked from channel to channel, but there was nothing she wanted to watch. She reached down and looked through the video cassettes; none of them were labelled.

She put one in the machine and pressed "play". For a moment she thought the tape must be blank, then a title appeared: "To Slash A Brunette". She laughed out loud. So he had copies of every video he was in! He was a typically egotistical actor after all. She figured she ought to watch it, it would give her an idea of the sort of thing she was getting herself into.

A woman was sitting on a bed in her underwear, reading a magazine. The setting looked familiar. It was the room she was in now. God, she thought, these must be really low-budget. Nothing happened for a minute, then the woman looked up. "Oh, it's you," she said. "Where the hell have you been?" Then she frowned. "What's that supposed to be?" She started moving backwards. "Look," she said. "This isn't funny, so stop it!"

Leslie rolled her eyes. That woman couldn't act her way out of a paper bag. She pressed "pause" and mentally went over the way *she* would have said those lines. With meaning. With *feeling*. She pressed "play" again.

The woman was screaming, "Stay away from me! Stay away from me!"

Leslie didn't think much of the script; surely they could have given her something more interesting to say.

A figure moved into the shot: a man wearing a long coat, leather gloves, and a tight-fitting black leather hood that zipped up one side and had holes for the eyes and mouth. He was holding a long knife.

That must be John, he told her he always played the slasher. The woman tried to run, but he caught her. She screamed and screamed. The man held her from behind, so that she was facing the camera.

This is so unrealistic, Leslie thought. He wielded the knife, and began to cut.

"OH YUCK!" Leslie said out loud. This was disgusting. They'd really gone overboard with the cheap special effects. She fast-forwarded through the disemboweling sequence, trying to find the obligatory scene where the hero (usually a hard-boiled private eye or a tough cop) is introduced. There wasn't one. There was a long shot of the woman lying dead and mutilated, followed by blank tape.

Leslie's forehead wrinkled in consternation. This couldn't be the whole film – maybe he just kept copies of his own scenes. Though he didn't seem to have any lines.

She put another tape in the machine. The title appeared: "To Kill A Call Boy". The same room, the same bed. A young man – about twenty years old, with bleached blonde hair and one earring – leaned back stretching his arms. "I've been waiting for you," he said. What followed was a repeat of the first film, despite some minor variations.

She ejected the tape and put in another. A woman again, only this time in the kitchen.

It was finally dawning on her. These were real. Real people. Real deaths.

Her stage experience came in handy; she was dressed in less than twenty seconds. She ran for the door. It wouldn't open. She picked up the telephone; it was dead. She went back to the door and pounded and screamed. The door was soft to the touch. So were the walls. The place was sound-proofed.

She ran to the window. She was fifteen floors up, but she could throw something down to the street to get attention. The windows were sealed shut. She picked up one of the metal chairs and swung it against the glass. The chair broke. The glass didn't.

"Help me!" she screamed. "Get me out of here! Get me out of here!"

There was a click and then a whirring. She spun around and looked where the sound was coming from. A panel in the wall slid back, revealing the lens of a camera.

The front door opened, and a black-gloved hand reached inside. She crouched behind the sofa, grasping the broken metal chair, and waited. One of them was going to be a star.

a sense of focus

The kitchen was a shambles. She shook her head. He wasn't like her – he couldn't just lie there and take it. To lie there and take it like she'd always done – to say nothing to anyone and then to *clean up afterwards*, removing every trace – that was strength: true strength. But he didn't have that kind of strength – he'd have to make noise, he'd have to put up a fight, wouldn't he?

The radio was on full blast. That was a trick she'd learned from him – he always played the radio when he hit her, and the neighbours never heard a thing. Never saw a thing.

He was quieter now, much quieter. She plunged the knife in one last time, and turned the radio off.

She took a black plastic bag from the cupboard beneath the sink. It wasn't big enough. She went outside, to the shed. She came back with some newspapers and an axe.

She carried half-a-dozen bags down to the cellar. She cleaned the kitchen with a vengeance, scrubbing every inch, washing and waxing the floor until she could see her reflection in it. The sight of her face in the shiny surface surprised her; she looked younger than she had in years.

Then she went upstairs and tackled his room. She emptied the ashtrays and piled his clothes on the floor, to be disposed of later. She wrinkled her nose at the smell of stale cigars and male sweat. Stepping gingerly over a pile of his possessions, she crossed the room to open a window.

She'd only had her back turned for an instant, but the room had changed. Brightly-coloured mobiles hung from the ceiling. There were pink curtains, trimmed with lace. Walls covered with scenes from Mother Goose.

A one-eyed teddy bear stood guard next to an antique wooden crib.

The sound of a music box tinkled in her ears. She threw out her arms, inhaling the sweet powdery smell of a new baby.

This was Jenny's room; it would always be Jenny's room.

Phyllis gasped for breath and opened her eyes. She'd been dreaming again. She sat up and checked the time. Three a.m. He was snoring; she could hear it through the wall. Her body tensed with anger; he was still in the house. He'd said he was moving out – why didn't he go?

She shut her eyes tight and the dream was still there, still lurking beneath closed eyelids. "Do it!" a voice inside her head screamed. "Do it, do it, do it, DO IT!" The words became a drumbeat. She picked up a pair of scissors.

She stepped into the hall, moving like an automaton, moving in time to the insistent rhythmic pounding: "Do it, do it, do it, do it." She stood outside his room for a long moment. She felt herself grow brave and strong. She opened the door.

The snoring stopped abruptly. "What the hell do you think you're doing?" His voice was a low rumble, seething with hatred.

She was no longer brave; she was no longer strong. Her courage and her strength had fled at the sound of his voice. She saw herself as he must see her, weak and alone and ridiculous, shivering barefoot in a freezing hallway. She hid the scissors behind her back. The drumbeat faded. "I... I..." she stammered, closing the door. "Sorry."

She examined her face in the bathroom mirror, gently fingering the yellow bruise on her cheek. She reached down and pressed the sore spot below her left breast. Three of her teeth were missing; one was broken. Her shoulders were hunched. Her eyes were bloodshot and puffy. Deep frown lines creased her forehead. Her hair was thin and mostly grey. She was only thirty-seven. She thought about the scissors in her hand, the knives in the kitchen, the axe she'd seen him put in the shed. She thought about Jenny. "Coward!" She spat at her reflection.

Then she slowly wiped the mirror clean.

She found him in the kitchen making breakfast. She paused in the doorway, fingering her terry housecoat. He turned and smiled. Perfect straight teeth, pearly white. Tall. Broad shoulders, straight back. Thick black hair. Perfect skin, hardly a wrinkle. Wearing jeans and a sweater, but expensive. He was two years older than her. "Sit down," he said. She hesitated; he handed her a cup of coffee. "Sit down," he said again. She sat.

A moment later, there was a plate in front of her. She picked at her eggs, watching him from the corner of one eye. He poured her more coffee; offered more toast, more jam. Later, in the living room, he ordered her to lie back on the sofa and take off her slippers. She did as she was told. He sat beside her and lifted her legs, resting them across his lap. He began to massage her feet. "Relax," he said. "You're so tense."

Don't fall for it, she told herself. You've been here before. You always believe, because you want to. You desperately want to believe that everything is going to be all right – you want to believe this is the real him, this is the way it's always going to be.

"I thought maybe we'd drive into town for lunch." He was smiling at her; his touch was expert, gentle. Every movement a caress. She knew the moment she opened her mouth the spell would be broken. But she had to open her mouth; she had to say it. "Why are you doing this?"

"Why am I doing what?"

She knew what would happen next. She braced herself. "Being nice to me."

He stood up, shoving her legs away roughly. "Well, I really like that, Phyllis! I try to do something for you – I try to do something for my fucking wife for Christ's sake! And what do I get for it? Insults! Fucking sarcasm! And you know what?" His twisted face was inches from hers. "You're too stupid and pathetic to insult anybody." He stormed out of the room.

She heard glass breaking in the hallway. She heard the front door slam. She waited until she heard his car pull away from the drive. Then she got up and surveyed the damage. Not too bad this time; he'd knocked some framed photos off a table. She swept up the glass and put the photos in a drawer.

It was late when he came back. She was in her room, with the door locked. She turned out the light, rolled over onto her side, and curled into an almost foetal position. She pulled the blanket up over her head and lay motionless, pretending to be asleep. She heard him moving around downstairs. She heard a crash. He shouted mockingly, "Oh honey! I'm home!"

His heavy tread moved up the stairway. She tensed, holding her breath. She heard the squeak of the doorknob as it turned. He shook the knob; she heard it rattle. She heard him kick the door. Once. Hard. So hard she thought the wood would crack in two. Then she heard his voice, low and menacing, "I loathe you. I absolutely loathe you." His steps moved down the hallway; she heard water running.

She exhaled. Her entire body, damp with perspiration, went limp. She rolled onto her back and went to sleep.

She has this recurring dream: she's in the kitchen; she hears Jenny crying. She does what she should have done, what she can never forgive herself for not doing. She runs up the stairs. She grabs the baby from him. She saves her. She takes her far away, where no one will ever find them.

She sat up, listening. He was snoring. She got out of bed, careful of creaking floorboards, careful not to make a sound. She tiptoed out into the hall and down the stairs to the kitchen. She desperately wanted a cup of tea, but she was afraid to use the kettle; it whistled. She boiled some water on the stove and lit a cigarette. Every movement was slow, cautious, and completely silent.

She'd met him at a party, when they were both students. They sat up all night talking. He agreed with everything she said. He laughed at her jokes. He turned up on her doorstep two days later with a dozen roses.

The first time he hit her, he begged her forgiveness. He got down on his knees. He swore it would never happen again.

She'd been young then. She had a job then; she was even pretty. She could have left him. But he had a sixth sense; he knew when she'd reached the point where she was actually considering it, where she was actually making plans, and then he went through a transformation. He was considerate, he was romantic, he was perfect. For a while.

It was his idea to move to a suburb where nobody knew them. A place just middle-class enough that people minded their own business. Where the houses stood just far enough apart so that no one could hear his shouting, her screaming, things breaking. But that wasn't what he said; what he said was he wanted to make a fresh start in a place with no unpleasant memories and no old associations (meaning her friends) to drag them down. The baby was his idea, too. A baby would tie her to the house, keep her in her place. But that's not what he said; he said a baby would give their lives a sense of focus. He said caring for a baby would teach them to care for each other. He said a baby would save their marriage. He knew someone who could arrange things. For a price.

It started one Saturday evening. She'd said or done something to make him mad; she wasn't sure what. He followed her into the kitchen. He was shouting; she was begging. He held a leather strap in his hand. He turned the radio up so the neighbours wouldn't hear. He wasn't drunk. He always beat her with a sober, methodical efficiency. He grabbed her by the hair and threw her face down on the floor. He kicked her, over and over. Suddenly he stopped. He switched off the radio, and stood there, listening. She lay sobbing on the floor. "Shut up!" he hissed. "Shut up or I swear I'll kill you!" She forced herself to be quiet. Then she heard it, too. The baby was crying. "That's *your* fault," he said fiercely. "She's always crying day and night, she's driving me crazy, and it's all your fault! You don't take care of her like you're supposed to; you're a rotten mother!" He left the room and bounded up the stairs.

She didn't do anything. She lay face down on the kitchen floor, hearing everything and doing nothing. At that moment, all she felt was relief.

Someone else was getting it instead of her.

He was sitting on the living room sofa, looking through old photo albums. "You're still here," she said.

"Of course I'm still here. I live here, remember?" He leaned back and sighed. "What's happened to you, Phyllis? You used to wear make-up; you used to dress so nice."

She stood in the doorway, clutching at her housecoat. "You said you were moving out. You said that months ago."

"Why would I want to move out? Where'd you get such a crazy idea?"

"You said you'd found someone else. You said you were leaving."

"You're imagining things. Why have you always been so insecure? Come here." He patted the seat next to him. She stayed where she was. "Come here," he said again.

She walked over slowly. She sat down on the sofa beside him, her jaw working nervously.

He reached over and stroked her hair. "There's no one but you, baby. There's never been anyone else. We took a vow, sweetheart: 'til death do us part. Remember?" He flicked through the album in his lap. "Look at those two smug faces grinning at the camera! We thought we had the world by the tail then, didn't we?" He reached around and gave her an affectionate squeeze. "There's so much that's been good between us. I want to try again. I want to win you back. And this time, it'll be different. I promise you it will."

"I've heard this before."

"No, I mean it this time. You know you're everything to me. You're my whole life; I'd do anything for you." He kissed her on the forehead. "Absolutely anything. And I'll prove it. Come on. I want to show you something."

He took her by the hand and led her up the stairs. He opened the door to Jenny's old room with a flourish. She stood in the doorway, her mouth open. The pink lace-trimmed curtains were back in place, several brightly-coloured mobiles hung from the ceiling, the walls were covered in paper cut-outs of cartoon characters. He'd brought the antique wooden crib back from the cellar; it stood in its original spot against the wall. His clothes were gone, the overflowing ashtrays were gone. The folding bed he'd been using for the last year was gone. She started shaking. "What is this?"

"We're going to adopt another baby."

"Another baby? After what happened?"

"Look," he opened the closet door and pointed to a black suitcase. "I've already been to the bank. Twenty-five thousand cash, in small denominations. The price has gone up, but forget that. Just think about what this means. We're going to be a family again, a real family."

"Another one. You want another one."

"Someone's bringing her tomorrow. Another little girl. Wait 'til you see her – she's gorgeous!"

"I can't…"

"Can't what?"

Who could she turn to? Who could she tell after all this time? How much sympathy could she expect from the police? From a jury? "I can't wait," she said.

He squeezed her hand. "It'll be different this time, I swear it."

"Yes," she said, slowly and deliberately. "This time is going to be different."

There was more blood than she'd expected. She kept the radio on while she cleaned and scrubbed. It took ages.

She vacuumed. She dusted.

She carried half-a-dozen plastic bags down to the cellar.

She took a train into town the next morning. She had her hair done; her nails manicured. She phoned a friend she hadn't seen in years and met her for lunch. She bought a new dress and wore it home.

At seven-thirty that evening, the front doorbell rang. She opened it to a man in a suit. He held something small close to his chest.

"Oh, she's lovely!" Phyllis clapped her hands with excitement. She handed over the suitcase. The man handed over the baby.

"I'm going to call you 'Jenny'," she said.

choosing the incubus

"Vivid dreams of a sexual nature?" the doctor repeated, nodding thoughtfully. He smiled at the twenty-something, red-haired woman sitting on the other side of his desk. "Lucky you. How long has this been going on?"

"About three weeks. Ever since I moved into my new flat."

He leaned back, making a steeple with his hands.

"Well, that explains it. Moving house is always stressful – these dreams are merely your subconscious's way of dealing with stress. And a jolly nice way of dealing with it, too."

"What about the scratches? The teeth marks?"

"You did those yourself. You'd be amazed what people can get up to in their sleep." He looked down, breaking their eye contact, and busied himself with separating the stack of papers on his desk into separate, equal piles. "Good day, Miss Baker. I have patients with real problems waiting to see me."

That night it happened again. Kisses. Deep, luscious kisses. Coral opened her mouth, responding to the tongue that gently probed; she moaned with pleasure as the tongue explored the rest of her body. The probing became harder; more insistent. A weight pushed down upon her, and her moans became screams of ecstasy.

Catlike, she stretched in the morning sun, her eyes still closed from sleep, her lips turned up in a satisfied grin. She rolled over, reached out and wrapped her arms around – nothing.

"Oh no," she said out loud to an empty room, "not again. Please not again!"

Gerald phoned from Vienna that afternoon; his seminar on "Accountancy in a United Europe" was over and he'd be flying back that evening. This weekend it would be his place.

She was in Gerald's kitchen when he opened his front door and set down his suitcase. "What's for dinner?" he said.

Later that night, moving on top of her, he whispered, "Vienna is an... amazingly... beautiful city... mmm, you would... have...," His voice raised to a shout, "uh! uh! uh! Aaaaah... loved the buildings." He rolled onto his back and lit a cigarette. "And the food! Those pastries!"

"Hmmm?" Coral said.

They spent most of Saturday out on the balcony. Gerald spent the day working on his seminar report for the other department heads. Coral read a book. After dinner, Gerald fondled her breasts and told her how the other departments were due for a real shake-up. "Ooh, baby," Gerald said before falling asleep.

She didn't want to go home alone on Sunday, but Gerald reminded her of their agreement that career came first. They never spent the night together when there was work in the morning. Gerald kissed her on the cheek and told her he'd see her next Friday at her place.

Coral's flesh rose up in tiny bumps the minute she walked into her flat. It was the middle of August; there was no reason why the place should be so cold. She walked into her bedroom and it was freezing. She turned on the heat and started to get undressed. Slipping out of her jeans, she felt strangely self-conscious, as if she wasn't alone. She put her jeans back on.

Armed with a knife from the kitchen, she searched every corner. Satisfied that she was alone and that every door and window was locked securely, she went to bed fully dressed.

The next morning, she found her jeans on the floor. I did that myself, she thought. I was uncomfortable and I took them off. That's all there is to it. I did that myself, she thought over and over.

She'd drunk six cups of coffee and was on her fifteenth cigarette when there was a knock on her office door. She jumped. "Who is it?"

The door opened and Abby, who had the office next door, marched in. Fifty, fat and twice-divorced, she had been Coral's self-appointed protector, advisor and surrogate mother-figure since the younger woman's first day on the job, a situation which Coral sometimes found annoying, but had come to accept.

Abbey stopped in front of Coral's desk, folded her arms across her chest, and glared. "Well? Are you going to tell me what's wrong?"

"I... I don't know what you mean."

"I thought we were friends, Coral. Friends talk to each other. They tell each other when something's wrong."

"There's nothing wrong."

"Nothing wrong? You've been holed up in your office all week, and if anybody so much as looks at you, you jump a mile!"

"No I don't," Coral said quickly.

"Ha!" said Abby, "pull the other one! What about yesterday? Poor old Henderson only had to say 'good morning' to make you knock over a stack of files. And the day before that, when you spilled coffee all over those computer disks? And..."

Coral raised a hand to stop her. "Okay, okay. Point taken. Maybe I'm a little tense, but it's nothing, really. I just haven't been getting enough sleep lately, that's all."

Abby's expression changed to a mischievous grin. "Don't tell me you finally dumped that horrible twerp and got yourself a real man? About time, girl!"

Coral's face turned red.

"That's it, isn't it?" Abby went on, deliberately misinterpreting Coral's reaction. She leaned across Coral's desk, lowering her voice to a husky, suggestive whisper. "No one ever gets a wink of sleep for those first few weeks, do they? Who is he? Do I know him? Not that it matters – anything's better than that last one of yours; I don't know what you ever saw in him."

Coral bit her lip, fuming. "You've made it quite clear you don't like him, but Gerald has many fine qualities of which you are obviously unaware," she said, struggling to keep her voice under control. "He's...

reliable. And stable... and honest, and... reliable. And if you had any idea how many two-faced bastards I've had to put up with in the past," her eyes began to fill with tears, "you'd realise just how important reliable is!" The tears were spilling down her cheeks. "Oh, damn!" She angrily wiped her face with the back of one hand.

"I'm sorry!" Abby looked around the room in desperation. "I'd offer you a tissue, but I can't find one! Where do you keep them?"

"Here." Coral reached into a desk drawer and pulled one out, loudly blowing her nose.

"Look, I'm really sorry," Abby repeated. "I was way out of line, talking about your boyfriend like that. I didn't mean it, love. Honest. I was only winding you up – I never thought you'd take me seriously. You know what a kidder I am! I like Gerald. He's a great bloke, really. And he makes you very happy – anyone can see that."

"Yes, he does," Coral agreed, sobbing.

Abby hesitated a moment before saying, "This doesn't mean lunch is off, does it?"

The weekend was a disaster. Coral couldn't relax in bed; she felt they were being watched. She nearly screamed for Gerald to stop – the room around them had come to life, watching with glowing red eyes, throbbing with jealous desire – but before she could say anything, he was already lying spent beside her, breathing softly with his head on her shoulder. Six months ago – even two or three weeks ago – she might have looked at him tenderly, or even kissed his forehead. He was good-looking, he had a well-paid job and a lot of ambition, and as far as she knew, he'd never cheated on her. That had been enough for her once. Now she just wanted him to leave. She wanted to be alone, to surrender herself, alone, to the feeling that permeated the room.

She lay there seething with frustration as Gerald snored beside her. She slid one hand along her inner thigh, moving upwards, and then she stopped, embarrassed. She was being watched; she knew she was being watched.

She slept all day Saturday. When she woke up that evening, Gerald told her he'd had a productive day; he'd brought his laptop computer with him.

Later that night, Coral's bedroom pulsated with anger and indignation. Gerald didn't notice. He climbed on top of Coral, and she rolled her eyes, grimacing in the dark.

When Gerald left on Sunday evening, Coral breathed a sigh of relief. She rushed into the bathroom and lathered herself with perfumed soap. She lingered in the shower, revelling in the way the water pounded against her skin. Then she got into bed and she waited.

By the middle of the week, everyone at work noticed that Coral seemed to be her old self again. In fact, they'd never seen her so happy – no one had ever seen her giggle over a group pension plan before.

She knocked on Abby's office door and offered to treat her to lunch.

"So what's all this about?" Abby asked, looking around the expensive restaurant Coral had taken her to. A uniformed waiter poured them each a glass of champagne.

"I'm celebrating."

"Celebrating what?"

"The fact that I've finally managed to accept something."

"And what have you accepted?"

Coral shrugged and raised her glass in a toast. "The fact that I've gone crazy. Stark staring mad. Bonkers. Utterly ga-ga."

"What?"

"I'm afraid so. I'm totally insane."

"You must be, ordering champagne on your salary."

"Oh it's not just that. It's things that have been happening. Fun things. Things that happen late at night, when I think I'm all alone, but I'm not... Or I think I'm awake, but I'm not. Oh here comes the food. Thank goodness, I'm starving."

"Fun things?" Abby repeated, starting to giggle. "Fun how?"

Coral told her. A man at the next table leaned so far over he fell off his chair.

Coral was wakened by the passionate mouth that forced her lips apart, giving access to that long and insistent tongue that she had come to know so well. She let out a groan of pleasure as her legs parted and the thrusting began.

She was awake. Though her eyes were still closed, she was definitely awake and she was being made love to. The weight that pressed upon her, moving in rhythmic waves, was real. There was no doubt about it. She could hear moans so loud they bounced off the walls, and they weren't all coming from her. Her body began to spasm, over and over again. She cried out and dug her nails deep into something above her. Something solid. Something that didn't feel right.

Gasping for breath, she opened her eyes. More than anything in the world, she wanted to run. She wanted to scream and scream until her throat had torn itself to shreds. She wanted to fall down on her knees and pray.

She didn't do any of these things because she fainted.

The alarm clock went off at seven. She reached over to shut it off and lay there for a moment, feeling drained. Her eyelids fluttered open and she stared up at the ceiling. Then she remembered. There was no time for a shower or make-up, she had to get out of there. She leaped out of bed, threw on some clothes with awkward, shaking hands, and ran out the door.

She phoned Gerald from a coin box. His voice was gruff and sleepy. No, he couldn't possibly take the day off. There was an important meeting that morning and he had to be there. He'd see her tomorrow, anyway, so what was the problem? Oh yes, he added, he might have a surprise for her. His alarm clock rang, and he hung up.

It was seven-fifteen in the morning and she had no family and very few friends. There was nobody she could run to; there was no place she could go except to work. She walked in circles for an hour and then she spent twenty minutes waiting outside the front door because she'd forgotten her key. She threw up in the toilet across from her office.

That afternoon, she knocked on Abby's office door.

"Coral? What are you still doing here? I thought you went home ill."

Coral sat down across from Abby. "I have been ill. But I didn't go home. I couldn't go home…" She bent forward, resting both her elbows on Abby's desk. She lowered her voice. "You remember those dreams I told you about?"

Abby laughed. "How could I forget?"

"They weren't dreams!" Coral leaned even further forward. "Do you know what an incubus is?"

"A what?"

"It's a demon. A male demon who has sex with mortal women."

"Coral, stop it right now. You sound positively medieval!"

"That's exactly it! In the Middle Ages, women who had sex with demons were burned at the stake."

"That was just superstition; there's no such thing as a demon."

"That's what I thought. But then I saw one. It's got burning red eyes, and leather wings, just like a bat. And it was in my bed!"

Abby nodded slowly, a tight little smile on her face. "Sure, Coral."

"Don't humour me, Abby! I remember reading about it at university, in a book about witch-trials in the middle ages. According to this book, in the fourteenth century, several unmarried women in a particular village gave birth to deformed children with wings! The women were tried for witchcraft and each confessed that she'd had sex with a demon, who she now realised had only been using her to reproduce its kind upon the earth. They all said the same thing: that a creature with black wings and eyes like burning coals had come to them in the night, every night. Sometimes several times a night. But the most important thing is this: after the women were tried and found guilty, the village they lived in was deserted – no one would live there any more. They thought the place itself was evil. And you know where that place is? Exactly where I'm living now!"

Abby raised one eyebrow. "In your flat? Stop winding me up."

"On that *land*. My flat's in a new development – I'm sure it's the same place because the land was empty until the developer bought it. It's been empty for hundreds of years. They were afraid to build anything there after what happened, don't you see?"

Abby thought for a moment before speaking very slowly and carefully, "Is there something you're unhappy about, Coral?"

"Something I'm unhappy about?" Coral repeated incredulously. She stood up, staring at Abby in wide-eyed amazement. "Of course there is! I'm unhappy there's a sex-mad demon in my flat! Wouldn't you be?"

"That's not what I meant," Abby said. "I mean, could there be something that on a conscious level, you don't want to face? Something you're pushing so far down inside you, that your subconscious decides it's got to make you face whatever it is – this problem you're denying – and the only way your subconscious can do it is to conjure up some image from your past, like this demon from a book you once read?"

Oh no, Coral thought, she's read something in *Woman's Weekly* and now she's an expert. "No," she said, shaking her head. "No, there's nothing."

"You're sure?"

"Of course I'm sure!"

"Coral, I'm no psychiatrist or anything..."

"But I thought you were," Coral interrupted sarcastically.

"All I'm trying to say is if you think about it, doesn't this demon of yours sound just a little bit Freudian?"

Coral brought her fist down on the desk. "I'm telling you there is something in my flat – not a dream, not a subconscious symbol – something one hundred per cent real and very, very physical!"

Abby leaned back and sighed. "I suppose you'd better come and stay at my place."

Coral arrived at Gerald's flat only a few minutes ahead of him. "I haven't had time to start the dinner – I only just got here."

"That's okay," he told her. "I was going to take you out for dinner, anyway."

Her jaw dropped in surprise. They never went out to dinner; Gerald always said there was nothing like good home cooking. "Really?"

He smiled at her reaction, and it struck her that he always looked so smug. "Really," he said.

After they handed their menus back to the waiter, Coral looked across the candlelit table and asked if this was the surprise he'd mentioned yesterday morning.

He shook his head. "I got my place on the Board. Sooner than I expected."

"Oh, Gerald, that's wonderful! You've been wanting that so badly."

"I know. And now there's something else I want. To make my life complete." He reached across the table and took her hand.

"And what's that, Gerald?"

"Children."

"WHAT?"

"I've been thinking about this for a while, Coral. Of course I didn't want to say anything until I was certain. But now, with this promotion, I think the time has come."

"Has it?"

"It has. Oh, we'll get married of course. And as soon as property starts looking up again, we can sell your flat and get a house in Sussex, near the Downs. It'll be great for the kids."

"Kids," Coral repeated. "That's a plural."

"I want at least four. Two boys, two girls."

"You realise this could make things a bit difficult for me at work, don't you?"

Gerald chuckled politely and squeezed her hand in appreciation. "You've always had such a sense of humour. Of course you'll quit your job. Being a wife and mother is work enough for any woman."

"But I've moved up very fast. I could be assistant district manager when Mr Henderson retires."

"Tut-tut, darling. You know you'll never get as far or make as much money as I will, so why bother trying? Of course, I'll let you keep working long enough to get some paid maternity leave..."

That night, Gerald asked her if she'd taken her pill and she said yes. Oh well, he told her, you can forget about those darn things as of tomorrow. She closed her eyes.

"Mmm, baby, baby," he said, pressing down on her in the dark.

"You're crushing my leg."

"Sorry." He shifted his weight.

"Not that one, the other one."

He moved again.

"Mind my... ow!"
"Now what's wrong?"
"You're pulling my hair!"
"Sorry."

He grunted, sighed, muttered something about re-joining the exchange rate mechanism, and went to sleep. She got up and took a long, hot bath, remembering the way every nerve-end had tingled with exquisite sensation only two nights earlier. Then she visualised herself, five years down the road, living with Gerald and Gerald's children, and never feeling that way again.

Saturday morning, she asked him if he enjoyed having sex with her. "What a stupid question," he said, patting her on the hand.

They spent the afternoon on the balcony and he told her what a great life they were going to have out in the country where there would be nothing to distract her from the joy of presiding over a brood of miniature Geralds. With the approach of evening, Coral noticed how the red light of the sunset reflected in his eyes, making them glow like a pair of hot coals. She couldn't stop herself imagining him with a pair of leather wings.

"You want to use me to reproduce your kind upon the earth, don't you?" she said.

He looked surprised for a moment, and then he smiled. "Well, I could hardly manage it without you, could I?"

She swallowed her pill when he wasn't looking.

"Fingers crossed," Gerald said later, doing a flying leap onto the mattress which broke the bedframe, throwing splinters in all directions.

On Sunday, for the first time ever, he told her that she didn't have to leave. "I can drive over and pick up the rest of your clothes," he offered, sitting on the mattress which now rested on the floor.

"No, Gerald," she told him. "I want to go home."

"Okay," he said. "We'll go to your place. This making a baby business does take a bit of effort, but I think I'm up to another go."

"No, please. I don't think my furniture could take the strain."

Her phone rang at eleven o'clock. It was Abby. "Are you all right? I thought you were coming back here tonight."

"I'm fine. And I don't think I'll be needing your hospitality after all. I'm going to stay right here."

"But... but you said there was an evil spirit in your flat that wanted to use you to reproduce its kind upon the earth."

"Did I say that? I must have been winding you up. Well, never mind. Everything's all right now. There's no problem... no problem at all." She put down the phone and turned off the light.

She lay alone in the darkness, laughing. That poor little demon from the fourteenth century would never have heard of birth control.

asleep at the wheel

Carrie and Eric were dancing around the living room. Carrie didn't remember the music starting. She didn't remember when or how they'd started dancing. She didn't even remember coming back to her parents' apartment. But there they were, slow-dancing by candlelight on the rug between the sofa and the TV set, and it seemed to Carrie like they'd been dancing forever. She rested her head on Eric's shoulder, closed her eyes, and floated in lazy circles.

"Carrie," Eric said, holding her close against him. "There's something we've got to talk about. Something I've been trying to tell you. Something important."

His voice was so soft and quiet, she could hardly hear him; it seemed to come from somewhere far away. "Hmm?" Carrie said, her eyes still closed. Still floating.

"Do you remember the night you went to a concert with your friend Gina?"

Carrie stiffened, no longer floating.

She opened her eyes and sat up in bed, shaking.

She'd had a dream that had upset her, obviously. But she couldn't remember what it was; it was gone. Completely gone. She'd been having a lot of those lately: dreams that vanished without a trace except for the fact that they left her wide-awake and shivering in the middle of the night.

She looked down at her husband, Jack, lying beside her with his mouth open. Snoring like a tank engine. She'd never get back to sleep while that was going on. She lightly pinched his nostrils together. He batted her hand away and muttered something she couldn't hear. "You were snoring," Carrie told him. He rolled onto his side and went back to sleep.

Carrie lay watching the back of Jack's head, waiting for dawn.

"I had another dream last night," she told him over breakfast in the morning. "Can't remember what it was about, though."

Jack stood up, gulping down the last of his coffee. "Gotta dash or I'll miss my train."

Carrie looked up to see her teenage daughter from her first marriage, Tanya, standing in the kitchen doorway.

Tanya didn't budge an inch to let her stepfather through – wouldn't even look at him. Jack had to turn sideways in order to squeeze past her, flashing an angry, disgusted look back at Carrie, the kind of look that said: "this is your fault". Tanya just stared at the wall.

Carrie looked down at the table, gathered the breakfast things and carried them to the sink, trying to drown the nagging voice inside her head with the clatter of crockery and splash of soapy water.

Tanya didn't move until they both heard the front door slam closed. Then she crossed the room to stand beside her mother. "I dream, too, you know," she announced. "I dream I'm dead. Sometimes I dream I was never born at all, that I'm not even real, not even human."

Carrie stared into the sink. "Would you like some cereal?"

"You're not listening to me, are you?"

Carrie turned and looked at her daughter. "I'm listening, but I don't like what I'm hearing. You're fourteen years old, you should be dreaming about your future – what you want to do with your life – not about death and never being born."

"You don't listen," said her daughter. "I try to tell you things – important things. But you never listen."

"What do you mean? I don't understand."

"No, I guess you don't," Tanya said, walking away.

Carrie knocked on Tanya's door and got no answer. She turned the knob and pushed it open. The window was shut, the curtains drawn. Tanya lay sprawled across her bed, fully clothed, eyes closed, mouth open.

"Tanya," Carrie said gently. "Tanya."

In the gloomy half-light of the room, the pale figure lying on its back before her looked more like a doll than a person, a stick-thin department store mannequin, stiff and bloodless. Carrie moved across the room, reached down and touched her daughter's cheek. Her flesh felt cool and powdery. "Honey, are you all right?"

"So tired," Tanya mumbled.

"It's a beautiful day outside. Don't you want to get some air?"

Tanya rolled onto her side, pulling a blanket over her head.

One evening, they'd been out (to a party, to a movie, for a pizza, where? Carrie tried to remember and it all became a blur) and when they got back to her parents' place, Eric sat down beside her and took hold of both her hands. "Carrie, there's something I've been trying to tell you for a long, long time, and the time has come for you to listen."

"Listen to what? I always listen, don't I?"

"No, Carrie, you don't," Eric scolded her gently. "But you're going to listen now."

"Okay."

"I want you to think back, Carrie. Back to a hot August night when you were seventeen years old."

"What are you talking about? I'm seventeen now."

"You went out with your friend Gina; you had tickets for a concert, and then you took the bus back home. Do you remember?" Carrie frowned and shook her head.

"Try, Carrie. Try to remember; it's important. You got off the bus at the corner of Belmont and Hamlyn. You only had to walk two blocks to get home…"

Carrie tried to pull her hands away. "Let go of me, Eric! You're hurting me! You're hurting me!"

Carrie sat bolt upright, drenched in sweat. She looked down at the mattress beside her. Empty. "Jack?" she whispered. "Jack?" she called again, more loudly. She got out of bed, threw on a robe, opened the bedroom door and stepped into a hot August evening in 1971.

Carrie sat down in front of the mirror, painting her lids with white eyeliner while Gina rolled joints and tried on one outfit after another. She finally decided on a long peasant dress and lace-up sandals.

Carrie chose a pair of brown hip-hugger bell-bottoms, an imitation suede vest, and a bracelet of silver bells.

It was late when she got off the bus. Moonless, dark, and still. She glanced up at a streetlight and saw a large moth flap towards the light, throwing itself against the burning bulb. She crossed the main road and started to walk the two blocks to the apartment where she lived with her parents.

She'd walked these same two blocks many times before, but tonight everything seemed strange and threatening. The jingling bells on her wrist seemed to echo off the walls of every building she passed. The sound made her feel strangely self-conscious, as if she was drawing too much attention to herself. Though the street appeared empty, she had a feeling she was being watched. She held the bracelet still with her opposite hand. The street fell back into eerie silence.

She was halfway down Hamlyn when the silence was broken once more. The door of a parked car swung open. Two men leapt out and she started to run. Then everything went black.

She found herself behind the wheel of her car, Tanya strapped into the passenger's seat beside her. She came to with a start; she didn't remember driving into the city.

A cold wave of fear travelled the length of her spine. She had just driven through the downtown business district at the height of the rush hour and she didn't remember any of it. She didn't even remember getting into the car.

She felt as if she'd spent the entire journey asleep at the wheel. What if a truck had come at them head-on? Would she have reacted? She tried to tell herself of course she would have, but the truth was she didn't know.

She shivered at the thought of all the dreadful things that could have happened, all the ways they might never have arrived. "We're here," she said, turning the car into Hamlyn Street, where her parents lived.

She rang the bell several times, but got no answer.

"The door isn't locked," Tanya said, pushing it open. The apartment was empty. The walls were streaked with grime, the floor covered in a layer of dust and leaves.

"I don't understand it," Carrie said, thinking Tanya was still standing beside her, "where are they?" She turned and saw she was alone.

Carrie found her daughter standing on the back porch, staring into space.

When Carrie was a little girl, she used to spend hours on that porch, watching the neighbours' laundry flap in the breeze, listening to their dogs bark, their televisions blare, their doors slam, their windows slide up and down. Now everything was empty: the neighbouring porches, the alley, every single window. Empty and silent. "I don't understand what's going on," she said. "Where is everybody?"

"I'm so tired of this," Tanya muttered more to herself than to her mother. "Tired of going through the motions. Tired of pretending."

"Tanya, honey, what's wrong? What can I do for you? Tell me."

Tanya turned to face her. "You really wanna do something for me? Then let me go. It's easy. All you have to do is wake up." She raised her voice to a shout. "Wake up!"

It was dark, and the street was empty. Carrie started to walk the two blocks back to her parents' apartment. The only sounds were those of her quick footsteps on the pavement, and the jingling of bells. Then she heard another sound: a constant tap, tap, tap, high above her head. She looked up and saw a moth, flinging itself at a streetlamp. Strange, she thought. How could she possibly hear such a tiny sound?

She tapped on her parents' window – tap, tap, tap, like a moth drawn by a light. She tapped on the walls and on the furniture. They didn't hear. She walked through the living room and the kitchen. They didn't see her. She touched them, but they didn't feel her.

Carrie stood on the back porch, clutching the wooden railing. Eric touched her on the arm. "Come inside."

"It's different this time, Eric. I remember the dream – or part of it, anyway."

"Really?" he said. "So what do you dream about when you go away?"

"I dream I'm old and I have a daughter who hates me."

Eric shook his head, looking puzzled. "Why do you think she hates you?"

Carrie thought a moment. "I'm the one who dreamed her into existence, I'm the one who makes her jump through hoops, and she knows it. Somehow, she knows it. The last time I saw her, she begged me to end it."

Eric leaned forward, touching her hand. "Then let the poor girl go, Carrie. Let her go."

Carrie closed her eyes and nodded. "I will."

"Do you remember anything else about your dream?"

"I think I had a husband, and he wasn't very happy, either…"

"Jack!" Carrie shook him by the shoulders. "Jack, wake up!"

He sat up. "Whattsa matter?"

"I just had the weirdest dream!"

He groaned and fell back onto the pillow. "You woke me up for that?"

"I've got to tell you now, while I still remember."

"Can't you tell me in the morning?"

"No! If I wait 'til morning, I'll forget it again." Jack sighed and made a face. "All right, what is it?"

"I dreamed that I died when I was seventeen years old, and that everything I've done since then, everything I thought was real – was the dream."

Jack scratched his head. "Let me get this straight. You dreamed you'd been dead for…" he closed his eyes and did some mental arithmetic, "…about twenty-five years. And everything you'd done over the last quarter of a century was just some dream you had after you died?"

"In the dream, I'd never left my parents' old apartment. I couldn't leave; I was a ghost. An old friend who died a long time ago was there, too." Carrie shrugged, embarrassed. "He was more than a friend, actually. We went steady all through high school, then he got killed in Viet Nam. Anyway, he told me we were there because we'd both died young and violently, but unlike him, I still hadn't managed to accept it, so I have this ongoing fantasy that I'm still alive."

"So what does that make me?" Jack asked, adding sarcastically, "According to your old dead boyfriend, that is."

"A fantasy," said Carrie. "A dead woman's fantasy."

"If I'm a fantasy, then how come you fantasised me with bunions? And why'd you give me such a crap job? And how come you fantasised a house with a leaky roof and a mortgage we can barely afford? Why couldn't you fantasise me rich and famous, huh? A rock star, maybe. I wouldn't have minded being a rock star."

"He said he thinks I must be punishing myself for something, that this was kind of like my version of purgatory, if not exactly hell."

"Your version of hell? If you're the one being punished, how come I'm the one stuck with the crap job and the bunions?"

"Yeah, I know," Carrie said, laughing. "And I'll bet Tanya might have a thing or two to say about whose hell it was, right?"

"Tanya?" Jack repeated. "Who the hell is Tanya?"

rules of engagement

Ruella, fifteen-year-old queen of Tanalor, slouched back on her throne, a dwarf in a jester's costume massaging her bare feet. A herald came in to the throne room. "Your Majesty," he said, kneeling before her with his head bowed.

"Yeah?"

"A messenger from the kingdom of Hala awaits without for your pleasure."

"Work work work. All right, send him in."

A young man with flowing black hair, large dark eyes, and extremely tight tights entered and knelt before her.

She quickly straightened her back, sucked in her stomach and kicked the dwarf out of the way. "Arise, sir," she said, sliding her feet into a pair of jewel-encrusted slippers. "Welcome to our fair kingdom."

"Truly thy kingdom is fair, lady, but I must say without fear of contradiction that the fairness of thy kingdom is nothing compared to the fairness of its Queen."

Ruella lowered her head slightly and raised one finger to her lips, regarding the young messenger with half-closed eyes. "So what can I do you for?"

"I bear tidings of great joy. My lord, the King of Hala, hearing of your great beauty and wit..."

"Wants me to marry his son," Ruella interrupted, rolling her eyes. "I get these proposals every day."

"If I may be so bold as to correct you, Your Majesty, the King of Hala does not wish you to marry his son. He requests your hand in marriage for himself."

"This is King Reynard of Hala you're talking about, right?"

"Yes, my lady."

"Seventy-five years old, no teeth, bad breath, with hair growing out of his ears?"

"Your description is cruel but I cannot deny its accuracy."

"And this is your idea of joyful tidings? Well, tell your King this for me. I'm not going to marry him because A: he's an ugly old man, and B: with an A like that, who needs a B?"

"My lady," the messenger said, looking her in the eye, "I would urge you to reconsider. My sire, King Reynard of Hala, is a man of enormous wealth, wealth beyond any your poor tiny kingdom can imagine. He can offer you a life of luxury beyond anything you could dream."

"Let me guess the next bit. All I have to do is give up control of my own tiny kingdom?"

The messenger shrugged. "And you'd have to sleep with him at least once."

Ruella burst out laughing. It amazed her that she had ever found this idiot attractive. "Get out of my sight," she said.

"One more thing, my lady," the messenger said. "I must warn you that if you refuse, your kingdom and even your fair self may be destroyed."

"I'll bet you say that to all the girls."

The messenger lowered his voice. "I must tell you my lord is a master of darkness."

"A what?"

"He has power over things that are not of this earth."

Ruella made a face. "I'm impressed."

"I warn you, lady, my father will not take kindly to your attitude."

Ruella raised one eyebrow. He'd said "my father". So this was Prince Merriller, heir to the Halan throne and inestimable wealth. On second thought, maybe he was kind of cute after all. "I pray you will forgive my hasty speech, Prince Merriller, but I didn't know who you were. I mean, it isn't every day a girl gets a proposal of marriage…"

"I thought you said it was," the prince interrupted.

"I was about to say from such a fine man as your father." She clapped her hands, and two guards appeared. "Show Prince Merriller to suitable quarters, he's going to be our guest for a while."

"But..." the prince protested as the guards carried him away.

In a cavern far below the palace, a hooded figure stood bent over a cauldron. It looked up as Ruella entered. "I've been doing a little checking on your latest suitor," it rasped.

"Oh yeah?"

"Yeah." It poured a vial of brightly coloured liquid into the cauldron, stirring it slowly, then dipped a fleshless finger into the bubbling mixture. "Needs more salt," it muttered.

Ruella reached for a container on a shelf. "So what did you find out?" she asked, handing it over.

The hooded figure tossed a pinch of salt over its shoulder. "Since when is Queen Know-It-All interested in what I have to say?"

Ruella rolled her eyes. "Try me."

The hooded figure dipped another finger into the boiling liquid. "Perfect," it said, removing the cauldron from the heat before crossing over to the shelves to dust its collection of jars labelled Poison. "It seems King Reynard started out with a little kingdom, not much bigger than this one. Then he married a neighbouring princess. Her father died shortly after the wedding, in mysterious and unexplained circumstances. A week after his new wife was crowned queen, she died, also in mysterious circumstances. Then he married another neighbouring princess, who died soon after in... guess what?"

Ruella made a face. "Mysterious circumstances?"

The hooded figure nodded. "He's done it five times. In five marriages – not one lasting longer than a year – he's managed to quintuple his lands, his power base, and his treasury." It picked up a jar of dead toads, gently polishing the glass. "So what do you think he wants with you?"

Ruella laughed.

"I told you you wouldn't be interested," the hooded figure said, putting back the jar.

"No," Ruella protested, giggling. "It's just that I know all this already. I've been studying up on Reynard for months, and I think it's about time someone beat him at his own game, don't you? It wouldn't be the first time a seventy-five-year-old man died on his wedding night. Nobody would suspect a thing, and Hala is so-o-o wealthy." She tilted her head to one side, licking her lips. "Who do you think sent him my portrait in the first place?"

"You shouldn't do things like that without telling me first," the hooded figure rasped in disapproval. "Some of these local sorcerers can be dangerous."

She waved her hand in dismissal. "Anything they can do, I can do better. Watch this."

She stood in the middle of the cavern, a look of concentration on her face. A pillar of flame shot from her fingers. "How's that?"

The other pulled back its hood, scratching a bare skull crawling with worms. "All right for a party trick. Next you'll be pulling rabbits out of hats."

"How about this, then?" She closed her eyes, intoning a series of strange harsh syllables. The ground below them began to shake. The rock walls of the cavern dripped blood. There was a sound of weeping and then a roar of fury. The air around them swirled into a red mist, reeking of sulphur. Ruella opened her eyes. The cavern split in two as the earth cracked open, spewing forth its dead. Ruella, breathing fire, grew impossibly large as a legion of corpses, soldiers of darkness ready to die and die again, bowed down before her.

"Better," the hooded figure rasped.

Prince Merriller stormed into the throne room. "You are foiled, lady!" he shouted.

In unison, without turning to look at him, the Queen, her guards, and each member of her court raised one finger to their lips and shushed him. Every eye was focused on a stage erected in the middle of the room, every ear was straining to listen. The prince tried to speak again. A guard placed one hand firmly over the prince's mouth.

On the stage, an actor and an actress were looking at each other intensely. "What is thy problem?" the actor said. "Thou knowest I need my space."

"Truly I know this, and have agreed on this basis to an open relationship," the actress replied, "but woe is me and triple times woe! For I fear I am great with child."

There was a dramatic musical chord. The actor turned to face the audience, looking startled.

The candles surrounding the stage were extinguished, plunging the actors into darkness. A chorus of singers began the theme: *Peasants, everybody needs good peasants...*

The prince broke free of the guard who was holding him. "Ruella!"

She shrugged, looking sheepish. "I know it's crap. But I'm hooked."

"You can keep me prisoner here no longer," Prince Merriller announced, thrusting his jaw forward in defiance.

"Why not?" she asked, yawning.

"While your guards were down here, watching this..." he gestured towards the stage, "... mindless rubbish, I made my way to the castle roof. From there, I saw the Halan army approaching, my father the King leading them to my rescue."

The Queen jumped up excitedly. "King Reynard's on his way? That's wonderful!"

"When I tell him the things I have witnessed and heard, how you have held me here against my will, how you cavort with undead skeletons..."

"Oh, shut up!" She moved closer to him, lowering her voice so that only he could hear. "Who do you think he's going to believe? You? Or me, when I tell him how you came to my chamber in the middle of the night, vowing to kill your father, take his throne, and marry me yourself?"

The prince's eyes nearly popped out of his head. He shook all over as he sputtered, "But, I didn't! I never...!"

Ruella winked and gave him a gentle nudge with her elbow. "I'll keep quiet if you will."

The chorus was still singing the theme from *Peasants*. "Will you guys clam up already?" They were silent. "And you can take tomorrow off.

I'm getting married!"

Ruella giggled as she put on her wedding dress. She was already thinking about her second husband. And her third.

women on the brink of a cataclysm

I felt like I was going through a meat grinder. Then there was a blinding flash of light – bright orange – and I felt like I was going through a meat grinder backwards. And there I was, back in one piece. Slightly dizzy, a little stiff around the joints. Swearing I'd never do that again.

The digital display inside the capsule read: 29 April 1995, 6:03 p.m., E.S.T. If that was true, then I was furious. Toni promised she would only set the timer forward by two minutes, and I'd gone forward by a year! A whole year, wasted. Didn't she realise I had work to do? And then I thought: oh my God, the exhibition! I was supposed to have an exhibition in July, 1994 – if I've really gone forward a year, I missed my one-woman show at Gallery Alfredo!

I opened the capsule door, bent on murder. And then I froze. This wasn't my studio.

I live and work on the top floor of an old warehouse in lower Manhattan, and I do sculpture. Abstract sculpture. I take scrapped auto parts and turn them into something beautiful. I twist industrial rubbish into exquisite shapes. I can mount a bicycle wheel onto a wooden platform and make it speak volumes about the meaning of life. I once placed a headless Barbie doll inside a fish tank and sold it for five thousand dollars, and that was before I was famous – I hear the same piece recently fetched more than forty.

I'd been working on a new piece called "Women on the Brink of a Cataclysm": an arrangement of six black and white television sets, each showing a video loop of a woman scrubbing a floor, when Toni Fisher rang the doorbell. I've known Toni off and on since we were kids. We grew up in the same town and went to the same high school before going our separate ways after graduation, in 1966. I went to art school in California, she got a scholarship to study physics at Cambridge in England. It would be twenty years before we met again, at the launch party for *Gutsy Ladies: Women Making Their Mark In The 80s*, the latest book by Arabella Winstein.

It was one of those dreadful media circuses; I remember a PR woman in a geometric haircut dragging me around the room for a round of introductions: "Hey there, gutsy lady, come and meet some other gutsy ladies." I was there in my capacity as "Gutsy Lady of the Art World" and Toni had been profiled in a chapter entitled: "Gutsy Lady on the Cutting Edge of Science".

I saw her leaning against a wall in the corner: a tall, stick-thin character with spikey blonde hair, gulping champagne. I could see she was a kindred spirit – we were the only ones not wearing neat little suits with boxy jackets – but I had no idea who she was; in high school she'd been a chubby brunette with glasses. She saw me looking at her, and waved me over.

We leaned against the wall together, jangling the chains on our identical black leather jackets. "I'm working on a calculation," she said, "that will show density of shoulder pad to be in directly inverse proportion to level of intelligence. I'm drunk by the way."

"I'm Joanna Krenski."

"I know who you are. I've still got the charcoal portrait you did of me for your senior year art project. The damn thing must be worth a fortune now; I keep meaning to get it valued."

That was the start of our friendship, the second time around.

Eight years later, I was sitting inside this metal egg, surrounded by my work and my tools and the huge amount of dust they always seem to generate, and Toni was shouting okay, push the button. Then I opened the capsule door and Toni was gone and all my work was gone and even the dust was gone.

I was in a huge, open-plan loft with floor to ceiling windows – that much was like my studio – but everything had been polished and swept and there were flowers everywhere. Flowers in vases, flowers in pots, flowers in a window-box. And then there were paintings of flowers. Dozens of delicate little watercolours depicting roses and lilies and lilacs completely covered one wall, each framed behind a pane of sparkling glass. Unframed oils on canvas stood leaning against every wall, apparently divided into categories: fluffy kittens, cute children, puppies with big sad eyes. I could have puked.

A woman was standing with her back to me, painting something on a medium-sized canvas mounted on a wooden easel. It looked like it was going to be another puppy. The woman had tightly-permed hair cut just above the collar – mouse brown gone mostly grey – and she was wearing a white smock over a knee-length dress. I also noticed she was wearing high heels. To paint.

Oh God, I thought, just like my mother. I remembered her putting on a hat and a little string of pearls to attend her first evening art class; she was like something out of a '50s TV sitcom. And how proud she was of her little pictures of birds. My mother used to paint birds: little red robins and yellow canaries, with musical notes coming out of their beaks. She hung them all over the living room walls. It was embarrassing.

I was going to have to handle this very carefully. The woman was obviously some old dear of my mother's generation and I was a disembodied head sticking out of a metallic egg. I didn't want to give the poor woman a heart attack. I cleared my throat. "Excuse me," I said, "Please don't be frightened, I'm not a burglar or anything." Even as I said it, I realised how stupid it must have sounded: a burglar in a metal egg.

The woman swung around, and I gasped.

"You again," she said, quite calmly. "I never expected you to turn up here."

I felt my mouth open and close half a dozen times, but no words came out. I just sat there, inside the capsule, gaping like a mackerel. The woman had my face. She'd let her hair go grey – something I've refused to do – and she was wearing a string of pearls just like my mother's and a dress I wouldn't be caught dead in, but based on her face – and even her voice – she could have been my sister. My twin.

There was an odd smell in the air; I'd noticed it the moment I opened the capsule door and now I realised what it was. It was bread, baking. Something very strange was going on here.

"I don't know how you did it," she went on. "Toni said we were both stuck where we were. She was very apologetic about it, of course." She put her palette and brush down on a table beside the easel, then crossed her arms and looked at me. She seemed angry. "Well, you can forget it."

I finally managed to get my vocal cords working. "Huh? Forget what?"

"Even if you've found a way, I'm not going back," she said. "No way am I going back. Ever. This is my life now, my world, and I like it. Though..." she paused a moment, and her face – my face – crumpled into a mass of lines. Oh God, I thought, I don't look as old as her, do I? She blinked hard, several times, as if she was trying not to cry. "How's Katie? Is she all right?"

I shook my head; the only Katie I knew was a drama critic, and I didn't think that was who she meant.

"The boys I don't worry about so much; they're grown up now, I know they'll be okay. But Katie... she's just a kid, isn't she?"

"Katie who? And who are you? I mean you look so much like... like my mother. Are we related or something?"

Her eyes opened wide. "You mean you don't know? But... but you've been there. Isn't that where you came from just now?"

"Been where?"

"But you must have! Or how could I be here?" This woman was talking nonsense; I figured she must be crazy, maybe even dangerous. Maybe she was one of those fanatical fans who get plastic surgery to look like their idols. Okay, maybe a forty-five-year-old sculptor doesn't have that kind of fan. Even a forty-five-year-old sculptor who appeared in two Warhol films and has had her picture on the cover of everything from *Newsweek* to *Rolling Stone* (twice) probably doesn't have that kind of fan. I still figured the only thing for me to do was to get the hell away from her in a hurry.

I leaned forward, trying to pull myself out of the capsule, but she grabbed me by the shoulders, shoved me back down inside it, and held me there. I struggled and swore, but I couldn't get up. I don't think she was any stronger than me, but she had the major advantage of not being curled into an almost foetal position inside a metal egg.

Her face hovered inches above mine, mouth twisted with rage, eyes narrow and shining with something that might have been hate or might even have been fear; I couldn't tell. It was like looking into one of those distorted fairground mirrors.

"But you have been there," she insisted. "You arrived there a year ago today. That's when the switch took place."

"What switch?"

"This switch," she said, slamming the capsule door down over my head.

It was worse the second time. My head was pounding; my whole body ached. It took a few seconds for my eyes to come back into focus – then I saw the digital display. I was back where I started; 29 April, 1994, 6:01 p.m., E.S.T. I sighed with relief. I was home and I still had three months to get ready for my show at Gallery Alfredo; I hadn't missed it after all.

I shoved the door open, expecting to see my studio, and Toni waiting by the capsule. I had a few choice words in store for Toni! But she wasn't there. And my studio wasn't there.

I couldn't tell where I was at first; it was dark. But as my eyes began to adjust, I saw that I was in a windowless room lined with crowded shelves.

"Hello!" I shouted. "Is anybody there?" No answer.

"Shit." I took a deep breath, gathered all my strength, and slowly began to extricate myself from Toni's infernal machine. I never felt so stiff and sore; I could hardly move. My jeans felt tighter than usual, as if my body was swollen. And my poor legs! I had to massage them to get the blood moving again, and then there was an unbearable sensation of pins and needles. I finally managed to stand up.

The shelves around me were stacked with jars of homemade preserves and chocolate chip cookies. There were bags of flour, a tinned baked ham, fresh coffee beans, baskets of fruit and vegetables, various pots and pans. It looked like some kind of a pantry.

I reached for the door, praying it wasn't locked. It wasn't, and I stepped into a kitchen that would have been the height of technology in 1956. The brand names were all ones I remembered from my childhood – the appliances were all big and white and clunky, except for the toaster, which was small and round and covered in shiny chrome, and the coffee percolator, which was switched on and bubbling away.

There was nothing in that room that would have been out of place when I was five years old. No microwave oven, no food processor, no espresso machine. There was a meat grinder and a coffee grinder, each with a handle you needed to crank. You needed a match to light the stove. You had to defrost the fridge. And it was all brand new.

"Hello! Anybody home?" I wandered through the dining room – a printed sign on the wall above the sideboard read, "Give us this day our daily bread" – and into a living room with a picture window and clear plastic covers over all the furniture. An embroidered sampler above the fireplace proclaimed, "Bless this house and everyone in it." I shook my head.

I looked out the window and saw women in cotton dresses hanging laundry, men in white shirts mowing lawns, kids on one-speed bikes with little tinkling bells and metal baskets. There was at least one big, gas-guzzling automobile in every driveway. It was 1950s suburbia, even worse than I remembered it. I had walked straight into an episode of *Leave it to Beaver*. I shook my head in disbelief; Toni's time machine had actually worked.

I heard a crash, coming from the kitchen. I ran back, pausing in the kitchen doorway. The back door was open. I looked around the room. There was no one there. Nothing seemed to be missing. I took a couple of cautious steps onto the linoleum floor. Then a couple more.

Everything seemed okay; the door probably wasn't properly closed in the first place, and a gust of wind had blown it open. It wouldn't be that unusual back in the '50s; we never used to lock the doors when I was a kid. I crossed the room and pulled the door shut. I realised I'd been holding my breath, and let it out.

There was a sudden high-pitched sound, and I nearly jumped a mile. I swung around, clutching my chest and cursing myself for being such an idiot. It was only the telephone.

The phone was mounted on the kitchen wall behind me, big and white, with an old-fashioned dial. I walked towards it, then decided to let the answering machine pick it up. I listened to it ringing and ringing, until it finally struck me they didn't have answering machines in the 1950s. I lifted the receiver. "Hello?"

"Joanna, what kept you so long? I was just about to hang up."

I knew that voice! "Toni? Oh thank God. How did you find me? How did you know what number to call?"

There was a long pause. "Joanna, are you all right?"

"I'm stuck inside a forty-year-old copy of *Better Homes and Gardens*, and you're asking me if I'm all right?"

"Joanna, you sound a little strange. Is Bob there?"

"Bob? Who the hell is Bob?"

"You're having one of your little turns again, aren't you? Now do me favour. I want you to sit down, or better yet, why don't you lie down? Take some good deep breaths, and try to relax." I could not believe the way she was talking to me, in this slow, soothing murmur, like I was some kind of nutcase. She might as well have been saying, "Now put that gun down, Joanna."

"You said you were going to send me two minutes forward, not forty years back! I don't want to lie down and relax. I want to get out of here! And what do you mean, 'turns'? I do not have 'turns'!"

"I'll be there as soon as I can, okay? Just try and stay calm; I'm on my way." There was a click.

"Wait a minute, Toni! Toni?" There was no one there; she'd hung up. I leaned against the wall, rubbing my throbbing temples. Nothing made sense. If I was really in the 1950s, and I'd left Toni back in the '90s, then how could she phone me?

I heard a door open and slam shut, then a man's voice: "Honey, I'm home!"

I didn't know what to do. One half of me said I should walk right up to the man, introduce myself and calmly explain what I was doing in his house. The other half said I should hide. I heard footsteps, moving towards me. Heavy footsteps.

I decided to hide.

I tiptoed backwards into the pantry, pulling the door closed behind me, trying hard not to breathe. I turned around and saw a second metal egg.

I raised a hand to my mouth and bit it to keep myself from screaming. Where had that other egg come from? I bent down to examine it. Like mine, the digital display must have been broken; it still said 1994. But this egg was nearly twice as big, and looked a lot more comfortable. It even had a padded lining.

So that was how Toni found me; she'd followed me back into time. She'd had a second egg the whole time, and she'd obviously saved the better one for herself, the selfish bitch. But if she was here, in the same house, then why did she have to phone me? And where was she now?

I heard the man's voice again: "Joanna, sweetheart! Jo-aaann-a!" Who was this guy and how did he know my name? "Joanna!" The voice was louder, he was getting closer. I heard footsteps moving across the kitchen floor. They stopped in front of the pantry door. I watched the doorknob turn. I tensed, unsure what to do.

"Who's there?" I said.

The voice sounded relieved. "Oh there you are! Didn't you hear me?" The door opened and I saw a middle-aged man with his mouth hanging open. "Oh my God, Joanna! What have you done?"

"Huh?"

"Your hair! What have you done to your hair? It's... it's purple!"

I couldn't believe it; this guy catches an intruder cowering in a closet, and his only reaction is to comment on her hair colour? And my hair isn't purple, by the way. The tint I use is called Flickering Flame, and the packet describes it as a deep burgundy red. The guy was so busy gawking at my hair, he didn't even notice the pair of metal ovals sitting in the middle of his pantry floor. I stepped out into the kitchen, pulling the pantry door closed behind me.

"You... you look positively indecent," the man went on, following me across the kitchen. "Look at you! Hair sticking up all over the place, like you haven't combed it in a week!" I positioned myself with my back to what I assumed was the cutlery drawer; I wanted to be within reach of something I could use as a weapon, just in case. "You look like some kind of a... a... a hussy! No wife of mine is going around looking like a hussy."

Wife? I thought, this man thinks I'm his wife?

"And where did you get those awful clothes? You look like some kind of a greasy mechanic!"

I was ready to punch the guy. First my hair, and now my clothes. There was nothing wrong with my clothes. I was wearing black designer jeans – strategically ripped at the knees – that cost me nearly five hundred dollars, and an understated, plain black tee-shirt that was a bargain at $57.99.

Hussy? I thought. Greasy mechanic? What kind of bigoted moron uses words like that, and more important, what kind of moron mistakes a complete stranger for his wife?

The man looked normal enough – almost too normal. Forty-something, thinning hair, brown tinged with grey, bit of a paunch, dressed like he just came home from an office.

"What if the neighbours saw you looking like that? And what about Katie?"

Katie. That rang a bell. "Ah," I said, remembering what the woman who looked like my mother had told me, "Katie's just a kid, isn't she?"

The man sighed and shook his head. "You're having hot flushes again, aren't you?" He touched my forehead as if he was checking for a fever. I slid my hand into the drawer behind me, grabbed hold of something I hoped was a knife, and waited to see what he would do next. But all he did was bend slightly forward, and stare open-mouthed at my feet. "You're wearing tennis shoes."

"Tennis shoes? I'll have you know these are Nikes!"

"Nikes?" he repeated, obviously confused. "But I thought you must be wearing heels..." His eyes moved upwards along my body, finally stopping at my eyes. "Joanna, I don't understand what's going on." Neither do I, I felt like saying, but I didn't get the chance because he carried straight on without a pause. "How could you possibly be taller?"

"Taller than who?"

"Than you were when I left you this morning. And you're thinner, too."

"Ha! Don't I wish." I took my hand out of the drawer. The guy didn't seem violent, just confused. And standing as close to him as I was, something about the guy was awfully familiar. I thought, I know him. If I could just see past the bald patch and the beer gut, and concentrate on the voice and the eyes, I knew it would come back to me. Then it hit me.

"Bobby!" I said, "Bobby Callahan! You took me to my senior prom."

His eyes went very wide. "Yes, dear," he said cautiously, "why are you bringing that up now?"

"I didn't recognise you at first; it's been a long time. It's gotta be twenty-five years. No, closer to thirty. God, Bobby, I can't believe it! So what are you doing with yourself these days?" I reached out to shake his hand.

Bobby went ever so pale. "Joanna, darling. I think you should lie down."

A few minutes later, I was leaning against a stack of frilly pillows, embroidered with sayings like "I Love Mom" and "Home Is Where The Heart Is", on one of a pair of narrow twin beds, separated by a twee little night table with two separate lamps and two individual wind-up alarm clocks, listening to Bobby clatter around in the kitchen below. He obviously wasn't used to cooking. My sudden appearance in the pantry apparently hadn't surprised him at all, but the fact that I hadn't made dinner seemed a shock beyond belief.

There was a loud crash, an "Ouch!" and a "Dammit!", then footsteps moving back up the stairs. Bobby poked his head into the bedroom and said he was driving down to the Chinese. The last thing he told me was that I should try and get some sleep.

I jumped up the minute I heard the downstairs door close; I had no intention of hanging around until he came back. Then the wardrobe doors flew wide open, and a hand shoved me back onto the mattress.

For the second time in less than ten minutes, I found myself staring open-mouthed at someone with my face. This one was even dressed the same as me: the same jeans, same tee-shirt, same Nike sneakers. She had the same blunt haircut, the same shade of Flickering Flame. "Snap!" she said.

I raised my head and took a long, careful look at her. I noticed two slight differences between us: she had a blue canvas shoulder-bag draped across her arm, and a bad case of sunburn. The sunburn looked painful; the skin on her nose was peeling. "Who are you?" I said, "Is this your house?"

"Let me address your second question first. If this was my house, do you really think I would be hiding in the wardrobe? And as to your first:

who do you *think* I am? I know it's a little difficult, so I'll give you a clue. Who do I look like?"

"Like me?"

"Bingo!" she said, "You got it in one." She flopped down on the other bed, stretching her arms high over her head. "God, my back is killing me!"

I swung my legs around and sat up, facing the other bed. "Let me get this straight," I said. "You're saying that you're me?"

She rolled onto her side, propping her head up with one arm. "That's one way of putting it. Though as far as I'm concerned, it's you that's *me*, not me that's *you*. A subtle distinction, I admit, but a significant one. To me, at least." There was something slightly different about her voice, too. It was a little deeper than mine, and a little harsher, as if she wanted to scream but was struggling to control herself. I guess the fact I didn't understand a word she was saying showed on my face, because she gave me a look of pure disgust. "Don't tell me you don't get it! Look, I'm an alternate you from a parallel universe, *capeche*?"

I couldn't believe what I had just heard. "A parallel universe?" I said. "Then how the hell did you get here?"

She got up and started looking through the various jars and bottles on the dresser. She opened one of the jars and spread some cream on her face. "How do you think I got here? The same way as you: inside that damn machine of Toni's. She made one in my universe as well, you know. A slightly better one, if you don't mind me saying so; I've seen yours down in the pantry, and it does look a bit poor."

I got up and stood by the window, watching wives in cotton dresses calling children and husbands in for dinner, and I knew this wasn't my universe, either. "So this is what the universe would have been like if I'd married Bobby Callahan."

"Oh get real!" the other Joanna said, disgusted. "Cultural and scientific stagnation is the basis of this type of universe, not who married Bobby Callahan."

"I don't understand how I got here. Toni's machine was supposed to send me forward in time, not sideways through space."

"That wasn't the machine's fault; it was that woman!"

"Woman? What woman?"

Her hands tightened into fists and her eyes became narrow slits. "The bitch that set the timer on Toni's machine to go backwards. Don't you see? As long you only move forward, you remain in the same universe. But if you try to go backwards, even by a fraction of a second, you end up in a parallel world. They tell me this is to stop you murdering your grandmother so you were never born. Anyway, she set the timer backwards on purpose to get me out of the way, so she could take over my life in my universe."

"How do you know this?"

"Because she told me! I met her. I talked to her; she's living in my studio, and I tell you she's ruined it. Cleared out all my stuff, and covered every available space with pictures of flowers and kittens. Disgusting!"

I sank down onto the nearest bed. "What did she look like?"

"Like me with grey hair and a perm, dressed in my mother's clothes. She's an alternate me from one of these oppressive suburban worlds and now she's living it up in mine, spending my money, using my name and reputation to exhibit her nauseating little pictures at all the best galleries."

Suddenly it all made sense. The woman in my studio, talking about a switch. "I've met her, too. She slammed the capsule door down on my head and the next thing I knew I was here."

"Isn't that always the way?" said the other Joanna, nodding in sympathy.

"But I still don't understand. I mean, how did she get there in the first place?"

"I have a theory about that," said the other Joanna. "I think one of us – meaning one in a world where Toni has invented a time machine – pushed the wrong button and went back by accident, maybe by only a couple of seconds. She ended up in a world like this one, and came face to face with her parallel self, a housewife who always dreamed of being an artist but never did anything about it. The Joanna like us explained who she was and how she got there. The parallel Joanna saw her chance at wealth and fame and stole the machine, leaving the other one stranded. Maybe this happened more than once, and one of these parallel Joannas ended up in your world and one in mine."

"Well, Toni will know what to do when she gets here."

"Toni? Here?"

"Yeah, she phoned just a little while ago. She said she was on her way over."

"Oh, you mean the Toni that lives here. You can forget about any help from that direction. Not the right sort of Toni."

"The right sort?"

"I've met most of the Toni's you get in this sort of world. Sometimes she's a widow with a grown-up son – usually in the army – sometimes she's a librarian, and if you're really lucky, she might be a high school science teacher."

"You've been in other worlds like this one?"

"Sure. I've been in loads of 'em. I always arrive on the same date: the 29th of April, 1994, and the same time: just after 6 p.m. Because that's when the first switch took place – in one of this infinite number of universes. And eventually, I'm going to be there when that first switch is about to happen, and I'm going to stop it before it does, and then none of this will ever have happened."

"How will you stop it happening?"

She smiled, patting the canvas bag that still hung from her shoulder. "I have my methods."

So she was going to make everything all right again. I should have been thrilled, but I couldn't help feeling resentful; I didn't like being made to feel stupid. Maybe I hadn't grasped all the nuances of quantum theory, and instantly figured out what was going on and how to fix it, but I was still a famous artist, and very rich. Didn't that count for anything anymore?

"I'm having an affair with a twenty-two-year-old male model," I said, leaning back on the bed. "We might even do a TV commercial together; they want him to play a gorgeous young man at an exhibition opening, and me to play myself. Then he picks up a bottle of..."

"Shut up!" she said.

"Ooh, hit a sore point, have I? In my world, I'm often seen with much younger men."

"Will you be quiet, there's somebody coming." She moved to one side of the window, flattening herself against the wall.

"Who is it?" I whispered, sitting up.

She raised a finger to her mouth to signal silence. I got up and headed for the window.

"Get back!" she hissed, then mouthed the words, "It's her." I flattened myself against the wall on the other side of the window from her, and peered cautiously around the frame. A woman was walking towards the house, struggling with several large shopping bags. She had my face.

I looked across to the other Joanna, and saw her reach inside her canvas bag and take out a gun. She reached in again, and took out a silencer.

"What are you doing?" I whispered.

She ignored me, raising the gun and taking aim at a defenceless woman. I couldn't stand by and let this happen; I picked up one of those twee little table lamps, and broke it over her head. The gun went off, missing the woman, but sending a bullet tearing through one of her shopping bags, spilling groceries all over the pavement. The Joanna that married her high school sweetheart stopped in her tracks, staring at the shredded bag.

"Move!" I shouted, "she'll kill you!"

Unfortunately, the lamp didn't knock my other self out, it just made her mad. She swung around, blood streaming from several cuts on her scalp, and pointed the gun right at me. "You stupid bitch! I fucking had her!"

"You were going to kill her!"

"I'll kill every one of them, until I get the right one. And no one's going to stop me."

I swung my right leg back and around, kicking the gun from her hand just as it went off a second time, sending chunks of plaster flying from the wall beside her. I'd taken a course in Ju-Jitsu about fifteen years earlier, and this was the first time I'd ever used it. Of course she'd taken it, too, and two seconds later I was being thrown head first over her shoulder. I landed on the bedroom floor with a thud, and looked up to see my other self with a gun once more pointed at my head. She was smiling. "It isn't murder, you know. It's more like suicide by proxy."

I closed my eyes, and waited to die. There was a sound like an explosion, and I thought, is that it? Am I dead? Then I thought, that can't be it; I've got a lap full of glass.

I opened my eyes again, and saw a grey-haired woman with my face, holding what was left of the second table lamp. Bobby was right, she was about an inch or two shorter than me, and maybe five pounds heavier. She reached down and picked the gun up from the floor beside the other, unconscious, Joanna, and pointed it at me. "I think you owe me an explanation, don't you?"

I told her everything. She didn't believe me of course, until I showed her the two metal eggs in her pantry. "I'm a bit of an artist myself," she said. "One of my paintings was in an exhibition at the town hall. Maybe you'd like to have a look at some of my paintings later; they're up in the attic."

Then there was the problem of what to do with the other Joanna. When we went back up to the bedroom, she was starting to wake up. "Wha'?" she said, "What happened? Where am I?"

Joanna Callahan and I stood on either side of the bed where we'd left her firmly tied down with a length of laundry line. She looked from one side of the bed to the other. "Who are you guys supposed to be, the Bobsey Twins?"

"Maybe I shouldn't have hit her so hard," said Joanna Callahan.

"I'd be dead if you hadn't," I reminded her.

"And so would I, if what you say is true," she sighed.

"What's going on?" said Joanna on the bed. "Who are you bozos?"

"Don't you know me?" I asked her.

"I never saw you in my life!"

"Do you know who *you* are?" Joanna Callahan asked her.

"Of course I do! I'm..." She frowned in concentration. "Oh shit."

"You stay with her," Joanna Callahan told me. "I'll just run and get my first aid kit from the kitchen."

Before I could think to ask her what she had in a first aid kit for amnesia, she was gone.

"Why don't I remember who I am?" asked Joanna on the bed.

"You've had a nasty crack on the head," I told her. "You fell down the stairs."

"Why am I all tied up?"

"To keep you from falling down again. Stay there, I'll be right back." I ran downstairs to the kitchen. The pantry door was open, and there was only one metal egg: the one I came in. Joanna Callahan had stolen the nicer one, with the padded lining. "Bitch!" I shouted, kicking the refrigerator. "Fucking bitch!"

Then Joanna upstairs started screaming for help. She was making a hell of a racket; someone would call the police if she kept that up. I ran back up the stairs and found the bed tipped over onto its side, and Joanna wriggling around on the floor, trying to break loose. "Help!" she kept screaming, "Somebody help me!"

The front doorbell rang, and Joanna started screaming even louder. I stuffed a pillowcase down her mouth; that shut her up.

The doorbell kept ringing and I heard a woman's voice call my name. "Joanna! Open up! Are you okay?" Toni.

I grabbed a scarf out of the wardrobe to hide my Flickering Flame hair, then I ran to the window. "Toni!" I called down, faking a yawn. "Sorry, I must have been asleep."

A large, dark-haired woman wearing a brown cardigan sweater over a white blouse and brown skirt looked up from the street. She was wearing a pair of horn-rimmed glasses so thick they reminded me of Mister Magoo. She had "small town librarian" written all over her. Definitely not the right sort of Toni.

"Joanna, are you all right? I thought I heard you screaming for help!" Joanna with the pillowcase in her mouth was trying to stand up with a bed tied to her back.

"I was having the worst nightmare! Hold on, I'll be right down." I ran down the stairs to the kitchen, then remembered something and ran back up again. The other Joanna was squirming around more than ever, making a lot of "Hmph!" and "MMMMMM!" sort of noises. I had to admire her determination. "Don't worry, Joanna, someone will untie you in a minute, I promise. But it won't be me." I put the gun back inside her blue canvas bag, and slung it over my shoulder.

I was halfway down the stairs when I heard Toni say, "Bob! Thank God you're home! There's something wrong with Joanna!" I reached the bottom just as his key turned in the lock. By the time they reached the bedroom, I was already in the pantry, squeezing myself back inside my uncomfortable, unpadded, metal egg. There was a lot of screaming and shouting going on upstairs. I heard Toni say she was calling the police, and then I heard heavy footsteps on the stairs.

I pulled the capsule door down over my head, and stared at a row of unlabelled buttons. I didn't have the slightest idea which one to press, so I pressed them all. I heard Toni's voice outside the capsule, saying, "What the..." and then I was ripped into a million pieces.

I pushed the door open and found myself staring up at a cactus. I was dizzy and more than a little nauseous; I waited for the cactus to stop spinning before I tried to sit up.

The moment I raised my head, the cactus started whirling again, faster than ever. I'd been broken down and reassembled for the third time in less than half an hour, and I didn't think my body could take a fourth; at least not yet. I pulled myself out of the capsule, fell to my knees, and vomited onto scorching hot dust. I crawled on all fours towards a clump of stunted bushes a few yards away, and rested in the tiny patch of shade they provided.

I don't know how long I was there; I think I must have fallen asleep. All I know is when I opened my eyes again, a man was standing over me, his face a mixture of surprise and concern. "You all right?" he said. He had white hair down to his shoulders, a full white beard, a round face with chubby red cheeks, sparkling brown eyes, and an enormous belly. Santa Claus in blue jeans.

"No, I'm not all right. I feel like hell and I don't have the slightest idea where I am."

The man knelt down beside me. "My house is just the other side of that hill. Don't try to move; I'll carry you."

"No, it's okay. I can walk."

"Now you just lean on me," he said, helping me to my feet. "And don't you worry 'bout a thing, my old lady'll get you fixed up in no time. She'll be interested to see you. Real interested, I'll tell you that for nothing."

"What do you mean, interested?"

"You'll see. Believe you me, you'll see."

A pair of large dogs – one black, one brown – lunged forward to greet us as we approached a large adobe house painted in a myriad of colours. Each of the outside walls was like a mural, one side adorned with children running through a field, another with a cityscape of high-rise buildings lit by a reddish-gold setting sun, another a series of geometric shapes in primary colours. Behind the house was another building, a bright red barn almost as big as the house.

"Down Horace! Get down, Charlemagne! Down boys," the man said as the dogs leapt around us, barking excitedly, "this here lady doesn't feel too well." Then he raised his voice to a shout: "Jo-aaannn-a!"

A woman appeared in the doorway. Wearing an ankle-length denim dress and a string of beads. Centre-parted, waist-length hair. Brown, streaked with grey. "Who you got there, Mark?"

"This lady's sick. Help me get her inside the house." She ran forward, and slid an arm around my back. I closed my eyes; I didn't want to look at her face.

"Oh my God, Mark," she said.

"Yeah, I know. Ain't it the strangest thing?"

I woke up with a dreadful case of sunburn; my face and arms were bright red. I raised my head and saw the woman who had introduced herself as Joanna Hansen standing in the bedroom doorway, holding a mug of coffee. Her salt-and-pepper hair was tied back in a long ponytail, and she was wearing sandals and a cotton kimono. I looked around for my clothes, and didn't see them.

"I put them in the wash," she told me. "Borrow anything you want from that closet."

I pulled on a pair of jeans and a denim shirt, and went down to the kitchen. Mark was making hotcakes in honour of my visit. He was under the impression I was a long lost cousin of Joanna's – at least that's what I'd told him the night before.

I'd known Mark Hansen back in 1967, when we were both art students in San Francisco. It was the Summer of Love, and he had long black hair and drove a VW van.

So there actually was a universe where I'd said yes when he asked me to go and live with him in the desert. In his day, he was every bit as gorgeous as any twenty-two-year-old male model. I wondered if there was a universe where he hadn't ended up looking like Father Christmas.

"I can't get over it," he said to Joanna, "all these years you had a cousin that's your spitting image and you never even knew she existed!"

"Yeah," said Joanna, eyeing me suspiciously, "I can't get over it, either."

I had told them both the most ridiculous pack of lies the night before, how I'd been on my way to visit Joanna and my rented car had broken down in the middle of the desert, and Mark, at least, seemed to believe it. I knew Joanna was waiting for the chance to get me alone; that's what I would have done.

Her chance came that afternoon, when Mark drove into town to get the shopping. We were sitting on the front step, sipping iced tea with slices of lemon, when she finally said it: "Isn't it time you told me the truth?"

"I don't know what you mean."

"I don't have a cousin named Annabel." (Annabel was the first name that popped into my head the night before; I don't know why.) "Not even a long-lost one, like you claim to be. So who are you, and what were you doing out in the middle of nowhere, covered in plaster dust and broken glass? And how come you look so much like me? I'm warning you, I want the truth."

"You'll never believe it."

"Try me."

"Okay." I put down my glass of iced tea, and looked her right in the eye. "Do you ever wonder what your life would have been like if you'd made some different decisions along the way?"

"I haven't done acid since 1975," she said when I was finished. "Don't you think it's time for you to give it up, too?"

"I told you you'd never believe me. Maybe if we could contact Toni; she might be working on something similar in this world. Maybe she even got it right in this one."

Joanna Hansen shook her head. "Toni's dead. She died a long time ago," she said. "O.D.'d."

"What? She can't be dead!"

"Why not? If I'm supposed to believe you, then where you come from, my two kids were never even born!" Mark had shown me pictures of them the night before: two extremely dishy young men, one twenty-five years old, the other only twenty-one. Then I remembered whose children they were.

"Oh yeah," I said, "Joanna Callahan apparently had some kids as well."

"And she just up and left them."

"More than once," I said. "I mean, more than one version of her left more than one version of them."

"How do you know I won't steal your machine, so I can be rich and famous in New York?"

"You don't know where I left it."

"You think I couldn't find it if I wanted to?" She laughed. "You ought to see your face, you've gone bright green. Well, you sit out here and worry yourself sick about whether I think being you is such an attractive prospect or not. Meanwhile, I've got work to do. Help yourself to anything you want from the fridge." And then she left me, sitting alone on the step.

I was still there when Mark came back, two hours later. The dogs leapt out of the truck and ran towards me, barking and wagging their tails. A second later, I was on my back, having my face licked. "I've never known those dogs to take to someone as quick as they've taken to you," Mark said. "It's like they've known you all their lives."

"I noticed," I said, pushing them away. "Where's Joanna?"

"She said she had some work to do."

"Then she'll be in her studio. Haven't you been in there yet?"

I shook my head.

"I thought she'd have given you the grand tour by now," he said. "Never mind. Help me get the groceries in, and I'll take you around."

A short while later, he led me around the back of the house to the large building I'd assumed was a barn. "Please don't think she's being rude, abandoning you like that. It's just that she's got this big show coming up in a couple of months, and she reckons she's nowhere near ready."

"Show? What kind of show?"

"Joanna's an artist, didn't she tell you?"

Of course, I thought, Mark and I had met in art school. So what was this Joanna's art like? More puppies and flowers? No, I thought, this one's an old hippie; I'll bet she weaves native-style blankets and sells them at craft fairs. Then Mark opened the door and my mouth dropped open.

This Joanna, like me, was a sculptor, and like me, she worked mostly in metal, and – this is a hard admission for me to make – she was every bit as good as me. Maybe even – this is an even harder admission – a little better.

I touched the twisted trunk of a metal tree with shiny flat leaves. Tiny men hung like fruit from its branches, each with a noose around his neck, each with a completely different and individual expression of pain or horror on his face. I wished I'd done it. Though in a way, I had.

"That one's already sold," Mark told me. "Some museum in Europe's offered her a couple million for it, and she's told 'em they can have it after the show."

At the sound of the words: "couple million", my heart almost did a flip-flop. It was all I could do not to clutch at my chest. I took a few deep breaths, counting to ten on each inhalation. "So where is this show of hers?" I asked him, trying to sound nonchalant.

"The Museum of Contemporary Art," he told me, adding, "That's in New York." As if I didn't know. And I'd been so worried this Joanna might want to trade places with me. "Didn't you see that TV show they did about her?" he asked me. "It was on prime time, coast to coast."

"I'm afraid I missed it."

We found her at the far end of the building, working on a rather familiar arrangement of six black and white television sets called: "Women on the Brink of a Cataclysm". She couldn't figure out why I thought that was funny.

Then she switched it on, and I saw that unlike mine, each of her screens showed a different woman doing a different repetitive task: one scrubbing a floor, one doing dishes, one hanging laundry, one ironing shirts, one chopping vegetables, and one slashing her wrists, over and over again, in an endless loop. I wished I'd done mine like that – though of course I would, now.

There was nothing in Joanna Hansen's work I wouldn't be proud to call my own. If I couldn't get back to my own world – and I was beginning to doubt I ever would – then this one would suit me just fine. But making the switch might be difficult with Mark around; it would have to be done gradually.

I offered to help Joanna in her studio, and learned exactly where she kept everything. I got her to tell me her complete history under the pretext of trying to figure out just where our paths had diverged. I got Mark to tell me everything I'd need to know about him under the pretext of finding him a fascinating conversationalist, which he never was, even when we were students. I went through every photo album and every scrap book, memorising the details. I sat through slides and home movies. And I nagged Joanna about her hair, told her it made her look much older than she was, and reminded her of all the photographers that would be at her opening party in New York. "Just trim the ends a little," I told her. "Just cover the grey." I finally convinced her to let me cut it – a much quicker process than waiting for mine to grow – but I couldn't get her to colour it; I had to let myself go grey.

Within three weeks of my arrival, Joanna Hansen and I were indistinguishable.

One morning when Mark had driven into town, I told Joanna it was time for me to leave. I put on the clothes I had arrived in, slung the blue canvas bag with the gun in it over my shoulder, and thanked her for everything. Then, as though it were an afterthought, I asked her if she'd like to see the time machine.

I led her out into the desert, to the spot where Toni's metal egg sat hidden behind a cactus plant. "That's it," I said.

"It doesn't look very comfortable."

"Why don't you try it for yourself?" I said. "Get inside, see how it feels."

"No thanks."

I pointed the gun at her. "Get inside."

"You can't shoot me," she said.

"I can and I will if you don't do what I tell you."

"No, you can't. That gun isn't loaded; I took the bullets out ages ago."

I pointed the gun straight at her and pulled the trigger. Nothing happened. "You bitch! You've been through my things!"

"Damn right. I did that the first night you turned up. You think I'm stupid or something? Now," she reached into one of the pockets in her denim skirt, "this gun is loaded." She was holding a little semi-automatic pistol. "As you were saying, Joanna, it's time you went back to your own world."

"Wait a minute," I said. "That was only a joke with the gun; I was never going to shoot you. What I was going to suggest is that we work together, sort of interchangeably. You could get twice as much done, and nobody would ever know."

"Good-bye, Joanna."

I got inside the machine, and the next thing I knew it was the 29th of April, 1994, a little after 6 p.m., and I was back in Joanna Callahan's pantry, with swollen joints and a raging headache. As I struggled to pull myself up, I noticed another metal egg. This one not only had a padded interior, but a row of little flashing lights along the outside.

Someone was coming. I ran through the kitchen and out the back door. I crouched down outside the open kitchen window and listened to the phone ringing, then my voice: "Toni! Thank God! How did you find me? How did you know what number to call?"

I was about to go back inside and talk to this woman, when I heard a car pull into the front drive. I crept along the wall towards the front of the house and saw Bob Callahan put his key in the front door. "Honey! I'm home!"

He'd head straight back to the kitchen and find the other me cowering in the pantry, where I'd left my only method of escape. I had to get back inside the house; I reached the door just before it swung completely closed, and crept into the hallway. I heard voices coming from the kitchen, then I heard Bobby say, "I think you'd better lie down."

I ran upstairs to the bedroom. It was different than I remembered. There was only one bed, a double. I looked out the window and saw a long-haired guy in black leather tinkering with his motorcycle, watched by a bunch of kids in baggy clothes and baseball caps worn backwards. I breathed a sigh of relief. This was more like the 1994 I knew. But it still wasn't the right one; Bobby Callahan was leading one of the alternate me's up the stairs.

"If this was my house, do you really think I'd be hiding in the wardrobe?" I said a short while later. "And as to your second question: who do I look like?"

"Like me, I guess. But older."

"Older?" I rushed over to the mirror. She was right. That grey hair put ten years on me, and my time in the desert hadn't done my complexion any good; I noticed several new lines around my eyes and mouth. I opened a jar of Joanna Callahan's moisturiser and spread it on my face.

"You look a lot like that woman who was in my studio," said the other Joanna – she was reaching for something inside a canvas bag just like mine, only hers was green. "Or at least I think it was my studio."

The downstairs door opened and slammed shut. Bobby couldn't be back already. I whispered to the other Joanna to stay where she was and keep quiet, then I tiptoed into the hall. A teenage girl with blonde hair, black roots, and thick black eyeliner, stomped up the stairs in a pair of platform boots. She had four or five earrings on each ear, and one through her right nostril. "Fuck off, Mom. Don't hassle me," she said, opening one of the other doors and slamming it behind her. So this was Katie. A moment later, the walls were vibrating with music by some band I'd never heard of.

I went downstairs and had another look at the house. There was a stack of videos next to the television, a microwave oven and food processor in the kitchen. All those "Bless This House" embroideries were gone, replaced by paintings of a grey-haired woman in varying states of depression. They weren't bad. I flipped one over and read the neatly-printed words: Number Three in a Series of Women on the Brink of a Cataclysm.

Well, Joanna, I thought, meaning both of them – the one I'd left upstairs, and the one who'd be home any minute now – you're on your own.

I opened the pantry door and sank down inside a padded machine with a row of lovely flashing lights.

The machine was a joy. I didn't feel a thing. No stiffness, no swelling, no dizziness. I opened the door and found myself back in the desert. April 29th, 1994, just after 6 p.m. New York time – the middle of a scorching afternoon out west.

I had been given a second chance. And this time I would do it right. I wouldn't let Mark see me; I'd get Joanna on her own and do the switch immediately. Then I'd have my exhibition, collect my millions, and give poor Mark an amicable divorce settlement – in this world, I could afford to be generous.

I climbed the little hill that hid the house from view and saw a shack. A dilapidated little house, like something out of Ma and Pa Kettle. I'm in the wrong place, I thought, I made a wrong turn somewhere out in the desert. Then two large dogs ran towards me, leaping and barking. One was black and one was brown. A man chased after them, shouting, "Charlemagne! Horace! Get back here!"

He looked at me and stopped dead in his tracks. "Joanna! Come outside!"

She appeared in the doorway, dressed in jeans and a transparent gauze top. "Wow!" she said.

They offered me a glass of home brew and a joint. Joanna told me she made native-style blankets and sold them at craft fairs.

I left after dinner.

I pushed the capsule door open, and breathed a huge sigh of relief. I was back in New York, surrounded by noise and dirt and traffic. I was home, though for some reason I wasn't in my studio. I had landed in an alley, surrounded by overflowing metal garbage cans and stacks of cardboard boxes.

I heard a rustling sound coming from one of the cardboard boxes – the closest one. Rats, I thought, cringing. I hate rats. I leaned forward to pull myself up, and came face to face with a pair of bloodshot eyes, staring through a little hole in the nearest box. My own eyes watered at the pungent, combined aromas of alcohol and stale perspiration.

"So you've come for me, at last."

Oh no, I thought. There was something horribly familiar about that voice. "Maybe," I said. "That depends on who you think I am."

"You're the angel of death, aren't you?"

"Your name isn't Joanna, by any chance?"

"You *are* the angel of death!" The box lid flew open and a woman rose before me. Toothless. Matted grey hair crawling with insects. Dressed in layer upon layer of dirty, ragged clothing: a winter coat over a man's shirt over a sweater over a dress over a pair of trousers. Eyes shining with madness, hands clutching a pair of heavily-laden shopping bags. "I'm ready. Take me to a better world than this one."

I slammed down the lid and pressed every button. I knew I must have arrived someplace else, but I couldn't bring myself to look. I just sat there, curled up inside my padded metal egg, and shook.

How could I have ended up like that? Me, Joanna Krenski. Talented, attractive, intelligent. Whatever could have happened to bring me down to that level? Homeless. Penniless. Living in a box. And then I realised why I couldn't stop shaking.

I, Joanna Krenski – *the* Joanna Krenski – was in exactly the same position. Homeless and penniless, living inside a box – it's just that mine was made of metal instead of cardboard.

Joanna the bag lady had lost her mind; how long would it be before I lost mine? If I dared to think about it, I knew I was already on the way.

All my life I'd thought of myself as an essentially good person, but all I'd been was comfortable. The moment I realised I'd lost my place in my world, meaning my material security (not the so-called friends I'd chosen on the basis of what they could do for me, not the young lover I only regarded as a trophy), I'd been ready to lie, steal and even kill. I had almost murdered the only alternate Joanna to treat me with any kindness. Now I thanked God the gun hadn't been loaded.

I felt disgusted and ashamed. I hated myself. Over and over again.

I didn't care where I had landed this time – the desert, the suburbs, my studio, a sewer – it didn't matter. I would stay curled inside my egg; I was never coming out again. And I wouldn't have come out, if someone else hadn't pulled the capsule door open.

"Please," a familiar woman's voice said in a whisper. "You've got to help me."

I lay back inside the egg, looking up at one of the Joanna Callahans. She was trying to squeeze into the machine with me. "Why should I help you with anything?" I said, wedging my legs across the opening. "Everything that's happened is your fault. If you didn't like your own world, you should have done something to change it from within, not try to steal someone else's."

"I know that now. I know," she whispered, leaning down over me, "and I'm sorry. Really I am. But you've got to move over. There's room in here for both of us. Please. She's killed the others, I saw her do it!"

So I had come full circle. One of me was killing off all the Joanna Callahans so the whole thing would never have happened. It didn't seem like such a bad idea to me now, and I said so.

"No, you don't understand! She's the one that started it! She's..." she looked up at something I couldn't see, a look of pure terror on her face. "Press the button," she said, slamming the lid down. "Save yourself!" Then I heard the most horrible scream: an animal sound that would haunt me forever, through every time and every universe.

I pushed the door open and raised my head in time to see a woman in a silver catsuit drag Joanna Callahan across the floor and through a giant hoop, by means of a grappling hook stuck into her back. As Joanna passed, howling, through the hoop, there was a blinding flash of light. She covered her eyes, shrieking and floundering helplessly. There was a final tug on the hook, and then she stopped screaming.

Joanna Callahan lay dead in a pool of blood at the feet of a woman with long black hair tied into a knot at the top of her head, a taut, muscular body, an unlined face with implanted cheekbones out to there, and the cruellest eyes I have ever seen. Me with plastic surgery, a personal trainer, and an advanced state of psychosis. She smiled at me and licked her lips; I slammed the capsule door shut and carefully pressed what I hoped were the right buttons.

I didn't want to switch universes this time, I wanted to stay in this one. Whatever this me was doing, she had to be stopped.

I opened the capsule just a crack; it was dark. I opened it a little further, and listened.

Silence.

The digital display inside the capsule read: 29 April 1994, 11:59 p.m., E.S.T. I had gone forward almost six hours. I stepped out of the capsule and examined my surroundings. I was in a large, square room with a bare concrete floor, furnished with a combination of electronic equipment and implements of torture.

The giant hoop leaned against one wall. It was about six and a half feet high, and three inches deep, lined with hundreds of tiny light bulbs. I still had no idea what it was.

I walked to the window and looked down at the twinkling lights of Manhattan. At least I assumed it was Manhattan; I didn't recognise any of the buildings. All I knew was I was very high up – at least ninety floors. I opened the only door in the room and peered down a long, dark hallway lined with doors. No lights on anywhere. It was a Friday night; she'd probably gone out.

I shoved the egg behind something that looked like an Iron Maiden with electrical cabling, and stepped out into the hall. Two Doberman Pinschers raced at me from the shadows, barking and growling. Stay calm, I told myself, dogs can smell fear. And then I remembered: smell. Joanna Hansen's dogs had taken to me because I smelled exactly like her. "Down boys," I said firmly, holding out my hand for them to sniff. They slunk away as if they were terrified.

I stood where I was, listening and waiting. Then I switched on the lights; if those dogs hadn't roused anyone, there was no one around to rouse.

I opened one door after another, peering into a seemingly endless succession of huge, opulently furnished rooms. This Joanna was seriously rich. Then I came to a door that had no visible lock or handle; on the wall beside it was a small glass plate showing the outline of a hand. I pressed my hand flat against it, a little sign flashed "palmprint cleared for access", the door slid silently open, and I stepped into an armoury.

There were guns of every description, hundreds of them, lined up on racks inside huge glass cases. There was every type of sword, machete, axe, knife and razor, also behind glass. There were stacks of drawers marked "ammo". And, mounted on the wall: the grappling hook, Joanna Callahan's blood still visible on two of its iron claws.

To get into the weapons cases required a voiceprint identification. That was easy, all I had to do was say "open".

I don't know anything about guns, so I just took one that felt fairly light and easy to handle, a smallish rifle. I loaded both the rifle and the handgun I'd stolen from that other Joanna back in the suburbs, and filled my canvas bag with extra ammunition.

I pushed the last door open, at the end of the hall, and felt around in the dark for the light switch. There was a slight humming sound, followed by a "whoosh", before the room came into view.

The walls, floor, and ceiling were velvet black; the only light came from inside the glass display cases scattered around the room. Each contained a moving, three-dimensional figure. They were better than any holograms I had ever seen; there was no angle at which they appeared to lose their definition, they were every bit as convincing from the back as they were from the front. And as I said before, they moved.

I stopped in front of one and watched a man pounding against the glass, his face contorted into a howl of hysteria. I could almost hear his screams, almost believe he was alive. I waved my hand in front of his face; he kept on pounding, his hands raw and bloody, his eyes glazed with desperation, staring at something I couldn't see. An engraved plate at the base of the display read: *Trapped*. J. Krenski, 1987.

I paused beside another case. Its occupant lunged towards me, holding a knife, and I leapt back, raising my rifle. I shook my head, cursing myself for being so jumpy, but the damn thing was incredibly realistic. The slobbering face pressed against the glass seemed to be leering directly at me. I looked at the title plate: *Slasher*.

In one display, a child was shooting up. In another, a hideous couple performed continuous sex, in another, an animal gnawed at its own foot, caught in a metal clamp above the title plate: *Trapped 2*.

There were rows and rows of cases, each more grotesque than the last. Finally I came to the arrangement of six glass cases, titled: *Women on the Brink of a Cataclysm: 6 Variations on the Theme of Suicide by Proxy*. Joanna Callahan was there, sliding across the floor with a grappling hook in her back. A version of Joanna Hansen was there, twitching at the end of a noose. A platinum blonde Joanna in a waitress uniform clutched at a knife in her chest. A brown-haired Joanna in a business suit appeared to be suffocating. One like me was in the process of being shot repeatedly, and one with black hair and fake cheekbones stood motionless, pointing a sub-machine gun directly at my chest.

"Drop the rifle, Joanna," she said.

I dropped it.

"And the bag."

The bag hit the floor. "I don't get it," I said. "What's the point of all this?"

"The point?" She raised both eyebrows. "The point, my dear, is art! I brought you here to be part of my exhibition."

"But how?"

"That was amazingly easy. When Toni first came up with the idea for her time machine, she decided it was extremely likely that at least one or two parallel versions of herself might be working along the same lines, and that at least a few parallel versions of myself might have one or two fundamental character flaws. So we sent out one empty machine, pre-set to go backwards, and it took exactly ten seconds to round up half-a-dozen of you, who'd been bouncing back and forth between your various universes, doing everything from ripping each other off to committing mass murder. And the minute you were all in one room, how you went for each other's throats! It was all Toni and I could do to keep you apart." She threw her head back and laughed. "I'd say every single one of you deserved her place here."

"You don't want me for that piece, though, do you?" I said. "I mean, you've already got one like me; I'd throw the visual balance off."

She shrugged. "You'll look different by the time I'm finished with you. Toni!"

Toni entered the room, pushing the giant hoop on a set of wheels. She had an American flag tattooed across her shaven head.

"What is that thing?" I asked.

"It's a three-dimensional camera," Joanna explained. "It photographs you from all directions at once."

The blinding light I'd seen was the flash going off. "So everything in here is just a photographic image, kind of like a 3-D movie."

"More or less, though we enhance it on a computer."

"So why did you have to kill them? Couldn't you just simulate the whole thing on a computer?"

She snorted in disgust. "That would be cheating."

I leaned against the 95th floor lobby wall, watching Toni set up. There was nothing else I could do with Joanna pointing a machine gun at me. As she'd already pointed out, there was no point in screaming because there was no one around to hear; this was an office building and no one else lived here but her, because she owned the entire block.

"Okay," Toni said. "It's all ready."

She had the elevator doors propped open. The 3-D hoop camera was wedged on its side inside the shaft, three floors down. The elevator car was stopped one floor above us.

"This is going to be such a brilliant image," Joanna said, motioning me towards the elevator shaft.

"How can you do this to me? I'm you, you stupid bitch! How can you do this to yourself?"

"No, dear," she said, shaking her head. "Only I am me. You are merely a variation on a theme. Now are you going to jump, or am I going to push you?"

I clung to the wall either side of the shaft with all my strength. "You're gonna have to push me."

I heard a horrible cackling laugh. That was Toni. Then I heard at least a dozen gunshots in rapid succession. I turned around and saw a bag lady holding an automatic assault rifle.

It turned out one of the other Joannas had landed in an alley and left her machine unattended for less than a minute. Joanna the bag lady turned out to be just as much a thief as the rest of us – thank God – and much better at staying out of sight, having had a lot more practice. She'd spent most of the last six hours under a stack of towels inside a cupboard, which she told me was a lot more space than she was used to.

We found her machine and the ones the others had arrived in, in a workroom behind the exhibition. They were each quite different – some weren't even egg-shaped at all. We used one of the larger ones to dispose of Joanna and Toni; we sent their bodies three hundred years into the future.

"So what will you do now?" I asked my bag lady self.

"Treat myself to a bath and a change of clothing," she said. "Then a long sleep, in a real bed, and breakfast in the kitchen in the morning. Maybe I'll just stay here permanently and stage an exhibition of my own. I'm a bit of an artist myself, you know. I mean, I am Joanna Krenski, and I seem to be extremely rich." She smiled and nudged me towards one of the eggs, at gunpoint.

I found myself back in the Callahan's pantry, pushing the door of my little padded capsule open just as Joanna Callahan herself was settling down into another egg directly beside me. "Don't do it," I told her. "On behalf of all your possible selves, I beg you not to do this." She ignored me.

I got up and walked through the house. The kitchen was shiny and white, the dining room decorated with watercolour paintings of daisies and the living room walls covered in pastel sketches of guinea pigs and bunny rabbits.

I went upstairs and found one of me sitting on the edge of a narrow twin bed. Bobby was right – her hair was purple. And so was her canvas bag. "She's done it again," I said, "She's stolen your egg. Why are we all so horrible to each other? To ourselves? I don't understand it."

"What did you say?"

"I said she's stolen your egg. Though I can't say I'm surprised. I'm not surprised by anything any of us do any more."

She got up and ran downstairs. "Wait!" I said, running after her. By the time I reached the kitchen she was gone.

I stared at the empty pantry floor for a minute or two and then I sighed. "Well that's it, then," I said.

I went upstairs and put on a cotton dress, a little big around the waist and hips. "Toni!" I said when she arrived, "I'm sorry if I sounded a little strange on the phone…"

I don't check the pantry for eggs any more; if anyone was coming, they'd have been here by now.

Bob's finally getting used to the idea that if he wants a shirt ironed or the house vacuumed, he'll just have to do it himself. And the same goes for sex. I don't feel sorry for him any more; his wife walked out on him more than six months ago, leaving him with a stranger from another universe, and he still hasn't noticed.

The Katie in this world is just too sweet for words: little brown pigtails, knee socks, freckles, and pleated skirts. I preferred the other one.

Bob Junior just turned twenty-eight. He and his wife live a couple of blocks away, and he has a little construction business. He helped me convert the garage into a studio, then he gave me a complete set of tools – including a welding torch – as a "studio warming" present.

My other son, Harold, lives in New York, but comes to visit most weekends. He wants to be my manager; he says he loves what I'm doing, especially the metal tree with the little men hanging from it like fruit. He says he doesn't know where I get my ideas.

I have an appointment with one of the major gallery owners tomorrow. I'm taking my latest piece to show him: a headless Barbie doll stuck inside a fish tank.

Well, it worked the last time.

learning to fly

It was the second four in the trulight, and Reedie was finally coming out of her flash. It had been a long one this time – she had no idea how long, and her head ached.

She was lying on a mattress in a room five floors above the street. The walls, ceiling and floor were covered with a thin layer of interleaved straw and brightly-coloured feathers. Several shelves had been mounted into the straw-covered walls, each holding a variety of small, shiny objects: everything from scraps of aluminium foil to crystal figurines and semi-precious stones. Tables, chairs, a chest of drawers, the counter dividing the main room from the kitchen – every available flat surface was crowded with items that reflected the light in some way: crystal balls, silver candle-holders, bangles, bells, and mirrors. Lots of mirrors. Reedie lifted her head and saw herself reflected over and over again: magenta hair tipped with black and green, and dark eyes that glittered as brightly as anything in her collection, round with fear.

She stood and picked up the nearest shiny object: a large round diamond. She rolled it between her palms, felt its solidity, its weight. Its reality. But it wasn't enough.

She was back home, in her room, but the flash had gone wrong – completely wrong. She closed her eyes and tried to clear her mind by visualising a white space, empty and silent, but she couldn't do it. Every time she closed her eyes, she saw strange sights, heard strange music and voices, coming from inside her head.

The flash was going on without her.

Lucy Weston felt an elbow in her ribs and a man's voice in her ear, "So what's with the bass player? Do you know the guy or something?"

Lucy's eyes fluttered open and she saw that she was sitting at a table in a crowded room. The room was dark and full of smoke. There were no windows – it had to be a basement. Oh yes, she remembered, we're in a club in Soho. The table was covered in bottles: two empty, one with a lit candle stuffed down its neck, one half-full of red wine. She thought for a moment about who she was, what she looked like. She was twenty-five. Chestnut shoulder-length bob, white blouse, grey flannel trousers, little string of pearls around her neck. Suburban. She turned to look at the man she was with: blonde, thirtyish, wearing a suit. "Hmm?" she said.

"The guy on bass. Do you know him?"

She blinked a few times, and the band came into focus. Three men, keyboards, drum, and bass. "No. I don't think so. Why?"

"He's been staring at you ever since we came in."

"Don't be silly."

"He has."

"Brian, please don't start." She was amazed he still could get jealous after all this time. "I never saw the guy before in my life, and he isn't even looking this way."

"Well, not now."

"Brian, please. You're the one who wanted to be friends. Let's just relax and have a good time."

"Yeah, you're having such a great time you can't even stay awake."

"I wasn't asleep," she said, reaching for the half-full bottle and topping up her glass. "I was just getting into the music."

"You were snoring!"

She rolled her eyes and emptied her glass in one gulp. "I was not snoring."

"You were making some kind of noise," Brian insisted.

"I was purring," she told him. "Like a cat that's tipped over a bird cage."

Brian was quiet a moment, apparently thinking. Lucy was relieved by his silence, all she wanted to do was listen to the music, get lost in the notes as they rose and fell – but it didn't last long.

"Lucy, you weren't having one of your... you know... just now? Were you?"

"No."

"You're sure? You're telling me the truth?"

Lucy sighed and leaned forward, covering her face with her hands as she rested her elbows on the table.

Brian's face creased with concern. "Oh no, Luce. Oh God, not again."

She straightened up, pushing her hair back from her face. "It's all right, Brian. I'm cured, remember? I've got it under control."

"It is not all right!" he shouted, his face turning red. "And you do not have it under control! Not if you're having these hallucinations of yours in public places!"

"Brian, please," she said quietly, picking up the almost empty bottle and filling his glass with the last of the wine, "people are looking."

He knocked the glass to the floor, where it shattered. "Let them look!"

Lucy stood up and walked away.

Reedie watched from her window as giant floodlights flashed into life from every rooftop, bathing the streets in a burnt orange glow. It was the first six in the falselight, the market would be open soon.

She put on a bodysuit covered with a fine layer of blue down and high black boots with long narrow feet divided into pointed segments – three at the front and one at the back, protruding behind the heel. She combed her hair flat and covered it first with a flesh-coloured skull-cap, and then with a head-dress made up of long dark blue feathers, some of which trailed down her back and others which she arranged across her cheeks and to a point between her eyes, so that her face was mostly hidden. She painted her fingernails – which were long and curved, like talons – to match the feathers on her head and face. The weather had been cold lately, so she threw a black feathered cloak over her shoulders, just in case.

She made her way through orange-lit streets that smelled of incense. Everywhere she looked there were shops and stalls, each selling a different brand of magic, but not the one she needed.

She turned into a darkened alleyway in the shadow between two buildings, and looked up. The walls of the buildings were lined with nests: real nests, where the true birds lived. She'd wanted to be like them; she'd wanted to fly, but had found herself more earthbound than ever. The flash had been a disaster.

Agreeing to see her ex-husband again had been a mistake, but Lucy had made a worse mistake back when they were still married: she'd told him something she never should have told him. About the power she had – how she could dream a whole world into existence.

"And you've done this, have you?" he'd asked her, obviously thinking she was joking.

"Oh yes," she'd said. "I've done it. I've done it many times. I dream something and the dream lives on without me."

But Brian refused to understand; he never dreamed. He had no imagination, no soul. Nothing beyond the five senses. She kept trying to explain, over and over, and he kept refusing to listen. One day, he told her she should see a doctor.

A woman sat behind a counter lined with skulls, some animal, some human. She was dressed in a combination of leather, suede, and imitation velvet, and had a huge pair of cordless headphones blaring music into her ears. "Zo Reedie," she said, slipping off her headphones, "Happens what?"

"Zo Lemma. Happens bad. I need Bangzhu."

"He's around somewhere," Lemma replied. "How come you need?"

"I did some flash powder in the early trulight, to fly yes? But my head didn't fly, it went somewhere I never saw before. Somewhere down, not sky. And this somewhere is still inside my head, and I can't flush it."

"The flash is in your head still?" Lemma asked, shaking her own head in sympathy.

"The flash is alive," Reedie insisted. "It lives in me, without me."

"Flash is always alive," Lemma told her. "Alive on wings."

"This flash has no wings. This flash lives with creatures that crawl in the mud."

She remembered the hospital as a series of corridors, twisting, turning, never-ending. She remembered walking with a shuffling gait, up and down, then up and down again. Keep walking, she'd told herself. Keep walking; don't let them get you. Don't submit.

She remembered a soothing voice – female – smooth and oily with hypocrisy, "Come with me now, Mrs Weston. It's time you got some rest. Don't you want to sleep? You'll feel so much better once you get some sleep."

Then she remembered arms – thick, male – lifting her clear off the ground. Landing with a thud on a cot in a room full of sleeping strangers. The jab of a needle, and then oblivion.

The air in the Garden of Sounds always smelled of jasmine, with the faintest hint of perspiration. The garden was located on the outskirts of the city, behind the great temple, beyond the reach of falselight. The sky above was velvet black. The only light in the garden came from flickering scented candles encased in blue glass lanterns that hung from every tree. The trees were silver, tinged with reflected blue, and had no leaves. They were tall and gnarled; their twisted trunks concealed the hidden speakers that gave the garden its name. And beneath every tree, there were groups of people, dreaming flash.

Reedie entered the garden through the temple, and walked along the pathways between speakers, listening to the variety of sounds on offer: sighs and whispers, the crash of waves, the plucking of a string, a quiet chanting of strange syllables, moans of pleasure rising steadily to orgasm. She walked slowly, always looking down, searching for a familiar face among the sleepers.

On the far side of the garden, beneath a tree that broadcast the sounds of calling birds – of course that would be his choice – Reedie found Bangzhu deep in flash. His body lay sprawled on a mat of tangled twigs and feathers. His eyes rolled wildly beneath his lids, his arms and legs twitched up and down.

All around the garden, she saw people flying in flash, just like the true birds. But Bangzhu wasn't flying; he was going into the mud for her, and she would stay with him until it was over.

The air was cold. She took off her cloak, and spread it across

Bangzhu's body like a blanket. Then she lay down beside him, to wait.

Eventually, Lucy had come to accept that it was all self-delusion. The doctor asked her when she first had the dreams, and she told him she was eleven years old.

"The year your parents got divorced," the doctor reminded her gently.

"Yes. When my parents got divorced."

"Your world was falling apart, so you felt you had to create a new one. A special world of your own. And you felt the same way when your marriage began to fail."

She'd told the doctor yes, it all made sense. She became firmly grounded in reality. She left the hospital and got a job and a divorce. Everything had been going so well until she agreed to see Brian again. She'd been all right – cured – for nearly a year. Then, in a smoke-filled basement jazz club, it had all come back to her: the feeling that something she'd once imagined in a dream had a reality of its own. It was stupid, she knew. A result of the tension that still existed between her and Brian, an attempt to escape an unpleasant situation by retreating into a dream world of her own. She couldn't have stood another minute with him, with his constant rehashing of everything that had gone wrong between them; she had no choice but to walk out.

She was less than fifty yards from the club when she heard running footsteps behind her. They caught her up within seconds, falling into a walking pace beside her. "Listen, Brian," she began without looking up.

"My name's not Brian," a deep voice interrupted. She swung around to see a tall, extremely pale man with waist-length black hair. He was dressed entirely in black: black tee-shirt tucked into tight black jeans, tucked into knee-high black leather boots. There were black feathers hanging from a string around his neck, and more feathers strung through his hair. "Zo, Lucy," the man said. "Happens good with you?"

"What?"

The man paused a moment, as if he were thinking, and then he smiled. "Hello, Lucy," he said, slowly and carefully enunciating every syllable, "How are you?"

"Do I know you?" He pointed back up the street, the way they had come. "You were the guy playing bass, weren't you?"

"I dreamed I was playing – what did you call it? – bass. I'm dreaming now. I'm dreaming about talking to you."

Lucy's eyes widened; she took several steps backward. The man was obviously insane. She turned, and began to run. She ran and ran, and when she finally stopped, gasping for breath and aching all over, she was in exactly the same place. There was only one place something like that could happen – in a dream. "Okay, you're right," she said, still out of breath and clinging to a nearby wall for support, "this is a dream. But it's nothing to get excited about. It'll be over soon, and then I'll wake up and get dressed for work."

"I don't think so," the man told her. "You see, this isn't *your* dream. It isn't even mine. Listen carefully, and I'll try to explain. You, and the world you live in, exist inside a friend of mine's head, and I'm afraid she wants you, and your world, out."

"I don't understand."

"I told you already. You're just a dream. It's like you said: nothing to get excited about, you'll be over soon, and then my friend can get back to work. She can dream a new world. Something better than slime and mud – a world of sky and flight."

"Sky and flight?" Lucy pursed her lips for a moment. Then she laughed out loud. "It's your religion!" she exclaimed, clapping her hands together. "You take a hallucinogenic powder that gives you the illusion of flight – it's called flash, and you believe it brings you closer to the birds, which you revere as the most sacred of animals. I know all about it, because I dreamed it one night when I was eleven years old and depressed about my parents splitting up. I'd spent the whole day watching the skies and wishing I could fly away from it all, like a bird. And then that night, I dreamed of gigantic orange floodlights that lit an entire city. I dreamed of a blue and silver garden... I wrote it all down in a notebook so I'd never forget. If I close my eyes now, it's all still there, inside my head. Don't you see? I'm not in your friend's dream – she's in mine!"

The man pursed his lips for a moment, then shook his head. "No," he said.

"Why not?"

"Because my world is real. I know this is true, because I can see it and touch it and taste it."

"You think I can't see and touch and taste?"

"Ah!" said the man. "The difference is: I *really* see and touch and taste, you just think you do."

"Ah!" said Lucy. "What about: 'I think, therefore I am'? What about the history of mankind? Of life on the planet? The origins of the universe, going back to the beginning of time? Literature, philosophy, politics? All these things – and so much more – are part of the world of my awareness. They're part of me."

The man shrugged. "My friend took a *lot* of powder."

"No," said Lucy, crossing her arms. "My world's the real one. You're the dream."

"No," said the man, crossing his arms. "You're the dream. All I need to do is snap my fingers, and you'll be gone forever."

"Ha!" said Lucy. "I can snap my fingers too, you know." She raised one hand and brought the fingers together with a click. "Just like that."

Nothing happened.

Bangzhu laughed, and snapped his own fingers.

Nothing happened.

Each stared at the other, looking puzzled.

The sky was murky red, partly obscured by noxious, dirty yellow clouds. The air was searingly hot; steam rose from a stagnant foul-smelling pond covered in slick brown slime.

The ground immediately surrounding the pond was reddish-brown, and consisted of a thin and watery mud not much firmer than quicksand. Hundreds of wriggling creatures hatched out from beneath the mud and struggled on tiny legs to reach firmer ground before the mud sucked them back under. Only a tiny fraction made it.

One of the few to reach higher ground stopped beside a stubby, thick-stemmed plant that smelled of sulphur. It opened its mouth and tore into the plant with pointed teeth as sharp as razors. The plant screamed and dripped blood. The wriggling creature with tiny legs gulped large chunks of shrieking, blood-soaked plant, and then it raised its face to the sky. Somewhere, far above, at the edge of the little creature's vision, something was moving: swooping and soaring through the air.

The creature continued its climb upwards, away from the mud that hatched it. It climbed and climbed, but no matter how high it went, its belly still brushed the ground.

At the end of its first day, the creature yawned and went to sleep. And while it was sleeping, a series of pictures came into its head, culminating with a vision of two huge, oddly-shaped animals, balanced on their hind legs and facing each other, making clicking sounds with their front paws.

The next morning, and every morning after, no matter how much the wriggly creature tried to shake them from its head, the strange huge animals were still there, snapping and clicking.

the final rushlight

She was there again at sunset, beneath a red sky, surrounded on all sides by high cliffs of red clay. She stood on the edge of a crater, watching grey mud bubble and pop. Steam and sulphur filled the air around her, scalding her lungs and her throat. The goddess Izanami bore these islands with her body; she bore the trees and the wind, and finally she bore the child that killed her: fire. Badly burned, in agony she made her way to Yomi, the Land of Gloom, cursing her offspring to suffer as she had: to know pain and to know death. Izanami swore to strip the land of all its inhabitants, destroying one thousand daily. Izanami, the mother of all life, became the mother of death.

Miko tried to imagine one thousand; she had never seen one thousand of anything.

The crater at her feet made her think of a gigantic eye, winking at her as it bubbled up, straining to watch her every movement. She wondered what it would feel like to touch it, to let it engulf her. She closed her eyes and felt its searing heat.

She stood on a porch beneath a black sky. A stone lantern hung beside the door, filled with one hundred burning rushlights.

She began the recitation. One hundred lines, one for each burning light. One hundred lines, pleading for him to return. With each line, another flame would flicker and die.

She extinguished the final rushlight, and waited in darkness. He didn't come.

It was sunset. The sky was red, the cliffs were red, the air was thick with sulphur.

Miko awoke beside the steaming hole that had carried her to Yomi.

A man appeared beside the stone lantern on the porch. He walked past one hundred lights into the room where she was waiting. "I've come back."

He was nothing like the man she remembered. The man she'd known was young and strong, with thick black hair and sparkling eyes. This man was old, with spindly legs and grey tufts sprouting from his nose and ears.

She placed a bowl of meat and noodles on the table. He reached for the bowl and his hand went through it.

"Woman, what is this?" His dark eyes narrowed. "You have not aged a single day! How can this be after so many years? Who are you? What are you?"

Miko would have answered, but she had no voice.

The old man reached for her arm. Miko watched her skin erupt into a thousand blisters; saw it blacken and fall away.

There was no pain, only the memory of pain. Of once having loved a young Samurai who abandoned her without a word. Of extinguishing the final rushlight, knowing he would not return. Of hovering at the edge of a boiling crater, wondering what it would feel like to let it engulf her.

She watched the old man's eyes widen in terror as his bony fingers closed upon themselves, grasping nothing, and she laughed, her eyes a lake of fire.

doris and angie and me

Doris says Angie isn't too bright. You'd think this would be a problem, but Angie gets by better than almost anyone I know, including Doris and especially Doris, who almost went to college and can even do division in her head.

Angie just bought herself a brand new Porsche, paid for it in cash, and had enough left over to treat me and Doris to dinner at a place where the menus are all in French. If Angie is dumb, then maybe we should all be dumb like Angie.

I know Angie and Doris from Ruggles, this club where we all used to work. Angie was the coat-check girl. It used to cost fifteen bucks to check your coat at Ruggles, but with Angie behind the counter, there was never any shortage of guys with coats to check. Even in the middle of summer.

Well, one night, this certain guy comes in, and he notices Angie right away. Which isn't too hard to do since her counter is right by the door. And also, I guess I've neglected to mention what Angie looks like. She's sorta tall and blonde and has a lot of teeth. Doris is always saying she can't understand why guys always go for these big blonde women with teeth. Personally, I wouldn't so much mind being tall and blonde and toothy, but I think there's more to it than that. For one thing, Angie's always wearing these itsy-bitsy little dresses.

So picture the scene: this guy comes in. He's about fifty, he's in an Armani suit, and he's talking on a mobile phone.

You remember that Angie is tall and blonde? Okay, so she's wearing this little black dress. It's very short and clingy, at least fifty per cent lycra. This guy puts away his phone and walks over to Angie's counter. He says it is obvious she is a very intelligent woman who is wasting herself checking coats. This is nothing Angie has not heard before. She smiles and waits for the next part, which is usually to do with the guy being a movie producer. You wouldn't believe how many movie producers come in to Ruggles. But this guy doesn't say that he's a movie producer. Angie is surprised. And so am I, because I'm standing a couple of feet away and can hear every word.

This guy tells Angie he's a marketing director for a big dog food company. Then he says he's been looking for an assistant, someone who really loves dogs, and Angie says I like the little cute ones, and he says that's great, maybe she'd like to come to his office for an interview. Angie says okay, and he suggests an interview over dinner.

That's how Angie became an executive.

Well, when I told Doris about Angie quitting the club to become an executive, she got more than a little bit upset. You see, Doris works in an office, too, and she figures she's really intelligent because she could have gone to college, but here she is getting nowhere. She spends nine-to-five Monday to Friday typing other people's letters on a computer, making pot after pot of coffee, and asking callers if they'd like to hold. For this, she brings home hardly enough to get by, so she works weekends at Ruggles, where she mostly just stands behind the bar and makes drinks with little umbrellas in them.

I guess she can't help resenting it when Angie gets a job that must pay four or five times as much when we both know that Angie is scared to death of computers because some hairdresser told her they give you wrinkles, and Angie didn't know the guy was kidding. I tried to console Doris by telling her that there's got to be a lot more going on than the occasional pinch by the water cooler, but that just made her more upset, and started her muttering about sexual harassment.

Maybe I should mention a few things about Doris. She's not so young like Angie and me. She's maybe thirty, but she doesn't look it. She looks twenty-three, twenty-four, so that's no problem. But to listen to her, you'd think it was. She's not tall and blonde like Angie, or even medium with blonde highlights, like me. She's short and brunette, with a little spikey haircut. She's about five foot one or two, and she wears these glasses. They've got red plastic frames, just like Angie's boss at the dog food company.

I don't think she's bad looking. She's what the magazines call "cute and boyish" and cute and boyish doesn't seem like such a hardship for her, judging by the number of guys at Ruggles that might go for her in a big way if she only gave them half a chance. But she says she's not interested in any of them, and sometimes I swear she goes out of her way to be ugly. I mean, she scowls a lot.

Doris used to be married. She got hitched right after high school, and that's why she never went to college. Her ex didn't like the idea. He said girls only go to college to meet men, and no way was his wife gonna go somewhere and meet men. Two weeks after her twenty-seventh birthday, he went to live with someone else. I'll betcha fifty bucks she was a blonde.

One time when the club wasn't too busy, I asked Doris why she doesn't go to college now that her husband's not around to stop her. She said I should mind my own business. Then she dropped a glass and it shattered.

I never asked her about college again.

Sometimes I don't know about Doris. She says I'm her friend, but she treats me like I'm really stupid. It seems like every time lately I open my mouth, she tells me to shut up because I don't know anything.

Okay, so I quit school at fifteen and all I've ever done is work in a bar. Maybe I don't know a lot of big words like she does. I've got this little tattoo on my right arm, and Doris says that was a stupid thing to have done. She says it over and over, but you know what I think? I think she's just too chicken to get one herself.

And then I think to myself that I don't have to get up in the morning, and I don't have to spend money on pantyhose and sensible little polyester suits in dark colours, and I don't have to stand on a crowded train in the rush hour, and I don't have to squint at a computer screen all day, every day, and get paid almost nothing for it.

And I make a lot more in tips than she ever will, because I always smile at the customers, while she's too busy feeling sorry for herself to smile at anybody. Doris would rather wrinkle her nose at you, like she thinks you smell bad or something.

And here's the most important thing: I don't cling to some goofy idea of who I could have been if it hadn't been for some guy I haven't seen in ages.

You tell me who's the stupid one.

Angie didn't stay with the dog food company long. It seems some bookkeeper started asking questions, and so did the marketing director's wife, and so, it seems, did the fraud squad. But in no time at all, Angie was an executive in another firm, and this time she never had to go near the office.

She met her new so-called employer, the head of an ad agency, when he came personally to the dog food company to sign them up for a big multi-million dollar contract. He told Angie then to phone him if she ever needed anything.

You've gotta give Angie credit, she must be really good on the phone. The night she took Doris and me out to dinner, she had us come back to her place so she could show us something she called "executive perks". When I saw what she meant by executive perks, I said I wouldn't mind being an executive myself. Doris, as usual, told me to shut up. By this time, I was getting a bit tired of Doris, and I told her so. But Angie just said have another drink and why don't you each try on one of my perks. So she hands Doris a mink that's much too big for her, and she hands me a silver fox. I try on the fox, and what does Angie say but I look so good in the coat, I can keep it. Then she turns to Doris and tells her she can keep hers, too. That's just the way Angie is. Generous. Besides, she says, there's always more where those two came from. And she can say this in the middle of a recession. You've really gotta admire her.

But then Doris had to go and ruin everything. She starts whining she can't possibly wear the coat, and Angie says you can have it altered, and Doris says that's not the point. The point is it's fur, and no one with a conscience wears fur anymore. I said I'd wear it, and Doris says see what I mean? Then Angie says maybe Doris is right; she'd never really thought about it. Then she says thank you Doris, all these furs are going right back where they came from, and I said so what are you gonna do, glue them back on the animals? And this time they both said shut up.

I couldn't believe it. One minute I've got a silver fox coat, the next minute I don't, and it's all because of Doris and her fake almost-went-to-college principles. I looked so good in that silver fox. I resolved right then and there that I would never be friends with Doris again.

I didn't tell Doris I wasn't her friend anymore. I decided to keep it my secret. I figured what's the point in telling her? Especially since she used to drive me home from the club after work every Friday and Saturday, which saved me five or six dollars in cab fare. See, I'm not stupid after all.

Though sometimes I wondered if it was worth it, 'cause all the way home I'd have to listen to her bad-mouthing Angie. She'd say Angie's no executive and never was one, she's nothing but a high-priced call girl. Then she'd call her all kinds of names. Terrible names. It was like she was so mad at Angie she could spit. And I couldn't understand why. I mean, who appointed Doris judge over Angie? What's it got to do with her what Angie does for a living? There were times I almost started to say something, even if it meant I'd lose my free ride home. I wanted to say: Angie's never done anything to you, so how come you're talking like you hate her?

But then I thought: who needs to worry about what Doris thinks or says about anything or anybody? Certainly not Angie.

And who's got bills to pay, and who could really use the extra five or six bucks she's saving in cab fares every week? Me.

So I kept quiet.

One night at the club, some guy leaned across the bar and tried to kiss Doris. And you know what she did? She punched him, hard, right on the mouth. Then she walked out of the club and she never came back.

Tuesdays are always my night off. Last Tuesday, I had nothing to do, so I figured I'd walk over to Angie's and see if she wanted to go to the all-night movies. I got there about a quarter to eleven. It's one of those high-rise buildings with glass revolving doors and a doorman who sits by the intercom in the lobby. Through the glass doors, I could see Angie and Doris getting into the elevator. Doris had her arm around Angie, and Angie had her arm around Doris.

I kept walking.

angel's day

Morning

Angel woke, shivering, in a cheap hotel room littered with condom packets. She stepped into her clothes: a wrinkled pink summer dress with a white lace collar, and a leather jacket, much too big. (She knew this guy once; his name was Ricky. She woke up shivering and hurting and *needing* on a morning just like this one. Ricky was gone and the dope was gone and all the money she'd made the night before was gone, but the bastard left his jacket.)

She paused in front of King's Cross Station, clutching the money in her hand, holding her breath, looking for the Italian. Then she saw him, outside the post office in Euston Road. He was leaning against the wall, dressed in expensive jeans and a black leather jacket, standing motionless. Hands in pockets, eyes hidden behind dark glasses, ignored by passers-by.

The light changed and Angel crossed a road filled with cars and taxis and buses. The night before – in the dark – she was pretty, with long brown centre-parted hair, big round eyes, and a tiny cupid's bow of a mouth, but now it was morning and she was ill. Trembling, shoulders hunched, face ashen and glistening with sweat, she stumbled on legs that were stick-insect thin, fragile as glass.

The Italian took his hands out of his pockets and stepped away from the wall, walking very slowly. Angel wiped her dripping nose on her jacket sleeve and slipped a damp, crumpled note into the man's outstretched hand. He spat, and a small foil-covered pellet landed on the pavement. ("Cops can't look in your mouth," Ricky once told her, "that counts as an intimate body search. If they grab you, swallow. If they put you in a cell, just make damn sure you don't shit for twenty-four hours, then they've gotta let you go; it's the fuckin' law.")

The Italian moved away, disappearing into crowds of morning people. He never once spoke, never even looked at her.

Angel bent down briefly, then stumbled back the way she came, fighting back waves of nausea.

In her tiny room near the station, she removes the wrapping from a chocolate bar and lets the chocolate fall to the floor; it is the silver paper she wants. She tears the cellophane from a fresh needle and lifts her dress, exposing the marks on her thigh.

Afternoon
Angel was out working when it started to rain. She headed towards a place she knew, a tunnel underneath a railway bridge north of the station, alongside some waste ground and a depot. She stepped into the tunnel and three women blocked her path. She didn't know them; she'd never seen them before. They were older than Angel, and big, with wide shoulders and muscular arms. "Where do you think you're going, little one?" asked the largest, stepping forward. She had shoulder-length black hair, parted on the side, and little piggy eyes smeared with blue make-up. Her face and arms were dotted with moles. She wore tight, ripped jeans and heavy, lace-up boots. "I asked you where the fuck you think you're going, bitch."

Angel stared at the ground. "Nowhere." Her voice sounded high and thin and faraway.

"Nowhere," the woman repeated in a tinny falsetto, mocking Angel's strained little-girl voice. The other two laughed. "Well, nowhere ain't around 'ere, love, is it?" She grabbed Angel by the hair and slammed her against the tunnel wall. The other two leapt forward, holding her there.

Angel looked around in desperation. There was no one around that she knew, none of the regulars – these three must have scared them all away. Now the bridge belonged to them and there was no one who would help her.

A car drove under the bridge, lights on, window open, hugging the curb. It pulled to a stop, distracting the women's attention. Angel bolted forward. "Get me outta here. I'll do anything you want."

The driver told her to get in.

The man drove a short way, then parked behind a derelict building with boarded-up windows and rainbow splashes of graffiti. He was blonde, in his late twenties. He wore a flashy suit – pure silk – and several rings: gold. "Well?" he said.

Angel's eyes went blank; something inside her switched off. She bent forward, reaching for the man's zip, but he stopped her, grabbing her hand and pushing it away. "You gonna tell me what that was about?"

Angel looked up, confused. "What?"

"All that bother under the bridge, what was it about, eh? If I'm gonna play a knight in shining armour, I want to know the reason why."

Angel shook her head. "I don't know."

"Dispute over territory, was it?"

Angel turned away, biting her lip.

"How long you been on the game?"

"Not long."

"You're a cute girl. How long you plan to stay that way?" Angel was confused. Men in cars didn't talk; they never talked, unless they wanted something extra. "How old are you?"

"Nineteen."

"Bollocks. But if that's what you want to tell me, I'll believe you."

"I am. I'm nineteen. Do you want me to prove it or something?"

"Nineteen," the man repeated, his eyes moving up and down, appraising her. He lifted a hand to her face. Angel tensed, ready to run. He wouldn't be the first man she'd met who got his kicks from slapping women around, but all he did was push her hair back from her eyes, ever so gently, and begin to stroke her cheek. Then he smiled, tracing the outline of her lips with the tip of one finger. "You don't even look fifteen, do you? You've even got a voice like a little girl. Some men like that, you know. Enough to make it worthwhile." He leaned back in his seat, staring straight ahead. The tone of his voice changed, became harder.

"So how much does it take a day, huh?"

"I don't understand."

He sighed and rubbed his temples. Suddenly he looked very tired. "Please don't play games with me," he said. "You think I can't see you've got a habit? Look at that thigh, love."

Angel tugged at her dress.

"So how much you need to make in a day? Minimum."

Angel looked down at her feet, making a face. "About a hundred."

He laughed and told her she could make twice that, easy, in just a few hours a night and all she had to do was sip orange juice and make small talk in that baby-doll voice of hers, and it was all completely legal. Then he asked her if she was interested.

Evening

His name is Brian and he treats Angel differently than anyone has treated her in a long time. He buys her a cup of coffee in a café, he talks to her. He asks her questions, he wants to know everything about her. He offers to buy her dinner, but all Angel wants is a bag of crisps and she can't even finish those. He eats and she watches.

When the time comes, he gets her what she needs. He follows her into her squalid room without comment, and at the sight of the needle, he averts his eyes. He raises a hand to his face for just a moment, and for that moment, Angel allows herself to imagine that he is brushing away a tear.

She stabs herself in the thigh. Squeezes. Angel leans back on the mattress, veins flowing with golden honey. Warm – the room is so warm. Alive with Brian's presence.

She feels Brian breathing, feels the beating of his heart. The air around him crackles with electricity; she can see the sparks, feel them explode against her skin. Even a blink of the man's eyelids sends shock waves across the room, making Angel shudder.

"We should be going," Brian said, looking at his watch.

Night

Two men walked down a Soho street, past nightclubs and restaurants, past neon signs promising food and liquor. But they'd had their fill of both and now they were looking for something more.

They turned down a narrow, badly-lit passage. A woman called to them from a doorway – the only doorway in that particular alleyway – and after a moment's discussion, the men headed down a steep flight of steps. The ceiling and walls above the stairway were painted a garish shade of yellow with the words: "Exotic Women" and "Live Strip" printed at intervals, in large black letters. A redhead in black hotpants sat behind a counter at the bottom, smoking a cigarette. "You here for the show? Three pounds each."

The men paid her and went inside, through a beaded archway. A dark-haired woman in a short red dress greeted them with, "Have a seat, the show will start in just a few minutes, aw'right?" Beside her stood the bouncer: a shaven-headed giant in a tight black suit. He crossed his arms and grunted.

The men sat at a candlelit table, noting the tiny stage in one corner, dark and empty, and the pale-faced man with thinning hair who stood behind the bar, slicing a lemon. There didn't seem to be any other customers.

A girl approached them for their drink orders. She was small and painfully thin, dressed in pink. She looked about fifteen. Her long hair hung from a centre-parting, nearly obscuring her face. "Good evening, gentlemen," she breathed in a little-girl, Marilyn-Monroe sexy voice. "What can I get you?"

She came back with two beers and something that looked like a glass of orange juice. She placed the drinks on the table and sat down, uninvited. The men exchanged amused glances. "Where are you from?" she asked them.

"Germany," they replied in unison, heavily accented.

"Are you here on holiday? Or on business?"

They told her they were in London on business. She asked a series of polite, general questions. The men answered distractedly, looking towards the empty stage.

A woman, tall and angular, with short-cropped hair bleached almost white and dark red fingernails like talons, appeared out of the shadows, brandishing a square of white cardboard. "Pardon me, gentleman, but I have to collect for the drinks." They nodded and reached for their wallets.

"That's two hundred and thirty-seven pounds, please."

"What?" the Germans shouted in unison.

"Two hundred and thirty-seven pounds," the woman repeated, adding firmly, "You'll have to pay that now. We collect by the round."

"But this is crazy!" one of the Germans shouted. "We have only two beers."

The giant in black moved closer; he was at least six foot six and weighed nearly twenty stone. "You raising your voice to the lady?"

"There is some mistake," said the other German.

"No mistake." The woman held the cardboard square up to the flickering light of the candle. It was a printed list of prices, and it was the first time that either man had seen it. "You had two alcohol-free lagers, at fifteen pounds each." She tapped the appropriate line on the menu. "That's thirty pounds. Plus one Satin Duvet," she tapped again, further down, "at fifty-two pounds fifty..."

"Wait!" one of the Germans interrupted. "What is this Satin Duvet?"

She raised one eyebrow. "That's the lady's drink." She made a point of emphasising the word "lady".

"But we didn't order..."

"You pay for the lady's drink," the giant informed them, cracking his knuckles.

"Plus one hundred and twenty pounds hostess fee," the woman continued briskly, tapping a line of small print across the bottom.

"But we never asked..."

"This is a hostess bar," she explained in a voice of patient indulgence, as if she was talking to a pair of not-too-bright children. "It says so quite clearly," she tapped the cardboard menu again, "here. And then there's VAT. Altogether it comes to two hundred thirty-seven ninety-four, but I'm dropping the ninety-four p." She spread her hands in a gesture of magnanimity, smiling sweetly. "Now you do have enough money, gentlemen, don't you?"

"We're not paying."

The bouncer shook his head. "You're paying," he said. "Turn out your fucking pockets."

Angel stood up and moved away. Brian appeared from a room behind the stage.

The Germans remained defiant. "We'll call the police."

"You won't call nobody if you don't get out of here alive," the bouncer reminded them.

The Germans looked up at the giant standing over them, looked at Brian looming behind him, the bartender moving in their direction. "Okay, okay," one finally said, "I have a Visa card."

Brian shook his head. "No cards. Cash."

The Germans paid and left, shouting threats, as a party of seven Japanese descended the stairs, chattering excitedly. "Three pounds each," the redhead told them.

It was late and the dark-haired woman in the red dress was taking her turn at the counter while the redhead sat with two men at a table, sipping orange juice and assuring them that the show would start in just a few minutes.

Angel was in the office with Brian. He opened his wallet and she saw that it was crammed with notes, more money than she had ever seen in her life. He counted out two hundred pounds, and handed it to her. He muttered that they'd be closing soon, and she didn't have to stick around if she didn't want to. She told him she wanted to stay a while longer, it wasn't like she had any other plans. He shrugged and handed her an empty glass coffee pot. "If you want to hang around, then make yourself useful."

Angel hesitated, staring at the pot in her hand. "Just fill it with water," he told her.

Angel giggled. "Oh yeah. Sure."

"Ta," Brian said a minute later. Then he smiled at her, and Angel felt her mind begin to spin. She started thinking, "What if?"

What if someone – someone with a smile like Brian's – wrapped her in his arms and never let go. Would it be enough to drive the demons out of her head? Would it be enough to make her forget all the things she needed so desperately to forget, the things that drove her to seek oblivion from the jab of a needle. She looked into Brian's eyes and imagined herself sinking into a different kind of oblivion.

"You all right?" he asked her, touching her arm.

"Yeah, sure." Angel trembled. His hand was still on her arm. She tried to pull herself together, tried to act as though nothing was happening, even though he was sending an electric current right through her. She wondered if he knew what he had done to her, what he was still doing. (Ricky used to tell her a junkie couldn't fall in love, but she always knew he was wrong.)

"Well, back to work," she said brightly, wanting Brian to notice how energetic she was, how eager to please, how quickly she had become indispensable.

Cold raindrops splattered the pavement. A man staggered around the corner into the narrow passageway where Angel stood waiting in a doorway. "If I were you," said Angel, "I'd want to come in out of the rain."

The man stopped in his tracks, swaying slightly. He was about forty-five, with bloodshot eyes, a large red nose, and puffy cheeks threaded with broken veins. He wore a crumpled beige raincoat over jeans and a polo-neck jumper. "I'll come in if you will."

Angel and the man sat down at a candlelit table. He didn't seem to care that there was no sign of a show; he never once looked at the stage. He was sliding a callused hand up Angel's thigh when the taloned manageress appeared with the bill, demanding two hundred pounds. "Wha'?" he asked, dazed, no different from any customer that night. The manageress repeated her demand, and he jumped up, roaring like a lion, knocking her back with a swipe of his hand.

The bouncer was on him in a flash; they rolled on the floor, knocking over chairs and tables and candles. The bartender leapt across the bar and into the mêlée. Angel ran towards the office, screaming for Brian. He opened the office door, shoving past her.

The bouncer and the barman got back on their feet, pulling the man up with them. They held him still while Brian punched him in the stomach, over and over.

He slumped forward; they let him go and he dropped to the ground. Brian went through the man's pockets, finding less than fifty pounds.

"Get the son of a bitch out of here, then lock the doors and bugger off home." He yawned, smiling ruefully, "I don't know about you lot, but I've had it for tonight."

Brian and Angel stayed for an hour after the others had left. Brian counted up the night's receipts while Angel swept up broken glass, emptied ashtrays, wiped down tables. "What are you doing, Angel?" he finally asked her. "What the hell do you want from me?"

"Nothing. I'm just trying to help, that's all."

"Why?"

"What do you mean why? You said yourself you were my knight in shining armour, didn't you?"

Brian sighed. "Let's get out of here, okay?"

Angel stood outside waiting, watching the neon lights of Soho wink out, one by one, while Brian pulled a set of metal gates across the doorway. The rain had finally stopped and the air smelled clean and scrubbed and full of promise. There was a pink glow on the eastern horizon; Angel imagined herself absorbing that glow. She felt beautiful and alive, like that first rush of liquid sky, when you feel like kissing God full on the lips. She wondered if it was possible to feel this way forever, feel this way watching a thousand sunrises with Brian by her side, feel this way without drugs. And then she thought, *I'd like to try*. She heard a padlock click into place, and turned to see Brian signal her to follow.

They turned the corner and were confronted by the leering face of menace. A man, his clothes torn, his face savaged, was waiting. Angel knew him at once; it was only an hour since his rough hand had worked its way up her thigh. He lunged at her, twisting her thin arms behind her back, and raised a steak knife to her throat. "I want my money." Angel couldn't believe this was happening; the man didn't have a knife an hour ago, he must have stolen it from a restaurant.

"You what?" said Brian.

"You robbed me! I want my money back."

"Piss off," said Brian.

Angel tried to say Brian's name, but she couldn't speak. She could hardly breathe; the serrated edge of the blade was pressed close against her windpipe.

"I'll slice her fuckin' head off."

Brian shrugged. "Be my guest."

"Huh?"

"Do you think I care what you do to her? She's just some piece of shit from the streets of King's Cross, does blow jobs in cars for a tenner. I only used her tonight 'cause I was desperate. I mean, look at her!"

"All I want is my money," said the man, "I had forty-nine pounds. That was all I had in the world." His grip loosened. Angel could finally breathe again. She gasped for air, scalding tears streaming into her open mouth as something inside her died forever.

"Forty-nine pounds!" Brian nearly doubled over laughing. "For her? Well, she's all yours now mate, do what you want with her." He backed away, palms up. "I'm off."

An ugly sound pierced Angel's ears, a cry that didn't sound human. Angel fell to the ground, hitting her head. Everything went dark for a moment, then there was another sound, the scrape of blade against bone. Her eyes slowly came back into focus; she saw Brian clutching at his chest. She watched him crumple.

The man in the raincoat turned towards her, the restaurant knife in his hand dripping blood. "I didn't want to. I never meant..." And then he was gone.

Angel's eyes darted from side to side; she was in a narrow alley, just before dawn, and there was no one around. No one anywhere. She looked up, saw empty windows. No faces, no prying eyes.

She crawled towards Brian on all fours. A puddle of blood formed beneath him, growing larger. She gently brushed the hair back from his eyes before stroking his cheek and tracing the outline of his lips with one finger, exactly the way he had touched her once – when was it? only a few hours ago? it seemed like a thousand years – back when he was a knight in shining armour and she, a beautiful damsel in distress. He made a horrible noise: a kind of gurgling. Then he didn't seem to breathe any more.

Angel reached into his jacket pocket and carefully removed his wallet.

neon nightsong

Empty streets and flashing signs – that's the only world I understand. Where old men huddle on the corner for warmth and subways are for sleeping on beds of broken glass while broken dreams stalk the streets in silence.

Where suburban boys keep trying their luck beneath a flashing neon light and everything glows red. Red in the glare of the neon night.

Bars are full of flashy people and everyone looks good, 'til they get outside with dull, tired eyes. They've lost something – deep within them. (Maybe tonight, maybe a long time ago.)

And it's four o'clock in the morning when I find myself leaning over a cracked cup of coffee at the greasy all-night counter – trying hard, trying consciously, to look like a painting by Edward Hopper.

An old woman in sneakers puts her last coin in the jukebox and slowly begins to sway to an old song by Tammy Wynette. She closes her eyes and she's a young girl again.

She doesn't hear the comments from the hooker in the corner. Someone drops a plate; she doesn't notice. She's far away by now, back home in Tennessee.

And I'm here, stuck in the present, with no place to remember even if I could close my eyes. But I understand the old woman – neither one of us can sleep. The song ends with the creeping dawn.

Formica counter reflects flashing neon: HOT EATS – OPEN 24 HOURS. Then it slowly begins to fade with the approach of another day. It's time to go. I button my coat and face the empty streets once more.

Dammit! It's all so ugly when the sun begins to rise. I can feel my life just slipping away, and I'm doing nothing about it.

I can swear to myself that tomorrow I'll change, but I know I'll be back here tonight, 'cause I can only live in darkened streets transformed by the neon sign.

ruella in love

Queen Ruella of the combined kingdoms of Tanalor and Hala, twice-widowed and still a virgin, opened her eyes to bright sunlight streaming through her window. She yawned and stretched like a cat; then she sat up and planted a big sloppy kiss on the Lord of Darkness poster mounted beside her bed. Of course most of his features weren't visible – just a single red eye glaring out from beneath a dark hood – but she'd smeared a bit of glue where she guessed his mouth should be, so every time she kissed the poster, it stuck to her lips and made a satisfied smacking noise that made her giggle.

She'd just had the most wonderful dream: she'd married the Lord of Darkness, who was madly in love with her, and she'd gone to live in his huge black tower, where orcs waited on her hand and foot, granting her every wish, and everybody, but everybody, addressed her as "Your Dark Ladyship." She winked at the poster and hugged herself in delight – it had to be a premonition, it just had to be.

She was standing in front of the mirror, trying out some new devastating poses, when there was a knock at the door. "Come in," she said.

A tall, skeletal figure in hooded black robes loomed in the doorway. It pushed back its hood, revealing a head divided into two sections – one half was bare skull, the other covered with rotting flesh – and fanned itself with a batwing mounted on a stick. The creature had one eye loosely hanging from a socket on the fleshy side. One long black string of hair, twisted into a perfect corkscrew curl, sprouted from what was left of its scalp. An occasional maggot could be seen crawling down its face. "Oh honey, it's like an oven in here," the creature said, "mind if I open a window?"

"Go ahead."

The creature crossed the room, pushed the shutter open, and sighed. "That's better." It turned back to Ruella, the fleshy side of its mouth raised into a smile. "So how's the birthday girl?"

Ruella shrugged. "I'm okay."

The creature grabbed her by the shoulders and planted a huge kiss on her cheek. "I could just eat you up! You know that?"

Ruella sighed and rolled her eyes, wiping bits of rotted lip off her face. "Oh please. Can we just get on with it?"

"Tetchy tetchy," said the creature. "All right, sit." Ruella sat down in front of the mirror. The creature positioned itself behind her. It shook its head, tsk tsk'ing and clucking disapproval. "Your ends are dry as dust! Girlfriend, you need some long-term intensive conditioning and you need it bad." Like so many of the hangers-on around the palace these days, the creature didn't have a reflection, so in the mirror Ruella's hair seemed to be moving around all by itself.

"Let's just worry about tonight, okay?"

"All right, all right. So what did you have in mind?"

"I want it all spikey on top, and then I want this bit here," she took hold of a large strand at the front, "to sort of come down over my forehead and cover one eye." She pulled the strand across. "Like this."

"Oh no no no! Look," the creature pulled Ruella's hair back, "you've got beautiful eyes and a high intelligent forehead – you don't want your hair hanging over your face. A nice upsweep, that's what you want."

"No it isn't!" Ruella snapped. "Stop trying to make me look like an old lady. Do what I tell you or I'll chop off your head!"

"Ooh, get her!" The creature placed its hands on its hips and rolled its one dangling eye. "That's your idea of a threat, is it? Well, let me tell you, Missy, I've been beheaded more times than you've had hot breakfasts! So you'll have to do better than that for a threat now, won't you?"

Ruella slumped down in her seat, pouting. "But it's my birthday!"

The creature pursed the fleshy side of its mouth. "Oh all right," it

Molly Brown

said, picking up a comb. "I can never stay mad at you for long, can I?"

There was another knock at the door, and another tall skeletal creature in black robes entered. It approached Ruella and leaned down, briefly pressing a fleshless mouth against her cheek. "Happy birthday," it said in a rasping voice not unlike the sound of gravel crunching beneath a pair of heavy boots.

Ruella brushed away a few worms the rasping-voiced creature had left on her face.

"Sorry," said the rasping voice.

"No problem. So what's up?"

The creature reached inside its robes and produced a scroll, which it unrolled with a quick flick of its wrist. "Behold the guest list for tonight."

Ruella scanned the list. "I don't see the Lord of Darkness – hasn't he RSVP'd?"

"Well, the Lord of Darkness doesn't go to many sweet sixteen parties."

"But this isn't just *any* sweet sixteen party! This is *my* sweet sixteen party!"

"I sent him an invitation. There's nothing more I can do."

"Don't worry, honey," said the one with the dangling eye, "he might still turn up." It turned towards the rasping voice, "You better put him on the list, just in case. You don't want him vaporising the guards or anything, do you?"

"You've actually met him, haven't you?" Ruella asked the dangling-eyed one.

"Once or twice."

"What's he like?"

"All seeing, never sleeping..." the rasping voice broke in.

"No, I mean is he cute?"

"Cute?" said the rasping voice.

"Cute?" said the dangling eye. "Honey, he's absolutely horrible! He's the epitome of evil! Cold and cruel without a shred of human decency or feeling. Of course he's cute."

"You think he'd be the type to mind that I murdered my father in order to take over the kingdom, then murdered my first husband in order to take over *his* kingdom, and then forcibly married my step-son

257

who was actually kind of cute but then committed suicide on our wedding night rather than consummate the marriage? I mean, if he and I were dating?"

"He'd probably take it as a recommendation," said the dangling eye. "Now hold still and be quiet; I'm almost finished."

"Why don't you put her hair up?" the rasping voice asked the hairdresser. "She'd look so pretty with her hair up."

The party was well under way long before Ruella came downstairs. The throne room was packed with sorcerers, wizards, lesser despots, and corpses in various states of decay, all bopping to the latest music. Dozens of dwarves were stationed on high platforms around the room, waving their hands in front of wall-mounted torches to make a strobe effect. Outside, a queue of nearly two thousand people and creatures waited in vain – the guards were under strict instructions: "If your name's not on the list, you're not getting in." And in the unlikely event that any woman or girl might possibly be considered even slightly prettier than Ruella, she was to be sent away immediately, list or not.

Ruella made her grand entrance at moonrise. After much argument, she'd finally got the hairstyle she wanted: huge back-combed spikes that stood out in all directions. She'd circled her eyes with black ash and dusted her face with Dead Body Shop Crushed Bone Powder (not tested on hobbits) to give her a super-chic pallor. She wore a gown of skin-tight black leather slit to the thigh, and carried a ten foot long bullwhip loosely coiled in one hand.

A hushed silence fell over the room; all activity ceased. Ruella leaned petulantly beneath a gilded archway, the hand with the bullwhip resting on her hip. She studiously curled her upper lip, giving the crowd the oh-so-mature-and-jaded, seen it all and found it too dull for words look she'd been practising in the mirror for the past two hours.

A rasping, gravelly voice rose from somewhere near the back and the entire throng joined in a rousing chorus of "Happy Birthday". Ruella dropped her jaded lip-curl and fell into a fit of giggling as a group of hooded figures lifted her above the crowd, bouncing her up and down sixteen times. They finally dropped her onto her throne, where she fell back, gasping for air.

"Speech! Speech!" the hooded figures shouted. Ruella stood up and signalled for silence. "I've only got one thing to say: Where the hell are my presents, you bastards!"

The hooded hordes rushed forward and swept her up again. "I'm sorry I asked!" she shouted as they carried her across to the stage. At the approach of a throng of hooded corpses, the musicians stepped aside, leaving the stage to Ruella, who'd been dumped stage-centre. "Okay," she said, looking down at her empty hands, "who's got my whip?"

"I do!" shouted a hooded figure surrounded by a haze of buzzing flies.

"You're dead, buddy," Ruella said, pointing a threatening finger.

"I know that!"

The room exploded into hysteria.

"I'm the one who's having the birthday!" Ruella whined in mock despair. "How dare you get all the laughs!"

Ruella had to stay on the stage as the guests trooped forward with their gifts, and she had to look grateful, though it wasn't easy. She'd never seen such a collection of rubbish: lengths of silk and emerald tiaras – real old lady stuff. Did they really think she'd be caught dead in a tiara? And then somebody gave her a solid gold spinning wheel! A spinning wheel? Who did they think she was, somebody's grandmother? "Gee, thanks," she said when it was all piled up in front of her.

"Make way! Make way!" a rasping voice shouted from the doorway. "Behold the beloved Queen of Tanalor and Hala's birthday present from the members of her household, for which we all chipped in!"

A hooded figure made its way towards the stage, leading a night-black horse.

Oh no, Ruella thought, not another horse. She already had a stable full of the damn things, and all they did was eat. "It's a horse," she said, trying not to sound too disappointed.

"This is no ordinary horse, my Lady," the rasping voice replied as it reached her. "This is what is known in the trade as 'souped-up'."

"Souped-up? What do you mean?"

"Behold the horse in first gear. It looks like an ordinary animal, does it not? Ideal for shopping or occasional leisurely jaunts to the country.

But when I do this..." The creature grabbed the horse's tail and turned it clockwise twice. The hooves split open, revealing a set of wheels. "That's only second gear," said the rasping voice, "wait 'til you see third!" It turned the animal's tail three more times. A pair of wing-shaped panels sprang out from the animal's sides; its nostrils belched smoke. "You control it here." The rasping creature picked up a section of the horse's mane. "This way's up, this way's down, the middle holds it steady."

Ruella clapped her hands and jumped up and down. "It's fabulous!"

Of course she had to try it out right away. She jumped on the horse's back and rode outside, where the unfortunate thousands were still queuing. They cheered when they saw her and then they gasped in unison; the horse had risen from the ground and was circling several feet above their heads. "My beloved people," Ruella shouted down at them, "thank you for coming out to celebrate my sweet sixteen. I'm sorry none of you will be allowed inside the palace tonight, but then you're peasants so you understand how it is. Now, if you'll excuse me," she said, turning the horse back towards the palace, "I've got some partying to do." The horse dropped something unpleasant on several members of the crowd. "Oops," said Ruella, stifling a giggle.

It was early morning, and from her bedroom window high atop the palace, Ruella watched the last of the revellers leaving. She stepped back into the shadows when she saw a wizard from Lithia step into the courtyard; he was looking straight up at her window. She'd been hiding from him for the last hour; she never should have gone behind the stables with him to smoke that Wizard's Weed – the guy seemed to think that meant they were going steady. She watched her guards usher him through the gate, and sighed with relief. She was tired and all she wanted to do was sleep.

She was just taking off her make-up when there was a loud knock at her door. "Oh no," she moaned, thinking the Lithian had found his way back into the palace. "Who is it?" she asked sharply.

"It's me," replied a rasping voice.

"Come in." She waited until the hooded figure had closed the door behind itself. "What's up?"

"I've brought you your birthday present."

"What? The horse?"

"No. The horse was a gift from all of us. This is a gift from me." The creature reached into its robes and pulled out a small round piece of clear crystal.

"What is it?"

"Behold the latest in communications. No longer need you rely on messengers that may not bring a reply for days – with this you can speak face to face with anyone you want to, instantly. Anyone who has one of these, that is."

"Wow," said Ruella. "How does it work?"

"You just tell it who you want to contact; it does the rest through a bit of minor sorcery."

"And you can see them and hear them and everything?"

"Yes. Provided they're at home."

"Nifty! And does the... um...," Ruella's cheeks were burning; she lowered her head and stared at her feet. "Does the...?"

If the rasping-voiced creature had eyebrows, it would have raised them. "Does the Lord of Darkness have one? Is that what you're trying to ask me?"

Ruella giggled.

"I believe he does. He has all the latest gadgets."

As soon as Ruella was alone, she combed her hair and put on a fresh coat of make-up. She tried on six different outfits before she changed back into the one she'd been wearing to begin with. She practised a new facial expression in the mirror – she wanted the casual, just called up to say "hi" look, which she achieved by baring her teeth in an open-mouth grin and opening her eyes a little wider than usual.

She took a deep breath, gathered up her courage, and approached the table where the creature had placed the crystal ball. "The Lord of Darkness, please," she said. "Calling the Lord of Darkness."

A woman's voice replied, "That ball is busy. Will you hold?"

"Uh... okay." Ruella rushed back to the mirror for a quick check. She couldn't go through with it; she couldn't possibly let the Lord of Darkness see her like this, she'd been up all night and she looked terrible.

"Putting you through now," said the crystal.

The crystal ball transformed itself into a giant red eye. "Hello?" boomed a harsh male voice. "Who's there?"

Ruella crept behind the table and threw a cloth over the crystal, breaking the connection. A moment later, she grinned to herself. At least she knew that he was home.

She called him three more times that day, just to make sure he hadn't gone out.

After a week of calling the Lord of Darkness and throwing the cloth over the crystal as soon as she heard his voice, Ruella got the brilliant idea that if she just happened to be riding past his Dark Tower – because she just happened to be in the neighbourhood – she just might run into the Lord of Darkness in person. First she made a quick call on the crystal ball, just to make sure he was home, then she got dressed.

With her new horse cruising in third at an altitude of about two hundred feet, it took her less than two hours to reach the Dark Land. It was everything she'd ever dreamed of, a stark land almost bare of vegetation, where sulphur mists rose beneath a blood-red sky. And it would all be hers, once she got over the minor problem of making the Lord of Darkness fall madly in love with her.

She brought the horse in for a landing about a mile away from the Dark Tower, and had it continue at a leisurely trot. As she approached the Dark Tower, she noticed a single red light burning in a window near the top. That had to be his chamber.

She rode past once, watching the window from the corner of one eye. Then she rode past again. Then once more, just in case.

Ruella was sound asleep when the round crystal began to make a ringing noise. "Wha'?" she said, opening her eyes.

"Hello, Ruella!" said a man's voice. "Remember me?" It was that moron from Lithia! Ruella had to think quickly.

"Ruella no here," she said, disguising her voice and hiding her face behind a blanket, "I yam de cleaner. Ruella go out, she no say when she come back."

"I see. Can you tell her I called, please?"

"Yeah, yeah. I give her message. You go now, I gotta clean." She threw her blanket on top of the crystal and sighed.

Sometimes, when Ruella rode past the Dark Tower, the red light moved from one window to another, but no one ever came outside. In fact, she never ran into anyone when she was in the Dark Land; if it wasn't for the moving light in the tower, she would have thought the whole place was deserted. She began to wonder if it was time to change tack.

"What does the Lord of Darkness like better than anything?" she asked the creature with the dangling eye.

"Desolation, I suppose. He's quite big on desolation."

"No, I mean like what do you think he'd like to receive as a gift? You can't give someone desolation, can you?"

"No," the dangling eye agreed, "but you can give them the means of desolation."

"Like what? I would have thought he's got all the means of desolation he needs."

"Yeah, but he likes to get gifts of soldiers. He gets through a lot of soldiers in a year – he can always use more."

"Soldiers," Ruella said. "I never thought of that."

The Lord of Darkness didn't even send a thank-you card. Ruella was sulking in her room when there was a knock at the door. "Go away," she said.

"It's me," said a rasping voice.

"I don't care who it is. Go away."

The door opened and the hooded figure entered. "I have urgent news," it said.

"I don't care," Ruella said, sticking out her lower lip.

"You must listen," said the rasping voice, grabbing her by the shoulders. "The Lord of Darkness has been defeated."

"WHAT?"

"He has been driven from his tower."

"But that can't happen! He's all powerful."

A sound like the scraping together of two boulders came from somewhere deep within the creature's skeletal chest; it was crying. "The Lord of Darkness has lost his powers," it said between sobs, "and with his fall, our own are greatly lessened."

"What are we gonna do?"

"I don't know."

Just then, the crystal made an awful ringing sound, loud and insistent. "If it's that Lithian again…" Ruella said, gritting her teeth. She moved over to the table where the crystal sat. "Hello?"

The crystal became filled with a single glowing red eye. "Ruella?" said a harsh male voice.

"Yes. Who is this?"

The eye moved backwards, becoming smaller. Finally, Ruella was able to make out a bald-headed man with a single red eye, a long crooked nose, and dark blue lips. He was holding a heart-shaped box of candy and a dozen roses. "It's me, baby. The Lord of Darkness. But you can call me 'Malcolm' – all my friends do."

"What do you want?"

"I was thinking maybe I could drop by tonight. I've been meaning to call you for a long time, but I've been so busy with this 'n' that, you know how it is. But now I've got some time on my hands, I thought we could get to know each other, know what I mean?" He winked and ran a forked blue tongue suggestively around his cracked blue lips. "You are one foxy chick, Ruella."

"I'm sorry," Ruella said, "but I'm busy. I'm washing my hair tonight."

"Oh, I see. Well, sure if you're busy." The Lord of Darkness paused a moment, thinking. "I know! How about if I just come over anyway, and kinda hide out in your castle for a while? You see there's these guys that are kinda looking for me…"

"Beat it, loser," Ruella said, throwing a cloth over the crystal.

"Your Majesty!" a herald shouted, rushing into the room. "The Knights of Light and Honour, led by the barbarian champion Glorioso, are heading this way! They should be here within four hours!"

"We're doomed!" said the rasping voice. "We don't even have an army any more, because you thought they'd make a nice gift!"

"Shut up and let me think," Ruella snapped. "Okay," she said, turning to the herald, "I want everyone in the throne room in fifteen minutes. Got it?"

"Got it," said the herald, exiting quickly.

"Don't worry," Ruella told the rasping voice as she pulled down her Lord of Darkness poster and scrunched it into a ball.

Fifteen minutes later, Ruella addressed her household. "I'm sure you've all heard the news by now. The Lord of Darkness is fallen, and the Knights of Light and Honour are marching this way, led by a champion. The way I see it, we've got two options: the first one is to go down fighting, but I'm going for the second. Or as someone much wiser than myself once said, 'If you can't beat 'em, join 'em.' But I intend to go one better on that second option, and make 'em think we were on their side all along. So what we need to do is this: dwarves, give the place a thorough going-over, and burn anything that might tie us with the forces of Darkness. And if anyone asks you anything, you don't know a thing, you're just the cleaners. Guards and heralds, go out to the stables, cover yourselves in shit and start working the fields – the Knights of Light and Honour never harm humble peasants, so hide your weapons and chew straw until further notice." She pointed at the undead hooded figures, "You lot, come with me."

In a cavern far below the castle, Ruella and the hooded figures discussed their plans. "So how much magic have we got left?" she asked.

"I still have one or two tricks left up my sleeve," said the one with the dangling eye. "Light the cauldron!"

While several of the hooded figures gathered around the cauldron, two of them ran back upstairs. Returning with several bolts of white cloth and a selection of needles and thread, they sat down in a corner and went to work.

Ruella watched in fascination as the creatures poured several brightly-coloured substances into the cauldron, all the time chanting in a strange forgotten tongue. Suddenly, they stopped. "It's ready," said the dangling eye.

"What's it for?" Ruella asked.
"It completely transforms your appearance."
Ruella made a face. "Do I have to drink it?"
"No. Sit down."

Ruella sat down next to the cauldron, surrounded by all but two of the hooded figures; they were still busy sewing. The hooded figures took turns dipping a large wooden ladle into the cauldron and saturating Ruella's hair with its contents.

At the end of one hour, they dipped Ruella's head in water and handed her a mirror. She gasped in amazement; her appearance had been completely transformed. She was a blonde!

The two creatures who'd been sewing presented her with a flowing white dress; the rasping voice placed a selection of dainty little flowers in her hair, which had been twisted into golden ringlets. The dangling eye placed both hands on its hips. "If this kid ain't a picture of innocence, I don't know who is!"

"Those Knights of Light and Honour won't know what hit 'em," said the one surrounded by buzzing flies.

"Yeah, but all the Knights of Light and Honour have to do is take one look at you guys..."

"We'll be okay," said the rasping voice. "We haven't lost all our powers; we can still do rudimentary shape-changing."

"Shape-changing? You mean you guys don't have to look like that?"

"No, of course not," said one with live rats scurrying around its ribcage.

"So how come you all look like refugees from a cemetery?"

"Fashion," said the one with the buzzing flies.

Far below the castle, Ruella held a last-minute inspection. She walked up and down, examining row upon row of golden-haired maidens in white dresses. "You," she said, pointing at a maiden's chest, "what are you doing with those?"

"What do you think?" asked the maiden.

"They're bigger than mine. Get rid of them!"

"Ooh!"

"I said, get rid of them!"

The maiden scowled, but her breasts shrank to half the size. "That's better," Ruella said. "Everybody got their rose petals?"

Each maiden held up a full pouch.

"Okay," said Ruella. "Let's do it."

The Knights of Light and Honour expected trouble when they crossed the border. They'd heard Tanalor was a dark and dangerous land, ruled by a an evil teenage sorceress and her undead minions. They were pleasantly surprised to find themselves greeted by scores of golden-haired maidens, blowing kisses and throwing rose petals.

The champion Glorioso pointed to the one he thought the fairest. "Come here, my pretty," he said, winking.

"I think he likes me," said the maiden with the rasping voice.